Dragon Emperor

Book Two of the Dragon Spawn Chronicles
By Dawn Ross
© 2021

"It is not in the stars to hold our destiny but in ourselves."
– William Shakespeare

Dragon Emperor

Book Two of the Dragon Spawn Chronicles

by Dawn Ross
Copyright 2021

Cover
Dragon art by Dmitrii Brigidov, purchased under the standard license agreement through istockphoto.com in 2017. Spaceship from freestyledesignworks purchased under the standard license agreement through 123rf.com in 2020. Eclipse image and starry background from NASA. Images combined by germancreative on fiverr.com.

Special Thanks
I'd like to extend a thank you to all the beta readers and editors who helped me make this novel shine. Special thanks to Brett Linley and Grace Bridges, who have been with me through every single book and have been instrumental in helping me make these stories so great.

Reviews for StarFire Dragons:

"A thoughtful novel that owes a debt to
Star Trek but works on its own terms."
—*Kirkus Reviews*

"A subtle space opera that explores the ethical
conundrums of intergalactic relations with main
characters who are worth rooting for."
—**Becca Saffier,** *Reedsy Discovery*

"Fans of epic sci-fi that look for realistic characters and complex
yet believable settings will find *Starfire Dragons*
a powerful introductory story that promises more, yet
nicely concludes its immediate dilemmas."
—**D. Donovan, Senior Reviewer,** *Midwest Book Review*

Dragon Emperor

Book Two of the Dragon Spawn Chronicles

by Dawn Ross

1
Attack of the Dragon

3791:023:12:35. Year 3791, day 23, 12:35 hours, Prontaean time as per the last sync. Two fairyfly drones drifted down the hall. Jori Mizuki crouched, remaining still but ready while the drone-feed played on his helmet visor. He honed his concentration as the tingle of adrenaline coursed through his veins.

The fairyflies turned the corner, revealing enemy soldiers. He signaled his team. *Three. Hold.*

The feed highlighted and labeled the enemies' weapons and gear. Jori's heart thumped steadily as he examined the information. Like him, the enemy wore sable nano-armor with energy-absorbent and bulletproof capabilities. Their headgear was of the Ribisan style with a pointed face and rounded ear guards. Small nondescript boxes clipped to their belt had no label, but Jori suspected them to be the source of their energy body-shields.

Though the enemy carried a decent selection of grenades, their M-TAK energy rifles were not as impressive. Jori liked the M-TAK's simplicity with its three firing options and three strength levels, but their smaller power cells meant they'd run out of power fast.

He steadied the weight of his own phaser rifle. The damned thing was hefty for someone only ten years old, but he liked the greater functionality of the RR-5. If the enemy hadn't set up the burn-barrier, he would have used the high-powered beam to sear through the metal walls and kill them. Still, he had the advantage with his seven senshi warriors.

Several attack options zipped through his head. Toss a grenade—too messy. Set off a smoke or flash-bomb—nope. His opponents wore enclosed helmets with high-tech functionality much like his own. Charge in—stupid without a way to distract them.

That's it—a diversion. Dorbs were perfect. The hovering balls had minimal firepower, but they shot quickly and in multiple directions.

He waved one of his men forward. As the senshi approached, Jori evaluated his own ready position. The recoil pad of his phaser rifle nestled against his shoulder. His hand tightened on the grip and his index finger poised over the trigger. He focused on the targeting system of his visor to sync it with the scope.

With a soundless hand signal, he ordered the senshi to send out two dorbs. The man launched them down the short hallway and the team rushed in. The silence shattered. Men yelled battle cries, boots clamored on the metal floor, the dorbs and phaser rifles popped like firecrackers.

The deadly music stopped as promptly as it had begun. The tangy scent of charred air twinged Jori's nostrils. He hustled in and followed the point of his rifle around the corner. The enemy was down. He checked the stats on his visor and noted two of his own men had also been taken out. *Damn*. He needed to learn how to win without losing his team.

He shrugged it off. They weren't real anyway.

"Five minutes," Sensei Jeruko said through his comm.

Jori tensed, but the steady mission-focus that always accompanied him during training stayed with him. He could win this exercise in five minutes. *Mushin*—no mind. *Fudoshin*—immovable mind.

He knelt behind his virtual senshi as they took point at the next corner. This hallway was too short. Ribisan-class spaceships had a longer hall here. Sensei Jeruko had likely modified the virtual schematics. The man's words echoed in his mind. *"Memorizing layouts is good, but you must expect the unexpected."*

With an eye-click to the left of his visor, Jori directed a fairyfly drone around the corner. It relayed a short, narrow corridor ending with a titanium blast door before the image blinked out. Only one thing would have terminated its feed.

Energy shield, he mimed to his virtual team. Getting this far had been easy, which meant his older brother was saving the best for last.

Jori pulled an RF weapon from his belt and tossed the thing out. He watched the feed from the remaining drone as the device skidded across the floor, halting when it hit the energy field. An energy barrier was only as good as its power supply. The RF kept it activated at full intensity until a bang followed by a fizzle indicated the shield had burned out.

"You'll never get inside," his older brother said through the comm on a private channel.

His concentration broke. Terkeshi's taunt meant he thought he was winning. "Chusho," he cursed to himself as he dropped his head against the wall. He had this victory already figured out. When he won, it would be the third time in a row. Terk would be pissed.

He didn't want his brother to be mad at him all over again. If he lost on purpose, though, Terk would know and resent him for it.

With his focus lost, his sixth sense expanded and caught hold of a familiar lifeforce.

"Chusho," he cursed under his breath. Father wasn't supposed to be watching.

He hoisted his rifle and eye-clicked his visor, selecting the mid-range beam setting. He aimed at the door control panel and fired a bolt. The panel covering popped off, exposing the electronic guts. After selecting the lowest single-burst setting, he shot into the mechanism. The door slid up.

The porcupine bomb would be the perfect weapon to throw in. When it exploded, it would shoot out super-heated darts. Depending on the proximity of its target, these bolts could overwhelm energy shields and sear through most armor. Terk wouldn't stand a chance.

Except Jori couldn't let Terk lose again—not with Father here. Terk likely had a few defense weapons ready and several of his own team members left, though Jori couldn't sense virtual players. He shrugged. *The best option is the worst option.*

After signaling his virtual men, he rushed in with weapons blazing. One-two-three energy blasts struck his energy body shield and the device shorted out. As he reached the threshold of the door, a fourth blast from Terk's weapon struck him. His visor flashed red and his weapon deactivated. In a real fight, he would have been dead.

The VR of Jori's armor reverted to the sim-suit. The simulation clicked off, revealing a vast empty room. He blinked to get reoriented.

Terk removed his helmet and glowered. "What the hell was that?"

Jori bit his lip as his sensing ability picked up on his brother's irritation and chagrin. "Father's watching."

Terk's emotions faltered.

Jori took off his head gear and stood at attention as their father emerged from the observation room. Terk planted his feet beside Jori's and puffed out his chest. At age fourteen, he stood broader and a head taller than Jori. Otherwise, they shared many of the same physical traits—dark hair, dark narrow eyes, and sharp facial features—although Jori's were still on the soft side.

Father's attributes looked as though they'd been carved with a razor, and his eyes cut like daggers as he glowered at Jori. "Boy, what kind of foolish stunt was that? Why didn't you use your arsenal?"

"I considered it, Sir," he said, careful to avoid an outright lie. Only cowards lied.

Father darkened. "Idiot. That was as incompetent as your brother's losses."

Jori's gut soured as Terk's shame brushed his senses. Terk's throat bobbed. "The sim game didn't—"

Father's attention snapped to him. "Save your excuses, boy."

"The sim game could have been programmed to give me the advantage," Jori said, hinting that Terk could have lost the first two games for other reasons.

"Are you saying you cheated to win and still lost?" Father stepped forward and clouted Jori across the head.

Jori clamped his mouth shut and stewed. He hadn't cheated. If Father thought he had, though, maybe some of the heat would be taken off Terk.

"Damned your incompetence," Father said. "Both of you. I will have Sensei Jeruko take over your duties today."

Terk stepped forward, his alarm pulsing into Jori's senses. "I can do it, Sir. My scores on operating the tactical station are excellent. I can handle this."

Father's mouth twisted. He seemed ready to speak when Sensei Jeruko approached from behind and cleared his throat. "Sire, I am confident in his ability, and he needs the experience."

Father's jaw loosened. "Very well, but if he makes the slightest mistake you will take over. I don't need him screwing this up."

Sensei Jeruko bowed. "Yes, Sire."

"Get changed," Father said to Terk. "We have a *real* battle to fight. I expect you on the bridge in fifteen minutes."

Father marched out with Sensei Jeruko. Jori and Terk headed to the locker room as their swirl of emotions fought for equilibrium.

"Why did you do that?" Terk said. "You could have won."

"I don't want Father to be mad at you anymore." Jori avoided Terk's eyes as a recent memory surfaced. Over a hundred days ago, he'd had the opportunity to destroy his enemies and chose not to do it. Father had considered it Terk's failure, though, instead of his. "And I don't want you to be mad at me anymore either."

"You dummy. You'd rather *Father* be mad at you than *me*?"

"Father's always mad."

Terk huffed. "Still. That was stupid. Pretending you're not good at this isn't fooling anyone. Not even Sensei Jeruko can beat you half the time."

When Jori sensed his brother's emotions soften, a slow smile stretched across his face.

Terk thumped him playfully. "Don't let it go to your head."

Jori beamed.

"Besides," Terk said as he unclasped the breastplate of his sim-suit. "We both know you wouldn't kill anyone in real life."

"I would too," he replied. "I've killed before."

"Yeah, in defense only." A shadow crossed Terk's mood. "You might fight better in a simulation, but you're too weak-minded to be a real senshi."

Jori's cheeks burned. Simulated opponents didn't have emotions that bombarded his senses. He bit his tongue to keep from arguing the point. Terk would only tell him to get over it, and he'd be right. What good was it to practice martial arts and assault tactics if he was too squeamish to use them?

Terk hung up his sim-suit. "If it wasn't for you, we would have captured that Cooperative ship and Father would be happy."

Jori focused on removing his suit, pointedly avoiding his brother's gaze. The enemy ship had escaped because of his sentiment. It seemed like the right move at the time. The Cooperative had saved their lives. To kill them or allow them to get captured didn't sit well, though—especially when it came to the enemy commander.

"You should have told Father it was my fault," Jori said.

Terk put on his uniform. "He still would have punished me. I was the one in charge of the mission."

Jori's throat hardened into an ache. Terk's punishment had been severe enough to require medical attention. Even now their father didn't let him live it down. No wonder Terk still held resentment.

If only he could go back and do things differently. Whenever he thought of killing Commander Hapker, though, his stomach squirmed like some creature inside struggled to get out.

He didn't have his brother's strength to do what was necessary. Terk was well on his way to being a fierce warrior, while Jori let his sentiment weaken him. Emotion is weakness, Sensei Jeruko always said.

Jori dressed in his uniform. The smooth texture of the black nanite-infused material made it easy to put on. It wasn't as thick as the uniforms worn in battle, but it had moderate energy and projectile defenses.

As he depressed the nodule that fastened his boots, a beep sounded through his comm.

"It's time," Sensei Jeruko relayed.

Terk clapped Jori on the back. "Now for a real battle."

Jori tried to look as eager as Terk felt, but all he managed was a half-hearted smile. The exhilaration of the sim-game abandoned him. His body turned heavy and sluggish instead.

They left the TTAC room and walked through the belly of the steel beast. The *Dragon* warship was the biggest and baddest of all Toradon ships. No other craft flew as fast or spewed as much firepower. The *Dragon* wreaked destruction as easily as its mythical namesake did.

There was a time when Jori had taken pride in living on this ship. He'd believed dominating and killing was his birthright. Now this belief wavered. Doubt had first appeared three years ago when he and Terk attacked the Gonoro space station. The incident with the enemy ship strengthened his uncertainty.

What the hell was wrong with him? He was a warrior, bred and trained to be the best. He should be excited. Instead, his stupid sentiment ran rampant.

"Emotion is weakness," Terk said, no doubt sensing his emotions. Their shared ability meant they couldn't hide anything from one another, but Jori liked how close it made them. "Find that same spirit you had when you helped plan this."

Jori sought that feeling. Not so long ago, his head had whirled with excitement. Planning the attack on Thendi was like untangling a mass of knotted wires, but more fun. He loved challenges—martial arts, strategic analyses, and space combat simulations.

Planning was different than attacking, though. He put his hand to his stomach as though this would stop the vortex churning inside it. "I don't want this to be like Gonoro."

He sensed Terk's emotions falter. He and Terk had enjoyed firing the weapons that demolished the space station. They might not have given the attack a second thought if their father hadn't taken them down to see the aftermath. The memory of the dead girl, blue and frozen by the vacuum of space, threatened to cripple him.

"It won't be like that," Terk said as they entered the conveyor. "We'll be fighting soldiers, not common people."

"Are you sure?" Most senshi on this ship never seemed to care who they killed.

Terk nudged him with his shoulder. "Don't be a baby. If you're getting sentimental, you can stay in your room."

His cheeks burned. The idea tempted him, but Father would be pissed if he didn't show—and he had to prove to Terk he was a warrior. As the conveyor took them to their destination, he summoned his resolve. *I can do this.*

The conveyor door opened to the command deck. *Emotion is weakness.* He repeated the mantra in his head until they reached the bridge.

He followed his brother in, then stopped short at the sight of the planet dominating the front viewscreen. Thendi was far more vibrant than any world in Toradon territory. It harbored deep blue oceans, enormous land masses, and icy patches that capped the poles like warheads.

The land's reddish-brown color bore highlights of wispy clouds that reminded him of coolant on rusted metal. Although there was a serenity to the planet's outer appearance, a war raged within its crust.

He wanted to ask the man at operations to zoom in onto Thendi's gouged terrain where its landmass was scarred from the violent clashes of grinding plates. Slashes of red marred it where the plates drifted apart, making the planet appear as though it had been ruthlessly stabbed.

Reports stated the Thendians were working with Prontaean Cooperative scientists to develop a powerful wave-emitting device that would temper the tectonic movement. Supposedly, this same device could be altered to cause planet-wide destruction—and Jori's father wanted it.

"Come on," Terk whispered. "You're gaping like an idiot."

Jori broke his gaze from the viewscreen and followed Terk to the tactical station. They both dipped their heads to their father as they passed.

Emperor Mizuki didn't bother to respond. He sat coolly in the throne-like chair at the center of the bridge. His broad shoulders eased into the back and his powerful hands lay casually on the armrests. He was far from relaxed, though.

Jori sensed Father's giddy anticipation. He also saw it on his face—the flared nostrils of his hawkish nose, the firmness of his angular jaw, and the glittering of his dark eyes. Jori sensed the same expectancy in Terk as he manned the tactical station, although in him it mixed with nervousness and determination.

Terk's brow drew inward as he examined the readings. He might not be as tall as their father, nor did he have a man's bulk, but Jori envied his fortitude. Even when he wasn't angry, the dark depth of his eyes reflected a strong will.

When Terk caught him looking at him, his mouth curled up. Being back in Terk's good graces filled him with warmth.

Terk pulled up the weapons stats. Jori noted the full cache. Energy cannons were primed. Projectile weapons were loaded. The artillery crew had reloads waiting in queue.

The *Dragon* and its sister warship, the *Basilisk*, slunk to the planet like mamushi snakes. The half-shadow on the planet's right side lay exactly where Jori had expected when he'd worked out the figures. The enemy most likely thought they would approach through the glare of the sun or from behind one of Thendi's moons. Advancing from a different direction had been his father's idea but Jori had done the calculations.

He glanced at Father, hoping for some hint of approval, but the man's fierce stare remained on the viewscreen. Jori's shoulders slumped.

As soon as the *Dragon* settled into position, a nervous heat flushed through his body. His uniform cooled to compensate, making him shiver. His mouth watered as nausea rolled in his gut.

Terk elbowed him and glowered. Jori clenched his jaw. He shouldn't feel this way. This foolish sentiment made him weak. He forced his emotions aside and focused on his duty and the hyped sensations of the other senshi.

"Passive sensors pick up three Prontaean Cooperative ships, Sire," the major at the operations station said. "Your diversion worked. The other ships must have pulled out."

Father sat erect. "Still no indication that they've detected us?"

"No, Sire," Major Niashi replied.

Jori held his head a little higher. His calculations had brought them close. Father's predictions about where the enemy would—or wouldn't—scan for potential threats seemed to hold. While the remaining Prontaean ships could only focus on a small portion of the vastness of space, the bridge crew of the *Dragon* knew precisely where to look.

Father's eyes lit up as though eager for an easy kill. "Zoom in and identify."

The viewscreen's image lurched inward and focused on a large bulky ship. Jori leaned in. Like most ships he'd seen, its gravity wheel and arc reactor dominated the overall shape. The propulsion units jutted out the rear while an array of weapons pimpled or indented its main body.

"A Tutamen-class battleship, Sire," Major Niashi said.

Jori marveled at the most heavily armed vessel of the Prontaean Galactic Force. The hull of the monster reflected a bluish tint. This rare metal was lightweight yet tough. At this angle, Jori couldn't see its bay doors where intelligence stated two squadrons of Pterodon jets could emerge. Since the virtual interface of those fighters weren't hindered by the g-force limitations of human occupants, they were faster and more maneuverable than the Toradon Asp fighters.

This PG-Force battleship was impressive, barely more powerful than the *Dragon* warship. Weaker races manned it, though. Various human cultures from all over the galaxy made up the Prontaean Cooperative, and only one or two were as fierce as the Toradon senshi. None matched the tactical brilliance of his father.

The next ship appeared on the viewscreen. This one was much smaller, but still amply armed.

"Fortis-class destroyer," Niashi said. "The Tutamen is called *Defender* and the Fortis is *Perses*."

"The third ship?" Father said.

Niashi tapped his console. The screen flicked again.

Jori's heart skipped a beat. *It can't be.*

It was an Expedition-class vessel from the Prontaean Colonial Cooperative. Although this PCC ship was nearly as large as the *Defender*, it didn't have as much armor and carried only a few basic defense weapons.

Niashi made a derisive noise. "It's just a civilian ship, your Eminence."

Jori clutched the armrest of his chair. "What's it called?"

"It's named *Odyssey*, young Prince."

Chusho! Of all the enemy ships out there, why did it have to be Captain Arden and Commander Hapker's ship?

"This had better not be a problem, boy," Father said. His expression was neutral, but his emotions radiated displeasure.

"No, of course not, Sir," Jori replied automatically. He masked his unease with what he hoped was determination.

The mask only worked on his outward appearance, though. He couldn't hide his emotions from his brother.

Terk glowered and shook his head. "Don't you dare go weak on me," he said low enough so their father wouldn't hear.

Jori swallowed. *Emotion is weakness.* Just because the *Odyssey* had once saved his and Terk's lives didn't mean he owed them.

He clenched his fists and summoned his resolve. He would not let Terk down by allowing his sentiment to interfere again. He was a senshi, and senshi didn't back down against their enemies.

Father stepped up to the viewscreen and clasped his hands behind him. "Tell the *Basilisk* to get ready."

Jori braced himself for battle.

2
Aid of the Odyssey

3791:023:13:37. Captain Silas Arden tapped his fingers on the armrest of his chair. The front viewscreen of the *Odyssey*'s bridge displayed a slowly spinning planet. It was the same planet it had shown every day for more days than he cared to count. Even the information scrolling across the bottom crawled, and it seldom changed.

Drumming his fingers had become a habit. Not because of boredom, though. Every time Major Esekielu was around, Arden could almost hear the hiss of an Indivian tarantula.

The major sat in the chair beside Arden's and methodically tapped his console, giving the impression of an articulated robot. Major Esekielu's critical black eyes flicked over the screen. Now and then his square jawline twitched, and his lips pressed into a nearly seamless line. No doubt he kept watch for a mistake so he could berate someone like an overzealous drill sergeant.

The major pushed away his console and snapped upright, reminding Arden of the expandable baton the man unnecessarily wore on his hip. "My shift is over, Captain. I will return promptly at zero-hundred."

"Very well, Major," he said, not bothering with the usual pleasantries.

"You may want to have your operations officer keep an eye on that QR gauge, Sir," Major Esekielu said with a barely concealed sour expression. "Arc emissions have neared the edge of specification levels twice now."

Arden bit back a sharp reply. It likely had stayed within specifications because Officer Chandly had already noticed and corrected it. However, his saying so had yet to register in the major's pointed head. "You get some rest. I'm sure we can handle things here."

The major left with a stiff gait. Officer Chandly scowled at the major's back, then caught Arden's eye and made a distressed look. Arden let out a lengthy breath and nodded in sympathy.

Their circumstances should normalize soon. His wife and the other civilians would return to the ship. Major Esekielu would go back to his post on the *Defender* and Arden would have his key people here again.

He glanced at the now empty second-officer's chair and shook his head. Some of the admiral's decisions had profoundly affected the spirit of the crew. Sending Commander Hapker to the planet was one. Replacing him and the *Odyssey*'s top security team with Major Esekielu and his lackeys was another.

Arden cupped his bearded chin and watched his people work. Now that the major's shift was over, shoulders fell, frowns eased, and a collective sigh lightened the air. Even so, the fresh and upbeat energy that once filled the bridge remained stale and edgy.

He missed Commander Hapker's affable manner. The commander's flexible yet firm mien brought out the best in his people, both in attitude and in the quality of their work. The major, on the other hand, was like a stick of stinkwood—unbending and with a scent that lingered despite his departure.

Director Jeyana Sengupta entered the bridge with an unusually tight posture and a pinched expression, signifying she had likely run into the major on her way in. "Captain," she said with a nod that made her black bushy hair bound.

He returned the gesture. "Good to have you here, Director."

Sengupta sighed as she sat. "Any difficulties?" she said in her Kochuru accent.

"Not this time," he replied, knowing she was referring to the major. "You?"

Sengupta pressed her lips together, confirming his suspicion. As Director of Intelligence, it was her job to know things or to know people who knew things. She had positive relations with all sorts, even those with questionable backgrounds. She was a people person, through and through—except, apparently, when it came to Major Esekielu.

"I never imagined I'd miss Major Bracht this much." She clasped her hands together and her eyes took on a far-off look.

Arden harrumphed. The Rabnoshk warrior could be stormy and demanding. But if Major Bracht had the demeanor of a lion, Major Esekielu was a rabid lion infested with fleas.

"Sir," Chandly said. "Why does Vice Admiral Belmont want Major Esekielu here anyway? Commander Hapker and Major Bracht are just as qualified."

He sighed. *Why indeed?* He suspected prejudice hid behind the admiral's rationale. Bracht was not entirely trusted by the Cooperative because of his Rabnoshk heritage, and Hapker had a history of insubordination. Assigning them to Thendi's ground defense kept them out of the way, especially since the admiral believed it was unlikely the Tredons would ever get as far as the planet's surface.

Telling his people this was unprofessional—not to mention that it would further lower their morale. "He felt they were better qualified to serve on the planet."

"It makes sense," Sengupta said supportively. "Commander Hapker has good interpersonal skills and Major Bracht is an excellent visual deterrent if the Tredons land, I mean Toradons."

Chandly's mouth twisted dubiously, but neither he nor anyone else commented.

Sengupta dipped her head toward the viewscreen. "Any changes?"

"All systems normal and no suspicious readings," he said.

"There's still no definitive word on whether the emperor is coming," Sengupta said regarding her informants. "There are rumors, nothing more."

He shifted in his seat, easing the ache in his tired back. "I'm surprised there's not anything from your contacts at the border."

"Perhaps the emperor won't come."

Arden shivered, imagining spiders scrawling in the shadows. "He'll come now that the admiral has sent half our force to that outpost."

Emperor Mizuki aptly styled himself the Dragon Emperor. Every report he'd read about this man had portrayed him as flying in like a dragon with fire blazing. Like a dragon, he'd take whatever treasure he wanted without hesitation or sympathy. This trait gave rise to his people being called Tredons for "tread on" instead of their proper name, Toradons.

Tredons were human, just like everyone else in the known galaxy. They might as well be alien, though, with their violent disregard for human life.

Sengupta's mouth turned down. "I don't doubt the emperor orchestrated that attack to diminish our defenses here, but those people need protection too."

Arden agreed. "An impossible choice, I know." *But it's just one bad decision after another with that man.*

It all began when the admiral decided the *Odyssey* must to be here. This ship wasn't a warship, as Major Esekielu had made disparagingly clear on several occasions. While its shielding and maneuvering defenses were nearly as good as those of a PG-Force ship, its weapons would be inadequate if Emperor Mizuki came. Or, as Esekielu put it, using the *Odyssey*'s weapons against a Tredon warship would be like using a child's squirt gun to defend against a flamethrower.

The admiral argued that the *Odyssey* was needed to help evacuate people from Thendi if the emperor attacked. Any PCC ship would be capable of the task, but it was Arden who had saved the lives of the emperor's sons.

If there was a chance this fact would convince the emperor not to attack and take the perantium emitter, then the admiral felt it was worth him being there. Arden mentally shook his head. Though there were factors about the Tredon Princes that gave him hope for the future, he had no delusions about the present.

"Sir! Two Tredon warships just came into view," Officer Chandly said.

His musings fled like debris from a supernova. "Shields up!"

The viewscreen flicked to a 3D graphic representation of the planet and surrounding ships. The warships appeared as glaring red dots. *Defender* and *Perses* lit up in yellow while the *Odyssey* was blue.

Several dashed lines burst from the Tredon ships, indicating a hailstorm of firepower.

"Defense sequence alpha," he called out.

The viewscreen flicked into the segmented view of every workstation. He kept his emotions steady as he took in the information. Sengupta set the ship-wide alert and monitored the ship's safety depots, where the crew buckled in and were protected by an additional hull layer and supplemental inertial dampeners. Lieutenant Wilshire readied weapons. Chandly coordinated with the helmsman and operations crew as they prepped the transport so people could be beamed up from Thendi. Officer Brenson alerted Commander Hapker, then switched the main comm channel to the speaker.

The bridge cracked with the trumpet of the admiral's broadcast alert. Arden maintained a pose of confidence as his crew reacted with practiced efficiency.

The pressure of Arden's harness increased as Officer Jensin manipulated the thrusters. A faint shift in his inner ear coincided with their port shields taking a hit. A glance at the helm stats indicated Jensin had nudged the ship back into geosynchronous orbit. Operations stats verified transport from Thendi was underway.

"Brenson, get Major Esekielu up here," Arden said.

His chair trembled as energy blasts from the enemy struck his ship. Each tremor angered rather than worried him, though. It was Admiral Belmont's fault that only two PG-Force ships remained to defend them.

A swarm of blinking dots representing space fighters spewed from the Tredon warships. "The Asps are hatched," a voice from *Defender* said.

"*Defender*, release the Pterodons," Vice Admiral Belmont broadcasted.

"It's 1v2 out there so hug your mamas," the air boss followed.

Arden gripped his armrests. Pterodon jets could outmaneuver Tredon Asps, but one-to-two odds would make it more difficult for the Pterodons to defend the *Odyssey* and two PG-Force ships.

"Sir," Chandly called out. "We have a set of evacuees ready for transport, but there's too much enemy interference."

"Admiral, we need protection," Arden relayed just as another blast from a Tredon warship made the *Odyssey* shake. For the dedicated transport platform on the planet to work, the ship had to be in nearly perfect synchronous orbit.

"*Perses*, cover line of sight," the admiral said.

Arden's knuckles whitened. The *Perses* might partially shield the *Odyssey* from the enemy's line of fire, but it wouldn't keep the Asps away. The smaller enemy jets could maneuver through ship shields and destroy targeting weapons or shield generators. The outnumbered Pterodon jet pilots had little chance of stopping them.

One portion of the viewscreen displayed the jets. He monitored the dots representing them as they engaged in battle. Lights blinked out as Pterodons and Asps alike were damaged or destroyed. Losing a virtually flown Pterodon jet was disappointing, but at least there would be no pilots to mourn.

"Port shields at sixty-five percent, Sir," Chandly announced.

Already? He glanced at his console. "Divert fifteen percent from aft."

"Two transports completed so far," another operations officer said.

He entered the data to share with the admiral and captains of the other ships.

"Fifteen percent of Pterodons down," Flight Commander Madan said through the comm.

He cringed inwardly at the number. The battle was moving much faster than any of their simulations had anticipated.

I wish Hapker was here.

At this point, though, he would settle for Major Esekielu.

"Chandly, which ships are we fighting?" he asked his operations officer.

"It looks like the *Dragon* and *Basilisk*, Sir."

The pit of his stomach shriveled into a hard rock. "Brenson, hail the *Dragon*." A distinctive beep indicated the comm was open. "Emperor Mizuki, this is Captain Silas Arden of the *Odyssey*..." He'd rehearsed the next part many times, but nothing he'd come up with sounded adequate. "I'm hoping that my recent interactions with your sons will allow us to open a dialog and negotiate terms."

Admiral Belmont had wanted him to mention that Emperor Mizuki's eldest son would have died without him, but Arden didn't like being so pretentious. If Rear Admiral Zimmer had allowed him to return the princes home rather than try to keep them in custody, there might have been a spark of hope.

The progress made in befriending the children during their stay crumbled when the princes had to fight to escape. The smoothness of their getaway should have alerted the admiral to the extent of Tredon cunning. As it stood now, the defense of Thendi unraveled fast.

"No response from the *Dragon*," Brenson said.

"Resend," he replied listlessly. This was a waste of time. Though the princes didn't kill a single person when they escaped, it was foolish to believe the emperor would exhibit such mercy.

"Seven transports accomplished," the operations officer said.

His shoulders tensed. There were still dozens to go. Over five hundred people were expected, along with key components of the perantium emitter.

"Fore-dorsal shields at sixty percent. Fifty-six."

"Divert another ten from aft," he replied automatically. "Do we know how the enemy shields are faring?"

"There's been a minimal effect, Sir," Chandly said. "They're still at over eighty per—Sir! They're releasing the Anacondas."

A wave of panic flooded his body. The transport-blockers prevented the Tredons from beaming their own people onto the planet but Thendi didn't have enough defenses to stop the Anaconda carriers. If the carriers entered atmosphere, they'd unload a horde of Rattler jet fighters and land their ground troops. "Brenson, alert Commander Hapker."

"Sir, all our shields are at less than fifty percent," Chandly said. "Port shields now at thirty-five percent."

Arden wiped the sweat from his brow and exerted confidence for the sake of the crew.

"The *Basilisk* seems to be out of the fight," an operations officer said.

Arden puffed, but his stomach still fluttered as he took full stock of the situation. The *Odyssey* had taken a few hits, but most operations remained functional. Shields slowly recovered and no serious injuries had been reported among his crew.

Transports continued but not quickly enough. He thumped his fingers loudly enough to disturb the collective reprieve and forced himself to stop. *Have faith.*

The viewscreen lit up with glaring dashed lines of incoming projectiles. He tensed as they headed to the *Odyssey*.

"Sir!" Wilshire called out. "Our defense cannons won't be able to stop all those torpedoes."

"Brace for impact!"

He gripped his armrests. His chair vibrated as a torpedo struck their port side. Four strikes followed in rapid succession, rattling Arden's teeth.

The ship settled. More dashed lines popped up on the screen. This time, they targeted *Perses*.

"Can we help them, Wilshire?"

"I'm afraid not, Sir. We have no clear shot."

He held his breath as the dashed lines closed in, then disappeared. Tension froze him as he waited for an update.

"Admiral," the captain of the Fortis-class ship said with a breathless tone. "*Perses* has sustained critical damage. We must move out."

Arden's body turned to ice. "Admiral, we must get those people off the planet." There were escape shuttles on the surface, but they'd be easy targets for the Tredon Rattlers and Asps.

"Sir, port shields are down," Chandly called out. "I believe an Asp has gotten through and taken out the shield generator."

"I'm redirecting aft shields to compensate," the other operations officer said, "but it won't be enough."

Oh no. "Brenson, alert Commander Hapker that we're unable to transport. Jensin, follow *Perses* out." He didn't like abandoning the people on the planet, but he still had those already rescued to protect.

He stabbed a button on his console. "Major Esekielu, where in the name of Tunrida are you?" All the hassle of dealing with that man and he wasn't around to do the most important part of his job.

"Our shields are down," the admiral said through the comm. "Pterodons, back to base. We must retreat."

Arden jostled violently as another energy blast struck his ship. His chair restraint kept him seated, but the belt bore down on his torso. Had it not been for the inertial dampeners, he would have been cut to pieces.

"Sir! We've taken a bad hit." Chandly's voice quavered, though Arden knew him to keep a level head in stressful situations. "The port hull's been breached and we're losing atmosphere."

"Seal the area," he ordered even though Chandly was probably already doing so.

"The aft-dorsal and rear shields are also down. All other shields are falling below five percent."

"Jensin, get us out of here."

Jensin moved as though drunk. His head bled profusely. Arden glanced at the other crew members. Even though they were secured by straps, some were disoriented by the violent jolt of the ship.

"Medical team to the bridge!" Arden called out as he struggled to unbuckle himself. The backup helmsman was unconscious, as were the only other bridge members who could pilot the ship.

"Auxiliary crew, I need you here now!" Arden's heart raced, but his body seemed to move in slow motion. Ship alarms sounded as he finally released his straps and stumbled to Jensin's station. Chandly called something out, but Arden didn't hear. The ship shuddered violently again. Arden lost his balance. He reached to brace himself on the edge of the communications console and missed. His arms flailed as the motion of the ship sent him flying in the other direction.

We're all going to die. The fleeting thought cut off at a sudden blow to his head. Blackness followed.

3

Dragon Horde

3791:023:14:02. Commander J.D. Hapker peered at the towering walls of sandstone. The Shovai Canyons were a striking sight with their multiple layers of red and orange hues. One layer recessed deep, allowing a stunning russet hawk to nest there.

Thendi had taken well to the terraforming process. It developed its own flavor after seven hundred years or so, but still had many elements said to be reminiscent of ancient Earth.

He let out a longing sigh. Living in space was certainly an adventure but sometimes he missed life on a planet—the feel of the breeze as he hiked the mountains, the smell of the ocean has he relaxed on the beach, and the sound of the river as he navigated its churning waters in his canoe. He nudged a clump of soft dirt next to his feet. This would have been an excellent place to camp or rock-climb if the canyon wasn't crowded with soldiers protecting the cave.

An alarm sounded through his comm, making his heart skip a beat.

"To your battle stations," the admiral broadcasted. "Enemy ships have arrived."

Adrenaline tingled through his body and sharpened his thoughts. He flipped his faceplate down and scanned the rim. Wavy purple lines tinted the sky, indicating the deflector shields functioned properly. Their half-kilometer range wasn't much, but better than nothing.

A green icon blinked in the top right of his visor as he examined the line of gun turrets stationed along the edge. Trusting their AIs to know when and what to fire didn't sit well with him, but reduced manpower increased their importance.

Lieutenant Hanna Sharkey stepped to his side. "You think we're ready?"

A wisp of her hair strayed loose from her tight bun. She had the same sandy-colored hair as him and stood nearly as tall. Their close friendship confused some people into believing they were brother and sister.

"As ready as we can be."

"Ready enough to hold off the emperor?" she said as she put on her helmet.

"Yes," he replied, hiding his doubt.

She smirked. "You're unending optimism is annoying sometimes, you know."

Her attempt to lighten the mood barely registered. Since they'd been friends through their schooling at the Prontaean Galactic Institute, he was used to her making casual conversation or telling jokes during stressful situations.

"The Asps are hatched," a voice announced through the primary comm channel.

"Here we go," he said.

She kept her pace with his as they made their way along the wall of synthetic barriers. The troops jumped into a flurry of motion. Everything was ready. It had been for some time, but the news roused everyone to high alert. Soldiers reexamined their phaser rifles. Artillery officers verified the readiness of their heavy guns. Squad leaders did roll call or checked stats on the MM tablets worn on their wrists.

Sharkey put her hand to the side of her helmet. "Did you hear that? The *Odyssey* is taking fire."

The knot in his stomach tightened. He should be up there. It made little sense to assign an officer of a civilian ship to lead PG-Force ground troops. However, both entities operated under the Prontaean Cooperative, and he had the qualifications.

He pushed thoughts of the *Odyssey* from his mind. Though he worried for his crew, people here needed protection too.

They came upon two robo-mules loaded with extra ammunition and additional supplies. Sergeant Mendosa paced between them, pinching his lower lip as he scowled at his MM. He tsked and removed the device so that it flattened and stiffened into the tablet form.

"Sergeant," Hapker said.

Sergeant Mendosa raised his head and saluted with a snap. His wrinkled brow smoothed, and his brown eyes flickered from dull to sharp. "Commander."

"You look troubled. Is something wrong?"

"No, Sir. Just wondering if we have enough sheepdogs to guard the sheep."

"At ease, Sergeant." He clapped him on the shoulder. "We've got a good team. Not to mention an outstanding weapons officer."

Mendosa bobbed his head. "Thank you, Sir."

He smiled in reply, hoping he conveyed confidence. "If the emperor makes landfall, all we have to do is secure the entrance until everyone can evacuate." He motioned to the broad doors that led into the facility where the construction of the perantium emitter took place.

"Yes, Sir. I can do that." Mendosa puffed out his chest and jutted his chin.

"Good man."

"Two transports completed so far," Sharkey added. "We'll all be out of here in no time."

Mendosa dipped his head. "Yes, Ma'am."

Hapker and Sharkey moved on to the sandbagged section of the barrier. It was an old-fashioned method of cover, but an effective one—especially when resources were thin. Sandbags held up against both energy weapons and projectiles, and this canyon had plenty of sand.

He half-listened to the chatter from the comm. The number of remote-flown Pterodons dwindled, but at least there were no casualties. They were up to seven transports. Ship shield strengths decreased, but it seemed both sides fared about the same.

Typed information scrolling along the bottom of his visor caught his attention. *Emperor not responding to hails.* Hapker's heart sank. He glanced skyward, hoping Jori wasn't up there having to take part in this.

Sharkey lightly touched his arm. "You're thinking about him, aren't you?"

He feigned indifference. "He made his choice."

She gave him a sideways look. "Anyone with eyes could see how fond you were of him—still are."

Hapker puffed. "You know me too well."

That fateful day when the Tredon ship crashed on the Cooperative planet had sent events on an unexpected trajectory. Everyone died except two boys who turned out to be the emperor's sons. Since the eldest was in a coma, Hapker was assigned to watch over the youngest.

"Jori started out hostile." He shook his head and laughed softly. "One time after he beat me at schemster, he said, 'You take too long to move. If this had been a real battle, you would've been dead much sooner.' He said it so coldly, it gave me chills. But he turned out to be alright, even at the end."

Sharkey's forehead creased. "Yet now he's up there in that ship doing who knows what."

"If he's taking part, I know he's only doing it because he has to." Hapker's stomach churned. "It's a pity. No child—"

Another alarm sounded in his ear. "Ground force alert," the general broadcast said. "Four Anacondas are on the move."

Sharkey's eyes widened. "Shit."

He agreed with the sentiment. Once those carriers entered Thendi's atmosphere, the responsibility of stopping the emperor shifted from the space force to the ground troops.

"How many Rattler jet fighters and infantry do those things carry?" she asked.

He broke out into a sweat despite the cool breeze of the canyon. "Too many," he replied, knowing her question was rhetorical.

Updates rolled in at the same time comm chatter increased. He noted it all while also doing calculations. Add the time for atmospheric entry to the time for their jets and ground combat ships to land. Then time for the warriors to reach the deflector shields and knock them out.

Not much time at all. Hapker announced the earliest estimate to the troops and ordered last minute checks.

"I bet you wish you were back on Pholatia," Sharkey said.

His homeworld. He harrumphed as he scanned the check-ins coming through on his visor. Being a Pholatian Protector certainly had been easier. Back then, he was a kitten batting at flies. As a PG-Force officer, he'd been a tiger taking down wild boars. Being a PCC officer balanced the two extremes—until now.

Ever since he had saved a friend when he was a boy, he knew he wanted to help people. Serving peaceful Pholatians wasn't enough.

He hated having to fight because of this greedy emperor, but he lived for this moment. Fighting alongside soldiers to protect the innocent strengthened his determination.

A restless buzz hung in the air and prickled his skin. When he scanned the troops, a panicked face grabbed his attention. He tapped Sharkey's shoulder and pointed. "Looks like we have a rookie."

They jogged up to find Sergeant Davis already handling the situation. The man loomed over Private Fresel. "You *can* do this, Private! Those bloody barbarians are gonna come down that wall and you're gonna stop them. Those worthless shites don't stand a chance."

Private Fresel nodded, but she looked to the ground rather than at Davis.

Corporal Harley elbowed her. "We've got your back, Fresel."

"Yeah," another officer said as he thumped Harley on the back. "We can't go wrong when we have hot-headed Harley on our side."

The dark-haired young man beamed. He obviously enjoyed the reputation of his name. Harley speedsters, known throughout the galaxy for both their power and speed, tended to be owned by the more maverick members of society. This young man wasn't a rebel, but he could be rash.

Fresel glanced at Harley with a half-smile. Her hazel eyes sparked, reminding Hapker of his childhood friend, Fadwa. Fresel had freckles and Fadwa had black hair instead of red. Yet looking at the private was like seeing Fadwa grown up.

"Do you know what those bloody barbarians do to women?" Davis continued.

Fresel looked down again. Hapker winced. It wasn't the way he'd go about motivating the private, but he had no justifiable reason to interfere. A forceful speech could be motivating. Unfortunately, it didn't seem Fresel bought into it. Her face paled and she hugged her rifle close.

If Fresel really was Fadwa, though, she'd be standing tall and glaring right back at Davis. Fadwa had been the daughter of a space cargo hauler. Her spirit was both resolute and adventurous. She was a marvelous wonder for a boy who'd never ventured beyond the continent, let alone the planet.

"You're not gonna let that happen, though," Davis said. "You're gonna shoot those worthless shites dead. You got that?" Davis clapped her on the shoulder.

Fresel jumped. "Y-yes, Sir!"

"Can you do this, Private?" Davis shouted.

"Yes, Sir!"

"Can I count on you?"

"Yes, Sir!"

"Good. Now get your arse back in line and ready that weapon."

"Yes, Sir!"

Fresel hustled and almost tripped back to her spot behind the sandbags. Sergeant Davis frowned at her back. He turned and met Hapker's eyes. Hapker dipped his head despite his dislike of the man, and Davis returned the gesture.

Davis' shoot-first attitude shared among many of his comrades was one reason Hapker didn't do well serving the PG-Force. Davis didn't much care for him either, but they respected one another well enough to do their jobs.

As Hapker moved to follow Davis out, he glanced back at Fresel and changed his mind. The woman swayed. Her hands trembled as she examined her rifle.

He pressed his lips. She still didn't have a grip. Time ticked away and he needed everyone at their best.

"Private!" he called out.

She snapped her gaze to his and gulped before coming over on wobbly legs. "Commander, Sir!" she said with a shaky salute.

"Private Fresel," he said in an even, unhurried tone. "Being nervous is normal. I'm nervous, too."

"Really?" she said.

"Really. But I've learned to push that nervousness to the back of my mind and focus on the task at hand. You will learn to do that too. Just watch your team. Do what they do. Do you think you can do that?"

She met his eyes, took in a deep inhale and let out a long exhale, then nodded. The shaking in her hands subsided.

"Good. I have no doubt you'll handle yourself well."

"Thank you, Commander," Fresel replied. "I, um, I also want to thank you for standing up for me the other day after I—"

"Say nothing of it, Private. You made a mistake, but you owned up to it and did what you could to fix it. That shows me you learn from your mistakes and you have integrity."

The creases of her mouth curved up, accenting the roundness of her cheeks.

"You'll do fine," he said with a smile.

As she returned to her station with a steadier gait, he glanced at the time on his visor. Each passing second tightened his shoulders. They were fully ready, but he couldn't help feeling there was more to do.

As he turned to leave, Davis met his eyes. "She's got to eat her fish head with a shot of whiskey, Sir."

He frowned. "I'm sorry, Sergeant. I don't understand."

Davis cocked his eyebrow. "She needs to toughen up, Sir, or she's not gonna make it."

Hapker's hackles rose from the hinted criticism against his easy manner, but he didn't have time for the man's opinions. "She'll be fine."

While he hurried through the ranks, offering words of encouragement or resolving last-minute issues, memories of the past interfered and triggered an acidic taste in his mouth. Though he had saved Fadwa, he also failed her. She'd made a mistake, one he considered forgivable. But nobody else, not even his own father, thought she was worthy.

Everyone deserved a chance—Jori too.

Regret replaced bitterness as his thoughts shifted to the boy. He'd saved then failed him, too. He glanced at the sky and hoped Jori was alright.

*****

3791:023:15:23. J.D. Hapker's faceplate automatically tinted as he looked up at the yellow sun and sky. A swarm of black-garbed warriors spilled over the red canyon wall like a raging flood. They rappelled downward, faster than greedy spiders descending upon their prey.

The PG-Force and Thendian troops opened fire on Emperor Mizuki's Dragon Warriors. The air flashed and shimmered as phaser fire struck their energy shields like rain splatter while the sound of projectile ammo resounded in a hailstorm.

Hapker aimed his phaser rifle at individual warriors and fired in rapid succession. Three blasts should disable their shields, allowing a fourth to wound or kill them.

"They're on the ground!" he yelled as several warriors landed on the uneven rubble of the canyon floor. "Major Bracht, focus on their artillery officers! Mendosa, fire the plat bombs!"

A blast struck his body shield, making him flinch. *That's one.* He aimed at a cluster of warriors and pelted them with phased energy.

A shock wave thudded his eardrums as the earth ahead erupted in rubble and smoke. He barely regained his balance when the tremor from the exploding plat bombs buckled his legs. He and Lieutenant Sharkey grabbed one another's arm as small bits of debris rained down.

A horde of Dragon Warriors spewed from the smoke like an infestation of cockroaches. Hapker's heart raced as he fired in rapid succession, draining the energy from his weapon. He coughed a dusty heat from his throat and reloaded. "Team! Stay with me! Protect the entrance!"

He took a quick peek at those around him. There were few, but they were skilled. Lieutenant Sharkey showed her teeth as she fired her weapon. It always amazed him how quickly her usual amiable and upbeat manner could turn so relentlessly fierce.

Major Bracht's mouth curled into a snarl and his throat rumbled like a lion. There had been a time when Hapker disdained the man's stereotypical traits of a Rabnoshk warrior. Now that he knew him, though, he was glad to have him fighting at his side.

Units of enemy warriors simultaneously expanded long black batons into large metal blast shields. They formed ranks in practiced efficiency and rushed forward as one machine.

"Aim for their legs!" Hapker shouted to his companions, knowing their weapons wouldn't be able to penetrate those physical shields.

The metal barbs accenting the enemy's black reptilian armor flashed with the reflection of exchanged firepower. They were Herculean men moving with deadly purpose, no doubt trained for battle since birth and supplemented with plenty of experience.

Another strike distorted Hapker's energy shield. *That's two*. He reached under his visor and wiped the sweat building on his eyelids, then pinpointed more targets. He gripped his phaser rifle and his muscles tightened, almost to the point of numbness.

Single-minded determination filled him. Some enemy warriors fell. Others slowed but overall, they kept coming. The dark narrow eyes of the enemy, charged with both hatred and battle lust, surged forward like an advancing tidal wave. Hapker's heart thumped in his ears too loudly to hear their battle cries.

He reloaded again. Lieutenant Sharkey did the same. Her face flushed and her brow furrowed over her striking blue eyes.

A cluster of approaching warriors protected by their blast shields inched closer to Hapker and his team. He took two opponents down. Sharkey and the others fighting around him eliminated three more. Only two of the original cluster of Dragon Warriors remained. They ducked behind their blast shields and waited for reinforcements. Within moments, several other warriors with black shields advanced.

Hapker glanced hurriedly down either side of the canyon. Their situation was hopeless. The initial planned pincher formation had been too weak to hold. It was now over a thousand against his remaining force of about two hundred.

"Retreat!" he yelled. Sharkey repeated the command behind him even though the order was relayed through the comms. Her sharp voice carried. The message echoed further back.

His troops promptly withdrew into the large recesses of the canyon wall where the facility had been built. The hundreds of scientists working within were likely already evacuated. The rear of the installation had elevators to take them up to a narrow canyon alcove where they could be transported away.

"There's too m—" Corporal Fresel's head snapped back and her body crumpled.

Hapker's heart lurched. He noted her cracked helmet but was too far away to check if she survived.

As Harley grasped her arm and dragged her back, Hapker protected their escape as best he could. He, Sharkey, and Bracht laid cover fire as the other troops retreated inside. Discharge from the enemy's weapons crackled around him. One struck and neutralized his energy body shield. *Crap, that's three.*

He ducked inside the facility. "Shut the doors!" he said needlessly since the thick heavy blast hatchway already descended.

Several shots burst through before the doors closed, but no one was hit. He let out a premature sigh.

"That won't hold them for long," an officer reminded him.

"Lieutenant Gardner!" he called. "Gardner!"

"He's dead, Commander," Sergeant Walden said.

A twinge of regret washed through him, but he pushed it aside. "Walden, get the bombs in place."

"Already on it, Commander," he replied.

"This won't stop 'em, Sir," Sergeant Mendosa said.

"We just need enough time to set another bomb on the device and get out of here," he replied.

"Another of the admiral's flimsy last resort ideas," Mendosa said sourly, but to himself. "I feel like a damned chicken trapped…"

His words trailed off as the troops hustled down the long corridor. Hapker got the gist. The admiral first suggested dismantling the device, but it took a stout Thendian scientist with a shrill voice to get the man to understand that even taking a few key parts would be difficult. The admiral retorted they should take what they could and blow up the rest.

He thought the statement had merely been a heated response, but a destruct-plan was implemented. When Captain Arden questioned it, the admiral cut him off. It would never come to that, he'd said.

Hapker ground his teeth as never turned into devastating certainty.

The second set of blast doors closed. A huge eruption from the first set thundered through the facility. The ground trembled violently beneath his feet. He and the others fell on one another. The walls cracked and crumbled around them. A sizeable part of the plastered ceiling dropped away, exposing the hard cave stone overhead.

He helped Sharkey to her feet. Her helmet had fallen off and she had a streak of blood running across her brow.

"You alright?"

"Yes," she said breathlessly.

"Commander Hapker," Officer Brenson's voice said into his comm. "We're unable to continue transport."

An invisible weight fell on his shoulders. "Everyone to the shuttles. Transports are down."

"Sir!" an officer behind him said. "The sky is full of Rattlers. We'll never make it away."

"It's better than staying here," he replied. "Get moving!"

"All ships pulling out," an anonymous voice announced through his comm. "The admiral's called for a full retreat."

The weight nearly sent him to his knees. He eye-clicked to a sub-channel. "Shuttle pilots, take your people to the backup locations."

"At least the admiral had the foresight to designate hiding spots on the planet," Mendosa said.

"Gag it, Sergeant," Major Bracht replied.

"Stay focused," Hapker added.

They shut themselves behind the third set of blast doors just as a reverberating boom took out the second. His troops stumbled but continued their swift retreat.

He entered the cavern last. It was more of a crevasse with a removable domed ceiling than a cavern, but spacious enough to allow several small transport ships to line up, one behind the other. Instead of ships, though, it held the giant emitter pieces intended for assembly in space.

The fourth set of blast doors closed him and the rest of the troops in. They retreated to the only exit—an elevator that could take them to another open cavern where hopefully at least one more shuttle waited.

"Get a barricade up quickly!" he yelled as the heavy stone around them shook violently from a blast taking out the third set of doors.

The troops scrambled to build a makeshift barrier from equipment, furnishings, and even tool bots.

"Bracht, you have command of the left wing," he said. "I'll take the right. Mendosa, how many grenades do we have left?"

"About two dozen, Commander."

He ran his hand down his sweaty face. Their resources were dwindling. "Divide them up."

He took a headcount. Fresel's icon was dead, which meant she was too. Most icons had gone dark. His chest tightened, but he ignored it and focused on those who still lived.

"Simmonds," he called to the *Odyssey*'s Chief Engineer. "What are you still doing here?"

A man with long sideburns pointed at a brown canister. "Sir, we can't get the bomb in place."

He groaned inwardly. Debris littered the area where they had initially planned to set the charges.

"Sir, we can put it over there," Simmonds said, pointing at a cylinder tower. "The coils won't be easily repaired or replaced, except by the Thendians later."

He nodded. Simmonds was no explosives expert, but his knowledge of the emitter helped with deciding where to set the bomb. "Hurry up, then get out of here."

Simmonds directed the PG-Force officer with the explosives to another spot.

Hapker turned to the Rabnoshk warrior. "Once Simmonds is done, you take him and leave. I'll follow."

Bracht didn't look like he cared for the idea of retreat, but he gave a curt nod and readied his men.

The fourth and final blast door rumbled to open.

"Get ready!" Hapker and the others ducked behind the barriers.

As the door rose, he fired his phaser rifle at the exposed feet of the enemy. The sounds of warriors in pain echoed into the chamber, but they weren't nearly as loud as their angry roars.

"It's set!" Simmonds called.

"Bracht, go!" Hapker ordered.

Bracht held his position as he directed half his group to retreat to the elevator. Simmonds stood to follow, then fell with a cry. Someone pulled him back behind the barricade. Simmonds clutched his lower leg but otherwise appeared alright.

Hapker's troops laid cover fire and threw grenades while the others escaped. Smoke from the explosions concealed them, but it didn't keep anyone from getting hit by the enemy. Energy shields failed and troops fell. Those who helped the fallen made for easier targets. He lost count of the casualties.

"Shiiit!" Corporal Harley flew back, his body armor dented by ammo.

"You alright?" Hapker asked.

"Yes, Sir!" Harley rubbed his shoulder and sat up with a grunt. After shifting his rifle to his other side, he resumed firing at the enemy onslaught.

Bracht and the last of his group hopped into the elevator. A stench of desperation permeated the air as Hapker's people fought and waited for their ride to return.

"I'm out!" an officer yelled.

"Get back! Go!" Hapker signed for him and half the team to leave.

A grenade flew over their barricade to the elevator. He ducked just as a searing burst sent a bulky shard of debris over his head. The ground and walls rumbled. Plaster and rock spewed forth. Sharp pains splattered across his back. His troops cried out in surprise, then some groaned in agony.

Sharkey and Harley fought with desperation etched on their faces.

"I'm out too," another officer said.

"We're trapped." Simmonds' tone was strained.

"Their grenades destroyed the elevator," Mendosa added.

Hapker noted the comments but kept fighting. He numbly pressed the trigger of his phaser rifle, aiming at the enemy swarm still at the open blast doors.

Someone touched his hand. "Sir," Sharkey said. "You're out too."

He turned his focus to his weapon. She was right.

"We're all out, Sir," Harley said, his voice winded. "What do we do?"

Hapker ducked behind the barricade. Everyone eyed him, but he couldn't make any words.

We're dead. We're all dead.

*****

3791:023:16:35. Zaps of enemy weapons sizzled through the air. J.D. Hapker met his friend's eyes with a pained expression and clasped her hand. "I'm sorry," he whispered. Lieutenant Sharkey gripped his fingers in return.

The boom of a Dragon Warrior's voice called out. Stark silence followed. Hapker's pulse thudded in his ears. He panted despite the smoky air that curled around him like writhing snakes.

He peeked over the barrier. The enemy warriors swarmed into the chamber unopposed. They waded through the littered remnants of battle with an ease of killer ants overrunning and devouring their prey.

He ducked and closed his eyes in silent prayer. When he opened them, a dozen warriors towered over him. They seemed much larger than they had in the canyon. Their reptilian uniforms conformed to their bodies, enhancing every ripple of muscle. Some soldiers built the muscular look into their armor with padding, but the Tredon warriors needed no such enhancements. Their glowers exacerbated his already swelling fear.

At the sharp command of a man with the bulk of a great brown bear, a pack of warriors manhandled Hapker and the others face-down on the floor. There was no time to resist as they bound his hands behind his back.

"Stay down," a warrior said as he slammed the butt of his phaser rifle into Hapker's shoulder. The warrior spoke in the Tredon language, but his comm automatically chirped the translation in his ear.

"Hey, look at this one!" a warrior with a missing front tooth said, slapping Sharkey's behind. "It's a woman," he laughed.

Heat flared in Hapker's chest. He tried to say something, but the weight of a boot pressed the air from his lungs.

"No wonder they lost so easily," the warrior standing on him said. "They have their women fighting for them."

"Knock it off, you dumbass brute," Sharkey growled. "You touch me, I'll rip off your balls and shove them down your throat."

Hapker winced yet admired her spirit.

The toothless man laughed lustily as he moved to mount her. Hapker growled and twisted.

"Duty first, Usagi," the bear-sized man said. The patch on his shoulder indicated he was a general. A heavy scar ran over his cheek and square jaw. His face was abnormally long, even compared to his gigantic frame.

As Usagi stepped back, Sharkey's shoulders sagged. Hapker puffed but the hardness in his stomach remained. The Dragon Warrior left her alone, but for how long?

"General!" a spindly Tredon called out.

The bear-sized man turned, and the skinny man wrung his hands. "They have a bomb set on the device, Sir. We've got five minutes before it blows."

"Disarm it," the general said as though it were simple.

"I'm not sure I can," the man replied. He wore a uniform, but it differed from the others.

"Then get it out of here."

"Sir," the skinny man whined. "There's not enough time."

Good. The thought of an instant death gave Hapker comfort, especially for Sharkey's sake.

The general forced a prisoner to his feet, and Hapker's hope for a quick death shattered.

"Do you know how to deactivate this?" the general asked with a rumbling tone.

The prisoner pressed his lips defiantly.

The general struck him in the jaw with a resounding crack. The man slumped in the general's grip and groaned.

Hapker jerked sideways, dislodging the boot. A jab to the base of his skull blackened his vision and curtailed his struggle.

"I ask you again, can you deactivate this?"

The man, a corporal who served on the *Defender*, shook his head. The general grabbed his chin and squeezed, making him scream in agony.

"Leave him…" Hapker gasped. "Leave him alone."

A knee pressed between his shoulder blades and the warrior on top of him grabbed his scalp. Hot breath burned his ear. "Shut it, chima."

"Are you sure?" the general demanded his prisoner.

The man whimpered and tried to speak, but his words came out garbled. The general snapped the man's neck, killing him.

Fire flushed through Hapker's veins as ice speared his chest.

The general yanked another officer up. "What about you?"

The prisoner shook his head. The general's muscles twitched.

"I w-will do it," Simmonds muttered. "I will do it!"

"Two minutes, forty seconds," the skinny Tredon said.

The general grabbed Simmonds. "You know how to disable it?"

Yellowish green vomitus dripped from Simmonds' chin as he bobbed his head. "Yes."

Hapker's gut clenched. "No, Simmonds," he managed to call out as the hand clutching his hair tightened. "He'll kill us anyw—"

The man gripping his hair jerked his head up and smacked it down. Pain exploded through his skull, sending tendrils of darkness through his vision. When his sight returned, the scene appeared calm. A warrior unceremoniously threw Simmonds to the floor next to Hapker.

"Please tell me you didn't deactivate it," Hapker croaked.

Simmonds' throat bobbed and his eyes turned down in guilt.

4
Second Betrayal

3791:023:16:36. Jori flushed with exhilaration as he and Terk exited the bridge. "That was intense."

"I know," Terk said with a cocked smile.

Jori swelled with admiration. "General Samuru couldn't have done better."

"I owe you one." Terk nudged him with his elbow.

Jori puffed out his chest as they headed to their next assignment with two of their personal guards trailing behind. After the enemy had crippled the *Basilisk*, their father slammed his fist on his console with a bellowing curse. A string of orders followed and Terk obeyed—almost without a hitch.

Some of his targeting coordinates were off and Jori discreetly pointed them out. Father noticed Terk's delay but seemed to have forgotten about it when the torpedoes and cannons struck the enemy's battleship. Not long after, the *Dragon* regained the offensive.

Jori had watched the viewscreen wide-eyed, taking in the stats and analyzing every maneuver and pattern of firepower. When Father ordered Terk to fire at the *Odyssey*, the rapid beat of his heart dropped to a hard throb. Worrying for Commander Hapker was foolish, but he couldn't suppress the feeling.

When the *Odyssey* escaped, thoughts of the commander had fled with it.

The *Dragon* won the day. Jori drew in a deep breath and let the heightened emotions of those around him bolster his elation. He cast a smile at Terk, and the corners of Terk's mouth curled in return.

The door to the conveyor slid open and Jori and Terk stepped inside. Their two personal guards followed and took their place on either side.

"Staging area," Terk said to the computer.

The conveyor jerked into motion. Every lurch brought them one step closer to their assignment planetside. Jori's heart drummed. The battle was mostly over, but maybe Terk would get a chance to prove himself.

What if an enemy survivor waited to ambush them? Jori's imagination played out a scenario where Terk sensed the man, then took him out before he made trouble. Father would be impressed, and Terk could join the senshi in their victory.

The daydream dispersed when the conveyor halted, but the elation remained. They exited to a wide corridor, following the grey lines worn through the dark epoxy coating by thousands of marching boots. Jori walked along the center with his shoulders pulled back and imagined the two personal guards behind him were a squad of senshi.

A ripple of goosebumps ran down Jori's neck as they entered a vast chamber. The staging area stood empty now, but the energetic vibe left by the senshi lingered. A dozen domed lights lit up the center of the room, creating deep shadows at the edges and hinting at the infinite might of the Dragon Warriors. A brighter light illuminated the blood red dais and the backdrop of a gold dragon on a field of crimson. Inspiration mingled with intimidation every time he watched Father address the troops from the platform.

A clatter followed by harsh laughter drew his attention. Two senshi stood over a figure huddled against the wall. The figure's jumpsuit labeled him a shokukin, a man from the worker caste. The man glanced up at his tormentors and Jori recognized Malkai's stark green eyes.

"Watch where you're going, dog," a senshi said as he shoved Malkai.

"I-It was an accident."

The senshi smacked Malkai across the head and pointed at the tools on the floor. "Pick up your shit."

Malkai bent low and the other senshi kicked him in the ribs.

Jori surged forward. "Leave him alone!"

Terk grabbed his shoulder and yanked him aside. "What the hell are you doing?"

Jori turned back, surprised at the intensity of his brother's irritation. "Malkai is here to do maintenance on the transport pad. It's a sensitive machine and we can't afford for it to malfunction."

"You know damn good and well that's not why you're interfering."

Terk shifted his darkened expression to the pair of senshi warriors. The men peered past Terk's shoulder at his personal guards and smirked. One barely dipped his head, then both sauntered away.

Jori sensed Terk's mood spike and matched his brother's indignation. Ever since their older brothers Dokuri and Montaro had died, the burden of trying to live up to the Mizuki name had fallen on Terk's shoulders. Terk had decent warrior skills but couldn't yet match Dokuri's fierce reputation, no matter how hard he fought for his authority.

Terk pulled Jori's arm. "Let's get going. Your damned sentiment has wasted enough time."

Jori swallowed the sting and walked with his brother into the changing room. They headed to their personal section off to the side while Michio walked around the room between the rows of lockers and checked every corner as a precautionary measure. Jori and Terk were reasonably safe on the ship, but there had been enough assassination attempts to warrant caution.

Jori opened the cabinet holding his battle gear. His uniform hung from a forked hook like a black pearl tree snake. The nanite-infused material had a slight gloss to it. It was only two millimeters thick, but like the sim-gear he wore earlier, it helped deflect, distribute, or absorb stabs, projectiles, and energy weapons.

The uniform slid on and conformed nicely. It fit him even as he grew—to a point. This material was technically superior to what the senshi had. He and Terk might have to prove themselves worthy before gaining the respect of the senshi, but their ancestry still afforded them certain advantages.

He reached over his shoulder to secure a strap. His senses told him Father was on the way.

Terk must have sensed it too. "You better hurry. That little stunt you pulled will make us late. You know how Father hates waiting."

Jori dressed and thought about what had happened and why he instinctively stepped in. The fear in Malkai's eyes was part of it. Mostly, it was the man's feeling of helplessness. Sometimes when Jori rested, he sensed someone else being hurt. It kept him awake, wishing he had the strength to stop it.

In that moment, several memories had popped in his mind. The time Dokuri slapped him so hard he had to be rushed to the infirmary, when Montaro beat him with a baton and locked him in a supply room—but Father's punishments were the worst. He shoved the visions aside before they overwhelmed him.

"Why do they treat them like that?" he said. "If not for the shokukin, we wouldn't have an operating ship."

"They're shokukin. You're a senshi. Act like it."

"Washi and Michio here are senshi too, but don't treat anyone like that."

Washi smiled. Michio returned from his rounds and shrugged. "Some thrive on harassing lesser men. I never saw the point."

"Unlike you, Washi and Michio have the respect of the senshi," Terk said, securing the girth of his armor.

"When you're older and stronger, they won't dare treat you like that," Jori said.

"It's not just about strength," Washi said as he helped Jori with another back strap. "Your voice was strong earlier, but your words were wrong."

"And giving them an order that you don't yet have the strength to back up makes you appear weak," Michio added.

Jori absorbed the information. He valued the input of Sensei Jeruko's sons. They'd been his personal guards since he was three. Like Sensei Jeruko, they always gave good advice.

"So what should I have said?" he asked as he put on his body energy shield and tested it.

"Make sure your face is stern," Washi said, demonstrating the expression. "Then say, 'I know you two have something else you should be doing,' This way you are not giving an order you can't enforce."

"And you're hinting at an authority without having to invoke anyone's name," Michio added.

Jori nodded. It made sense. Terk's eyes followed the conversation but he said nothing.

Michio handed Jori his phaser rifle. It was smaller and easier to carry than the one he used in simulation. It didn't have as much firepower either, but it had enough.

He checked the rifle over to make sure all the functions worked. When he finished, he stood alert with his feet together, his shoulders pulled back, and his chin up.

Michio regarded him, then raised his brows. "Impressive, young Prince."

Jori grinned.

"Ah-ah," Washi said, putting up his finger. "Keep your expression hard. You may be small, but no one will mess with you so long as you carry that weapon like you mean to use it."

Jori hardened his resolve. The chances of him having to fight were slim. Neither he nor Terk had earned the right to take part in a ground battle. This assignment was partly for training and partly for show—but maybe they'd get lucky.

*****

3791:023:17:10. Smoke wafted through the canyon, creating an acrid haze. Jori blinked his watery eyes and stepped carefully. His heavy boots protected his feet as he crunched over the occasional smoldering debris left over from bombardment.

An enemy corpse lay in their path, but Father strode over it as though it was another piece of wreckage littering the ground. Captain Renzo kicked the dead man aside, revealing a pool of curdled blood. General Nezumi's lips curled as his eyes scanned over the bodies, making his face look even more rat-like.

Lifeless husks lay all about. The stench of fire and death singed Jori's nostrils. The enemy fighters were soldiers, but they were still dead because of him. He clenched his hands and swallowed the rising bile.

He shouldn't have come, but what choice did he have? He was either a warrior or he wasn't. Unlike the sons of some planetary lords who had enough sway to allow them to be indolent, Jori and Terk had to prove themselves worthy. Strength would hold the empire, not emotional weakness.

Jori gritted his teeth. He would not be weak. Besides, the battle was over. The senshi had risked their lives and won the day. He should honor them by holding his head high and walking among the dead without puking.

He scanned over the senshi searching the field for survivors. Two men carried Senshi Pachin between them. A scorch mark on his lower abdomen indicated his energy shield had failed but his body armor held up.

Another senshi found an enemy survivor and blasted him in the head. Jori broke out into a cold sweat as the sensation of the man's death bombarded his senses. The intense feeling ended quickly, but it carried the lingering pain of a dried and bloody bandage being ripped from his skin.

He glanced at Terk, who kept his eyes firmly forward. Though Terk had the same unique sensing ability, he seemed unaffected.

"Doesn't the pain of death bother you?" Jori asked quietly.

"Unlike you," Terk said, "I can't afford to let sentiment hinder me."

A stony lump formed in Jori's throat. Damn Commander Hapker. It was his fault he had confusion about emotion being a weakness.

After the failed mission that ended with Terk in a coma and them both in the Cooperative's custody, Jori had spent a lot of time with the enemy commander. Something he said stuck with him— emotions themselves weren't a weakness *unless you lose control of them or let them control you.*

When Terk awoke and it came time for them to escape, Jori let his feelings for the commander guide his actions. He insisted on not hurting anyone. Instead of killing their enemies, they used stun weapons. Rather than commandeer the ship, they escaped to the *Brimstone* warship and left the *Odyssey* to defend itself.

His stupid emotions had gotten Terk in trouble and threatened to do so again. He tightened his fists and attempted to quell his feelings. "I won't let it happen again."

"You better not."

Jori firmed his jaw and matched Terk's confident stride. He took in his brother's sense of resolve and let it bolster his own. It wasn't easy to keep his eyes forward as they continued through the litter of dead, but he managed. If he focused on the surrounding warriors, the emotions of the dying barely touched the edge of his thoughts.

A glimpse of the sensations coming from Father sent a shiver down his spine. The man liked to criticize Jori for being emotional. If that was true, though, why was Father always so bad-tempered?

He should be happy this battle had gone so well, but his emotions were full of nothing but disdain for the dead he trod over.

General Samuru met them at the cave entrance. "Sire. We've secured only a small group of prisoners. Most appear to be fighters."

"Chusho!" Father cursed. "How in the hell did you let all the scientists escape? You know we needed them to help with the device."

Samuru dipped his head at the appropriate ten-degree angle for a general and Father's lifelong friend. "They had a good escape plan laid out, Sire. Four sets of blast doors protected them, and they escaped up an elevator shaft."

The eyes of his father ignited with fire. His face tightened and his jaw worked.

"Kujira is tracking two shuttles that left the area, but it's not—"

"I know what he said," Father said. The heat of the man's emotions doubled in Jori's senses. No doubt Father wasn't just upset with his men. His decision to let the *Odyssey* escape while he concentrated on the surface attack got him the device but no scientists to fix it.

"Tell Kujira to make sure he captures the shuttles. We need those people alive." Father turned to Terk. "Terkeshi, take a team inside and search the bodies for survivors. Don't kill them. I will determine their value later."

Terk snapped into a stiff posture of attention. "Yes, Sir," he said eagerly.

Jori gave Terk a small smile. It wasn't enough to prove his worth, but it was something.

Terk wordlessly directed Washi and Michio and two senshi to join him. As Samuru and Father headed down the main hall, Terk led Jori and the others through an offshoot door. Most likely, the warriors had already cased each room, but everyone had their weapons poised in case.

Terk took the lead, checking each corner and crevice with the coordinated and fastidious air of strict training. Jori mimicked him, though he was at the rear and not likely to encounter any trouble.

"I don't sense anyone here," Jori said.

Terk made a sharp nod and dutifully searched the room anyway. They investigated two more rooms with no results.

As they approached a fourth door, a sensation of life struck Jori's awareness. "There's at least one person alive inside. He's conscious and deathly afraid. Probably not a warrior, but he could still be armed."

Terk entered with the others. His method of searching didn't change. As Sensei Jeruko taught, knowing someone was lying in wait should always be handled the same as not knowing.

"Out!" Terk said as he aimed his energy rifle around the corner. "Put down your weapon and come out."

Jori sensed the man's overwhelming terror. It must have been enough to freeze him because he didn't respond.

"Come out, you chima!" Terk fired a short burst. "If I have to drag your ass out, I will flay the flesh from your bones."

A sound like a sob broke out. "Please," the man said. "I don't want to die."

"Get your ass out here and you'll live," Terk said. "I have orders not to kill. But if you don't come out, I'll make you wish for death."

The man pushed aside metal shelf, making it screech as it scraped across the floor. The sensation of his terror soared, but it willed him forward.

"Please, please," the man said with a whimper as he came forward. His head hung low, but a spark of recognition made Jori's breath catch.

The man's skin had a bluish-grey tint and his lips puckered like a fish. Jori had only met him once, but never forgot a face— especially not one as ugly as this. The man was human, but he might as well be an alien with his unnatural skin tone and colorful eyes.

"He's from the *Odyssey*," Jori said. An ache grew in his throat and he tried swallowing the dryness from his mouth. If someone from that ship was here, then others might be too.

Terk gave Jori a hard look of warning.

If the grey man recognized him and Terk, he didn't show it. Washi took his arm as Michio checked for hidden weapons. Terk and the two others finished searching the room.

Jori didn't help this time. He concentrated on keeping his emotions under the surface. No one else here had survived. The senshi had shown no mercy. Two women held one another in a deathly embrace. Normally, senshi left the women alive for later use, but these two were older, one with entirely white hair.

Their eyes were glazed open. The white-haired woman had a singed dot of phaser fire through her temple while the other's head was a bloody mushy mess. No doubt some senshi had taken joy in stomping it in.

His mouth swirled with a sour taste and his stomach lurched.

Terk exited the room. "You better not throw up."

Jori clenched his jaw. "They didn't need do that," he said quietly.

"At least they're not children," Terk replied.

The memory of the girl with dead eyes struck him. She had died because of his actions. Father would have killed her anyway, but he still took part. "How can you stand this?" he asked.

"I do what I must, as should you. Now shut up and do your duty or leave."

Jori's cheeks burned. He averted his eyes from his brother's glare.

Terk turned to search the other rooms. Washi put his hand on Jori's shoulder. "It's alright, Jori-chan. I feel it too, sometimes. But your brother's right. We have a duty to do."

Jori numbed his emotions and closed off his senses as much as possible. The last rooms were searched, but they found no more survivors.

He followed his brother and their team to the main room where their father waited. The perantium device took up a great deal of the sizeable space. Under other circumstances, Jori would have been fascinated by all the components and data-filled screens.

Terk threw the grey man at Father's feet. "He's definitely not a warrior."

"Is that all you found?" Father said accusingly.

"That's all we found *alive*, Sir." Terk shot a pointed look to Samuru and the other senshi.

Father growled, then turned to the men. "Start dismantling this thing." A flick of his hand at the large central emitter initiated a flurry of activity. "Yemon, download everything you can get from these computers. Samuru, what's your assessment of these prisoners? Are any of them qualified to work on the device?"

"One, possibly two," General Samuru said. He led the emperor over to the group.

Jori should be helping skinny Yemon but followed giant Samuru instead.

Samuru lifted a prone man by his hair. The long-sideburned man cried out, and the sensation of his fear washed over Jori's senses.

"He helped disable a bomb and his insignia indicates he's a PCC chief."

"What's your duty?" Father demanded.

"I-I-I'm an en-engineer," the man said.

"Keep him," Father replied.

Samuru threw him back to the floor, then grabbed another. This man didn't cry out. He stood tall and lifted his chin.

Jori's heart stopped. The scene froze as he took in the man's features. He had short sandy hair, hazel eyes, and a long face. His most distinguishing feature was his lopsided lips. Though Jori usually saw this man with a crooked smile, it twisted into a frown this time.

"What the hell is *he* doing here?" Terk said just low enough for only Jori to hear.

Despite Terk's earlier hardness, dismay emanated from him now. It seemed he, too, was unsettled by the appearance of Commander Hapker.

5
Prisoners

3791:023:17:42. J.D. Hapker clenched his teeth and silently bore the pain as the general gripped his hair.

"This one's insignia shows he's a PCC commander," the general said.

"What ship do you command?" Emperor Mizuki had the same domineering bulk as his warriors. He stood tall and bulging muscles broadened his frame. The intensity of his gaze emphasized the sharpness of his facial features.

"I'm second-in-command of the *Odyssey*," Hapker replied.

The emperor's glower sparked. "The one responsible for imprisoning my sons."

Hapker scowled. "We saved them."

The emperor stepped in close enough for him to see the obsidian and bronze flecks in his eyes. "You kept them against their will."

"That's not the whole story."

"You *thought* you could use them against me."

"No. We *helped* them. They would have died—"

The emperor snatched him by the throat. "I will enjoy killing you."

An ache expanded in Hapker's chest as he strained for air. This was it. The end. He twisted and jerked with the resistance of a rabbit caught in a wolf's maw, but the hold didn't break. Although spots flashed in his vision, he matched the emperor's glare with defiance.

The emperor released him. "A prolonged death is more appropriate."

Hapker's heart spasmed as he gulped in oxygen. The image of Sharkey suffering a *prolonged death* by the hands of those men emboldened him. He had to stay alive long enough to get her out of this. "Kill me, then," he choked out. "It's not like Prontaean officers have to know engineering and physics to operate a spaceship."

The emperor's nostrils flared. "You think your life is worth saving just because you know a little science?"

"We all do." Hapker tilted his head toward his fellow officers. "It's why they stationed us here."

"Ha!" the emperor barked. "You're only saying that so I won't kill you."

Hapker pulled back his shoulders and glared. "I'm not afraid of death. Kill me or not. It's up to you."

Everything froze as he and the emperor locked into a silent battle. A warrior with a pinched expression whispered in the emperor's ear. The only word Hapker caught was *scientists*.

The emperor's eyes narrowed. "Boy, come here," he said without breaking eye-contact.

"Yes, Sir."

Time crawled as Jori approached. They'd been friends once, but there was no sign of that friendship now. The boy's face was as flat as a volcanic lake.

"Do you have sentiment for this man, boy?"

"None," Jori replied tonelessly.

The word stabbed like a lance through Hapker's heart. Their friendship had stopped Jori from killing him once before. If only it could save him now. *Please sense how much I still care about you, Jori.*

"Good," the emperor said. "Is he telling the truth about them having science and engineering skills?"

The way Jori's brow furrowed gave him hope. When the boy returned to the same placid look he knew all too well, his heart sank.

"Well?" the emperor demanded.

"Speak again," Jori said to Hapker.

Hapker weighed his words. Although he didn't want anyone to fix the emitter, he cared about his people. He couldn't let them be killed, not when a chance of rescue was possible. "Some of us have skills in electronics, some in programming or engineering." He sighed. "Someone here might even have knowledge in laser physics." He held his breath, hoping Jori wouldn't point out his evasiveness.

Jori's deadpan air didn't waver. Hapker's heart pattered so rapidly, he thought it would burst.

"He's telling the truth, Sir," Jori finally said.

Hapker's relief cut short at the sight of Terkeshi. A black expression filled the elder prince's face as he pinched the younger's shoulder. Jori turned to his brother with a pleading look. Terkeshi pressed his lips. Jori's brows tilted further, emphasizing his widened eyes. Terkeshi let out an irritated sigh but said nothing.

Even as Hapker's captor unceremoniously tossed him back to the floor, the heaviness in his chest lifted. He craned his neck and explored his surroundings. Rescue might not be far off, but perhaps there was something he could do now.

Canthidius curled in a fetal position and mewled like a lonely calf. What was he doing here anyway? The pale-skinned man should have left with the Thendian scientists.

Defiance, however, etched the faces of Lieutenant Sharkey, Corporal Harley, and others. He counted on them to put up a fight, but not with all the rifles targeting their heads.

He locked eyes with Jori. The boy's face remained impassive. *He didn't expose me, though.* Maybe Jori had a plan.

"Terkeshi, get a biometric scan of these chima," the emperor said.

"Yes, Sir," Terkeshi replied. "Major Awamori, have you scanned anyone yet?"

"Not yet, my Lord." A middle-aged warrior with blue eyes gave Terkeshi his scanner.

"Biskol," the emperor called.

A warrior with a foxlike face stepped forward. "Yes, Sire."

"Access the satellites and find a Cooperative database. I want to know exactly how much value they have."

"Yes, Sire," the fox-faced warrior replied with a bow.

Terkeshi peeked over his shoulder as the emperor headed toward the perantium emitter. The prince's grip on Jori tightened even more. He said something to Jori with a dour tone, but Hapker's translator didn't pick it up.

Jori took the scanner with a frown. Terkeshi's scowl deepened.

"Terkeshi. Jori," Hapker whispered. "It's good to see—"

Terkeshi kicked him in the temple. "Do not pretend we are friends," he said through his teeth.

It stunned Hapker into silence. There was no trace of concern on the elder prince's face. Jori held a hint of disquiet but didn't explain why he covered for him. Instead, he gave an almost indiscernible shake of his head.

Hapker's body chilled as the young princes methodically worked together. Terkeshi roughly twisted heads and arms as Jori used a hand-held device to scan faces and fingertips.

Hapker pressed his forehead to the gritty floor. Jori had said once that it wouldn't be the same if their situation was reversed. He'd been right.

The irony of being bound and helpless again because of these boys was not lost on him. A tightness in Hapker's chest impeded his breathing more than the dust in the air. Despondency had pawed at him before, but this helplessness gripped him tighter than the bonds on his wrists.

Jori was just a boy. The sternness of the emperor gave him no room to deviate from his obligation. It saddened him to see someone so young and with so much potential being twisted into a monster.

The emperor barked an order, and the general enforced it with threats. No one else spoke, but the pace of work increased. Hapker glanced at the exit, hoping a storm of PG-Force officers would arrive to stop this.

He closed his eyes and slumped his shoulders. If rescue came, the emperor would realize it long before anyone got through that door.

"Father, I'm ready," Terkeshi said. "I'll work with Biskol to match the data."

"Go." The emperor barely took his eyes off the Tredons who dismantled the perantium emitter. "Take the prisoners with you and put them in the aft cells. Dispose of the ones who are of no use."

"Yes, Sir," Terkeshi replied.

Terkeshi's dark eyes looked much like the emperor's, scowl and all. Hapker swallowed hard. He didn't know Terkeshi as well as he knew Jori. Even if the elder prince hadn't been in a coma during most of his time on the *Odyssey*, he doubted they ever would have gotten as close. Terkeshi had a hardness to him he dared not provoke. Seeing the young man now and hearing the indifference in his voice when he acknowledged his father's orders, Hapker had little doubt that he'd kill without hesitation.

"The woman's mine." Usagi flicked his tongue through his missing tooth.

"Fine," the emperor replied.

"What!" Hapker shouted, forgetting about his own impending death. "You can't!"

A swift boot to the gut kept him from saying more. Hapker buckled from the blow and struggled for air. He coughed and gagged as a Tredon warrior dragged him from the room.

6
Sibling Rivalry

3791:023:18:23. Jori calmed his rumbling thoughts and focused forward as he transported onto the *Dragon* with Terk and the others. With most of the warriors on the planet, the corridors laid empty and eerily quiet. No one spoke as the heavy boots of the senshi echoed off the walls.

He dared a peek at the emotions coming from the prisoners. They radiated grim but bold attitudes. All but one man walked with their heads held high. His father had said the Cooperative people were weak, but the bravery of these officers impressed him.

He unintentionally delved into Hapker's emotions. The man's mood matched theirs but spiked with an emotional hurt.

Jori's gut tightened and he swallowed down the sour taste rising in his throat. *I did warn him.*

The memories of his time spent with Hapker on the *Odyssey* kept pushing their way forward. While Terk lay in a coma, Jori stood alone against the enemy. Only Hapker treated him as a friend.

He had grown to like the commander, admire him even, enough to feel comfortable calling him by his first name. He couldn't call him J.D. anymore, though. Not after his betrayal where he almost killed him. He had a phaser set to kill aimed at his head. Though he told himself it was Hapker's own fault for not allowing them to go home as promised, the truth was Terk had already convinced him to do his duty. Now he had to betray Hapker again by letting him be tortured to death.

"Kelar, take them to the holding cells," Terk said. "Remove their comms. I'll have someone give the survivors limited translators later."

Kelar dipped his head and led them away. Two other senshi hauled Lieutenant Sharkey in another direction. A burst of commotion erupted. Commander Hapker and two Cooperative officers yelled and broke free. Kelar struck Hapker with a hard crack. Jori winced as the senshi beat him into submission.

Lieutenant Sharkey struggled too, but with less success. Kesatsu Yushino punched her in the gut, then threw his huge fist into the side of her head. She released a strangled sound and dropped to her knees.

Jori remained firm despite his desire to step in. He remembered Sharkey from the Cooperative ship. Though he had never spoken to her, she was one of the few people on the *Odyssey* who didn't harbor any malice against him. The thought of what Usagi would do to her made his stomach writhe.

The disturbance settled and the senshi conveyed the prisoners to their designated fates. Jori touched Terk's elbow to stop him from following.

Terk turned and swatted his hand away. "What in the hell did you think you were doing?" he asked in their secret language so Washi and Michio standing a few steps back couldn't understand.

The fury in his eyes froze the words in Jori's throat.

"You lied," Terk said.

Jori shook his head. "Not really," he replied in the same secret language. "Everyone who lives in space has to have some knowledge about science and engineering."

"You know good and well that won't be enough."

"I-I couldn't help it."

Terk growled. "Damn it, Jori. If your sentiment gets me in trouble again..." He balled his fists but didn't finish the threat.

"I'm sorry. It just came out." He hung his head. Conflicting emotions clashed like swords. "We can't let Usagi have her," he said quietly.

Terk's anger wavered. "It's too late. He's already claimed her."

"It's not too late." He locked eyes with his brother. "You can use that stuff we used last time. I know Terena keeps it handy."

Terk sighed. "You can't save everyone. Eventually the men will catch on."

Jori's brow furrowed. "She didn't hate me like many of the others. When he hurts her, I won't be able to block it out."

"You *must* learn." Terk kept a stern expression, but Jori sensed his discomfort. Neither of them had learned to rebuff intense emotions.

"I try, but it's hard. You know how it feels."

Terk emanated a sourness that matched Jori's distress. Echoing footsteps from around the corridor grabbed his attention.

"You coming, my Lord?" Tokagei asked Terk testily.

"I'll be there shortly," Terk replied with a huff.

Tokagei scowled but dipped his head appropriately.

Jori clenched his teeth. Of all their personal guards, Tokagei was the worst. He did his job in protecting them, but he wasn't the friend that Washi and Michio were.

Terk glared at Tokagei until he left. "Alright," he said to Jori, switching back to their secret language. "I will get the stuff from Terena, but *that's* all." Jori nodded. "I don't know what you hope to achieve by this," Terk added. "I'll have to kill her and the commander when Father learns how useless they are."

Jori tried to push his sentiment aside, but it gripped him so hard he almost couldn't breathe. "I can fix it so it looks like they have what we need," he said carefully.

Terk's eyes narrowed, then darkened. "Was that your plan when you lied to Father?"

"I didn't lie."

Terk threw up his hands. "You omitted the truth and that's just as bad! As soon as we put them to work, it'll be obvious they have no idea what they're doing."

"I can fix that too."

Terk crossed his arms. "No. You're not doing this to me again."

"Please," he said, reaching out for Terk's arm. "I helped you earlier. Please help me now."

Terk's nostrils flared. "You think that makes me obligated? So if I don't let you do this you won't help me again next time?"

He shook his head emphatically. "I will always help you. No matter what."

Terk's outrage dwindled. A touch of the closeness they'd shared before Dokuri's death peeked through his emotions. He released an exasperated sigh. "Chusho. If we get caught—"

"We won't."

Terk pressed his lips together and scowled. "You're being a coward. So what if it hurts a little when you sense people die? Death happens all the time. You'll have to learn to live with it."

Jori's emotions exploded to the surface. "I can't!" The sharpness of his voice echoed in the hall. He glanced at Washi and Michio. Washi raised an eyebrow at his outburst but showed no indication that he understood the secret language. Jori cleared his throat and regained his composure.

Terk bared his teeth. The heat of his anger swelled into Jori's senses. "Damn you, Jori. Have you already forgotten what Father did to me because of you?"

Jori gulped. It was supposed to be a simple mission. Go to a space station, purchase the perantium prototype, and return home. They'd accomplished the first two, but their ship was shot down by greedy Grapnes. If not for the Cooperative, they'd be dead.

"I lost our ship, I lost our crew, and I lost the device. All because of *you*." Terk jabbed his finger at Jori's chest.

His cheeks burned, but he didn't want to back down. "None of that was my fault—or yours."

Terk's throat rumbled. "Maybe not, but I could have made up for the mess if you'd let me deliver the Cooperative ship to General Sakon. Because of you, I came home with nothing. Because of you, Father still thinks I'm a failure."

"I'm sorry," he said. "If I had known, I would've—"

"No, you wouldn't have. Do you know why? Because you're weak."

Terk was right. This sentiment for Hapker shouldn't interfere with his duty. The desire to give in pressed on him, but the thought of letting Hapker die bore down on him more. "It's not fair," he said with a dry throat.

Terk growled again, but this time in a resigned way. "I get that you want to save him, but there are two of us, remember? Father only needs *one* son."

Jori suppressed the urge to shiver. "He needs both of us." Though he tried to sound certain, they knew better. One moment, their father saw Terk as incompetent. The next he saw Jori as weak. Their brother Montaro had been both incompetent and weak, and it had cost him his life.

"I want to believe that," Terk said, "but—"

"You don't understand what it was like," Jori replied. "Everyone on that ship hated me. Everyone except *him*. You were dying and there was nothing I could do. He helped me. He helped *both* of us. I want to do the same for him and Lieutenant Sharkey."

Silence lingered. Jori swallowed while Terk panted as though trying to calm himself.

Jori bit the inside of his lip and pressed the issue. "If Father finds out, I will take the blame."

"Don't be stupid," Terk said. "I don't want you to be punished either."

"Father's always looking for something to punish us for. At least this time it will be worth it."

Terk rubbed his brow. "This is a bad idea," he said to himself. "I can't believe I'm letting you talk me into this again."

"So I can do it?" He resisted the urge to bounce on his toes.

Terk huffed. "Do what exactly? What is your plan?"

His stomach did somersaults as he laid out his scheme. "Biskol will need my help. He can probably hack into a satellite on his own, but not quickly enough to please Father. After we download the information, I'll alter the records on our end. Then I'm—"

Terk put up his hand. "How long will that take?"

"Not long. I promise."

Terk groaned. "One condition."

Jori's heart skipped a beat. "What?"

"You need to convince Sensei Jeruko first."

A mixed sense of both relief and misgiving rolled over him. If anyone could be convinced, it was Sensei Jeruko. The man had served Jori's father since his youth and was loyal, but he had also been Jori's primary teacher since he was three. Jori cared about him far more than he cared about his own father, and he was sure Sensei Jeruko felt the same, but would he keep another secret for him?

"Deal?"

"Deal," Jori replied.

"Good. Now hurry up. You're supposed to be on the planet helping with the perantium device."

Jori didn't wait for Terk to change his mind. He turned about and headed to Sensei Jeruko's dojo with Washi following behind.

"The things I do for that little brat," Terk muttered just loud enough for Jori to hear.

7
Dojo Debate

3791:023:18:47. Jori stepped into the conveyor.

Washi followed him in. "You look troubled. You two were talking about the Cooperative commander, weren't you?"

"Deck fourteen," Jori said to the computer. He clasped his hands behind his back but didn't answer. He trusted the man but didn't want to discuss the matter again until he spoke to Sensei Jeruko.

Washi radiated concern but didn't push the issue. Both remained silent during the ride and the walk to the sensei's personal dojo.

"I'll wait out here," Washi said as he took a guarded stance outside the opening door.

Jori stepped past the threshold into the dojo. His pattering heart eased as he took in the serene surroundings. The open space was spanned with genuine sugi wood. Its orange tone with grains of rich brown gave this room a pleasant glow. The evenly spaced windows along the sides were fake, but they radiated a soft light through the rice-paper-like screens.

Although this room was used for training, it was a place of peace. Unlike the common dojo of the senshi or the dojos of other specialized trainers, Sensei Jeruko's was fastidious and reverently cared for.

Jori studied the four large and vertically rectangular white sheets of shodo hanging above the mantle. The calligraphy was in an ancient style of writing that only a rare few could read, but Sensei Jeruko had made sure his students understood each of these four mindsets and took them to heart.

Sensei Jeruko didn't react to Jori's entrance. Jori clasped his hands behind his back and waited as the man's body flowed from one martial form to another. Each of Sensei Jeruko's moves floated like a feather, yet with the sharp precision of a nano-cutter.

The man's movements showed no indication that he was crippled. A graceful sweep of his bad leg rolled smoothly into the solid stance of the final form. Jori stared in awe. Even this ordinary pose exhibited the power of Sensei Jeruko's skill. He was older and walked with a limp, but he could still outfight nearly every senshi on this ship.

Sensei Jeruko finished up with his fist to hand and a bow toward the mantle. "Enter," he said gruffly without looking Jori's way.

Jori approached and again waited as the man stood in meditation. Silver streaked through the ebony of the sensei's hair, especially at the temples. The thin mustache that extended just beyond the edge of his mouth had no sign of grey. Nor did the single arched eyebrow over his left eye.

A thick scar etched across the other brow. Healing devices could fix scars, but Sensei Jeruko had said he kept his to remind him of an important lesson to never turn his back until he was certain the enemy was defeated.

Sensei Jeruko turned to him with a bearing full of authority. "Shouldn't you be helping your father?" The man's expression hardened, though Jori knew it as a mask. His air always came across as uncompromising and irritable. Underneath, though, he was objective and collected.

Jori kept his composure just as austere. "Yes, Sensei, but something has come up and I need your guidance."

"Speak," the man replied in his usual deep tone.

"Father captured about a dozen people. One is Commander Hapker." He braced himself for a reaction.

Though Jori sensed Sensei Jeruko's emotions jump to surprise, his face remained impassive. "I see," he replied.

Jori's skin itched as he waited for the man to finish his thoughts.

"That is too bad," Sensei Jeruko finally said.

His heart fell, but he didn't give up. "I want to help him."

Sensei Jeruko frowned. "You can't help him."

"I will alter his records to show he has the skills needed to work on the perantium device."

"You're going to lie."

Jori hesitated. "It's the only way. You said yourself that I owe him a life debt."

"But not at the expense of your honor. Your first obligation is to your father, then to your brother."

"This feels like an obligation too."

Sensei Jeruko shook his head. "You can't honor this man *and* honor your father."

"Why should I care about my father? He doesn't care about me."

"Watch your mouth, boy. Your father carries the weight of worlds on his shoulders. He is the emperor. More than that, he is your blood."

Jori doused the heat that had risen within. He had no love for his father. Sensei Jeruko was more of a father to him.

He considered the man's unwavering sense of honor. "The commander saved my life. Father has never done that—not even when necessary." His tongue twisted with bitterness as a memory flashed through his brain. Jori had been kidnapped and tortured when he was only seven years old. Father not only refused to pay the ransom but also didn't send anyone to rescue him. He had three other sons, after all.

Sensations of outrage and sympathy radiated from Sensei Jeruko as he likely recalled the same incident. "Your father felt you needed to find your own way out."

"*You* didn't, though," Jori replied. When he had managed to escape on his own, it was Sensei Jeruko who came and brought him home.

"I understood your conflict," Jori continued. "You wanted to help me but couldn't disobey Father. I'm not disobeying. I'm merely making him think the man has uses when he has little. Father doesn't lose or gain, either way."

"Lying and going behind your father's back is dishonorable."

Jori swallowed the knot in his throat. "Not sparing a man who saved my life is a larger dishonor, is it not?"

Sensei Jeruko's severity melted away. "You've already created a well of dishonesty. You can't keep digging it deeper or you'll never get out."

Jori nodded. When Jori and Terk told their father about their time on the *Odyssey*, they made it seem they'd been mistreated. Though a few had tried to hurt them, they kept the extent of the captain and commander's goodwill hidden from him.

He wanted to look away from Sensei Jeruko but forced himself to remain firm. "You think I'm a coward for not telling Father the whole truth?"

"No. Not cowardly. Prudent, perhaps—with a sense of honor worth admiring." Sensei Jeruko lay his hand on Jori's shoulder. "I concede your point. If your father finds out, though, he will see this as a betrayal. I cannot risk losing you, Jori-chan. What you are wanting to do is too dangerous."

"I've heard you say, 'The tough and daring die young but live stronger while the weak and timid die later but live in wretchedness.'"

"Do you really want to die for this man?" Sensei Jeruko frowned but there was no harshness in his emotions.

"No, but I think it's cowardly if I don't at least try and help him. You're always saying I shouldn't let fear hold me back from what I want."

"There's a difference between cowardice and prudence."

"I don't see anything prudent about Father killing him."

"That is not for me to judge. Nor you, for that matter." Sensei Jeruko sighed. "So long as your father is emperor, this is not the right time to be merciful."

"It's the *only* time."

Sensei Jeruko's firm posture didn't change but Jori felt the man's surety fall. "So what is your plan after that? He'll be killed when he isn't able to fix it. Even if he does manage, he will still die. You are only prolonging the inevitable."

"I don't have a plan yet but—"

"Only a fool goes to battle without a plan."

"Sometimes when battle is thrust upon you, you must act on wits alone."

Sensei Jeruko glowered. "Do not throw my words back at me, boy."

Jori bowed. "Forgive me, Sensei. My only plan at this time is to hope."

"You are putting me in another impossible position," Sensei Jeruko said. "I didn't tell your father about your experience on the Cooperative ship because he never asked. If he asks me directly about any of this, you know I cannot lie."

"I know."

Sensei Jeruko's mouth pressed into a thin line. "If you know, you shouldn't be telling me."

Jori's heart fluttered. "I need your help."

"Help!" Shock reverberated through Sensei Jeruko's emotions. "Now you are asking me to risk my honor?"

A knot formed in Jori's stomach. "You could never lose honor in my eyes."

Sensei Jeruko's expression melted. "Jori-chan…"

"All I'm asking is that you help me talk to the commander. There's no dishonor in that. If I tell him what to expect, it will reduce the chances of Father finding out."

Sensei Jeruko groaned as he brought his hand to his forehead. "Boy, you'll be the death of me."

Jori stilled in tense anticipation as he waited for a definitive answer.

Sensei Jeruko looked up and sighed. "My loyalty lies with you first and foremost. I'll have Washi and Michio arrange a visit."

Jori flushed. He could always count on Sensei Jeruko and his sons. "Are you sure we should involve them too?"

"I know where their hearts lie. You need allies and it's our job to protect you."

Jori broke out into a wide grin.

"Get that look off your face, boy," the man said as he snapped into a cross expression. "This is not the time to celebrate."

Sensei Jeruko was right. As the fourth mindset said, he shouldn't celebrate his victory until he was sure it was complete. He let his face go blank again while inside his hope swelled.

8
Ghondorian Venascabia

3791:023:18:48. Two giant men gripped Hanna Sharkey's arms like hydraulic clamps. They hurt her, but she dared not give them the satisfaction of letting them know. She pressed her lips in grim defiance as they escorted her down an empty corridor. She had no choice but to walk with them. It was either that or they'd drag her.

The reality of what was about to happen hit her when they stopped at a door of someone's living quarters. She dropped her weight and jerked her arms, hoping to catch them unprepared. They tightened their grip instead.

Adrenaline shot through her system. She thrashed about to no avail. Before she had time to consider another move, they took her inside and cuffed a wrist to a metal ring connected to the post of the bed. The ring was an ominous sign that they'd done this before. Sharkey's heart pounded in her ears.

"No point in fighting it, sweetness," one man said with a smile that made her cringe. His eyes glinted with lust. He moved to grab her chest, but the other man stopped him.

"Usagi will kill you."

The lustful man glowered. "To hell with Usagi."

"Don't be stupid. You'll get your turn. Besides, she's not much to look at—hardly worth risking your neck over."

The man grunted in agreement.

Sharkey trembled. After they left, a wave of dizziness swept over her. She clutched the metal ring with both hands to keep from falling. *Breathe, damn it.*

She sucked in air and filled her lungs, hoping to calm her nerves, and nearly retched instead. The room reeked with a mixture of sour body odor and rot.

She forced herself to breathe and her heart eventually slowed. Her thoughts coalesced and she took in her surroundings. The small room was beyond dirty. The floor's thin carpet had grime trampled into the fibers, making it flat and smooth. Empty liquor bottles and half-eaten food littered the floor and furnishings. Even the bed had trash on it.

A closer scrutiny of the bed revealed grossly stained sheets. Sharkey suppressed a sob. *No, I won't cry.*

She pulled at her wrist, but the cuff wouldn't budge. She jerked harder, back and forth, ignoring the pain.

"You bastards!" she yelled. Despite the promise she had just made to herself, Sharkey cried in earnest. She had no hope of breaking free. Her energy drained, leaving her listless.

She wept a little longer before she got a hold of herself and resolved to be brave. *If this is to happen, I won't give him the pleasure of crying.* Pretending disinterest and acting lifeless might discourage him.

No, she wouldn't allow herself to be used. She would fight no matter how pointless her situation.

The chamber door opened. Sharkey's heart jumped to her throat. A tall shadow hovered in the frame. When the man entered the room, her mind reeled.

The first time she met Terkeshi on the *Odyssey*, his intensity unsettled her. There was an air of danger about him that made her wary but not fearful. This bad-tempered young man never filled her with trepidation until now.

Terkeshi stood only a little taller than her. His black uniform emphasized his strength, and his deadpan expression enhanced his sinister appearance.

Somehow, Sharkey found her courage. She spewed curses at him. "You worthless shit! You're not man enough to take me. I bet your balls haven't even dropped yet," she screamed.

Terkeshi scowled but said nothing in reply.

It was foolish to antagonize him, but she couldn't help herself. "We should have let you die when you were on our ship! You don't deserve to live, you warted pig."

Terkeshi's face darkened as he approached her. She tried to strike him but, he deflected all her assaults effortlessly.

"You won't take me without a fight, you bastard!" she yelled.

"I don't want you," Terkeshi said with a menacing growl. "By the time I get done with you, no one else will want you either."

Before she could reply, Terkeshi forced her against the wall. His strength utterly subdued her. Her heartrate tripled. She met his eyes and nearly lost hold of her bowels at how cold and unwavering they were.

Instead of groping her or forcing her to the bed, he pressed a hypospray to her neck. The hiss of it died away anticlimactically. He let her go and stepped back.

Sharkey tentatively touched her neck.

"I've just injected you with a pseudo-strain of Ghondorian venascabia," Terkeshi said. "You'll develop a purple rash across your chest in moments. When Usagi sees it, he'll be pissed. He'll beat you, but he won't touch you in any other way."

She swallowed. Her racing heart slowed to a guarded thud. "Um, thanks," she replied.

"Don't thank me. The beating will not be pleasant," he said dispassionately, handing her another hypospray. "This is for the pain. Hide it as best as you can."

With that, Terkeshi left. A moment later, Sharkey's chest itched. Ghondorian venascabia was a disgusting sexually transmitted disease—and she was grateful to be infected.

9
The Emperor

3791:023:19:32. Clunk. Clang-clang.

Emperor Kenji Mizuki regarded the source of the sound. Hisho Yemon mumbled a curse. The tall, skinny man pointedly looked away from Mizuki's glare as he picked up the metal piece and hurried to put it back on the device.

"Chusho! Be careful," Mizuki yelled. "You break anything, you'll pay for it in blood." He gave each of the workers an enraged look to emphasize the threat, but none would meet his eyes.

"Are you sure your clerk is up to the task, Sire?" the man beside him asked.

He glanced at his old teacher. Sensei Aki had gained much weight since Mizuki's youth. His face was wrinkled now, and his rheumy eyes sagged.

"Who would you suggest?" Mizuki asked rhetorically. "Besides Jori, he's the only one here with enough scientific knowledge." The shokukin didn't have the means, and most warriors didn't have the inclination.

Sensei Aki grunted.

Mizuki looked around. "Where is that boy, anyway?"

"I haven't seen him."

He ground his teeth. Jori was about as obedient as a stray dog.

He tapped on the MM clasped round his wrist intending to check his whereabouts, but the time grabbed his attention. "Move faster!" he said for all the room to hear. "And not so fast that you blunder. We must hurry before the Cooperative returns with reinforcements."

"Don't worry, Sire," Sensei Aki said. "Defeating those weaklings was easy. This will be too."

"Yes, but it would be easier if those cowards hadn't gotten away with their key people." *Something I should have accounted for.*

"You will get this thing up and running in no time. I'm sure of it, Sire. Then you'll regain the supremacy of your grandfather and be the greatest emperor in Mizuki history."

Mizuki's chest swelled with yearning. He wished he had met his grandfather. The man was a true dragon in battle, Sensei Aki had said, an unstoppable force that everyone feared.

"Did I ever tell you of the battle of Tamaki?" Sensei Aki said.

"Many times, my friend," Mizuki replied.

"Of course, I have. The raze of Tamaki was his greatest feat. It was the greatest because it was the most difficult. He fought against three times his force and with the cunning of a fox and the ferociousness of a blackbeast."

Although he'd heard the old man ramble through this story many times, Mizuki listened in rapt attention. Pride filled him no matter how many times Sensei Aki talked of the late great Mizuki emperor.

"Lord Shiro was the last to ever oppose him," Sensei Aki finished.

The last until Mizuki's father's reign. His grandfather's greatness never failed to remind him of his father's failings.

His father was a blathering drunken fool with no battle sense—or any sense at all. If not for his wealth and the ability of his generals to oust his enemies, he would have been deposed. Thanks to him, Mizuki had inherited a weakened empire with enemies lurking behind the smile of every pompous lord.

Even making an enemy of Lord Enomoto and others couldn't compare to his father's biggest blunder—losing the entire Pentam system. Mizuki had been trying to make up for his father's inadequacies ever since. He made sure his ship was strongest and his men were the fiercest. He showed his face in every battle and kept in top physical condition.

"Once you have this device, the Pentam system will be yours," Sensei Aki said as though reading his mind. "No one will dare stand against you."

"First, I will deal with Fujishin," Mizuki replied darkly.

Sensei Aki shook his head. "I still can't believe he left."

"Left?" Mizuki growled. "He betrayed me. All these years of service and he runs off to join a band of rebels? What would my grandfather think of that?"

"Pah." Sensei Aki flicked his hand. "He is nothing, Sire. A flea on a blackbeast only."

A surge of pain sharpened in Mizuki's chest. Colonel Fujishin's betrayal incessantly burned inside him. The man was no mere senshi. He had been one of his closest advisors—and his friend.

His gaze flicked to General Samuru, then to Sensei Aki. If Fujishin could betray him, who was next?

Surely not Sensei Aki. Of his five—now four—advisors, known singly as Talons and collectively as the Emperor's Claw, Sensei Aki was the oldest. He had served under Mizuki's grandfather and father with an unyielding fervor.

Even after Mizuki's father relegated the man to a teacher, he spoke of nothing but the glory of the Mizuki house. His idealistic view had spurred Mizuki on since he was a child.

"Your grandfather had enemies aplenty," Sensei Aki added. "Did I ever tell you about Majimi?"

"Many times, old man."

"Then you know your grandfather defeated him," Sensei Aki replied as though oblivious to Mizuki's darkening mood. "Fujishin will die just as badly for what he's done. When he's gone, you can reclaim the Pentam system without the worry of Lord Enomoto scheming behind your back."

Mizuki's head pounded. Too many enemies, too many schemers. and too many betrayers.

"No, no, no!" Yemon said to Rushiro, a senshi conscripted to help the workers with the emitter. "You need to remove that valve first, and not with a hammer either." Turning to another man, he yelled, "Telock! It doesn't turn in that direction. It goes the other way." Then back to the other man, "Put that hammer down!"

Mizuki frowned. A mere clerk should not oversee a crew that was half senshi. *Where the hell is Jori?*

"Damn it, Rushiro!" Yemon said. "I told you not to use the hammer."

The man made a face and struck with the tool anyway.

"Rushiro!" Mizuki said. "If I see you with that hammer one more time, I'll break your arm off and beat you with it."

The man tossed the hammer aside without complaint and gave Yemon a dirty look that told him he'd get even with him later.

Yemon would cry and whine, but Rushiro knew better than to hurt the man badly enough to keep him from doing his job.

Yemon cursed and bossed people about, but his words tickled rather than stung. Normally Mizuki couldn't care less, but this device was too important. *Where the hell is Jori?*

He checked his MM. Jori had a curious mind that absorbed intellectual and physical information faster than a ship at full power spent its fuel source. Yet despite having a potential greater than any of his other sons, he was also the most troublesome. Terkeshi, though not as intelligent, did what he was told. Jori questioned too much and was often squeamish over the simplest things. His stubbornness had a way of making Mizuki's blood boil and evaporate his ability to reason.

The MM opened to the status section. Before Mizuki tapped Joris name, Yemon rubbed his brow and groaned.

"What is it now, Yemon?" Mizuki demanded.

Yemon snapped his hands to his side. "Nothing, your eminence. These louts are merely trying my patience."

"And you're trying mine," he replied. "I put you in charge because you told me you could handle this."

"Oh, Sir. I can," Yemon said in a servile tone as he licked his lips. "It's just—"

"Then do it and quit whining about it."

Yemon made a jerky bow. His compliance came out in a hurried jumble as he jumped back to work.

Mizuki shook his head and mumbled under his breath. Could no one be trusted to do their damned job? *Where the hell are you, boy?*

His intention to check the MM fled with the beep of his comm. "Your Eminence," Colonel Bakuto, the leader of the senshi force, said. "The Thendians regrouped. We have them closing in from both sides."

"Chusho!" he cursed. Bakuto's report meant he needed Mizuki's expertise. To give that, he needed both a tactical update and visual view of the fighting.

"Samuru, with me. Awamori, you're in charge here. Make sure they hurry without breaking anything." As an afterthought, he added, "And find out where the hell my youngest son is and tell him I said to get his ass down here."

10
Alterations

3791:024:01:50. J.D. Hapker clenched and unclenched his fists. His body trembled with uncontrollable rage. Lieutenant Sharkey was a close friend. What those men would do to her… The throbbing in his temples interrupted his bleak thoughts.

He dropped onto the pallet in his cell harder than intended. The extra gravitational setting of this ship seemed to compound the heaviness of his predicament. This was a disaster, a complete disaster.

He hung his head and covered his eyes. He held the position for some time as the storm of his emotions swirled.

After they subsided somewhat, he sat up. The smell of excrement burned his nose. The floor of his cell was sticky and the walls grossly stained. Scum caked the outdated food and water dispenser. The toilet, a mere bowl-shaped hollow in the floor, had a sickly yellow tint streaked with putrid brown.

Hapker glanced down at his pallet and grimaced. The bed was a rickety thing with a mattress splotched in the color of rotten fruit.

Still, he felt isolated despite sharing a cell with Simmonds and Harley. The men sat on beds across from him, each lost in their own thoughts. Harley's brows hooded over his sparking green eyes even as he stared at the ceiling. His bow-shaped mouth bent down. Simmonds absently nursed his injured face. The legging of his uniform was stained red from where a projectile had grazed him.

Sergeant Mendosa paced in the cell across from them. Sergeant Davis stood in the next unit over with his arms folded. The man's eyes flicked with edgy vigilance. Canthidius lay curled on a bed behind him. Everyone else sat, some slumped against a wall and others leaned forward with elbows on knees.

They'd all been unceremoniously shoved into their prospective cells in no sense of order. No one spoke. The silence mirrored their sullen moods. The emperor would have no use for the PG-Force officers. Though Hapker was technically a PCC officer, his command derived from his experience with the PG-Force. His future was just as dire. Canthidius and Simmonds might survive a little longer, but not in comfort.

Sharkey's predicament was worse. The thought of her fate had his body shaking. He was like a mother zebra that stood helpless as a pack of hyenas disemboweled her foal.

Hapker forced his despair aside. He rubbed his wrists where the guards had removed the bonds. Harley sat up and did the same. His eyebrows were dark, almost black, and thick but not bushy. They matched his wavy close-cut hair and complemented his darker skin. "We're going to die, aren't we, Sir?"

"It certainly seems so," Hapker replied, too glum to sugarcoat it for the young man.

"Surely, Captain Arden will come for us," Simmonds said.

Hapker nodded. It was a small spark of hope. Captain Arden would argue for a full-on rescue mission—if he survived. *All these people dying in vain.* Private Fresel was just one of many. He rubbed the ache from his chest.

"I can't believe those boys acted that way," Simmonds said. His mustache turned downward with a frown. "After you were their friend."

Harley's brows wrinkled. "What do you mean?"

Hapker's thoughts switched gears. Leaning against the wall, he rested his chin in his hand and set his elbow on his knee. "We had the two princes on the *Odyssey*—"

Harley's green eyes bulged. "What? When?"

"A little less than a third of a cycle ago." Hapker put up his palm to keep Harley from interrupting. "They were returning home after running an errand on the Depnaugh space station when Grapnes attacked them. Their ship crashed on a planet we were checking the terraforming process on."

"I bet the Tredons had kidnapped their people or something. They're always raiding and taking slaves." Harley curled his lips.

"We assumed it was that or they stole something. It turns out it was neither. The Grapnes found out the two boys were the emperor's sons—"

Harley made a wry expression. "And those devious little scavengers thought they would profit from capturing them."

Hapker harrumphed. "It cost them," he said, without offering details. It didn't seem the right setting to tell Harley about his first encounter with Jori.

He hadn't expected survivors when he investigated the crashed Tredon ship. Four Grapnes had gone down to the planet too, hoping for an easy steal. They met with a firefight instead. A Tredon survivor took out all four of them before Hapker could intervene. To his astonishment, it was a ten-year-old boy.

Hapker shook his head. Jori fought alone against odds that even he himself might not have been able to overcome if their situations had been reversed.

"Only the two princes survived the crash," he said. "We had no idea they were the emperor's sons, though—not yet. They were given medical care and overall treated fairly well, almost as guests."

"Then they repaid us by taking over our ship," Simmonds said with a sourness contrary to his joyful character.

Hapker shook his head. "I doubt they had much choice."

Harley's mouth hung open. "They took over your ship? By themselves?"

"They were certainly more than we anticipated." Hapker made a face. Jori was full of surprises. His high level of maturity, his talent for sensing the emotions of others, his brilliant mind—one that was both coldly calculating and enthusiastically observant. Add in his strategic ability and advanced fighting skill, and the boy was a recipe for disaster. Learning he was the son of Emperor Mizuki, though, was the biggest surprise of all.

"We intended to return them home," he continued, "even after we discovered they were the emperor's sons. Then Rear Admiral Zimmer ordered us to bring them to him for questioning. Though the boys were a security challenge, we didn't have any real problems until they found out they were prisoners."

"Oh shit," Harley said. "I mean… Sorry, Sir. I didn't mean to curse."

"It's alright, Corporal."

"So what happened after they took over your ship? How are you all alive and not Tredon slaves?"

"Surprisingly, they didn't kill a single person during their assault."

Harley's eyes popped again.

"They could have. I have no doubt of that, but for some reason they chose not to. And when they escaped to a Tredon ship, they left a means for us to defend ourselves against it."

"The commander made a good impression on them," Simmonds said. "Especially the younger one."

Hapker tapped his chin. Feelings of both warmth and hurt filled him whenever he thought of Jori. "The older one was in a coma until the very end of their visit. Since Jori was so young, the captain said he needed a guardian. I spent a lot of time with him and so I got to know him." *And care for him.*

He learned the hard way that their growing friendship went only so far. While his superiors had forced him to detain the boys rather than return them home as promised, Jori had his own obligations.

It shouldn't have been a surprise when they fought to escape. Yet something nearly broke inside him when Terkeshi knocked him to the ground and Jori tied his hands behind his back.

He lay paralyzed for a time while Jori and Terkeshi took out their guards and took over the bridge. However, some things Captain Arden, Sharkey, and even Jori had said spurred him to break free.

He met Jori on the way to the bridge. When the boy confronted him with a kill weapon, he was sure it was all over. Instead of shooting him, though, he fired the phaser above Hapker's head, making him duck, then escaped with his brother when a nearby Tredon ship transported him off.

"He wasn't the stereotypical monster everyone expected him to be," Hapker added. "We became close."

Harley's tanned skin darkened. "Not close enough, apparently."

Hapker shrugged. "I got the impression they never told their father how their visit was with us."

"Somehow I doubt it would make a difference," Simmonds said.

Harley harrumphed. "The Tredons are a bunch of murdering cutthroats."

"They're just boys," Hapker said. "They have no choice but to do what their father, the emperor, commands."

Harley turned away with a frown. "They are monsters—the lot of them. You never should have helped them."

"I don't regret what I did. Maybe they'll return the favor." Hapker tried to sound hopeful, but his optimism was a facade. Jori chose duty before, there was no reason to think he wouldn't choose duty again. Besides, what could a boy do against his ruthless father?

Hapker scrunched his eyes, wanting to block the memories of the people he saw die today. Too many deaths, and all because the emperor wanted to turn a life-saving device into a planet killer.

Before he could dwell on it further, two big warriors entered the brig. They had an identical build, and their facial hair style was the same mustache and patch under their lip. They looked nothing alike, though. One had round eyes and a dimpled chin while the other had narrow eyes and a slenderer face.

The two warriors peered into the cells and stared longer when they came to Hapker. "You." The one with the dimpled chin pointed. "Come."

Hapker's pulse quickened. He stood reluctantly as the slender-faced warrior unlocked the thick transparent door and slid it open. The man maintained a posture of guardedness.

The warrior with the round eyes and dimpled chin beckoned him. As Hapker stepped forward, he considered charging the man and fighting his way out to find Sharkey. Should he try it knowing the chance of success was slim, or bide his time? Before he decided, the warrior grabbed him by the arm and twisted him around.

Harley stood and tensed as though he wanted to jump in and help, but the narrow-eyed warrior squared his shoulders daring him to try. Hapker subtly shook his head at Harley then let them cuff him and take him away.

"Where are you going with him?" a guard standing just outside of the brig asked.

"The chair. Prince's orders," the dimple-chinned warrior said. "You got a problem with that?"

"No, Sir," the guard replied in a deferential tone.

Apprehension mixed with Hapker's hopefulness as they marched him down a long, doorless corridor. The chair sounded ominous, but the warrior had also mentioned the prince. He hadn't said which one, but Hapker pictured Jori. Perhaps the boy had found a way to help him.

The two men led him to an isolated room and clamped him into a cold metal chair. Lumpy crusts dotting the armrests could have been rust but looked more like scabs.

The warriors faced him but didn't make eye contact. Their hard expressions brooked no room for conversation. Their alert posture reminded him of how Jori had often stood, with feet planted at shoulder width, chest out, and hands clasped behind the back.

Hapker worked his tongue to wet his dry mouth. He concentrated on his breathing in a determination not to show his anxiety.

The longer he waited, though, the greater his trepidation became. Jori wouldn't torture him, would he? Would Terkeshi? It saddened him that the boys could be capable.

The handle to the metal entrance door clicked. Hapker tensed as the door creaked open. When Jori entered, he exhaled but his muscles remained taut.

Jori bore his usual unreadable expression. He stepped forward and took a stance that mirrored the two warriors behind him. "I told you that if our situations were reversed, you would not be treated the same," Jori said evenly. "If it were up to me, this wouldn't have happened. But it's not."

"You didn't tell your father how we helped you," Hapker rasped through the dryness of his throat.

"It would do more harm than good," Jori replied. "He believes sentiment is a weakness. It's probably best he doesn't know about our connection."

Hapker glanced at the two guards.

"Don't worry about them," Jori said. "I told them everything, and I trust them with my life."

Hapker struggled to read their blank faces. "So what happens next? Are you going to kill me?" His gut twisted as he imagined being killed by this boy, a boy he cared about.

"I wouldn't do that, even if Father ordered me," Jori said, again without emotion.

"Torture me then?" The words soured his mouth.

"I won't, no. You will be tortured, though. Terkeshi may be compelled to take part. Trust me when I say it is not something that either of us wants to do."

Hapker swallowed the lump in his throat. "So you've come to tell me we're still friends."

Jori's expression twisted into a fleeting look of hurt.

Hapker didn't give him time to respond. "I understand. We were both forced to do things we didn't want to do. I forgive you. I hope you can forgive me too."

Jori's hard demeanor faltered. "Damn you, Hapker—"

"It's alright," he said soothingly. "I know this isn't your fault. Whatever happens, I don't blame you."

Jori's forehead wrinkled. "I am sorry. I wish things could be different."

"Me too."

Jori sighed. "I may not be able to get you out of this, but I *have* done something that might help you."

Hapker perked up.

"Don't' get your hopes up," Jori said. "I altered the records we downloaded to show you may be useful in getting the emitter set up. This tactic only prolongs the inevitable, though."

"What about the rest of my people?"

Jori dipped his head. "I changed Lieutenant Sharkey's records too."

"What about the others?"

Jori grimaced. "I'm risking a lot already."

Hapker slumped in his chair. He considered arguing, but Jori's placid expression turned into a pained stare. "I know, and I appreciate it."

"If Father finds out I've even done this much…"

"I understand." Hapker shook his head. "But I am responsible for them. If you can't help them, don't help me either. I think Sharkey would agree."

"You want me to let my father kill you?"

"I don't want to die, but it doesn't feel right to save myself and let everyone else die."

"You told me once that emotion is not a weakness," Jori said heatedly. "If you let yourself die because of this foolish sentiment, you're weak."

"Do you really think my desire to help my people at any cost is weak?"

"You can't help them if you're dead."

"I can't help them at all if your father kills them."

Jori nodded and his expression softened. He turned to a guard. The man dipped his head. "There's honor in his request."

"I'd ask the same if in his place," the other guard said.

Jori faced Hapker. "I'll see what I can do to help your people, but no promises."

"What are the risks to you?"

The guards exchanged a look but Jori didn't react. "Don't worry about me."

The pit of Hapker's stomach twisted. He hated the idea of Jori being punished but he had to do whatever it took to save his people. "If you make it look like we all have at least a little technical expertise, it will give us some time."

Jori shook his head. "It won't be pleasant. My father *will* make sure you're properly motivated."

"What about Sharkey?" Hapker asked. "What that man will do to her isn't right."

"We have a way to keep it from happening and Terkeshi is taking care of it now. She will still be hurt, though."

Hapker sagged with relief. *Better than being used by those brutes.*

Another thought occurred to him. "There is one major problem. Most of us don't have the knowledge to so much as tighten a screw."

Jori's brow furrowed. "You'll need to fake it as best you can."

"Are you sure your father wouldn't let us go if he knew how we treated you?"

"I'm sure. You mustn't say anything to anyone either. Only Sensei Jeruko and Washi and Michio here know," he said, indicating the two guards. "If my father suspects Terkeshi and I have a concern for you, he will keep a closer eye on us."

"Or worse," the warrior with the round eyes said gruffly. "He'll order the boys to torture you to death to force any such sentiments they have out of them."

Jori regrettably agreed.

Hapker's stomach roiled. What kind of monster would do such a thing?

"Don't tell your people how they've come to be recognized as experts," Jori said. "I don't want anyone accidentally blurting anything. Understood?"

"Yes. They will probably think the Cooperative had something to do with it."

"Good. Now I suggest that when we take you back to your cell, you act like you're in pain or someone will wonder what happened here."

"Thank you," Hapker said with sincerity. "I know you can't do much, but I appreciate your help. And I'm glad we're still friends."

Jori gave a disheartened look in reply.

11
Resentment

3791:024:02:13. The conveyor doors closed. "Bridge peripheral," Silas Arden said to the computer.

The transition to movement was smooth, but his head reacted with a stabbing pain. He massaged the area around the pulsing knot left over from when he'd fallen. The throbbing subsided, but a constant ache hovered behind his eyes.

He had regained consciousness on the bridge in time to hear Major Esekielu announce to the admiral they were away. He tried to regain his feet and take command, but the major insisted he report to the medical bay.

It was a wise decision, yet a twinge of resentment lingered. If he had known he'd be cleared for duty with nothing more than an offer for pain reliever, he never would have put Major Esekielu in charge.

When the conveyor opened, Arden stepped out. His head pounded with each hurried stride. He should have taken the meds, but others had a greater need.

As he walked, he skimmed the reports on his MM. Though most of the crew had strapped themselves into the safety depots, the hull breach meant he'd lost some of his people. Thank goodness his wife and other non-essential personnel and civilians had been left at a nearby space station.

He entered his conference room to find Major Esekielu already dominating the scene. The stiff-postured man stood in front of the viewscreen, blocking the view of the admiral from those sitting at the table behind him.

Arden purposefully took a stance next to the major. Neither the major nor the admiral acknowledged his presence.

"We secured several people from the planet before having to leave," the major said to the admiral.

We? Arden masked his irritation. His feelings were unfair. Even he would use the term *we*, but the major sounded like he was taking credit.

"Who did we rescue and what components did we get out?" Admiral Belmont's mouth turned down and his bottom lip protruded in a pout, though it was a permanent feature. The dark-complexioned man had close-cut greying hair that receded deep into his temples. Although he and Arden were the same age, the admiral had deeper wrinkles.

"We did not retrieve any components, Admiral," Major Esekielu said.

The admiral's lip stuck out further. "Survivors?"

"At least three-hundred people so far, including Doctor Huang and all but four of his team, Doctor Orlov and her assistant, and two other key scientists."

The admiral's frown lifted.

Arden glanced at his MM. "I didn't see Doctor Lahti's name on the recovery list," Arden said.

"Doctor Lahti and three top engineers are still unaccounted for," the major said.

"Since we still have a few shuttles that haven't returned yet, he could be there," Arden added.

Admiral Belmont's gloomy expression returned. "I pray it is so. Hopefully, we've hindered the emperor enough that he can't make the device work. As soon as we assess our losses, we need to focus on getting it back or destroying it."

"Yes, Sir," Arden and the major replied at the same time.

"What's the status of your ship?" the admiral asked.

"We had a hull breach—" Arden started to say.

"Our shields are depleted," Major Esekielu said. "Two need immediate repairs. A propulsion unit needs recalibrating..."

Arden scowled and peeked at the officer who should have been giving the damage reports. The man removed his MM and flattened it into the tablet form. His brows drew inward as he perused the device, but it could have been a look of concentration rather than irritation. The others worked, too, as though used to the major sidelining them.

Yes, Major Esekielu had their reports, and perhaps it was more efficient if he gave the overview himself, but Arden hated seeing his crew being treated as afterthoughts.

"It will take twelve hours for us to complete all the repairs," the major said.

Us? As if the major would do anything but micromanage. If Arden didn't know any better, he'd think the major was overcompensating for not being there when needed.

He silently berated himself for being petty. They were a team, after all—or they were supposed to be.

"You're in better shape than we are, Major," the admiral replied. "Our arc drive was severely damaged on the way out. We almost didn't escape."

A heat ignited behind Arden's temples. Was the admiral hinting that waiting for the *Odyssey* almost cost him? No, he couldn't be. Arden shouldn't let his mood get the best of him.

"As soon as you're done, approach the planet cautiously," the admiral said. "If the emperor is no longer there, retrieve any survivors and assess our losses. If he's still there, employ hit-and-run tactics, but avoid direct conflict. He can't have that emitter."

"Yes, Sir," Major Esekielu snapped.

Arden's mouth fell open. "Hit-and—"

"Hold out until reinforcements arrive," Admiral Belmont continued."

"You want to use us like a battleship?" Arden blurted.

"That's what Major Esekielu is there to do," the admiral replied in an annoyed tone. "There's no time for anything else."

"Sir, we are not equipped to—"

"You have your orders."

Arden scowled. "I must protest, Admiral. One major doesn't turn this ship into a battleship."

"Your disagreement is noted, but lives are at stake, Captain," the admiral said with finality.

Arden fumed but held his tongue. The man presided over both Prontaean Cooperative branches and could do whatever he wanted—even if it was absurd.

"Shouldn't I reattempt negotiations with the emperor?" he said instead.

"You had your chance. It's obvious it won't work, anyway," the admiral said. "If we still had his children, we would have leverage. As it is, there's nothing else to offer."

Arden braced himself against the unfair criticism. He supposed it was the admiral's way to deflect from his own faulty decision to divide their forces. *To hell with him and his pet major.*

He filled his lungs and slowly exhaled. Let the admiral play his political games. Arden had far more important things to worry about.

12
Only Cowards Lie

3791:024:07:27. Terkeshi shook his head as he scrolled through the information on his MM. To fabricate engineering and science skills for *all* the prisoners was pushing it. Then again, maybe his father would be happy to have skilled workers.

The perantium emitter had been successfully dismantled and brought aboard some hours ago. The *Dragon* was en route to Toradon territory with no Cooperative ships in pursuit. Father's plan had gone perfectly, except they hadn't captured many actual scientists.

Terk transmitted the info to his father, then glanced down the hall at Tokagei, the man who'd most likely snitch if he discovered what Jori had done. He turned to Sensei Jeruko and Michio with a frown. "I can't believe you agreed to let Jori do this," he whispered.

"Your brother made a valid argument." Sensei Jeruko spoke confidently, but Terk sensed his uncertainty.

"What argument is that? Going behind Father's back is a good idea?"

Sensei Jeruko's brows drew down. "It's an unfortunate circumstance with few options. If this deception gets discovered, I will take full responsibility."

Terk's heart skipped a beat. "I can't let you do that! Father will kill you."

"Perhaps not. We've been good friends for many years."

Terk scoffed. "Father would never let friendship get in the way of a good killing."

"If it comes to that, so be it. I honor my position as your protector and I would die for either of you, even for your brother's sentiment. But your father can't do without you, and you and Jori can't do without one another."

"You have my support," Michio said.

Terk huffed. "Both of you should be discouraging this emotion of his. Where's the firmness you used on me? You never let me get away with such blatant disobedience."

Sensei Jeruko's eyebrow rose as if to say Terk knew better. "It's true I'm not as strict with your brother, but he's a different person."

Terk twisted his mouth. "You mean he's *special*."

"I was about to say more stubborn." One side of Sensei Jeruko's mouth curved up. "But he's also the youngest. He doesn't have your burden."

"I didn't have this burden at his age either, yet you were still hard on me."

"I always knew Dokuri was too reckless and Montaro didn't have what it takes. You are not them, and better for it."

Terk flushed. "That still doesn't explain why you encourage his sentiment."

"As you said, Jori is special. His sentiment ensures he will support you in the same way my sons support one another."

Terk's eyes widened. He hadn't thought of that. Dokuri had killed an older brother to become first heir. Jori's skill level meant he could do the same someday. There were only two ways to keep him from becoming a rival—keep him on his side or kill him before he got too strong.

Terk's gut soured at the latter option. He shook the feeling away. "This is dangerous."

Sensei Jeruko put his hand on Terk's shoulder. "There is honor in what your brother wants to do. I'm grateful to this commander as well. If it weren't for him, who knows what would've become of you two."

Terk sensed the warmth of the man's emotions and shifted uncomfortably. "You realize Jori altered the records of *all* the prisoners, not just the commander."

Sensei Jeruko grunted.

"His emotions went too far," Terk added.

"Mercy has its merits," Michio said. "Look at General Seiko and General Brevak."

Terk conceded Michio's point. Both generals had been criticized for showing mercy, but their reputations garnered them more respect than disdain. When Terk had visited Brevak's ship, he felt the love and loyalty of his men. Although the *Basilisk* warship had a fierce reputation, a serene mood filled its interior. Even the shokukin lived in contentment. "My father would not see it that way."

Sensei Jeruko cocked his eyebrow. "There was a time when he would have."

Terk scoffed. "When?"

"Before Jori was born. Before the attack."

Terk nodded. Traitors had made attempts against his father's life many times, but Sensei Jeruko referred to the incident that still threatened to end the Mizuki line. A saboteur had injected Father with something that corrupted his DNA and left him unable to sire more children. Because past abuse of genetic engineering and cybernetic enhancements gave people an unfair advantage, he couldn't fix the corruption without provoking the most powerful lords into a revolt. This left Jori and Terk as the last of the Mizuki heirs.

"He has changed much since that time," Sensei Jeruko continued. "Dokuri's death followed by Fujishin's betrayal has made it harder for him to find mercy."

The thought of Dokuri brought a bitterness to his tongue. Even dead, his older brother was a pain in his ass. Terk couldn't make a single mistake without being reminded of him. "Yeah, Dokuri," he muttered.

"Do not despair, Terke-chan," Sensei Jeruko said. "Your father has forgotten what Dokuri was like at your age. Together you and Jori are far more formidable than him."

"Formidable?" Terk said with disdain. "Between Jori's sentiment and my…" He couldn't bring himself to say his lack of prowess.

"Do not give in to your father's criticism. You *are* skilled. The only thing that made Dokuri appear strong was his cruelty."

"And you are not cruel," Michio added. "Neither is Jori. The men see this, and they will love you more for it."

Terk grunted and glanced down at Tokagei. "Not all men."

Sensei Jeruko shared a look with his son. "The ones that matter."

Terk took in the features and qualities of the father and son before him. They were both powerful and well respected. Not even the brutal Samuru or the sinister Nezumi would dare cross them. "Let's just hope we all matter enough that Father won't gut us if he finds out."

"We will make this work, Terke-chan."

*****

3791:024:08:01. Terkeshi pulled back his shoulders and entered his father's office. A massive picture of a red and gold dragon hung on the wall. The fearsome claws of the beast held a golden crown. Though Father would never wear such ridiculous gear, the symbol hovered over his head while he sat.

Even sitting behind a desk, Father dominated the room. His blazing eyes and hooked nose with wide nostrils promised no quarter. He wore a perpetual frown that creased his face with age, but no one mistook him for an old man. Father was as powerful as any warrior, if not more so.

"I just sent you the results of the records we pulled on the prisoners, Sir."

"How many?" Father asked brusquely in his usual deep-toned voice.

"Eleven, Sir," Terk replied.

"Eleven alive or eleven total?"

"Both."

"Both?" Father said. "Damn it, boy. I told you to kill the ones who were of no use."

"There are two with questionable value, Sir," Terk replied without a hint of the nervousness he felt. If he got caught lying… *Damn you, Jori.* "But considering how limited our own knowledge and resources are, I kept them alive for now." At least this part was true.

"Define questionable."

"The report shows two corporals with only a little engineering training." Not a lie since Jori altered the records.

His father's eyes narrowed. "You think this is worth keeping them alive for?"

"Even a minor education is more than most of our men have." Another truth.

Father studied him. Terk stood motionless, though his stomach fluttered. He suppressed the urge to swallow so the movement wouldn't be noticed.

Father tapped his deskview screen and perused it. "Very well. We will keep them alive for now."

Terk hid his relief.

"But give them a taste of what will happen if they don't cooperate," Father said. "Gather them all in the arena at o-seven."

"Yes, Sir," Terk replied. A hardness fell in his gut. Competitions usually took place in the arena, but they occasionally used it to implement punishments and set examples.

"One more thing," Father said. "What was your brother doing earlier today?"

Terk's heart skipped a beat. "What do you mean?" he asked, knowing full well what his father meant.

"He was supposed to help dismantle the device and catalog the parts, but Tokagei said he came with you here instead."

"He did."

His father's features darkened. "Why?"

"He said he needed to help Biskol hack the satellites."

"I don't recall Biskol asking for help."

Terk floundered for a half-truth. "It wouldn't surprise me if he did, Sir. Jori's skill surpassed his long ago."

"Jori was with Biskol the entire time?" Father asked.

"I believe so, Sir." The lie singed his tongue, and he silently cursed his stubborn little brother.

"Damn it, boy. You knew he had another task to do. You're supposed to be a leader someday, but you can't even control your own brother."

Terk's throat tightened. "I thought he came with me because your orders changed." *Another lie.*

"Why in the hell would they change?" his father said.

"I assumed that since we didn't capture any scientists, checking these prisoners was a priority." *Chusho.* This was getting out of hand.

"You assumed wrong." Father's eyes glinted with heat. "We could have pressured them for the information."

Terk's heart rate increased. He clenched his fists to keep his emotions in check. "I didn't think of that, Sir."

"You didn't think at all, apparently. You're no Dokuri."

The sting of his father's words tightened his chest. "I'm no Montaro either," Terk mumbled, referring to his next eldest brother.

"If you were, you'd be dead too," Father said with a growing sense of aggravation.

Terk swallowed. After Dokuri died gloriously in battle, Montaro became heir. Later, he ran from a fight, leaving his men behind to die. Then he had the audacity to return home with whiney excuses. Father had been furious.

The memory of Montaro's resulting death seared Terk's soul. Both he and Jori still had nightmares about it. Tradition or no, it was stupid that only the strongest of the emperor's sons should live. Terk wasn't as intelligent as Jori. Nor did he have Jori's martial and strategic skills—which meant he might be next. Unless Jori's sentiment got him in trouble.

"Dismissed," Father said.

Terk left. His thoughts churned, and he forced them to focus on planning the spectacle in the arena. After what Hapker had done to protect Jori, he didn't want to torture him—but the man *was* his enemy. Terk couldn't afford to let sentiment get in the way. Whatever Father wanted him to do, he'd do it.

Jori didn't have his strength. This wasn't the first time he'd gone behind Father's back to help someone. One of these days, his little brother would get caught and he didn't want him to die any more than he wanted himself to die.

Damn you, Jori. Why do I keep enabling you? He should just put an end to the prisoners and be done with this mess. *Except I'm no Dokuri.*

13
Torture

3791:024:18:56. Dour-faced warriors tromped out an ominous beat. J.D. Hapker and the prisoners remained silent as the impenetrable wall of towering men escorted them down the corridor. Though the width of the hall allowed seven people to walk abreast, these Tredons had chests nearly as broad as two men.

Hapker's stomach fluttered. *Where are they taking us?* Had Jori's plan fallen through? Were they marching to their deaths? He forced his anxiety aside. No reason to worry. The emperor needed them to work on the emitter.

A thick armored shoulder jostled Hapker into the hefty Corporal Barslow. He mumbled an apology but Barslow kept his eyes firmly forward. His ruddy cheeks paled, and his throat bobbed up and down, yet he walked tall.

Not as tall as Sergeant Walden. Even the Tredons barely reached the man's great height, but Walden had only a quarter of their width. Despite this, he glowered at his captors. His stark white hair and golden eyes made him look as fierce as an eagle. Davis and Harley's black looks projected the same fortitude. Only Canthidius conveyed defeat.

Hapker generally loathed the man, but now he pitied him. As the leading science officer on the *Odyssey*, Doctor Canthidius had the best chance of survival. Yet he hadn't spoken a single word since being dragged and dumped into his cell. His head hung as the Tredon warriors hauled him along.

In his own domain, the doctor strutted like a cocky rooster with a yellow tuft of hair instead of a red comb. This time his pale skin and puckered lips made him look as lifeless as a fish on a dinnerplate.

The wicked smile and glinting eyes of the guard next to him made Hapker's neck prickle. He twisted his wrists, trying to put feeling back into his cuffed hands. As they continued through the dimly lit halls, he considered his options. With more prisoners than guards and an element of surprise, they might overpower these men. Although Barslow, Walden, and the others seemed ready for a fight, Canthidius, Simmonds, and Sharkey were not. Plus, the warriors outmatched them in size, weaponry, and likely in skill.

Hapker clenched his fists. He had to do something.

The moment passed when the Tredon guards stopped at a wide set of doors. As they slid open, an acrid scent escaped and burned Hapker's nose. He took in the vast room and swallowed the knot in his throat.

Tiered seating along the walls reminded him of the ruftbol stadium back home, only this court had ash-colored flooring and— Hapker's blood drain from his face—a looming structure in the middle. Heavy steel shafts made up the rectangular framework of this contraption. The metal might once have been burnished, but it was dull now with blotches of dark stains. A thick chain hung from the center with two iron shackles on the end.

The source of the smell became evident. Hapker nearly gagged from the scent of sweat and blood mixed with a cleaning agent. He wanted to spit out the taste, but his mouth was dry. Jori told him they'd be tortured, but he had assumed it would only be if he and his crew didn't cooperate.

Sharkey groaned. *I'm sorry*, he mouthed to her. When the Tredon guards had thrown her into his cell earlier, he was sure Jori and Terkeshi had failed to keep her from being used. Her clothes were torn and her face bloodied.

Harley had found the hypospray in her hand and injected it. She became a little more alert and told them what Terkeshi had done. Hapker's relief barely offset his guilt over the beating she'd received—and now she had to suffer further.

A warrior gripped Hapker's arm and pulled him inside the room. He lost his balance, but the vice grip forced him along until he stood in front of the contraption. The warriors lined him and his crew before it, then made them kneel on the cold hard floor.

A warrior with a shaved head yanked Walden to the structure.

Hapker leapt to his feet. "No! Take me ins—" A jab between his shoulder blades sent him crumbling to the floor. Someone grabbed his hair and forced him back to his knees.

Sergeant Davis' face turned as red as his hair. "Leave him be, you bloody barbarians!" A punch to the side of his head cut his protest short.

Walden struggled and yelled, but he couldn't do much against the giant men. They shackled his hands and pulled the slack from the chain until his arms stretched far over his head and his toes dangled. He stopped yelling and hyperventilated.

"The man will piss his pants before we even get started," a Dragon Warrior standing behind Hapker said.

"This oughta be good," another said. The man made a sucking sound, then sent a glob of spit splattering to the floor. "Let's make these pussies sing."

The room filled with derisive comments from the deep-voiced warriors—some lewd, others hateful, and a fair few sounded gleeful.

Hapker's body flushed with heat. He moved to stand again, but strong clawed hands on his shoulders kept him down. "You can't do this! We saved your sons' lives." When he jerked his torso, he broke free and lunged forward. A round-nosed warrior swung his fist in his gut, making him double over.

"Leave off 'im!" Sergeant Davis jumped from his knees and butted his head into the chin of the man behind him. "I'm gonna kill you worthless shites!" He elbowed another warrior in the sternum and earned himself more strikes to the head. "Leave off 'im!" he said as he front-kicked a man in the hip at the same time as Hapker rolled away from his attacker.

Another warrior clipped Hapker in the ear, sending a powerful twinge into his skull and down his neck. The next fist bashed into his temple and sent him sprawling. A heavy boot slammed on his chest, knocking the wind out of him.

As he choked for air, a warrior grabbed Davis' foot and jerked it with a snap. Davis yowled, then shouted obscenities and threats. The warriors pummeled him until he stopped.

Hapker rolled to his knees. Two men snatched him by the crook of his arms and threw him face-down to the floor, then pressed their weight on him to keep him from moving.

The other warriors stepped back from Davis to reveal the heap of his body and the splatter of his blood. Sergeant Davis groaned. The warriors whooped and jeered like an eager pack of hyenas. All of it stopped at the command of Emperor Mizuki.

"I have no patience for protests or procrastinations." The sound of the emperor's voice sent a shiver down Hapker's spine. The man spoke sharply, though his tone was deep. His dark eyes glowered at the prisoners. "I expect each of you to put forth your best effort to complete this device. You will work hard as if your life depends on it because it does. Just so you know how serious I am, I've invited you here so you can appreciate my resolve."

The emperor gave a curt nod to a warrior carrying a long metallic rod. The man stepped forward and used it to send a spray of blue sparks at Walden. Walden cried out as the blue charge crackled over his body. It lasted only a few moments, but Walden's scream lasted longer.

"No!" Hapker struggled but couldn't get out from under his captor's weight. "I'm the leader. Please! Take me instead."

Hapker continued to plead as he watched in horror. Walden took two more strikes before breaking down into a sob. Hapker stifled his own well of anguish. Walden was an exemplary officer, and a good man. He had a wife and a lovely daughter, both of whom he talked about often. The way his face lit up every time he shared a story about them made even the stoic Captain Arden smile.

Walden didn't deserve this. No one did. Hapker ached for them. Helplessness racked him as he struggled to keep his composure.

They tortured the Cooperative officers one after the other. Davis, Barslow, and Harley spewed curses through the first few strikes, but ended with cries. Meanwhile, Hapker's stomach clenched with a mixture of fear, anger, and guilt. These were his men. He was responsible for them, so it was his fault this happened.

No, not my fault. It's his *fault.* A surge of hate for the emperor washed over him. After getting to know Terkeshi and Jori, Hapker had realized that not everything he'd heard about the Tredons were true. However, Emperor Mizuki's dark eyes and baleful frown seemed to embody all the terrible stereotypes.

His heart clenched at the sight of the two boys standing on either side of him. Jori and Terkeshi resembled their father in many aspects, but neither glowered the way he did. Instead, they held wooden expressions. Were they enjoying this or hating it? He hoped this sickened them as much as it did him.

Harley's torture ended. The guards removed him from the hanging shackles. He slumped into their arms and they dragged him away. The warriors didn't move to get anyone else. Was it over? He and a few others hadn't had their turn yet.

The warriors mumbled among themselves. A few glanced at the emperor. Hapker struggled to see what had their attention.

"Now!" The emperor's angry voice silenced the room.

A warrior moved just enough for Hapker to look past him. Jori and Emperor Mizuki glared at one another. A quiet tension froze everyone in their place.

Jori fearlessly faced the man twice his height and width. Neither spoke. The emperor's fist tightened. Hapker held his breath.

"I'll do it." Terkeshi stomped over to the prisoners. "Get him up!" he said with a head tilt toward Simmonds.

Simmonds paled. Two guards jerked him to his feet. Terkeshi snatched the rod from the torturer. He looked very much like his father now with his brow furrowed, and jaw clenched.

Hapker's gut tightened. It was bad enough that the emperor forced his children to watch, but this was even more depraved.

After the warriors secured the engineer, Terkeshi unleashed the blue electricity. Simmonds cried out. "Please! Why are you doing this after we—"

Terkeshi struck again. The man tried to say more but Terkeshi kept at it.

Soon the man was a blubbering mess. Terkeshi slapped the rod back into the warrior's hand and stormed to his father's side.

A warrior took Simmonds down. Hapker watched the interaction between Jori and his father. He couldn't hear what they said, but the emperor undoubtedly expected Jori to do what his brother had just done.

Jori shook his head. The emperor grabbed his arm. His other hand balled into a fist. He bent low to put his face in Jori's and said something, probably something threatening. Jori didn't cower and his eyes continued to reflect his refusal. Hapker choked on the lump in his throat as the emperor raised his hand.

The strike didn't come, though. "Get out of my sight, coward." The emperor jerked Jori's arm away so harshly that Jori almost fell. Hapker sighed in relief as Jori marched out of the room. Terkeshi's eyes followed as his brother left. The boys could be hard to read, but Hapker was certain worry etched Terkeshi's face.

The warriors shackled Sharkey next. They hooted and hollered as she hung in chains. She groaned as she waited, then screamed when the shock hit. Hapker trembled violently as dizziness came over him. He gritted his teeth and strived to move. It was hopeless. His throat tightened as Sharkey cried out.

Hapker jerked again and managed to prop himself up by the elbow. "Leave her alone!" he croaked. "You monstrous fu—"

A heavy boot cut him off. Sharkey screamed again, then passed out. The warriors took her down and another warrior yanked Hapker up. He was the last one, either by chance or by design because he was the highest in rank. His chest constricted as they forced him into the chains. His heart hammered, but he refused to show them his fright. They pulled him upward until his toes barely touched the floor. *I won't cry out. I won't cry out.*

When the blue electricity hit him and surged across his body, a warbled sound escaped him. He'd broken his leg once while on a hike. He suffered for hours before rescue came, but that pain was nothing like this. It was like every part of him was being torn to shreds. Even after the first shock was over, agony continued to saw through his muscles.

Just as the pain subsided, another jolt blasted over him. This time he screamed.

It happened again several more times. Hapker wasn't sure how long it all lasted, but he was certain they tortured him more than they had the others.

When it ended, he felt like a shattered window. As soon as the Tredon warriors released the shackles, he fell into their arms the same way Harley had done.

The warriors unceremoniously dropped him to the floor. Hapker embraced the coldness of it.

"Luckily, the empire has a use for you," the emperor said to the prisoners. His voice intruded into Hapker's newfound respite. "This is nothing compared to the real torture I have planned. Ankgar has some creative ways to bring about enduring agonizing pain. The last man I sent to him lived for weeks after being flayed alive. You will be his next victim if you fail me."

Hapker cringed and swallowed the bile rising from his throat.

14
Princes and Prisoners

3791:024:21:22. The extra gravity pulled J.D. Hapker down like a giant elephant in a graveyard as he lay face down on his hard cot. A throbbing ache steeped throughout his body while his thoughts spiraled an empty void. Something cold touched his neck. A hiss followed. Hapker jerked awake to find Terkeshi kneeling over him with a hypospray.

His mind cleared and his pain eased but he still didn't have the strength to do more than slouch against the wall. Corporal Harley's face darkened. He moved to stand, but a Tredon guard Jori had said could be trusted nudged him back down with the point of his phaser rifle. Simmonds curled in a fetal position on his bed and warily eyed the guards. Sharkey stirred but nothing more.

Jori stood with his brother, both with a disciplined posture and neutral expression.

"You've got to help us," Simmonds said with a whine.

Terkeshi's face twisted. "Don't be ridiculous."

"But we saved you."

"This is all you get," Terkeshi replied as he indicated the stack of read-only devices they held.

Jori stiffly handed Hapker an MDS and tossed three more onto the beds of the others. "I have uploaded a section of the emitter specs onto each of your devices," the boy said tonelessly. "Your portion is specific to your specialty."

"Our specialty?" Harley asked.

"You've worked with transmitter technology before," Terkeshi said.

Harley's brow tilted. Hapker gave him a nod indicating he should roll with it.

"Uh, yeah." Harley looked closer at his MDS screen. "I have uh two years of experience in mecha—uh—tronics."

Hapker lowered his face in his hand. Maybe keeping the others from knowing what Jori had done wasn't such a good idea.

"Yeah, dumbass," Terkeshi said. "That's what your records say."

"You changed our records?" Simmonds asked.

Hapker glanced warningly at the engineer, but the man didn't seem to notice.

Terkeshi growled and gave Jori a penetrating stare. "This is a stupid idea," he muttered.

Simmonds sat up slowly. "Why torture us, then help us?"

"I've been asking myself that same damned question," Terkeshi said with another pointed look at Jori. "I should just kill the lot of you and end everyone's misery."

Simmonds' throat bobbed. "You-you would do that?"

Terkeshi stared coldly in reply.

Harley muttered a curse.

"B-but we helped you," Simmonds said.

Harley crossed his arms. "You think they care about that?"

Terkeshi's attention snapped to the young corporal.

"Not our choice," Jori said before his brother could say anything.

Simmonds' eyes darted about, as though looking for answers. "Surely your father knows we saved you. Surely that should count for something."

Terkeshi's fists tightened. "My father has no sentiment for the likes of you."

Simmonds gulped.

"We can't fix that emitter," Sharkey replied, barely audible.

"If you wish to live, you will *act* like you can," Terkeshi said.

"For how long?" Hapker asked. "We can't keep up this ruse."

"Do you have a plan?" Simmonds glanced back and forth between each boy.

"Not yet," Jori replied.

"No," Terkeshi said as he shot a glare at Jori. "There is no plan. There's nothing we can do for you."

Harley bared his teeth. "Except torture us." He jabbed his finger at Sharkey. "Look what you did to her. She served on the ship that saved your life, and this is how you repay her? Ungrateful brute."

Terkeshi's eyes blazed. "Talk about *ungrateful*. Maybe I owe her, but I owe *you* nothing. Yet here I am keeping you alive, and at great risk."

Harley scowled but didn't reply. Terkeshi held his glare until Harley broke eye contact.

"Jori," Terkeshi said. "Go with Washi to the other cells and hand out the rest of the MDSs."

Jori and Washi, the dimple-chinned man, left.

"I do owe you." Terkeshi's features calmed as he spoke to Hapker. "I even admit that you have a lot of admirable qualities for a Cooperative officer. I don't want to see you die, but helping you is risky. If something happens to Jori because of you, I will not hesitate to kill you."

Hapker nodded.

Harley harrumphed. "Why should your brother's life be more important than ours?" he mumbled.

"Because you're nothing but a worthless piss-ant," Terkeshi said.

"And you're a damned—"

The elder prince grabbed Harley and slammed him against the wall. Terkeshi's hand pinched the man's throat in a white-knuckled hold.

Hapker jerked upright, ignoring the searing pain in his body, and stopped short as Michio's rifle aimed at his head.

"Terkeshi, please don't," Hapker said in a tone that was calmer than he felt.

Terkeshi's unyielding stare into Harley was as unforgiving as his grip. Harley flailed and struggled to breathe.

Crap, that boy is strong. Hapker swallowed down his surging dread as Harley's face purpled. Terkeshi released him and stepped back to let the man fall forward. Harley dropped and sucked in air only to hack it back out.

Terkeshi turned to Hapker. "Tread *very* carefully, Commander. And make sure these people do the same."

15
Incessant Stinkwood

3791:024:23:41. Silas Arden resisted the urge to massage his temples. Though his wound had been healed, the uncertainty of the new situation set his nerves on edge. The Tredons had gone, but they left a mess in their wake. Debris littered the facility—concrete, equipment, and a smattering of personal items. Attempts had been made to clear pathways, but disorder remained.

The emitter room was the clearest place. With it gone, the once energetic and hopeful facility turned into an empty promise.

They'd lost more than the emitter. Outside, medics searched in vain for survivors while others gathered the dead. The rising death toll here was just the beginning, though. If the emperor got that device working, the hundreds would turn to millions.

The veins in Arden's head throbbed as people disembarked from the last shuttle that had escaped during the fight. He put on a pleasant smile and greeted them. The weight on his shoulders lightened as the passengers walked out with nothing more serious than a few lacerations.

"Welcome, Mister Largos," Arden said to a grey-haired man wearing a mechanic's uniform. "I'm grateful you've returned safely."

Largos grasped Arden's outstretched hand. "Thank you, Captain. It's been a wild ride. Did the Tredons get our emitter?"

"I'm afraid so."

Largos hung his head and shook it. "It's a shame. I don't know what we'll do now."

"We'll do everything we can to help." The hollow comfort made Arden feel like a fraud, but he had nothing else to offer.

Largos looked away and sighed.

Arden swallowed the lump in his throat. "I believe Mister Donal is in his office. Please check in with him."

Before Arden could welcome the next passenger, the sound of Major Esekielu's shrill voice caught his attention.

"Not a single part?" the major said. "You didn't spend a few minutes for one piece?"

The Thendian project leader's jaw dropped. "There wasn't time. I was barely able to get our people—"

Major Esekielu's lips curled. "The plan was to take those parts before leaving."

The project leader ran his hand through his hair. "I'm telling you, there *wasn't* enough time. One moment we heard the Tredons were attacking, the next moment—"

"Now the emperor has everything he needs." Major Esekielu's wooden posture strained to the point where it might snap. "And you've got nothing. While he's out destroying planets, yours will be in the process of destroying itself."

The project leader clenched his fists. "That's your fault. Not mine. You were supposed to protect us."

Major Esekielu's face purpled.

Arden stepped between the two men. "You are correct, Doctor. None of this has gone according to plan, but I'm glad you and your people escaped. As I understand it, not one person from your project was taken." He turned to the major. "This means the emperor doesn't have anyone to set up the emitter, let alone reconfigure it."

"That's right," the project leader said with an emphatic nod. He huffed as though glad to have the heat taken off him. "That device is far too complicated. It will take the Tredons years to catch up to our level of expertise."

"Thank you, Doctor," Arden said. "Although the emperor took none of your people, I understand you've lost a few. My condolences to you and their families."

"Thank you, Captain Arden." The project leader bowed, then dashed away.

Major Esekielu pressed his lips as though holding back a spray of fire.

"These are civilians, Major," Arden said with a fire of his own. "It's not their job to sacrifice themselves for the sake of a mission."

"Obviously," Major Esekielu said. "They're a bunch of—"

"I have had enough of your pretentious attitude, Major. If you're so damned good at your job, then *do* it. Quit wasting your time laying blame and work on a solution instead."

Major Esekielu flashed his teeth, but quickly masked it with a tight smile. "Yes, Captain," he said with mock politeness.

"Sir," Major Bracht interrupted.

Arden dismissed Major Esekielu with a curt nod, then turned to Bracht with relief. "It's good to see you, Major."

"And you, Sir. Unfortunately, I come with bad news."

Arden frowned. "I haven't seen Commander Hapker," he said, guessing. "Several people remain unaccounted for."

The Rabnoshk warrior's at-ease posture made most formal military stances look lazy, Major Esekielu's being the exception, yet his mien seemed dispirited now. "The commander and a dozen or so others were still fighting when I retreated as ordered. An enemy blast destroyed the elevator before they could follow."

Arden sighed. "He must have been captured, then. We didn't find his body. Was Lieutenant Sharkey with him?"

"Yes, Sir."

Arden glanced at his MM tablet. Unlike the list of those confirmed dead, the list of missing people dwindled when the last shuttle came in. He sent Bracht the information.

Bracht's brows turned down as he reviewed his own MM. "I didn't see Doctor Canthidius, but these others were with the commander."

Arden nodded. Either they had overlooked the doctor in the headcount or the Tredons had captured him too.

"I shouldn't have left them, Sir," Bracht said with his usual harsh tone.

"You did the right thing," Arden replied. "If you had stayed behind, they might have captured or killed you as well."

Bracht opened his mouth to protest, but Arden forestalled him. "I'm glad you're here, Bracht. I need your help getting them back."

"I'll do whatever it takes, Captain." Bracht sounded eager to redeem himself.

"I know you will. First, see to it you and your people get some rest. I need you refreshed."

"Yes, Sir." Bracht snapped a salute and left.

Arden rubbed his forehead. Too many dead, too many dying, a handful missing, and little to be done about it.

His comm beeped. He tapped the small device taped behind his ear. "Captain Arden here."

"Captain, we've repaired the *Defender* and we're on our way," Admiral Belmont said.

"That's good news, Sir."

"Also, two of our battleships are heading to the Tredon border. You and Major Esekielu will meet them there and assist in the search."

Arden froze. "Sir? Major Bracht is here. He can—"

"Just until I catch up to you. There's no time to waste. I've already informed Major Esekielu of the plan."

"Major Bracht knows this ship best, Admiral. And he's part of our team."

"Those involved in the ground fighting lost a lot of friends. They are to be put on leave."

Arden understood the reasoning, but not the timing. "Sir. We can put them on leave when this is all over. I need my major."

"You have your orders. Belmont out."

A sharp pang in Arden's head broke him out of his shock. His headache burst like the climax of a Rabnoshk opera. It made no sense to keep Major Esekielu in charge. That Bracht was being pushed aside by this incessant piece of stinkwood once again was unacceptable.

He clenched and unclenched his fists to quell the tempo of his thoughts. There was nothing he could do about it. Arguing would make him sound petty. Although pettiness wasn't something he tolerated, the desire remained.

He set his jaw, determined to take his own advice to quit wasting time and work on a solution. Get his people back.

16
The Nurse

3791:025:08:11. Hanna Sharkey kept an easy pace as Terkeshi led her down the corridor. Two Tredon warriors followed silently. Although they didn't say anything, she felt their eyes. She had heard enough lewd comments from other warriors to suspect they leered at her ass as she walked.

The elder prince never said where he was taking her. Yet despite his harshness with her before, his presence put her at ease.

"Wait outside," Terkeshi told the two guards when they reached the infirmary.

The sterile smells permeating the room were much like any other sick bay she'd encountered, but the primitive quality of the place raised her eyebrows. It could have been a salvage yard. Older-model medical devices and idle med bots cluttered the corners.

Beds occupied by injured warriors crowded the lobby, creating a dangerous maze. Only two men were connected to monitoring systems. One person tended to the patients, though he looked more like a warrior than a medic.

"Come with me," Terkeshi said. He led her through the lobby and into a private room with a single examination bed. "Sit down."

After she sat, he leaned against the wall and crossed his arms. The silence that hung between them niggled at her nerves. She shifted her weight. "So why are you helping me?"

His eyes penetrated hers as the silence lingered. Finally, he spoke, "Let's just say I don't think Usagi deserves a woman."

"Pffft. You got that right."

Terkeshi didn't respond. She picked at her fingernails and tried to think of something else to fill the stillness. "That stuff you used," she said as she clasped her hands to keep from fidgeting. "How did you know it would work? Have you used it before?"

Terkeshi's eyes tightened. She discreetly worked her tongue to wet her dry mouth as he studied her.

"Jori says you looked out for him while I was in a coma," he spoke at last.

"Yeah. Some people were giving him a hard time."

He tilted his head to the side. "Why would you care?"

She raised her brows. "He's just a kid."

"Not just *any kid*."

She shrugged. "Hapker believes in him and I believe in Hapker."

Terkeshi nodded slowly. "Jori learned about the pseudo-strain and found a way to get some."

"That quickly?"

Terkeshi looked at her as though she was daft. "It's been in use for a while. The medic you are about to meet is the only other person who knows about it, so you had better not blab about it to anyone."

She emphatically shook her head. "I certainly don't want that secret getting out."

An older man arrived, halting their conversation. Dark age spots speckled his balding head and clean-shaven face. His fatness contrasted greatly with every other Tredon Sharkey had ever seen. The man met her with gleaming eyes. His lips curved in a way that made her skin crawl.

Terkeshi's expression darkened. "Get Terena."

The man blinked and his manner shifted into subservience. "My Lord, your father ordered me to examine her."

"He ordered that she be examined. He did not specify that *you* be the one to do it."

"But surely I'm the most qualif—"

"Damn it, Fink!" Terkeshi snarled, sending a shiver down Sharkey's spine. "Do not argue with me. Get Terena now."

The man bobbed his head and backed quickly out of the room.

Terkeshi returned to his position against the wall and silence fell again. Although he wasn't looking at her, his dark eyes sparked with annoyance. Despite how he helped her, his sudden shift in temper made her nerves vibrate.

An older woman entered the room. Her grey hair streaked with black hung loose, as did her robe, or dress, or whatever she wore. Its plain brown material seemed held together by a simple belt at the waist. The knuckles of the woman's aged hands bulged. Her wrinkled face crinkled more when she smiled.

She bowed. "My Lord."

"Terena." Terkeshi nodded and stepped aside. "This is Lieutenant Sharkey."

"Hanna. You can call me Hanna," Sharkey said.

Terena's smile widened. The genuine kindness of it made Sharkey smile back.

"It is good to meet you, Hanna." Terena grasped Sharkey's hand with her gnarled one. Her touch was gentle and as reassuring as her eyes. "Go ahead and lie down now, dear."

Sharkey let Terena guide her down, but she glanced nervously at Terkeshi.

"My Lord?" Terena said as though she noticed Sharkey's unease.

"There are two choices," Terkeshi said to Sharkey. "I can stay in here or I can leave." Sharkey almost answered but Terkeshi held up his hand and stopped her short. "My choice depends on you. If I am to leave, you must give your word that you will not make any trouble here. Terena is one of the very few on this ship who wants to help you, and I won't have her hurt in some feeble escape attempt."

"I promise I won't try anything," Sharkey replied.

Terkeshi stared at her a moment as if analyzing her. "Good. I have work to do. Let me know when you're done," he said to Terena.

After Terkeshi closed the door on his way out, Terena did a basic medical examination. "How are you doing, my dear?" she asked as she checked Sharkey's eyes with a light pen.

"I itch like crazy."

"Mmm," Terena said. "I'm sorry about that. It's an allergic reaction to the pseudo-virus. I will give you something to help before you leave."

"So pseudo means fake, right? I don't really have Ghondorian venascabia, do I?" Sharkey spoke quietly even though the door was closed.

"No, you don't." Terena shared a reassuring smile as she continued her examination. "This strain can be easily cured by your doctors. All they need to do is give you a katharos of some kind."

"I'll tell them, assuming I ever get to leave here. Will I? Get to leave here, that is?"

Terena sighed. "It doesn't seem likely."

"What about the other doctor, the creepy man? Won't he be able to check the scans and see I really don't have it?"

"Don't worry. I've taken care of the scans. Besides, Fink isn't smart enough to figure out it's a pseudo-strain. If by some miracle he does, First Prince Mizuki will handle him."

"Hmm. He *does* seem capable. Too bad he can't use his power to keep others from hurting us."

Terena prodded Sharkey's abdomen with a gentle touch. "He has enough pull to help a little. Unfortunately, doing more would only put him and his brother in harm's way. If that happens, they wouldn't be able to help anybody."

"So they help other people?" Sharkey asked, wondering if she read too much into Terena's words.

Terena only smiled in reply as she ran the healing pen over the bruises Usagi had made. Sharkey gasped at the vibrating relief. It didn't take away all her aches, but it helped.

"You're a woman," Sharkey said.

"Yes," Terena replied.

"I didn't know Tredons allowed women to become doctors."

"I'm not a doctor. I'm a nurse." Terena moved the pen over the bruises on Sharkey's ribs.

"Still."

"Medical personnel are in short supply and I have enough skill in treating the emperor's concubines that he tolerates me."

Concubines? She should have known. "How did you come to be here in the first place, if you don't mind me asking? Surely he didn't just hire you."

"No, dear. I was a concubine of the previous emperor." Terena pulled Sharkey's shirt down and picked up a scanner.

Sharkey's eyes widened and she bolted upright. "Are you the emperor's mother?"

"No." Terena put a comforting hand on Sharkey's shoulder to lay her back down. "I wouldn't even call myself his stepmother since I had no part in raising him."

"What a life," Sharkey replied. "I can't imagine living on this terrible ship."

"Oh, I don't have it so bad as some." Terena browsed the results on the scanner's screen. "Besides, there are a few good things about this place. And even a few good people."

A bitterness filled Sharkey's mouth. "Really? Like who?" Though Jori and Terkeshi had spared her from utter humiliation, all the ogling and nasty comments from the other warriors made her leery.

Terena smiled and patted her shoulder. "Your exam is over, dear. Let me get you that antihistamine and you can be on your way."

Sharkey sat up. When the door slid open, Terena ran into a big ugly warrior.

"Pardon me, Senshi Usagi," Terena said with a bow.

The man pushed her aside and stepped in. A sickening smile spread over Usagi's face as he ogled Sharkey. She clenched her fists and broke out into a cold sweat as nausea rose from her gut.

Terena regarded Sharkey with a crinkled brow. "I will call Prince Mizuki now that we're done."

Usagi frowned and grabbed Terena by the arm. "Is she cured?"

Terena lowered her head. "I'm sorry, Senshi Usagi, but it will take some time for her to recover."

"I want her healed, woman!"

"It will be done, Sir," Terena said with a remarkable calmness that Usagi might have mistaken for meekness. "I have orders directly from the prince."

Usagi tightened his grip. "Good. Make it happen soon."

Terena dipped her head. "Yes, Senshi."

Usagi jerked the old woman out of the way and made for Sharkey. She pulled up her feet and kicked out. "Get away from me, you fucking animal!"

He grabbed her by the ankle and laughed. As he shoved her legs aside, she readied her fists. As soon as he got close, she struck out. He deflected her hand with ease and laughed.

"You will be mine," he said as he grabbed her jaw and pinched her chest.

She pushed against his strength to no avail. Her body had weakened after the torture, and her muscles protested from Usagi's previous beating.

The pace of her heartbeat quickened. She held her breath and ground her teeth through the pain. Usagi's eyes glinted as he waggled his tongue. Despite the pain and terror that seized her, she refused to cry out.

"First Prince Mizuki says he's on the way," Terena said.

Usagi let go and stepped back. "I'll have you soon enough, Sweetness."

He turned away and backhanded Terena. She yelped and hugged the corner.

As soon as the door closed behind the man, Sharkey's body broke out into a tremble.

Terena rushed over. "Are you alright, dear?"

"Y-yes. You?"

"Don't worry about me. Some like to hassle me bit, but it's been a long time since they abused me." She eased Sharkey's face to the side and tenderly ran the healing pen down her cheek. "It will be alright. If the prince has gone through all this trouble to keep Usagi from having you, you will be safe."

"Good. Because I'd rather die than let that man touch me," she replied vehemently.

Terena patted her shoulder and Sharkey got the feeling she might have to make that choice soon.

17
Estimates

3791:025:08:12. The entrance slid open and a warm gust swept past Jori's face. He stepped in and scanned the five platforms that spanned the auxiliary docking bay. Earlier, this place had been a noiseless expanse. Dignitaries hadn't visited here since his father abolished court about ten years ago—after the attack that corrupted his genetic coding and left him unable to sire more children.

Jori paused and drank in the noise and activity that filled the bay now. Pounding hammers, zings of electric saws, and drills resounded throughout. The buzz and hum energized the place.

The emitter lay in about a dozen pieces, most large enough to tower over the workers. Jori made his way to the antenna and stopped by the group of shokukin building scaffolding to keep it steady.

"Malkai," he said to the green-eyed worker.

Malkai set aside his hammer and dipped his head. "Yes, Prince Jori."

"I still haven't received your report." Jori tapped his MM.

Malkai's eyes widened. "I sent it, my Lord. I swear."

Jori sensed his truthfulness. "You may have sent it to Yemon, but not to *me*."

Malkai's panic swelled and he rushed to get his tablet. "My apologies, Sir. I thought I sent it to you as well."

Jori's vexation left him. Malkai hadn't slighted him on purpose.

The worker tapped his device, and Jori touched the alert that came to his MM. The report opened and he scanned the information. After reviewing the key points, he added Malkai's report to his own and forwarded it to Father.

"Excellent," he said with a nod. Malkai bowed back and resumed his work.

As Jori left the bay and headed to his father's office, his stomach wriggled. Though the state of the emitter wasn't surprising, Father would be displeased.

He reached his father's door and pressed the comm button. "Jori here, Sir."

The door slid open. Jori stepped inside and stood in front of the desk in a stiff at-ease stance and waited. Father sat in his ornate chair and perused his deskview. Most sensations emanating from him indicated deep concentration, but spikes of irritation protruded through.

The dragon illustration hanging on the wall behind him shared his stormy expression. This detailed art glittered with minuscule jewels of mostly red and gold. The ancient piece had been created shortly after Earth explorers settled on Jinsekai, the primary Toradon planet. It supposedly inspired the naming of his people as Toradon Nohibito, Dragon People, and passed through many hands before ending up with the first Mizuki emperor.

Jori loved this picture, but the weight it signified sometimes overwhelmed him. Perhaps the dragon's fierceness and its bloody color had something to do with it. Learning to be a warrior was easy—the prospect of killing was not.

Father looked up. "Status."

Jori sensed Father's temperate mood. Perhaps he could bring up the information he put together from the emitter spec files. First, he needed to get past the unacceptable time estimate.

"We've successfully set up each of the major components, Sir," Jori replied.

"How long before it's ready?"

Jori suppressed the urge to fidget and spit the words out. "At least four periods, not including the time it will take to set it up on the special gun ship."

Father's brows pinched inward. "That's over a hundred days!"

Jori's heart jumped, but he didn't react outwardly.

"I thought the Thendians were nearly done," Father said.

"They were. They've been working on this project for about five years, so from their perspective a half year means almost done."

Father's piercing brown eyes hardened. Jori steeled himself. He had worried his tone would sound flippant and attempted to control it, but it was difficult because his father seemed to take everything as a personal insult.

"Work the men harder," Father demanded.

"It will be difficult, Sir." Jori's heart thumped, but he kept his expression calm. "The Thendians had a team of specialists."

"*We* have eleven new specialists."

"The prisoners have skills, but they need to catch up on this project before we can make any progress."

"Chusho!" Father slammed his fist down on his desk.

Jori didn't react this time. Father's anger wasn't as bad as he'd expected.

The man sat back in his chair and examined the report on his deskview. As he stroked his chin, Jori remained rigid despite his spiked nerves.

Before he could gather the courage to bring up the other topic, Father locked to his eyes. "All your studies are to be put off. I want you fully focused on this project. And if you sense that any of these men are slacking, you will tell your brother and let him handle it. Is that clear?"

"Yes, Sir."

"Dismissed."

"Sir, there's one more thing," Jori blurted. His heart hammered.

"What?"

Jori sensed Father's impatience surge but pressed on. "In looking over these specifications, I think it would be easier to convert the emitter into something that can help us mine the ores from Tymnar."

"I'm not interested in a mining device," Father said with a twist of his mouth.

"If we do these modifications—"

"If we do these modifications, I won't be able to use the emitter on Pentam."

Jori steeled himself. "This emitter will need people to maintain it. Why not create more wealth with an excavation machine first? We can use it to entice scientists to work for us and expand our military at the same time. With a greater stream of income and a permanent team of specialists, we will eventually be able to purchase the materials needed to make the emitter."

"Don't be an idiot. It's not that simple."

"Yes, actually. I think it can be. If the emitter—"

"Damn it, boy!" Father bolted to his feet and leaned over his desk with a menacing glare.

Jori resisted the urge to quail and held his father's stare. It really was simple. If they used this device as a mining tool, it would reduce the need for slave labor and ores would be extracted more quickly.

Jori had crunched the numbers, and their profits from Tymnar alone would double. Modifying the technology for their other mining operations would help make them profit almost as much. He had been sure the idea of making more money would appeal to his father. He had it all worked out. If only Father would look at it.

Jori didn't bother pointing out the file. The look in Father's eyes told him it would do no good.

"Get your ass back to work," Father said. The man sat, but his glare made it clear what would happen if Jori persisted.

Jori turned about and left. As his trepidation subsided, the annoyance at his father for not listening grew.

Maybe he could find a way to change Father's mind. If the modifications needed to turn it into a weapon couldn't be done...

He tucked the notion away. First, he had to figure out how to save Hapker.

18
The Clerk

3791:025:14:42. J.D. Hapker's brow drew down as he studied the MDS. These specifications made no sense. Despite all the studying he had been doing in his cell, he couldn't see how the resulting energy transfer came out as it did. Based on his current understanding, it shouldn't have been so high.

The pressure of massaging his temples and brow eased his developing headache for only a moment. He stopped and a shockwave of pain washed over his forehead, then settled back down to a dull throb. He blinked his tired eyes and continued studying.

"Do you get any of this shite?" Sergeant Davis said.

Hapker shook his head at the red-headed man beside him. "The more I look at the numbers and formulas, the more they all seem to melt together into a jumbled mess."

Davis grunted in agreement. Hapker wiped his brow. Jori's plan wouldn't work. All this information was too convoluted. His desperation, though, kept him from tossing the MDS across the room. He had to understand this, at least for the sake of pretense.

The unnerving silence in the cargo area made it difficult to concentrate. Hapker almost tasted the surrounding tension. Dozens of hawk-faced warriors watched over the Cooperative prisoners. The black-garbed men stood motionless yet were as alert as a pack of wolves on the hunt. If not for their towering bulk, their dark uniforms might have made them less conspicuous as they lingered in the shadowy gloom.

Not all Tredons kept guard. Hapker labored alongside men of the shokukin caste. They shared many of the same features as the warriors but had a leaner physique.

Hapker glanced over to where Jori worked. The boy had the smallest stature, but something else set him apart. His posture projected a level of interest and self-assurance that no one else here matched—worker or warrior.

Jori stepped away from the emitter and inspected the workers.

"Watch out, Sir," Sergeant Davis said. "Here comes the li'l rotter."

Hapker resisted his desire to defend the boy. Simmonds might have figured out Jori was helping them but the less the rest of the team knew, the less likely the secret would come out.

Despite Jori's casual stride, he walked like a general with a manner as flat as a frozen lake. Canthidius cringed at his passing, but the boy paid him no mind. Harley made a hateful face. Jori ignored him as well. He didn't stop to check out Sharkey's work even though she'd whispered to him the other day that she needed help. She seemed busy now—busier than most. No doubt it was a pretense to avoid unwanted attention.

Jori carried authority here, but a wiry man named Yemon acted as though he was in charge. Yet while Yemon irritated them like a pesky flea, he was otherwise ineffective. Still, he presented a danger. Like a flea, he jumped on everyone. Since he knew how this device worked, he had a reason to bite at their inadequacies.

Hapker took in the man's features. His wiry frame towered over Harley's shorter but stockier one. The round-faced man had no chin, lips so wide and narrow they'd look more natural on a frog, and the slitted eyes of a half-sleeping cat.

"What are you doing, you idiot?" Yemon said to Corporal Harley.

Harley's face reddened and his dark brows turned down.

"What kind of senseless moron puts a capacitor on backward?" Yemon continued. "Whatever you lack in muscle, you certainly don't make up for in brains."

"Funny, that's *exactly* what I heard one of your men say about you," Harley replied.

Sergeant Davis stifled a laugh. Hapker groaned inwardly.

Yemon's nose flared and his skinny chest puffed out. "Don't you dare talk to me that way."

Harley smirked, which seemed to infuriate Yemon further. "You might be important where you come from," Yemon said through clenched teeth, "but here you're an insect. And if you act up, I'll have you exterminated like one."

Harley huffed in derision.

"You don't believe me?" Without turning away, Yemon spoke to a guard, "Kelar, take this man to the arena and have him whipped."

"Yemon, we don't have time for this," Jori said before Hapker intervened. "He must keep working."

"I will not be spoken down to by Cooperative scum. He must be punished."

"Excuse me?" Jori replied. "Are you telling me what to do?"

Yemon flinched, but his scowl quickly turned into a sneer. "No, Sir."

"Then you will address me properly and do as you're told without argument."

"But, Sir—"

"*Without* argument. Do your job and report any problems to me. Understood?"

"Yes, Sir," Yemon said in a mocking tone.

Jori's face darkened. The resemblance to his father made Hapker's skin prickle.

Yemon's sneer left his face. "Yes, my Lord," he said in a more respectful tone and with a bow.

Jori's scowl remained. "Good. Now get back to work. Both of you," Jori said to both Yemon and Harley.

Yemon turned away in a snit. Harley gave the man a triumphant smile. Yemon stopped short and opened his mouth to say something, but Jori cocked an eyebrow and he flicked his tongue over his lips instead.

Harley's face shifted into a self-satisfied smile but darkened to a glower when Jori eyed him. Hapker sighed. If the young corporal insisted on not appearing chastised like Yemon, there would be trouble.

"That Harley's got a bit of a mouth on 'im," Sergeant Davis said, "but he's got pluck."

"Yeah, well, I need him and the rest of us to stay alive until we get rescued."

"Rescued?" Davis harrumphed. "Not bloody likely. The way I see it, we're gonna die anyway. Might as well gut some o' these wankers while we got the chance."

"No. We hold out."

"Yes, Sir. If you change your mind, just gi'me the go. I'll end 'em—and the li'l blighters too."

Hapker cringed at his reference to Jori and Terkeshi. He could let him in on how the princes were helping them, but he didn't trust Davis. "We're not killing children, Sergeant."

"If you say so, Sir."

"I do."

Davis headed to his next task. Hapker went back to trying to figure out how the data all fit together. The first part of the calculation inversely affected the third part. Apply the coefficient here. Add this one to that one and multiply the product by this other one. So far, so good. Only a couple more steps to go.

"What are you doing?" Yemon asked.

Hapker startled and all progress he'd made scattered like leaves in the wind. "Testing these energy transfers to make sure they're correct."

Yemon snatched Hapker's MDS and peered at the screen. "This isn't hard. I don't see what's taking you so long." He handed back the device.

"You're right. It's not hard, but it is time consuming." Hapker shifted his stance to ease his nerves. "Each piece of information interrelates and if one part is wrong, all of it is wrong."

Yemon squinted his eyes and asked about the figures. This was the same problem he'd been trying to wrap his head around. He spit out an answer.

Yemon frowned. A heap of dread fell on Hapker's shoulders.

"Either you Cooperative scum are not as smart as you think you are or you're playing dumb. Don't think that playing dumb will save you."

"Sorry," Hapker replied quickly. "You put me on the spot. I got nervous."

Yemon's mouth twisted. "Very well. Try again."

Hapker cleared his throat. Sweat formed on his brow as his mind raced.

"Well?" Yemon said and crossed his arms.

Hapker licked his lips. "Uh…" As he studied his screen, an urgent message icon flashed. "If the first part…" He tapped the message and skimmed its content. It was the answer. He peeked over to where Jori worked. The boy didn't acknowledge him, but he was the only one within earshot.

Hapker repeated the message, then deleted it.

Yemon frowned as though disappointed. "Well then. Maybe you're not as stupid as you look."

He likely meant the remark to be an insult, but Hapker smiled and discreetly wiped the sweat from his palms.

"I suggest you not let your cowardice interfere with your work," Yemon continued. More quietly he said, "If you mess this up, I'll have you whipped no matter what the little know-it-all says."

"What was that, Yemon?" Jori said as he approached.

Yemon jumped and turned around. "N-n-n-nothing, my Lord."

Jori replied with a raised eyebrow. Yemon stuttered an apology, then rapidly retreated.

The corner of Jori's mouth curved upward before turning serious. He leaned in. "You best study more on this. I can't protect you if he realizes you don't know what you're doing."

"I'm trying," Hapker responded.

Jori cocked an eyebrow. "Try harder."

19
Firefight

3791:025:15:23. Silas Arden fought to keep his eyes open. He forced himself to focus as they scanned the depths of space for any recent arc-signatures that might give them a clue to the whereabouts of the Tredon warships.

"LRS shows nothing," Chandly said for his hourly update.

Arden glanced at the data on his console, then rubbed his brow. This entire endeavor was fruitless. Space was too vast to monitor and long-range sensors could only detect so much. Not to mention that anything they detected would be several hours old.

"Sir!" Brenson said. "We're getting a distress call from the *Defender*."

Arden straightened. "Put it on."

Brenson tapped his console. "We've encountered a Tredon warship and need immediate assistance," the *Defender* captain's voice rang out, followed by a computerized statement of the coordinates.

"Jensin, get us there immediately. Maximum arc." Arden's stomach did a little tumble as the arc drive engaged.

"Shall I call in the major?" the lieutenant at the tactical station asked.

A sourness bit into Arden's tongue. If only Major Bracht and the others who survived the planetary battle hadn't been put on leave. He stabbed the comm on his armrest. "Major Esekielu, I need you here now."

Major Esekielu entered the bridge a few minutes later. His inky eyes scrolled the information on the viewscreen as he marched straight-backed to the commander's chair.

"Report coming in," Brenson said before the major could demand an update. "Captain Richforth says the *Basilisk* was waiting for them. He hasn't confirmed it, but he guesses our people and the emitter are on the *Dragon* and the *Basilisk* is covering the retreat."

"Forget about guesses," Major Esekielu said. "What's the status of the *Defender*?"

"I haven't received that information yet, Sir," Brenson replied in a flat tone.

Moments passed. The major didn't move, but the edginess of his posture indicated he wanted to get up and take over Brenson's job.

Brenson pressed his earpiece. "I'm getting something now, Sir. The *Defender* shields are at fifty percent. Their energy cannons are nearly depleted while the *Basilisk* seventy percent shield strength remaining."

Major Esekielu tightened his fists. "Lieutenant Wilshire, charge our cannons and fire as soon as you have a target."

"Yes, Sir," Wilshire replied.

Arden cringed inwardly. The firepower of the *Odyssey* wouldn't be adequate against a Tredon warship. Entering this firefight was a bad idea but lives were at stake. Since he was a peacemaker, not a warrior, he bit his tongue and let the man with the experience take over.

The bridge remained silent as they approached the destination. Backs straightened, eyes focused, and hands hovered over consoles. When Jensin announced their arrival, the crew sprang into action.

The ship came out of arc, making Arden's gut twinge again. Chandly and others swiftly gathered data and displayed the updated results on the viewscreen. For once, Major Esekielu didn't berate them as they worked.

Information from the *Basilisk* confirmed what Brenson had reported, but the *Defender* now had a much lower shield percentage.

Major Esekielu secured himself in his seat. "What's the status of our other battleships?"

"The closest is over thirty minutes away, Sir," Chandly replied.

"Damn it!" The major slammed his fist on his armrest. "When will we be within firing range?"

"Twenty—" The *Odyssey* shook. "We're taking in heat," Chandly said. "Their weapons have a longer reach."

The major's face turned purple. "Helmsman, lambda maneuvers now. Tactical, fire when ready."

"In range now, Sir," Lieutenant Wilshire said. "I'm targeting their port side."

The release of the *Odyssey*'s energy cannons jostled the ship. A violent shaking followed.

"Sir, we're taking heavy fire," an officer said.

"Obviously," the major replied. "Shield status?"

"Eighty… No, seventy-seven percent." Chandly's hands darted over the console as he kept up with the operations of multiple stations.

"Our energy cannons are ineffective," Lieutenant Wilshire said. "The *Basilisk*'s port shields are still at fifty-five percent."

"The *Defender* has taken a crippling blow." Brenson's brow furrowed. "Captain Richforth is reporting a hull breach."

"I said lambda maneuvers, helmsman!" Major Esekielu's mouth twisted into a snarl.

"I'm trying, Sir, but we're being barraged. Course corrections are ineffective."

"Our shields are at sixty-nine percent," Chandly said. "The *Basilisk* is now at fifty percent and they're still firing. Our energy cannons are dangerously low. We won't be able to—"

The *Odyssey* convulsed. Arden's teeth chattered.

"Sir, our port shields are down!" Chandly braced himself. "We've taken a direct hit."

"Zeta maneuvers, now!" The major's expression radiated wrath. "And no excuses."

The ship groaned and strained under the firepower. Arden's stomach lurched.

Brenson's forehead wrinkled. "The *Defender* is defenseless."

"Keep fir—" A thunder both heard and felt cut Major Esekielu off.

Arden gripped his armrests.

"The structural integrity of our ship is weakening, Sir," Chandly said. "We can't take another hit."

The thunder subsided. The bridge quieted as though passing through the eye of a storm.

"Chandly?" Arden said, his voice strained.

Chandly jerked from his frozen position and checked his console. A frown creased his brow and he tapped again. "Sir? You won't believe this, but the *Basilisk* is pulling out."

The major put on a predatory smile. "We hurt them more than we thought."

The muscles in Arden's neck and shoulders eased. "Or we're not a worthy target."

Major Esekielu glared. "Helmsman, set in a course to pursue."

"Belay that," Arden said. "We stay and assist the *Defender*."

"The *Defender* can help itself." The major bared his teeth. "Go after the *Basilisk*."

Arden smacked the arm of his chair. "Don't counter my orders, Major."

The major snapped off his harness and jumped to his feet. Arden stood too and towered over the man. "The battle is over, Major," he said in a low tone. "You're no longer needed."

Major Esekielu tilted his head up to match Arden's stare. His attempt at intimidation was pointless. Arden wasn't a warrior, but he had faced Rabnoshk warriors with more violence in their hearts than Major Bracht. Major Esekielu was a little boy throwing rocks at birds' nests in comparison.

The Major broke eye contact and scrutinized the bridge crew. He turned back to Arden with a hateful gaze. "We need to talk."

"There's nothing to talk about," Arden said. "This is *my* ship."

20
Scheming

3791:026:09:46. Jori resisted the urge to strangle the skinny man before him.

"I'm sure it goes here, my Lord," Yemon said.

Jori sensed the man's irritation, and it grated his own. "For the last time, Yemon, it makes no sense. If you put it there, the emitter will barely have enough power to penetrate an escape pod, let alone travel through the planet's crust."

"No. Look at my calculations, my Lord."

Jori reviewed the formula on Yemon's tablet, then pointed to a number. "You rounded your coefficient. It should be point two-five-one, not point three."

Yemon huffed. "A point zero-four-nine difference couldn't possibly change this so much."

"It can. Watch." He changed the value and handed back the device.

Yemon's lips moved as he reexamined the formula. Realization emanated from him, then shifted to agitation. "Well, if this is how you want it, Sir," he said with a fake smile that pricked Jori's nerves.

"It is," he replied through gritted teeth.

He turned away from the annoying man and knelt beside Benjiro. The straggly bearded shokukin stuck his tongue out to the side as he concentrated on attaching a component. His head-mounted lamp lit inside the tight workspace.

Jori studied his work. "Ben, why did you switch those two pieces around?"

"Wrong place," Benjiro said.

Jori frowned. "Wrong by the old specs or wrong by the new configuration?"

"Wrong," Benjiro replied. "Thingamajig go here."

"Why do you bother asking that idiot anything, my Lord?" Yemon said. "He can't even put on his own shoes."

119

"He may not be able to do everyday things, but he knows engineering."

Yemon sniffed in a way that made Jori want to punch him.

Terk approached. "How is it going?"

Yemon flinched. He straightened into the deferential military stance he neglected to use with Jori.

Jori scowled. He opened his mouth to answer Terk's question, but Yemon replied. "Well, my Lord. Except these men, or whatever you call them, have no clue what they're doing."

"They do," Jori said, trying not to sound defensive. "It's you who doesn't."

Yemon looked like he wanted to reply, but Terk glowered at him. "Why don't you go find something else to do."

The man nodded and bowed courteously, but Jori felt his indignation as he stepped away.

"I told you this wouldn't work," Terk said in their secret language.

"Chief Simmonds and Doctor Canthidius are doing alright."

"Yes, but for how long?"

Jori sighed. "I'll come up with a way to keep them safe."

"What do you mean you'll come up with a way? You better not do anything else. You've done enough."

"If I can find a way that won't get me in trouble—"

Terk's nostrils flared. "Or me. Or Sensei Jeruko. Or anyone."

"Maybe Yemon," Jori said, half-joking.

Terk growled. "Damn it, Jori. This isn't a game."

"I know," Jori muttered. "I can't help but think about it."

"Yes you can. You're just not trying hard enough."

"If I can do it so *no one* gets in trouble—"

"No." Terk's eyes hardened.

Jori replied with a pleading look.

Terk pressed his lips together. "It's impossible. You know very well that Father will find someone to blame."

Jori frowned. Terk was right.

"Quit scheming and keep your head where it belongs," Terk said. "The only way they have a chance to survive is if this thing gets fixed."

Jori deflated and stared at the device. If only Father had never heard of this stupid emitter. Jori and Terk wouldn't have ended up in Cooperative territory, met the commander, or taken him prisoner.

Terk let out a heavy sigh and put his hand on his shoulder. "Maybe when this is done—*maybe*—we can convince Father to send them somewhere else to work. And maybe we can arrange it so the ship that picks them up takes them back to the Cooperative instead."

Jori straightened, then smiled.

"Get that stupid look off your face," Terk said.

Jori flattened his expression.

Terk shook his head. "It's a good thing no one else here can sense your emotions. Don't get your hopes up, though. You must still deal with Yemon. That little worm is always scheming." Terk darted a dirty look Yemon's way. The man was too busy harassing a Cooperative prisoner to notice. "No doubt if the emitter doesn't work, he'll shift the blame onto you. And of course, if the emitter does work, he'll take all the credit."

Jori nodded. "He sticks his nose into everything. I keep telling him I'm watching the prisoners, but he doesn't take me seriously."

Terk grunted. "He's been acting above his station lately. Do what you can here. I'll have a private talk with him later."

"Thank you."

"You're a real pain in the ass, you know," Terk said in mock anger. Jori smiled. Terk rolled his eyes and muttered, "Brat."

21
New Mission

3791:026:12:02. Silas Arden examined the ship's damage and personnel injury reports that came in from all over the ship. Director Sengupta, acting in the place of Commander Hapker, assisted with coordinating the repair tasks while Major Esekielu stewed in blaring silence.

"Captain," Brenson said. "I have the admiral on the comm."

Captain Arden and Major Esekielu stood at the same time. Arden matched the major's stance, but no one could imitate the major's strict posture. "Put him on."

The admiral appeared on the viewscreen.

"Captain Arden of the *Odyssey* reporting to Admiral Belmont," Arden said before the major could dominate the conversation.

"Report," the admiral said with his usual sulky expression.

"Sir, the *Basilisk* escaped over the border," Arden replied. "We've sustained heavy damage—"

The major stepped forward. "Our shields are down, but the crew says they can have them operational in an hour. I recommend we pursue."

Director Sengupta arched an eyebrow Arden's way, no doubt disbelieving the major's audacity.

Arden kept his expression wooden. "I disagree, Admiral. This ship is not equipped to handle a Tredon warship."

Major Esekielu thrust out his chest. "If I may, Sir. I am a military officer, and I will do whatever it takes to get my people back."

The cords of Arden's neck tightened. "As will I. The only difference is I'm more prudent about how we do it."

The admiral frowned. "Is there a problem here?"

Major Esekielu's hard bearing turned self-important. "Sir, Captain Arden intervened during our engagement with the *Basilisk*. If he hadn't, we might have—"

"The battle was over, Major," Arden said. Damn this man for making him sound like a bickering child.

"We should have pursued." Major Esekielu's mouth twisted as though he'd just found an insect in his food.

"I want a full report." The admiral's bottom lip protruded, turning his expression into a stern pout. "We can discuss this later. For now, Captain, understand that Major Esekielu is there to assist you with any military matters."

Arden clasped his hands tightly behind his back. "Begging your pardon, Admiral, but Major Esekielu is not as familiar as we are with what this ship can and cannot do."

The admiral dipped his head. "Noted, but the next time you need to engage in battle, Major Esekielu has complete discretion."

Arden bristled at the unconventional order. A PCC captain was superior to the PG-Force presence on his ship, except in times of war and war had not been declared, but he had no grounds to overrule the admiral's orders. "Yes, Sir."

Major Esekielu jutted his chin. Arden bit the inside of his cheek.

"We have two of our battleships on the way now," the admiral said. "I'd like to tell you to chase the bastards down but crossing into Tredon territory is not something we're prepared to do… Yet. Councilor Greymore is pushing for war. Hopefully, it won't be long before he convinces the others."

Arden groaned inwardly. He wanted his crew back and he wanted the emitter out of Emperor Mizuki's hands, but he didn't want war. "Perhaps I can find a way to contact the Mizuki Princes."

"We've already tried that."

"We've tried to contact the emperor, Admiral," Arden said. "I know things didn't end on the best of terms with the children, but I believe there may still be a chance they would help us get our people back."

The admiral's frown deepened. "They're just children, and probably ungrateful ones at that. Besides, how would you contact them without going through the emperor?"

"I might have a way."

"How?"

"It's thin, at best, but it's worth a try since I can't be much help in the military side of this." Arden motioned for Director Sengupta. She clasped her hands behind her back and stepped beside him.

"Director Sengupta knows the commander of the Chevert outpost very well."

"This man is a talented collector and disseminator of information," she said. "He has contacts all over the sector and might know someone who has connections to the emperor's sons."

The admiral's lip protruded further. "You're right, Captain. This is thin, but it's also true that your ship won't be much help if we're given permission to pursue the warships into Tredon territory. Contact this man and get any intel you can on the emperor's military status and plans. I want to know everything that bastard is up to."

"Yes, Admiral. Such information may come at a price, though," Arden said.

"If the information you get is valuable, pay it. I'll increase your commerce budget."

"Thank you, Admiral. I'll be on my way as soon as my ship is repaired. I shall return Major Esekielu to you straight away."

The admiral took on a thoughtful look. "Keep him a while longer. The Chevert outpost is not the most hospitable place. You may find the major to be helpful."

Arden opened his mouth to argue, but the admiral put up his hand to forestall him. "This isn't over yet, Captain."

Arden nodded sharply and imagined Major Esekielu's pointed head swelling into a red giant.

22
Spotlight

3791:026:23:33. Terkeshi stifled a yawn and frowned. Whose idea was it to keep the lighting low on the bridge anyway? He wasn't the only one tempted to take a nap. Half the crew moved slower than an overloaded cargo vessel making port while the other half twitched and fidgeted in a fight to stay alert.

Terk shifted in his seat to ease the ache in his back. Standing and stretching would feel good but doing so would arouse the yawn he tried so hard to keep at bay. Maintaining the same alertness and focus expected of the crew wasn't the only reason to suppress his fatigue. General Samuru scrutinized every little thing he did—or didn't do. The man was like an incendiary device, ready to detonate at a moment's notice.

Terk regarded Samuru as he sat like a giant boulder, both hard and unyielding. The red puckered scar running down the side of his long face flared as menacingly as his eyes.

"Time to make a log," Samuru said.

Terk scowled. "I was just getting to it. It doesn't have to be right on the mark, you know."

Samuru returned the dark look. "It's called an hourly log for a reason."

"The ship won't spiral into chaos over a few seconds," Terk replied, trying to keep the petulance from his tone.

"If a leader is too lazy to do his job properly, that laziness will filter down to the rest. Is that what you want?"

Terk clenched his teeth. It was a few damned seconds, barely enough time to spell the word lazy. He yanked the console from the side of his father's chair in front of him and pounded in his report. *Nothing has changed since the last time I made a log. Not a single damned thing. All systems normal and all bridge crew acting accordingly, except for the giant blackbeast turd sitting beside me.*

With his frustration spent, Terk backtracked and rewrote it into something more appropriate.

Why did Samuru have to be such a hardass? The man flaunted his authority the same way he flaunted that stupid scar of his. Well, maybe he didn't flaunt his authority so much as he wielded it. Woe to anyone who made him angry. He was a hammer mill, pounding slaves and warriors alike until they were a mess of blood and guts. Even now when his essence lolled, he reeked of a rabid blackbeast.

Terk folded the console to the side. "Nothing is happening. I can manage here."

"Something *might* happen, and I need to be here when it does," Samuru said with irritation in both his voice and emotions.

"I don't need babysitting. I can handle whatever comes."

Samuru harrumphed. "You don't have enough experience yet."

Terk shot him a glare. "How can I get experience if you won't let me do anything?"

"We *did* let you do something, remember?" Samuru replied regarding Terk's failed mission and capture by the Cooperative.

Terk growled. *That wasn't my fault.* "I handled the tactical station during the battle perfectly."

Samuru scoffed. "Pressing a button when your father tells you to is nothing to brag about."

Terk simmered. It was a lot more complicated than pressing buttons. What in the hell did he have to do to show he was as good as Dokuri? He could plan and lead a battle just as well if only they'd give him a chance. At least he worked on the bridge. Dokuri never did. Terk was a better pilot too. Another year of training and he'd be as good at close-combat fighting as his much-beloved and now dead-as-a-rogue-planet older brother.

Terk studied the readouts on the screen. QR gauge—still optimal. Arc-flow—still normal. Engine temp—still in the green zone, though creeping into yellow. Time to destination—too damned long.

"Edo, the A-P output is high," he said to the bridge worker. "Make the necessary adjustments."

"Yes, Sir."

Edo's forehead furrowed in concentration, then turned frustrated. Terk sighed with annoyance. The readings on this sensor needed to be compared with three other components, and Edo struggled with the calculations.

Jori should devise a program to help, but he was too busy. Although Biskol wrote programs, he was an amateur at best. Toradons were not known for their intellect—unless they were a ten-year-old boy who excelled at everything.

Terk pushed his jealousy aside. Jori could be a pain in the ass know-it-all sometimes, but he was a good brother. A few years ago, they and their mother had made a pact not to interfere when Father punished one of them. Trying to stop him just ended with all of them hurting and no one able to provide comfort.

Jori held to the pact when Father disciplined Terk for his failed mission, then broke it later by acting out whenever Father said something derogatory to Terk. One incident stood out. Terk smiled inwardly. It wasn't funny at the time but looking back, Jori's behavior had been absurdly out of character.

About twenty days before the attack on Thendi, Father had berated Terk for failing the mock battle set up in the TTAC room.

"Dokuri could have won this with his eyes closed," Father had said. "Hell, I bet your little brother can do this better than you."

Samuru reset the simulation. The lights in the observation room dimmed and the scene blazed to life. Terk fumed. Jori had already defeated this contest twice. This time, he'd do it with Father here.

Only he didn't. Jori sent his entire sim-team in the worst direction while he stayed behind to lay cover fire. His generally accurate aim struck everything except a target. Terk's mouth hung open. Jori hadn't been this awful since he was six.

The clincher came when the battle ended and Jori jumped over the wall and yelled obscenities. When he extended his impression of his childish older brother, Montaro, by stomping his feet and sticking out his bottom lip, Father backhanded him and sent him sprawling.

Since then, Jori held back whenever Father watched them in the grand dojo or the TTAC room. Terk's gratitude matched his shame. It wasn't fair. He practiced just as hard and as often. His little brother shouldn't be better.

A beep from the external comm scattered his musings. The corner of the bridge viewscreen indicated the communication came from the *Basilisk*.

Terk pressed the comm button on his chair and stood. Sensei Jeruko had said addressing a high-ranking official while sitting projected laziness and arrogance. Standing marked his authority and signified his respect.

A man in his mid-forties popped up on the screen and bowed his head. "First Prince Mizuki, General Brevak here."

Terk dipped his head in return and glanced at the *Basilisk*'s readings scrolling along the bottom of the viewscreen. "General, you look as though you've encountered more trouble."

"Yes, my Lord," Brevak replied.

Brevak, one of the best warrior-leaders of his father's fleet, came from a family long dedicated to the Mizuki Empire. Unlike many of the lords who tended to get lazy and leave the work of fighting to lesser-born men, his family maintained a strong warrior heritage. The general was an excellent strategist, skilled in space combat, and the master of all the basic weapon types and several forms of martial arts.

His skills were not what Terk admired most about him, though. Nor was it his unwavering loyalty to the Mizuki line. His leadership style earned him the devotion of his men. While the senshi here on the *Dragon* grumbled and complained but did as they were told, Brevak's men served eagerly.

"We engaged two enemy ships just before crossing the border and suffered additional damage," Brevak said.

"Repairable?"

"Yes, my Lord. Within about six hours."

"Injuries to your crew?"

"Minor."

"And what of the Cooperative ships?" A mental image of the *Odyssey* being destroyed sent a twinge to his gut. He shoved it aside. *Jori's damned sentiment is rubbing off on me.*

"They sustained enough damage to keep them from following us over," Brevak said. "I will need assistance, my Lord, if you want me to finish them off."

"Assistance is a few days away yet. Repair your ship and monitor the border to make sure they don't sneak in."

"Yes, my Lord."

Terk ended the communication and the viewscreen returned to its data display. He sat carefully to hide his relief. This soft emotion that kept coming over him every time he thought of the Cooperative irritated him. So what if they saved his and Jori's life? That made them stupid. As was Jori's sentiment for them. He should've killed those prisoners when he had the chance.

Terk's mind wandered and he caught a drift of Jori's essence. His little brother worried about something as he headed this way.

When Jori entered the bridge with Tokagei, Terk stood and faced him. "What are you doing here?"

"Father summoned us."

"What about?"

Jori shrugged.

Terk focused his senses and found his father more irritable than usual. There was no point in guessing why. It didn't take much to piss him off.

They made their way to Father's office with two personal guards in tow. "I'm sure it's nothing," he said to Jori in their secret language so Tokagei couldn't understand.

They reached the office located right outside the bridge and entered with an identical bearing—heads high, chests out, hands behind their backs. Father and Nezumi didn't bother looking up, their focus intent on the deskview.

"I recommend this one, Sire," Nezumi said, pointing at the screen. The man's normal pinched expression was as rat-like as his essence—a dead rat in the throes of putrefaction.

Dokuri had undoubtedly learned his cruelty from this man. Nezumi had been Dokuri's first general until Dokuri got himself killed. Now the man was semi-retired—or whatever you called it when a man got too old to fight but not too old to get pleasure from inflicting torment. The rat-faced bastard might not kill with the force of Samuru, but he left as much gore. Except he didn't always kill his victims. The longer they lived in their suffering, the more he enjoyed it.

Terk's gut churned. If a man needed to die, just kill him and be done with it. That's how the other three Talons did it. Or *had* done it. Colonel Fujishin was gone. Terk had rather liked him. He was an incessant complainer, but not cruel.

Sensei Aki wasn't so bad either. He jabbered more than Fujishin complained, but never spoke or did ill. The only Talon Terk would keep when he became emperor, though, was Sensei Jeruko. Jori, of course, would become one of his Talons.

His father snapped his head up. Terk's mouth dried from the mental stab of Father's anger.

"Yemon came to me with a disturbing complaint," Father said.

Chusho! Terk's blood turned cold. He'd meant to speak to Yemon as soon as his shift on the bridge ended.

"He says the Cooperative crew members don't know what they're doing," Father continued.

"Some are more knowledgeable than others," Jori replied with a calm Terk knew he didn't feel. He and his brother's nervousness intensified, though neither let it show. Their father couldn't sense emotions the way they could, so their ability to hide how they felt withstood the spotlight put on them.

Father's jaw clenched and his nostrils flared. "He says they're *faking* it."

Terk scrambled to think of an excuse but Jori beat him to it.

"I find it hard to believe they faked the records we pulled, Sir," Jori said. "Besides, if they lied, we'd sense it."

Terk marveled at how his brother answered without speaking an outright lie.

"Terkeshi?" Father said. "Have you sensed any deception in them?"

"N—" His voice cracked as a truthful answer eluded him. "No, Sir." *Damn it.* Jori was making a coward out of him with all this lying he had to do.

Father glared at them while Nezumi's expression seemed to pinch even more. Terk suppressed the urge to swallow as the men scrutinized them. He stood in a stiff at-ease stance, hoping he reflected calm and confidence.

"Just to be sure," he said, "get Amarante… Now!"

Terk barely kept his face straight this time. He and Jori acknowledged Father's command and held their composure despite the rising tension.

Their mother's ability to sense emotions and lies was much more precise than Terk and Jori's combined. It kept her close while Father's other concubines eventually got passed on to the men.

Jori and Terk cleared the office with Tokagei and Washi following behind. "If Father finds out what you've done," Terk said to Jori in their secret language, "he'll be beyond pissed."

Terk should have been angry at Jori for getting him into this mess but worry gnawed at his gut. Not worry for himself. Jori would suffer the most.

"We will be alright," Jori replied in the same language. "Mother won't say anything."

"Maybe not," Terk said in a calm tone. "But the more people you bring into this, the harder it will be to keep it from Father."

A sensation of distress emanated from Jori and he shared a worried look.

"I can't keep lying for you," Terk continued. "One of us is expendable, remember? I don't want to die, but I certainly don't want you to either, especially not over that damned Cooperative officer."

"It won't come to that," Jori replied.

"How can you be so confident?" Terk said as they came to an intersection and turned left. "You might be smarter and a better warrior, but if you keep refusing to torture or kill anyone, Father might take your punishment too far."

The double-chill of both his and Jori's emotions ran down his spine at the thought of Montaro's fate. He pushed these dire thoughts out of his mind as they entered the conveyor. He and Jori would get through this and they would get through it together.

The conveyor took them to the bottom level. When the doors opened, Terk stepped into the threshold to keep the door open. "Warn the commander," he said to his brother in their secret language. "Washi," he said so the man could understand him. "Go with Jori to get a prisoner. Preferably the leader."

Washi nodded.

"I'll talk to Mother," Terk whispered.

Jori took one step and stopped short. He held the comm taped behind his ear and listened. Terk sensed a sharp panic from him. "Yes, Sir," Jori transmitted.

"What is it?" Terk asked.

Jori paled. "Father called me back."

Chusho. Jori can't warn him. "I'm sorry," he said. "This may be the end of it."

"Maybe Mother—"

"Maybe. Or maybe we'll get caught." Terkeshi glowered, daring Jori to protest.

Jori didn't say a word, but the emotions emanating from him said it all.

Terk returned to the conveyor with a huff. "Harem," he said to the computer. Anyone looking at him would have thought him furious, but inside his gut churned like a giant planetary vortex.

*****

3791:027:00:17. Jori's stomach ground like a stone-crusher machine. Father's mood didn't bother him. But if he found out about Hapker… Everyone he cared about was at risk. Was Hapker worth it?

Father leaned over the desk with a fiery glare. Jori's muscles twitched, provoking him to fidget, but he steeled himself for whatever came.

"Why do the prisoners have so much information on their MDSs?" Father's voice boiled with anger.

Jori's nervousness fled and he cocked his head. It was no secret the read-only devices were full of data. "Although they have general knowledge on emitters, they aren't familiar with this project."

"They're supposed to be experts. What's the point of keeping them around if they can do the same thing our workers can do?"

Jori kept his tone from sounding peevish. "Their records show they have a higher level of education, yet they still only minored in the technology. I gave them references they could turn to so they wouldn't mess up."

Father heaved a breath. His irritation was palatable, but his suspicion seemed to abate. "Yemon thinks you're protecting them."

The rocks in Jori's stomach tumbled again, but he maintained a placid expression. "Yemon is jealous because he knows I'm smarter than him."

Father raised an eyebrow. "So you're not helping them?"

"If I help them, it's to make sure they're doing things properly."

"And I suppose you're not protecting them either?"

Damn Yemon. It wasn't surprising the man was causing trouble, but that he had the nerve to go to his father with such accusations irked him. "Protecting them how? And why?" Jori replied.

"By not properly motivating them," Father said through clenched teeth.

Jori gut twinged. He should have allowed Yemon to punish the prisoner. He kept his eyes locked to Father's. "Yemon's desire to exert his newfound dominance over them is counterproductive."

Father balled his fists so tight that his hands turned white. "Is that your sentiment talking, boy?"

"It's simple sense, Sir," Jori replied. He lifted his chin in a way he hoped reflected a confidence he didn't have. "I don't like having to work with our enemies and the more Yemon wants to punish them, the longer this will take."

Father's fists unclenched. "So you're taking it easy on them for the good of the empire?" His tone hinted at skepticism, but Jori sensed his acceptance.

"Why would I do otherwise?" he replied without lying.

"Then it won't bother you if I sign them up for another round in the arena."

"Not at all, Sir," he said truthfully. He hated feeling others in physical pain, but he'd experienced enough of it in his life to know it was short-lived and manageable.

"Good. When Amarante is done, I will make the arrangements."

Father stared at Jori, as though looking for a reaction. Jori's stomach twisted, but he let nothing show.

"Since you hate the Cooperative so much," Father continued, "I expect you to participate."

The blood drained from Jori's face, but he forced himself to keep the hateful look. This time, it reflected how he felt about his father. "You know I won't."

Father snarled. "Then when I am done with them, *you* will be next."

Nervousness and outrage rumbled together but Jori defiantly held his father's stare. *So be it*, he almost said out loud. Just because his Jintal training taught him to endure pain didn't mean he welcomed it.

Father growled. "Damned your stubbornness, boy."

23
The Empress

3791:027:00:36. J.D. Hapker awoke from a deep sleep as two hulking silhouettes entered his cell. He blinked the gumminess from his eyes and rose to prop himself on his elbows. "What—"

The burlier warrior grabbed his arm and yanked him to his feet. "Come with us."

Before Hapker could catch his footing, the man twisted him around and pushed his face to the bed. The cold metal of cuffs clamped about his wrists, bringing him to alertness.

"What's going on?"

The warrior jerked him upright and swung him toward the cell exit. The palm jabbed between his shoulder blades sent him stumbling to where the other dark form waited. This smaller man, who was still taller and more muscular than him, stepped aside and caught him before he fell.

Hapker's toes dragged along the floor as he struggled to keep up with his captors' single-minded pace. The burly warrior on his right bore a forbidding expression as he pinched Hapker's arm. Washi, on his left, gripped him but not painfully.

They entered the conveyor and Hapker recovered his footing. The car lurched, then clanked as it climbed. The level to the docking bay passed as they continued up. Hapker tensed. Were they taking him to the arena?

The conveyor jerked to a halt. Gears and cranks drummed from the outside. The car jolted into motion. Hapker caught his balance as they traveled horizontally. If not the arena, then where?

He regarded Washi, but the man stared forward, offering no hints. The other warrior wore a dour expression that deterred questions.

The conveyor stopped. Though rough hands led him out, he kept pace this time. He cast about for any clue of where he was. The lusterless walls and subdued lighting were the same as everywhere else. They rounded a corner and came upon a long row of plasti-glass windows looking into a dark room. Some lights came from the consoles along the walls. Large viewscreens hung above the stations and a great holographic table sat in the room's center.

The war room. It had to be, which meant they brought him to the command level. They stopped before an ordinary door. As it slid open, a crack of light fell through as though trying to escape. Hapker's heart skipped a beat. Inside, the emperor stood behind a massive desk. A brightness from above cast upon him, immersing his eyes in shadow and darkening the lower half of his face.

The burly warrior thrust Hapker in. He stumbled, but Washi kept him upright. The emperor remained stiff and silent. The intensity of his piercing expression reminded him of a tiger ready to lunge.

Hapker's skin prickled. There was a time when he'd first met Captain Arden that the flight part of his brain fought for dominance. But where Captain Arden incited a quick duck and hide, the emperor roused a stampede.

The emperor donned a black-armored vest that somewhat resembled the type Terkeshi and Jori wore, except embellished with added metal spikes and gold trimmings. His arms bulged with muscle and he towered over his two sons, who stood on either side of him.

Hapker met Terkeshi and Jori's eyes. Was there a hint of worry in them? *Wishful thinking.* As usual, their expressions betrayed nothing.

A woman waited behind Terkeshi. She dressed in yellow, of all colors. Hapker's brow furrowed. Every other crew member he had seen on the *Dragon* wore brown, dark grey, or black.

"Do it," the emperor said.

Terkeshi stepped aside and Hapker's breath caught. The woman was tall, about Terkeshi's height. Her broad shoulders matched the width of her hips, giving her a curvy figure. Her jet-black hair contrasted nicely with her olive skin, full lips, and dark narrow eyes.

As she came forward, her yellow dress rippled like a warm breezy day. Hapker's jaw hung down and he clamped it shut with a snap. She bored into his eyes and he fell into hers.

She reached for his forehead. The movement flowed, urging him to lean toward her rather than pull back. Her soft touch sent a heat throughout his body. An inaudible buzzing filled his head. The comfortable sensation reminded him of the vibrations of a Nordian massage chair.

"You will answer all questions truthfully," the woman said.

The statement was ludicrous since he couldn't imagine ever lying to her.

The emperor loomed over from behind her. "Do you and your men have the required knowledge to complete this emitter?"

An urge to tell the truth rolled over him. He opened his mouth to speak, but a shock of not-quite pain came through the woman's touch. His fear sharpened. Something about her set his nerves on edge.

Lie, a whisper in his head warned him. He shivered. The voice was feminine. "Yes, I believe we do," he said compulsively.

Jori's stony face gave way to a look of relief. The boy glanced at his father, but the man's scrutinizing gaze on Hapker probably meant he didn't notice.

"Do you intend to fix the emitter?" the emperor said.

Lie. The whisper in his head was light—surreal—but unnecessary. He'd rather die than help create a planet killing weapon for the most violent man in the galaxy. "We have no choice," he replied evasively. He wasn't ready to die just yet.

"Answer the question, yes or no," the emperor said.

Hapker hesitated. The strange feeling from the woman's touch sharpened again. *Lie.* "Yes."

The emperor's frown deepened. "So no procrastination, no pathetic attempts to escape?"

Speak truly, she said in his head.

Huh? He fought the urge to speak.

The emperor's posture hardened.

The buzz in Hapker's brain intensified. "We've been considering both but have no plans so far."

"Why?"

"Impossibility. Your men are too attentive, we don't want to be tortured again, and we have no means of escape." Hapker snapped his mouth shut to stop the flow of words. *Why does she want me to tell the truth?*

The corner of her lips curled up. *To make your lies more believable.*

Hapker swallowed hard. Jori had admitted once that he could sense the emotions of others. He'd also said his father couldn't. *Did he get this skill from this woman, his mother?* If so, her ability seemed stronger than just reading. She had to be an imperium-animi, a person who read and commanded thoughts.

His spine tingled. A dry lump formed in his throat. Worse than the idea of someone rummaging through his brain was knowing she could compel him to tell the entire truth.

The emperor eyed him. "You're certain he's being honest?"

She dipped her head. "Yes, Sire."

"I sense no lies in him," Terkeshi said.

"He's too afraid," Jori added.

The emperor didn't look convinced. "Is there a chance he can resist your touch?"

"I feel no indication that he has this kind of training, Sire."

"Yes or no, woman."

"No, there's no chance."

The emperor commanded her with a head movement, and she stepped back with her eyes downcast. An internal sensation like a snap broke Hapker from her spell and he gasped.

As his nerves settled, he noted the progressive similarities of the four people before him. The empress, or whatever she was called in the Tredon culture, resembled Jori. Jori, in turn, looked like Terkeshi and Terkeshi was a younger version of the emperor.

"Test his knowledge," the emperor said to Jori.

Hapker braced himself but calmed when Jori asked questions he knew the answers to.

The emperor's posture relaxed, though his mien remained unforgiving. "You will finish this emitter. If I see any hesitance in you, or any sign that you don't know what the hell you're doing, I will have this woman turn your mind so you think you're a dog. From there, you will serve my soldiers in any capacity they wish no matter how painful or humiliating."

Hapker shivered as a cold sweat swept over him.

The emperor stomped to the door. "Get him back to work. Woman, with me."

She nodded meekly and followed. Her eyes remained down until the last moment when she turned and smiled at Jori and Terkeshi.

24
Pissed

3791:027:02:51. Terkeshi clenched his jaw to both stifle his yawn and force out the pressure building inside him. Someone was taking his damned time. Calling the man to his father's office should have made him scamper over to curry favor. What good was it being the heir if no one, not even a lowly clerk, took him seriously?

To hell with him and everyone else. Terk tapped the desktop harder than he ever would have dared if Father was here. Fortunately, Father had left for his scheduled sleep cycle hours ago. Terk should have gone too, but something—someone—needed taking care of.

His jaw hurt from biting down on his teeth, but too many thoughts hurtling through his head made the pain register as nothing more than a nuisance.

This headache was Jori's fault. Terk practically fought with a ship's navigational controls against a planetary tempest when it came to Jori. One wrong move and his ship would spin out of control, then crash. Another failure would burn his reputation into a smoldering ruin.

More likely, though, it would be Jori's ruin. Either was unacceptable.

Father almost discovered our ruse. His fists tightened. He had to get this situation contained and put Yemon under his thumb.

He clamped down on his teeth so hard that pain shot down his neck and to his arms. His knuckles turned white. *That skinny little snake went behind my back!*

He slammed his fist on the desktop, imagining it as Yemon's face. If only he could pound that bubble-headed bastard into oblivion.

No. He needed cold composure, not a hot temper. Terk breathed deep and imagined his turbulent emotions coalescing into a calm lake. If he beat Yemon, Father would wonder why. Besides, Yemon must be more than just afraid. Terk had to convince him of a better way.

The plan, hashed out with Sensei Jeruko's help, played out in his head. The tension in his jaw relaxed somewhat, but he didn't completely release his ill temper.

He sensed Yemon's approach and sat straight and tall in his father's chair. He clasped his hands to keep them still.

Yemon's nervousness wafted from the other side of the door but lessened when he entered and saw only Terk. The snake let out a sigh that made Terk hiss. His internal fire flared, and his face twisted with menace. *I can be just as tough as my father, little man.*

Yemon averted his eyes and licked his lips.

The corner of Terk's mouth twitched. *Good.* He restrained the impulse to yell and kept his tone steady. "Do you know why you're here?" he asked through gritted teeth.

Yemon shifted his feet. "No, my Lord." He flicked his tongue again. "I'm doing the best I can, considering the inferiority I must work with."

Terk's frown deepened at Yemon's lack of self-control. If he had ever fidgeted in front of Father like this, he'd get the shit beat out of him. "My father proved the Cooperative crewmen know what they're doing, *and* that they're cooperating."

Yemon frowned. "Really?"

Terk leaned forward and glared. "Do you doubt him?"

"N-no. Of course not, my Lord. It's just that, well, I don't see how it is possible."

Terk sat up straight again and gave Yemon a blank expression. *Put him at ease*, Sensei Jeruko had told him. *Let him talk first, then pound the hammer.* "So you think they're worthless?"

"Completely, my Lord." Yemon met his eyes. Terk kept his face neutral as Yemon continued. "When I ask them questions, they barely know the answers. They have no clue which tools to use. When they do pick the right ones, they use them wrongly. I am constantly fixing their mistakes."

All True. *Damned this man for being too smart for his own good.* Terk resisted slapping Yemon upside his head. He kept his tone light as he played out Sensei Jeruko's advice. "You don't believe their ignorance is an act?"

Yemon puffed out his lean chest and lifted his chin. "Not at all, my Lord. I think they're lying to save their skin."

Time for the hammer. Terk raised his eyebrows. "So you're able to complete this emitter all on your own?"

Yemon blinked. His mouth hung open. "Um, y—"

Terk let his mask fall and his scowl return. His tone deepened. "Don't lie to me, Yemon."

Yemon paled. "Well… No," he said. More quickly he added, "I can do it with more help. With real help."

Terk gritted his teeth. "It is *not* available."

"But these men are useless." Yemon's shoulders slumped and he glanced away, never meeting Terk's eyes.

"Wrong." Terk slapped the desk hard and stood. Yemon flinched and took a wary step back. "They *can* help you."

"How?" Yemon shifted from foot to foot.

Terk approached from behind the desk, keeping his posture tall and rigid. "Let's pretend we kill the Cooperative men now and leave it all to you. When the emitter can't be fixed…" Terk stopped in front of Yemon and stared hard into the man's eyes. "… Who will my father blame?"

Yemon's eyeballs bulged. His apprehension flooded Terk's senses. Terk puffed up in response but kept his smugness from showing.

"B-but it won't be my fault. I don't have enough help," Yemon said with a whine.

"He will still blame someone." Terk's scowl deepened and his nostrils flared. "My father might put some fault onto Jori. But of the two of you, who is more expendable?"

Yemon's Adam's apple bobbed.

Terk suppressed a smile. "This is what I propose. Even if these Cooperative men don't know all of what they're doing, let's try to squeeze as much usefulness out of them as we can. Who knows, perhaps we'll get lucky. If not, lay the blame at *their* feet."

"Yes, Sir."

Yemon's shoulders fell, but his relief was fleeting. Terk wasn't done yet. After all, he had to build his reputation. "One more thing."

"My Lord?"

Terk leaned in nose-to-nose and gave the man his most menacing glare. "Jori is your immediate superior in this." He lowered his tone. If he spoke any louder, it would come out as a growl. "You report any problems you have to *him*."

Yemon took a step back. Terk moved forward. "If he thinks it is important enough, he will talk to me and *I* will go to Father."

Yemon stepped back farther, eyes widening and his throat bobbing.

Terk followed. "If you *ever* go over my head again, I will toss you into the sewer vat and flush your shitty carcass out into space. Do you understand me?"

Yemon hit the wall behind him. Terk held his glare.

"Yes, S-sir."

Terk pulled back and made his face go blank to keep his self-satisfaction from showing. "Good. Dismissed." He returned to his father's chair.

Yemon straightened and fiddled with the front of his uniform as though trying to regain his composure.

Terk frowned. "Why are you still here?"

"Sir, one thing," Yemon said. He licked his lips again and cleared his throat. "I'm worried that the young prince is helping the prisoners."

Terk shot out from behind the desk. Yemon squealed as Terk grabbed him by the neck. "If you ever do or say anything to get my brother in trouble, I will personally rip out your guts and choke you with them."

A sharp smell stung Terk's nostrils. The stench of Yemon's fear had expelled itself from his bladder.

Terk tightened his hand around Yemon's throat. The man's face paled, then reddened, and his eyes dilated.

"No. I have a better idea," Terk continued. "If you breathe even a whisper of this *ridiculous* accusation to my father, I won't kill you."

Yemon struggled for air. Terk loosened his hold a bit.

"Y-you won't?" Yemon blinked and tried not to meet Terkeshi's hateful look.

"No. I will send you to Ankgar." Terk growled through his bared teeth and shook with wrath. "And I will stand there and watch as he peels away your skin, patch by patch. I'll smile as he slowly dips you into a pot of boiling water, only to pull you out again so you can live on. You will cry out in agony while I laugh with joy as you live the rest of your life in *perpetual pain*."

Yemon trembled. Terk let go. A sense of triumph came over him, but it wouldn't last. Yemon was just one problem. There were many more to overcome. *Damn you, Jori.*

25
Three Talons

3791:027:09:45. Kenji Mizuki stood like a sentinel at the outer edge of the auxiliary docking bay. A delightful quiver sprouted in his stomach as he took in the machines before him. Each enormous piece took up the space of a small transport ship. There were oscillators, buffers, power amplifiers, modulators, and a bunch of other parts that Jori had named in his report. The only one he recognized was the antenna.

Soon, all these pieces would be put together and he'd be back at the top where he belonged.

"Hmm," Nezumi said. "Perhaps we need more guards."

Mizuki frowned. About a hundred warriors patrolled the perimeter—twice the number of shokukin and prisoners combined. With them spread out over five large docking bay platforms, though, it only put twenty senshi in each spacious section.

"It will have to be enough," he replied. "If I split the warriors into two long shifts rather than the three, they won't have time for their military exercises. I need them honed for battle."

The pinched expression on Nezumi's face indicated he didn't agree, but the man wisely kept it to himself. Of his four remaining Talons, he liked Nezumi the least. The man was loyal and effective, though—more loyal than Fujishin, apparently.

"The warriors are spread thin," Jeruko said, "but it's a ten-one ratio on our prisoners."

"The shokukin need only have the senshi present to inspire them to work," Samuru added.

Mizuki nodded at his two other Talons. The men couldn't be more different. Both were Mizuki's age and had served by his side since his youth. However, where Samuru was brawny and hot-tempered, Jeruko was sinewy and coolheaded.

Fujishin had followed him since then as well. All together, they had been a fearsome team. While Mizuki's father kept losing battles, he and these three friends picked up the slack.

Friends. Mizuki's gut churned. The word meant nothing to Fujishin. How could he do this to him?

A sharp movement captured his attention. The clerk towered over someone, jabbing his finger. Mizuki strained to hear but caught only high-pitched tones.

"Nezumi," he said, "Go see who Yemon is yelling at."

Nezumi left to check, then returned with a sour expression. "It's the woman."

Mizuki's lips twisted in disgust. He never understood why the Cooperative worked so closely with their women. He found it laughable that she had been a part of the firefight on Thendi. A woman had her place, and it wasn't on the battlefield.

"She shouldn't be here, Sire," Nezumi said. "She's a distraction."

"Agreed," Mizuki replied. "But Cooperative records show she's an expert on transmitter technology."

"Pah." Nezumi waved his hand. "I find it very hard to believe a woman can be so well-versed in such technology."

Mizuki said nothing. He wasn't so ignorant to assume women weren't as intelligent as men. Amarante's mind-warping gift wasn't the only reason he chose her as a mate. Her intellect coupled with his own had produced the child-genius of Jori.

His attention fell on his youngest son. The boy's brow furrowed as if in concentration. He was diligent, and Mizuki didn't doubt his intelligence was greater than Yemon's. Yet Jori's sentiments made him appear as spineless.

Mizuki scrutinized the two prisoners closest to him. They all appeared to be working, but he had no way of knowing their level of competence.

Suspicion crawled through his brain. He clenched his jaw, sending a jab of pain to his skull. If he had Amarante's ability, he'd feel the boy's deceit. *Why would he help the Cooperative, though?* It made no sense, yet Yemon's accusations lingered.

No. His sons wouldn't betray him, at least not like Fujishin did—going behind his back. If Jori and Terkeshi ever betrayed him, it would be face-to-face, the way Mizuki had done with his own father.

He stepped from the edge to patrol the docking bay and directed his three accompanying advisors to do the same. His deliberate stride prompted the workers to work harder and the senshi to be more attentive.

Five shokukin and one Cooperative prisoner worked on the antennae. This prisoner was the engineer. He didn't look like much. His leanness matched the workers, but he stood a head shorter. What he lacked in height he made up for in his work. The man's immersion in his task kept him from noticing Mizuki passing by.

A tall shokukin with a hunched shoulder worked on another part of the emitter. He held a scanner of some type as he peered into the guts of the machine. He rose as though done but saw Mizuki and jumped back to work.

The next platform held two components, still large, but not as big as the others. Sometime soon all these parts would come together. With any luck, the workers would finish here at the same time he finished refitting his other ship to house the super-sized device.

Mizuki stopped by Jori. Only the boy's eyes moved as he scanned the schematics on a portable computer. He likely sensed his presence but seemed too preoccupied to acknowledge him.

Jeruko stood at Mizuki's side. "His level of intellect never ceases to astound me."

"What is your opinion of Yemon's claim about the prisoners?" Mizuki said low enough to keep Jori from hearing.

"Yemon's newfound authority is inflating his self-importance, Sire," Jeruko replied. "He probably considers them all inferior."

Mizuki grunted. "What of his accusation that Jori is helping them?"

"Yemon is jealous of your son."

Mizuki chafed. "So you believe he is trying to undermine him?" That damned clerk shouldn't get above himself.

"I doubt he's doing it on purpose," Jeruko replied. "He's worried. If your son's aptitude surpasses his own, then he is back to being just a clerk."

"Hmm. So you do not think Jori is helping the prisoners?"

"He's assisting them in a way," Jeruko said.

Mizuki narrowed his eyes.

"He's doing whatever is needed to ensure they fix the emitter," Jeruko finished.

Jeruko's distaste for lying abated Mizuki's suspicions… Somewhat. "Then why does Yemon keep scolding the prisoners?"

"Yemon doesn't know how to control his emotions. He's impatient. Jori is not."

"Not impatient, as in, he'd rather help them than motivate them?"

"Your son has never been fond of using force."

Mizuki let out a slight snort. "No doubt a doing of his mother's. I should have pulled him away from her sooner. The boy is far too womanish."

"He's still young, Sire. Still learning."

True. Jori irritated him a great deal, but he had time to mold him. "I want you to have a long talk with him about not befriending our enemy."

Jeruko nodded. "Yes, your Eminence," he replied.

Mizuki gave Jeruko a dismissing nod. "Get Bishamon and escort him to my office," he said.

Jeruko bowed and left. Mizuki stepped out of the at-ease stance and crossed his arms. Jeruko was probably right, but he had to be sure. Bishamon came recommended by Samuru and seemed eager to please. Having this man watch his youngest son wouldn't hurt. The more eyes on this situation, the better.

26
Helpless

3791:028:11:04. Hanna Sharkey narrowed her eyes and steadied her hands as she touched the tiny probes of her multimeter to each end of the trace.

"Position 17c. Zero," she said into the recorder. *Only several hundred more to go.* Unless she got lucky and found the problem.

Then again, she didn't need that kind of luck. Canthidius had mentioned a quicker way of finding the issue but looking one-by-one took longer, and they needed all the time they could get.

She kept one probe in place to keep track of where she was and rotated her other shoulder. A spasm burned through her biceps.

With the stiffness alleviated, she returned to her work. She read and recorded trace after trace until the strain in her eyes grew into a piercing headache.

"Are you done yet?" a voice said.

Sharkey flinched. "Shit! Damn it, Doctor. Don't sneak up on me like that. You made me lose track."

Canthidius' mouth puckered. "You're not done? I need to get this working soon."

"You really want to fix this doomsday device?"

The doctor's eyes widened, and he hunched into a cower. "Not fixing it will get us killed."

"We're going to die anyway," she said in a whisper. "We might as well protect the rest of the galaxy by not fixing this stupid thing. Besides, the longer this takes, the better chance we have of being rescued."

"How?" Canthidius frowned. "How do you think they will rescue us? The Cooperative won't go to war. The way I see it, the best plan for survival is to prove we're indispensable."

"Easy for you to say. You're not the one being lusted after."

Sharkey caught sight of the ugly brute with a missing front tooth. "Shit." Why did she have to jinx her luck? Now he headed over here.

"Hey, eel-guts," Usagi said to Canthidius. "You're wanted over at the antenna."

Canthidius bowed deeply and scurried away.

Usagi smiled, displaying the blackened gap in his mouth. "Well, I guess it's just you and me, Sweetness."

Sharkey quivered at his repulsiveness. "I've got work to do."

"Go ahead. I don't mind watching." He leaned against the device and leered her up and down.

Sharkey swallowed. "What's wrong with you, anyway? Doesn't this ship have a slew of slaves you can harass?"

"Oh sure, but none of them are Cooperative women." He made a sucking noise through his teeth.

A sinking feeling filled her gut. She tried to concentrate on her work but couldn't ignore the heat of his eyes at her back. A pinch and a slap to her butt triggered a reflexive jump and swing of her arm. Her fist struck his jaw with a thwack.

Usagi's nostrils flared and his smile turned wicked. "You're stronger than you look, Sweetness, but not strong enough."

"Leave me alone, damn it!" She held the multimeter up in front of her as though it were a weapon.

Usagi laughed. "C'mon, now. We can take a little break and have some fun."

Sharkey glanced over his shoulder, then over her own. Jori and Terkeshi were nowhere around. She saw Hapker and her heart jumped. She could take care of herself, but as a prisoner with no weapons—and the brute's cohorts ready to step in—she needed help.

Hapker wasn't paying attention, though, and he was too far away to hear her if she yelled. She frantically scanned for others.

Usagi stepped forward, forcing her to step back against the emitter. She tossed the multimeter at him, then ducked and dived through the wide gap on his left side. His giant paw snatched her by the shoulder and pulled her into his clutches. She yelped and struggled. Her arms were pinned, so she snapped her head into his face with a satisfying smack.

He let go with a growl that rolled into a chilling laugh. She lunged away, but he grabbed her arm and turned her about. He slapped his body into hers and pressed her against the emitter. She jabbed her palm toward his chin. He blocked her before she made contact and seized both her wrists. His strength kept her from twisting out of his grip. His weight pushed on her and thrust the air from her lungs. Her pounding heart was the only part of her moving.

Usagi put his mouth to her ear. "The more you squirm, Sweetness, the more it turns me on."

She cringed as the hot stink of his breath moistened her ear.

*****

3791:028:11:26. Jori's concentration broke with a snap. Lieutenant Sharkey's terror skewered his senses like a spear. He tossed aside his scanner and headed to the other side of the bay.

Chusho! Usagi was the worst when it came to women. Jori shivered from the memories of all the times he had to suffer the mental intrusion of this man's acts. This time would be different though. This time he had the means and the excuse to stop it.

He turned the corner and caught sight of Usagi smothering Lieutenant Sharkey against the emitter. Her red face twisted with a grimace as Usagi bent his head into her neck.

Jori's stomach wrenched two times over—one for his own concern and the other from the sensation of her writhing emotions.

Jori quickened his pace, side-stepping workers and mechanic bots while aiming toward his target. Someone grabbed his shoulder and broke his focus.

"Not this time," the man said.

Jori regarded Sensei Jeruko and scowled.

"You can't interfere anymore." Sensei Jeruko's stern tone matches his expression.

Jori's blood turned hot. "Why not? Usagi—"

Sensei Jeruko calmed. "I'll handle it, boy."

"I'm not a boy. I—"

A blur rushed by them.

"Chusho," Sensei Jeruko muttered as Hapker ran by.

The guards shouted and moved to chase but weren't quick enough. Hapker rammed his shoulder into Usagi, forcing the big man to stumble back. Usagi's eyes widened for a split second, then his face contorted into a snarl. Hapker's fist smashed into his nose. A spray of blood burst.

Jori almost called out in elation at seeing this side of Hapker.

Usagi seemed off balance. Hapker punched him again. Usagi raised his arms to deflect and Hapker jabbed him in the gut. Usagi doubled over. Sharkey snap-kicked him in the face.

Senshi from all around closed in.

Jori stepped forward. "Stop!"

Sensei Jeruko grabbed his shoulder.

Jori broke his hold and continued onward.

Hapker aimed his fist at the back of the man's neck, but Senshi Kelar plunged in. He deflected Hapker's arm with one hand and struck him in the face with the other. Hapker's head jounced. Another senshi grabbed Sharkey and tossed her to the ground.

Sensei Jeruko moved in front of Jori, halting him.

Jori balled his fists. "Get out of my way."

Sensei Jeruko remained firm. Jori prepared to dart around him, but someone else yanked him back.

"Stop, you idiot," Terk said as he panted heavily from the exertion of rushing over.

The two brothers glared at one another. Jori braced himself for an evasive maneuver, but Terk's hot temper kept him in place.

*****

3791:028:11:29. Terkeshi pressed his lips together and gave his brother a reproachful stare. "Don't."

Jori's nostrils flared and his eyes burned.

Terk balled his fists. "Don't do this, Jori. You've gotten us into enough trouble already."

Jori's expression flashed with irritation, but his body lost some tension. Terk uncoiled his hands. Jori turned and marched from the scene.

Terk and Sensei Jeruko put their attention on the fight. Sharkey had been restrained, but several senshi continued to pummel Commander Hapker like a pack of blackbeast on a deer. Yet despite the abuse being heaped upon him, the man's will remained.

Terk clasped his hands behind his back and watched with admiration. Whatever weak sentiments the commander had, at least his strength kept him on his feet as he took a beating.

Hapker held his elbows to his sides and blocked his face as the barrage continued. He held his ground for a dozen round of punches, but a blow to the side of his head sent him to his knees, then to the floor. The warriors added in a few mighty kicks but still couldn't diminish the commander's defiant determination.

"What is this about?" Terk asked Sensei Jeruko.

"Usagi was harassing the woman."

Terk's gut soured. *Damn that man.* What the hell was wrong with him? Had he no self-control?

Terk glanced over at someone else who needed to exercise restraint. The prisoner named Davis twisted and jerked, trying to break free from the senshi holding him.

"Let me go, you wankers!" Davis yelled. "I'm gonna kill the lot of ya!"

Terk made a face. The man's life-essence was almost as dark as Usagi's but for a different reason. While Usagi's aura felt like a slimy mud pit, Davis' was a black inferno of hate. Why the senshi weren't beating the shit out of him instead of Hapker, he didn't understand.

After the warriors threw a few more kicks into the commander, Terk unclasped his hands and approached them. Sense Jeruko followed close behind. "That's enough!"

Senshi Kelar and two others punched or kicked again, before realizing the others had stopped.

"That's enough," Terk said in a normal tone. "We need these people to work."

The bloody-faced Usagi stepped forward. "Sir! Look what this filthy do-gooder did to me. Let me take him to the arena for further punishment."

Terk's blood simmered. "I think you all have punished him enough. Besides, you're the dumbass who let him get the best of you. How in the hell did this happen, anyway?"

"He surprised me, my Lord."

Terk shook his head and tsked. "He *surprised* you. It sounds like you weren't doing your job."

Usagi's brows crossed with uncertainty. His eyes darted to Sensei Jeruko, but if he was hoping for some support, he wouldn't get it there.

"Perhaps Usagi should be sent to the arena, my Lord," Sensei Jeruko said.

Terk pretended to contemplate. "No. You're off the hook—for now. If I find out you're not doing your job and you're keeping the workers from doing theirs again, I'll cut off the source of your distractions."

Usagi shifted his stance. Terk felt the pang of his discomfort and almost smiled.

"Get back to work, all of you," he said.

The senshi disbursed. Hapker coughed and pushed himself to his hands and knees. With an effort that Terk sensed, he stood and hobbled to his station.

Terk nodded at his strength of will, then turned to Sensei Jeruko with a low growl. "This is getting out of hand. You're supposed to keep Jori out of trouble."

Sensei Jeruko rose an eyebrow. "I stopped him, my Lord."

"Not soon enough. Bishamon saw the whole thing and he will report it to Father. Now, we will be seen as coconspirators."

Sensei Jeruko emitted a sense of worry but kept a wooden expression. "Jori thought he should investigate the commotion. I told him not to concern himself."

"That's flimsy and you know it." Terk's jaw tightened. *Damn it, Jori. Damn you and this pit of quicksand you've sucked us into.*

Sensei Jeruko's brow wrinkled. "I'll have a very stern talk with him."

Terk harrumphed. "As if that will do any good. If you don't quit spoiling him, he'll get himself killed."

"Unlikely, my Lord." Sensei Jeruko's stance strengthened and Terk sensed his conviction. "Your father sees his weaknesses, but he also recognizes his intelligence and fighting potential."

"Yeah, he's a brilliant little brat," Terk mumbled.

"You have your strengths as well. Together, you two are stronger and your father knows it."

The tightness in Terk's shoulders subsided. "Still, his insistence on protecting our enemies is dangerous. I should end them."

"Perhaps. However, at this point it's probably better if your father does it, not you. Your brother idolizes you."

A bitter pang rumbled through Terk's gut. Jori would never forgive him if he killed Hapker. The brat could be a stubborn pain in the ass sometimes, but that didn't mean Terk wanted him to hate him.

"Perhaps you're right," he said, "but things can't go on like this. Something has to be done."

"Agreed."

Terk waited for Sensei Jeruko to bestow some wisdom, but the man remained silent. He likely didn't have a solution for this mess either.

Chusho.

27
Persuasion

3791:028:23:42. Another long day of working on the emitter dragged J.D. Hapker down like a slow-sucking pit of mud. The pain of his bruised body doubled with every throb of his heart.

He turned the knob one click to the right. The slight movement sent a twinge through his hand. His bloody and swollen fingers didn't hurt as much as his head and ribs, though. Still, the beating was worth it. They'd stopped bothering Lieutenant Sharkey. He glanced at the woman beside him and smiled—or tried to.

Her eyes twinkled as her lips turned upward in return. "Your face looks like a giant pomegranate."

Hapker suppressed the laugh that would cut into his sides. How did she do it? How could she make jokes after what almost happened? Her resilience amazed him.

He refocused on work and noted the numbers on his scanner. An increase of two-point-five-seven degrees. He documented the change, then turned another click.

So far, they had given him simple tasks, but life as a prisoner pressed against his hopefulness. Every day highlighted more problems, none concerning the emitter itself. A battle ensued inside him. On the one hand, he wanted to survive long enough to find a chance of escape. The longer they stayed here, though, the more likely Usagi would take Lieutenant Sharkey against her will.

Not that they should fix this device anyway.

"You need to have a chat with Sergeant Davis," Sharkey whispered.

"Why? What's wrong?" he replied with the same conspiratorial quietness.

"His mood is getting ugly."

"Ugly how?"

She bent her head to his ear. "He's talking about killing some 'bloody' barbarians. I think he's planning something."

"Does he have a plan with a chance of succeeding?"

Sharkey shook her head. "He said that since we're going to die anyway, we should kill some before we go."

Hapker suppressed a curse. "I'll talk to him the first chance I get."

"There's more, Sir."

"What is it?"

"He said something about ending the tyranny and he said it while glaring at Jori."

Hapker's heart clenched.

"Someone might have mentioned your fondness for the boy," she continued. "And he's telling everyone you don't have the balls to get us out of this."

"Crap." Davis was criticizing his leadership again, this time behind his back. Worse, he had his sights set on Jori. "If I don't get a chance to talk to him, you must tell him his orders are to stand down until I can inform everyone of a solid plan."

"Do we have a plan, Sir?"

Hapker sighed. "No. The odds are against us. Davis is right about sacrificing ourselves to stop our enemy, but I'm considering another idea."

Sharkey cocked her head.

A buzz sounded throughout the bay, stopping him from answering her. Time to return to their cells for a meal and rest. A coppery flavor still lingered in his mouth and his tongue stung from being bitten earlier. Perhaps he should skip the food and go straight to sleep.

Hapker held his ribs as he limped. Each step sent a stab of pain down his left side, making him unable to keep up with Sharkey, let alone reach Davis.

"Hurry it up," a guard said to him.

When Hapker quickened his steps, a hand on his shoulder stopped him.

"I'll take care of this one," Washi said.

Hapker sighed. Thank goodness it was him and not the merciless warrior named Kelar.

Washi kept an easy pace that allowed Hapker to walk in moderate comfort but let the other prisoners to get well ahead.

"That was brave," Washi murmured. "You'd almost make a good senshi."

A bitterness filled Hapker's mouth. "Except senshi don't protect. They abuse."

"We're not all like that horny dog."

Hapker accepted the response. Terkeshi's intervention had been a surprising welcome, and neither Washi nor Michio had created any difficulties with him or the others.

His personal escort veered him down another hall.

"Where are we headed?"

"The infirmary."

Hapker almost thanked him, but remembered the man wasn't doing this out of generosity.

They entered the medical bay. It was much smaller than the one on the *Odyssey*, and nowhere near as organized. Stained grey blankets were piled in the corner. The drawer of a med bot lay open, revealing a jumble of various instruments. A used bandage hung over the edge of a garbage chute.

The clutter decreased as Washi led him through the main room and down an empty hall. They stopped before a heavy curtain and slid it open. The lights switched on and he found himself in a cleaner room with an older-model healing bed.

"Sit," Washi said. "Someone will be here shortly."

Hapker leaned against the edge of the bed and carefully hoisted himself up. His bruised muscles protested but he settled into position without a sound of complaint.

Washi grasped the curtain to close it but stopped short when a diminutive figure appeared.

"My Lord," Washi said. "You shouldn't be here."

Jori acknowledged the man with a dip of his head, then faced Hapker in his formal at-ease stance. "I came to check if you're alright."

"I'm fine. Sore but still alive."

"Good to hear." Jori didn't make eye contact, which was unusual.

The boy glanced round the room, as though taking it in, but Hapker suspected he had more to say and waited.

Jori finally met his eyes. "I'm sorry I couldn't step in to help Lieutenant Sharkey."

Hapker nodded.

"I'll leave you to it then." Jori stepped back.

"Wait," Hapker said.

Jori stopped.

"Can I talk to you?" Hapker asked.

Jori glanced at Washi. "Wait down the hall."

"That's not a good idea, my Lord."

"I'll be fine."

"Perhaps, but if your father finds out you're here—"

"He won't."

Washi shook his head, then regarded Hapker. "If you make trouble, you'll wish for a beating as light as the one you got earlier."

Hapker raised his bruised hands. "Even if I wanted to, I doubt I could."

Washi nodded and stepped outside.

Hapker waited until he thought the guard was out of earshot. "Something has to be done about Usagi."

"Agreed. We're doing what we can, but I must be careful. My father suspects I've helped you."

"Is that why your mother questioned me?"

Jori's brow drew down. "How did you know she's my mother?"

"You resemble her." The memory of her voice in his head triggered a sensation like crawling spiders over his skin. "She's imperium-animi, isn't she?"

Jori nodded.

"She could have made me do or say whatever she wanted." Hapker attempted to keep his tone flat so he wouldn't sound accusatory.

Jori hesitated. His face was unreadable. "Yes."

Although he had expected the answer, the imaginary spiders wriggled down his spine. "Are you and imperium-animi?" he asked.

"No. I didn't inherit her full ability. Neither did Terkeshi."

Hapker sighed. If Jori had been able to command thoughts, his stay on the *Odyssey* would have gone much differently.

Jori's cheeks colored. "She's not like those other imperiums. She only uses it when Father makes her."

Hapker nodded. Still, his stomach fluttered anytime he recalled her touching him with her power. People throughout the galaxy feared skills like hers. Using such an ability was illegal in

Cooperative territory. Cooperative citizens capable of it had to register themselves with a security division devoted to finding and monitoring them.

Hapker ran his hand down his face and stroked his chin. "I hate to consider this then… Can she use her ability to convince your father to let us go?"

Jori shook his head. "He's been trained to resist it, and he'd kill her if she tried."

Hapker sighed. *We're never getting out of here.*

"I wish none of this happened," Jori said.

"I know," Hapker replied.

"If I could do more, I would."

Hapker remembered what he wanted to talk to Jori about. "There is something else you can do."

Jori's brow furrowed.

"There's more at stake here than either me or Lieutenant Sharkey. If we fix that device, your father will use it to kill millions of people."

Jori's expression remained impassive, but his throat bobbed. "I can't do anything about that."

"You understand how the emitter works, so you can figure out how to make it not work."

Jori shook his head. "Yemon will realize what I've done, and he'll fix it."

"I get the impression you can outsmart that petty little man."

"Maybe, but why should I? I'm not like you. I'm a warrior. Killing is what we do."

"Is that how you really feel?" Hapker asked, suspecting Jori was putting up a front. "I seem to recall you being sincerely upset when you told me about a certain space station you and your brother helped destroy."

Jori paled. Hapker pressed on. "Laren's family was on that station, remember? He tried to murder Terkeshi because of what you did."

Jori darkened. "That wasn't my fault. You said so yourself."

Hapker conceded with a nod. "You were too young to understand what you were doing. But you know now, just like you know what your father will do with that weapon."

Jori looked away. "I can't help you. I made a choice, remember? My duty is here, to my brother and my father."

"Even if your duty includes killing children?"

Jori turned back with a scowl. "Don't, Hapker. I've already taken a risk keeping you alive. Breaking the emitter would be in direct conflict with my father's wishes. I won't betray my family."

Hapker leaned forward. "There's a better way, Jori. The fact that you're here talking to me means you recognize this."

"But I can't do anything about it, damn it!" Jori balled his fists. "This is how it is."

Hapker let the matter drop. Pressing the boy would push him away. If he got him thinking about it, something beneficial might come out of this fiasco. If not, the galaxy was doomed.

28

Blackmail

3791:029:00:27. Jori jabbed an icon on the tablet. He never should've visited the commander. Why did he do it? Did he feel guilty? None of this was his fault. Hapker asked too much.

The file opened and the slew of data Hapker had collected earlier appeared. Jori scrolled through but didn't really see it. Working on the emitter after the prisoners left was usually easier. He didn't worry about anyone messing up in front of Yemon, and no glum moods crept into his senses. Yet his mind wouldn't focus.

A slapping sound grabbed his attention. Kelar boomed out a laugh as Benjiro stumbled. Benjiro nearly regained his footing but Kelar kicked into his backside, making him land with a smack on the hard metal floor.

"No. You make me break thingamajig," the simple man said as he cradled a component in his arm and moved to get up.

"What's the matter, idiot?" Kelar replied with mock concern.

"My name's Benjiro now."

Jori tilted his head. *Benjiro now?* What did he mean by that?

Kelar raised his boot. "Your *name* is *idiot*."

"Kelar!" Jori scowled. "Let the man work."

Kelar smirked and kicked Benjiro in the side anyway. Jori's blood turned hot. If only he had the physical ability to put Samuru's toady in his place.

While his mind raced through his response options, Pachin and Biskol stepped in. They helped Benjiro to his feet and escorted him to his station. If only more senshi were like these men. They didn't take liberties with their authority, and they had brains.

I bet there's an inverse correlation between level of intelligence and brutish behavior. Jori considered saying as much out loud, but Kelar didn't care that he was a dumbass bastard. Until Jori grew stronger, dealing with bullies like him was difficult.

He made a mental note to get advice from Sensei Jeruko later, then returned to analyzing the data. The numbers were exactly where he expected them to be. Now to determine what to adjust.

The distraction of the senshi didn't help his restless mind focus. Instead of feeling the thrill of solving a puzzle, he crunched the numbers and gauged the death toll. Hapker's suggestion kept resurfacing, adding a shade to his already somber mood. Along with it came a flashback of what he helped do to the space station.

It wasn't my fault! He growled and slammed the tablet onto the workstation. A hard knot tightened in his gut as the memory replayed.

He and Terk had taken turns calculating trajectories and firing weapons at the space station. The first projectile that breached the station spewed an impressive amount of debris and atmosphere.

Three years had passed since then, but Jori still remembered his elation—and it ate at him now.

He might not have given much thought to what he'd done if his father hadn't taken him to the station afterward. Gored and frozen bodies floated in zero gravity. Most had been ordinary people, not soldiers. The one body that still dominated his nightmares was the girl with dead eyes.

He should have known his actions would kill people. Hapker had told him he was too young to grasp the consequences, but his gut said otherwise. He had killed that girl—and many others.

This was different. He wouldn't be the one targeting the emitter. It wouldn't be his finger pressing the fire button.

But it was *him* fixing it.

He mentally shook himself. He had no choice. If he didn't do it, Yemon would. Either way, the device would still become operational.

He studied the data. Yemon didn't understand thermal dynamics well enough to determine the proper settings.

Ideas on how to undermine the project spun through his head. The knot in his gut tightened again. Father would punish him— worse, Terk would never forgive him. Terk needed the emitter to prove himself, for he would command the new ship.

Maybe he could sabotage it so they wouldn't find out it was him. He glanced around. So long as he left the programming and certain components alone, Pachin and Biskol wouldn't realize it either.

As he contemplated, an acute sensation poured in and his spine prickled. Someone was watching him.

His gaze drifted to the guards along the edge of the bay and fixed on a sparsely bearded warrior named Bishamon. Bishamon averted his eyes and seemed to take a sudden interest in a passing shokukin. The man sneered and yelled something at the worker, sending him scurrying away.

Jori tightened his jaw. *Damn all these brutes.* Bishamon and Kelar were both bullies favored by Samuru. The only differences between them were Kelar was stronger and Bishamon was a scheming worm.

Jori marched over to the man. "Bishamon. You can stop pretending. I know what Father ordered you to do."

Bishamon bowed. "I'm merely doing as I'm told, my Lord."

Jori huffed. The prisoners weren't even here. Why did Father want this spy here now? "Well, pretending you're not watching me—when you are—makes you look like a coward."

Bishamon made a fake smile that reeked of spitefulness. "Be mindful, little one. You speak in the presence of *men*."

Jori jutted his chin. "I'm aware of your exploits. Most of your kills are of women and slaves."

Bishamon darkened and his face contorted into a snarl. "You—"

"Careful." Jori showed his teeth. "I won't be small forever." He held his glare until Bishamon's fake smile returned. If only he had the strength to slap that smile away.

Another pompous attitude intruded on his senses. He groaned inwardly and met the approaching man at his workstation.

Yemon wore a smug expression. "My Lord. I must show you something."

Jori narrowed his eyes and glowered. "What?"

Yemon jutted his chin and raised his eyebrows. "Oh, I think you'll want to keep this private."

Jori tightened his lips and ground his teeth. "This had better be good."

"Oh, it *is*. Just you wait and see."

Jori's heart kicked up a pace as Yemon led him to a control room.

As soon as the door closed behind them, Yemon handed him a tablet. He gave the man a dark scowl and Yemon replied by widening his smile. The pounding in Jori's chest intensified.

He took in the information. His heart stopped and an icy sensation ran down his spine. "What's this?" he asked, though he knew the answer.

An irritating smirk crossed Yemon's face. "I thought it was rather suspicious that all the Cooperative crew members had skills with this technology, so I did some research on my own."

Chusho. Jori's stomach tumbled and twisted. His heart pounded like a jackhammer, but he'd be damned if he'd give Yemon the satisfaction of seeing fear in him. Jori set his jaw and gave Yemon a menacing stare.

The skinny weasel ignored the look. Amusement emanated from him. "I realized Terkeshi couldn't have done this. He doesn't have the skill and there is only one person on the ship who does." Jori clenched his teeth and held the glower on his face. Yemon continued, "If your brother finds out you've used him…"

Yemon had this part wrong, but it was still too much. Jori balled his fists and tried to keep his breathing even.

Yemon put up his finger. "Oh, but it would be a lot worse if your father found out." The triumphant smile on the man's face made Jori want to stab a dagger into it.

The weasel might as well be threatening his life. Jori considered the knife he kept sheathed at his thigh. The weapon practically burned to be used, but did he dare?

Death surrounded him. He couldn't count the number of times he'd watched Father or the senshi take lives. It was easy for them. Some relished in it to where their emotional bloodlust made him queasy. This sensation compounded with the pain of the victim's death usually overwhelmed him to the point of vomiting and tears.

No wonder his father and Terk thought him weak.

He was bred, born, and trained to kill. Even at his young age, he was physically capable of it. Besides his murder of the people on the space station, he'd killed in self-defense on two other occasions.

So why couldn't he do it now? Yemon certainly deserved it. His hand twitched over the sheathed blade, but he didn't grab it. "What do you want?" he said in a quiet tone.

Yemon held up his fingers. "Two things. The first one is easy." He clasped his hands behind his back and puffed out his chest. "I want assurances that if the emitter doesn't work, the Cooperative crew will be blamed."

Jori didn't so much as nod.

"I don't want any blame put on me," Yemon went on. "If your father tries to blame me, I expect you to say it was your fault, not mine."

Jori remained silent.

Yemon smiled as though Jori had accepted his first stipulation. "Second, I should get paid for my silence. The more the better."

Jori's face darkened at Yemon's insolence.

"Oh, don't worry," Yemon said, his tone condescending. "You don't need to pay me all at once. Just a little at a time. Not enough for anyone to notice it's missing, but enough for me to buy a few high-class whores whenever we go planet-side."

Jori's blood burned. His fists clenched at his sides. His fear and anger jumbled together so tightly that his stomach twisted like a raging storm. Of all the people to disrespect him today, Yemon was the most unexpected.

Heat swelled in his cheeks. He wouldn't do what this weasel wanted, but he couldn't let his father find out either.

His knife called to him, but his hand still wouldn't move. There had to be a way out of this.

Nothing came to mind. After a long moment of silence, Jori nodded in agreement. "You'll have your money soon," he said through clenched teeth.

Yemon walked away with a cocky gait. Jori struggled to keep his chin up against the demeaning heaviness piled upon him. Giving him money wouldn't be difficult, but the weasel would undoubtedly never release him.

29
Mother's Love

3791:029:01:04. Jori stormed out of the control room. He should have gone back to work but left the docking bay with a flurry of emotions. Tunnel vision narrowed his sight, but he maintained a purposeful stride.

How dare Yemon threaten him. The humiliation of being blackmailed by that conniving pitiful excuse of a man boiled his blood. He would have screamed if his chest hadn't constricted.

Yemon's power over him was too dangerous. Something had to be done, but what? His shame kept him from telling Terk or Sensei Jeruko.

"My Lord!" Michio called after him.

Jori quickened his pace but Michio still caught up. "What happened? What did Yemon do?"

Jori clenched his jaw. Confiding in Michio or Washi was as good as telling Sensei Jeruko.

"If that skinny little bastard hurt you," Michio said, "I'll pound his face in."

"He didn't hurt me."

"Then what was that about?"

"It's not your concern."

Michio sighed. "You can trust me, Jori-chan."

Jori swallowed the lump in his throat. He trusted Michio but didn't trust himself to speak. He turned into the conveyor and stopped in the doorway. "Don't follow."

"I must," Michio replied.

Jori pivoted around and scowled. "Bishamon is trailing me. If you want to protect me, keep him away."

Michio's lips pressed into a thin line, but he dipped his head and left.

Jori traveled to a restricted area of the ship. After exiting the conveyor, he entered a short hallway that ended with a secure door.

He put his hand on the handkey device and remained motionless as the biometric authenticator swept over his face.

The machine beeped and the heavy double-doors slid open to reveal another security room. Jori entered and tapped his foot as a second ultrasensitive biometric system verified his identity.

The next set of doors opened, revealing an antechamber like no other place on the entire ship. Rather than cold titanium walls, the ones here held colorful tapestries. The elegant furniture compared starkly to the run-down desks, beds, and shelves that resided in the soldiers' quarters. Instead of the metal flooring that dominated most of the ship, the floor here incorporated radiant tiles.

It even smelled different here. Jori took in the fresh, clean scent. His shoulders fell as his tension eased. His pounding heart subsided to a light tapping.

The comfort of home washed over him. Father had forbidden him from visiting here anymore, but he'd long since reprogrammed the authentication devices. This was one of the few places where he felt at peace.

Sevana, a girl a little older than Terk, greeted him with a pleasant smile. "Hi, Jori," she said. "You here to see your mother?"

"Yes." Jori replied, surprised his tone sounded so calm. His thoughts still jumbled about but knowing he'd soon spill it all out to his mother lessened his anxiety.

Sevana waved her hand down the hall and Jori walked down the orange-flowered runner rug to his mother's private room. The sensation of her grew with each step so that by the time he reached the entrance to her chambers his heartrate returned to normal.

Her door opened automatically. She had undoubtedly sensed him coming and greeted him with a sunny smile and open arms.

He fell into her warm embrace. Her soft but sweet perfume brought forth an image of a garden.

"I'm sorry, Mother," he said into the crook of her arm.

Mother caressed his head as she held him. "For what?"

"For making you lie to Father."

She patted his back. "It's alright. I know that man is the one who saved you and Terk. He has goodness in him. It's strong."

Jori swallowed the lump in his throat. "I don't want Father to kill him."

Mother sighed. "I know." She eased him back and looked him in the eyes. "Be careful, though. What you're doing is dangerous."

Jori cast a glance to the floor. He understood the risk, but he didn't think getting caught would come about this way. What would he do if Yemon got Hapker killed? Despite how things ended on the *Odyssey*, Jori still cared about him. Terk made him do what he did. He felt terrible about it, but Hapker's recent forgiveness was a boon he hugged close.

The commander's compassion reminded him of the day in the *Odyssey*'s infirmary when Terk had almost died. Terk was in a coma when his heart went erratic. As the doctors rushed to stabilize him, Jori struggled to hold back the flood of emotions. When Hapker embraced him, though, all his fears and worry spilled out. His mother was the only one who ever held him. It was like she was with him in that moment—her comfort and concern shared through Hapker.

"I had to do something," he said.

"I hope you can trust Sensei Jeruko and his sons as well as you think."

Jori nodded. "They care about me."

"I sense that, but I also feel the deepness of Sensei Jeruko's loyalty to your father. The secret you're asking him to keep troubles him."

Jori shifted his feet. He never should have involved them. Yemon wasn't just risking Hapker's life, he risked theirs too.

Mother gently squeezed his shoulder. "What's wrong? Your emotions spiked earlier. Did something happen?"

"Yemon," Jori said.

Mother waved her hand to a plush upholstered chair. Jori looked at it in askance. He hated how this chair smothered him, but it was her favorite way of talking with him.

She sat in the chair across from him and leaned in. "Tell me everything."

Jori told her all about Yemon's blackmail.

Her expression pained. "I wondered what had put you in such a state."

"I don't know what to do," Jori said.

Mother bit her lip and seemed to contemplate the situation.

"Killing him is the only thing I can think of," Jori added.

She frowned. "That isn't the answer to everything."

"He's a threat."

"Is this what you really want to do?"

She didn't say it with an accusatory tone, but he sensed it. Imagining himself hurting anyone, even Yemon, brought an acidic taste to his mouth. "No, but why would it be so wrong?"

"Ending someone's life because you don't like what they're doing is very different than killing to protect yourself."

"But I *would* be killing to protect myself."

She raised her eyebrow. "You know what it feels like both here and here." She touched his head then heart. "Taking lives shouldn't be as easy as your father and others make it out to be. It takes a toll on your soul."

Jori swallowed. Would the memory of the space station ever leave him?

His train of thought led him to the conversation with Hapker. Would fixing the emitter be as bad as being the one to use it? Either way, people would die—and it wouldn't be in defense.

He pushed the idea away. He already had too much to think about.

"Is there something you can use against him?" Mother said, snapping him back to the situation with Yemon.

He fell against the chair in a huff. "He's a weasel and a coward."

"I'd say he's greedy too. Use that."

"What's to keep him from asking for more?"

Mother clasped her hand around his and smiled. "You're an intelligent young man. I'm sure you'll come up with a plan."

Jori chewed his lip stared at the ceiling.

She touched his cheek. "You're not like your father, Jori-chan."

He frowned. He had hoped to find answers here. Perhaps even a small part of him wished she would tell him to kill Yemon.

At least he felt better. Worry still lingered, but his emotions settled. He met her eyes. "Alright. I'll work on a plan."

She grasped his hand tighter and gave him an approving smile. They sat in silence for a few minutes when something Hapker had said popped into his head.

"Can you use your power on Yemon? Make him forget what he found?"

"You know I don't like doing that. Besides, it's impossible for me to get to him. The only time I'm allowed to leave here is with your father." She spoke without any inflection but Jori sensed the swell of the sadness she always carried.

"What if I find a way to help the commander escape… And you go with him?"

She shook her head. "Your father will use his new weapon to exact revenge. As much as I'd like your friend to live, you can't help him—or me."

"Why not?" he asked, ignoring her point and replacing it with wishes. "The *Odyssey* is a nice place. You would sleep peacefully without all the negative emotions, and you'd be free to do whatever you want."

His mother's reluctance didn't waver, so he continued, "Maybe you could live on a planet and visit different places—parks, museums, shops. You could go horseback riding, just like you did when you lived on Jinsekai."

Mother smiled wistfully. "Those were wonderful days. My brothers and I had a lot of fun on our father's estate."

Her expression turned serious. "But we were children then. Things have changed."

"Your older brother is Lord Enomoto now," he stated. Father's enemy. One of the many his father wanted to destroy with the emitter. Jori's stomach hardened.

Her eyes lost their light. "He's no longer the brother I remember."

She never talked about it, but he'd heard the rumors and seen some results. Supposedly, Lord Enomoto killed his own father—an act all too common with Toradon nobility. Then he forced his sister, Jori's mother, to marry Jori's father. He did it to elevate his status, and it worked. It worked too well. Lord Enomoto's power rivaled Jori's father's—not enough to start a war, but enough to create friction.

Jori had met Lord Enomoto once, before Father decided he was an enemy. Jori played in the same garden his mother had said she played in when she was his age. He visited the stables and convinced Father and Lord Enomoto to let him ride a horse. It was an exhilarating experience. The emotional connection to the animal that carried him combined with the wind in his face and the warmth of the sun was something he would never forget.

Most of his memories at Lord Enomoto's estate were happy. The man didn't seem like a brutal killer. He questioned Jori about his mother and seemed pleased to hear she was doing well. When Jori asked after his mother's little brother, Enomoto replied he was working on a project elsewhere. Jori had sensed his truth.

"Just because Lord Enomoto didn't tell me what happened to your brother, doesn't mean he's dead."

Her brow wrinkled. "He was special—a genius in certain things—but he was childlike. A simpleton, my father said. So if he isn't under the protection of my older brother anymore, then he's probably dead."

Every time his mother talked of her younger brother, Jori imagined Benjiro. The man fixed just about anything, even with junk parts. He spoke with only a few words, though, and he didn't understand how to defend himself. If he hadn't been lucky enough to find himself here and for someone to recognize his intelligence, he'd likely be dead too.

"But it doesn't mean Lord Enomoto killed him," Jori said.

She touched his hand. "I hope that's true."

The depth of her depression made Jori want to fall in it too. "Sorry to make you sad."

"It's alright."

"Maybe you can't go back, but you can find happiness again. If we can't fix the emitter, Father can't come after you."

She shook her head. "Too risky. If something happened to you, I would never forgive myself. My freedom isn't worth your life."

"But you're a slave."

"So long as I have you, I'm happy."

She told the truth, but the sadness of it pierced his senses.

The two sat for a while longer, holding hands, talking about mundane things. She smiled warmly at times and nodded in understanding. Her depression lifted a little and his worries drifted to the back of his mind.

He eventually left. Though he still had no answers, he slept peacefully that night.

30
Mounting Suspicion

3791:029:06:55. Kenji Mizuki planted his elbows on his desk and glared at the report on his computer screen. He flexed his fingers, making them crackle, then clenched them into fists.

Damn Fujishin. This had to be his doing.

Three lords had taken over Lord Kami's estate. One was Fujishin's cousin. Nobles ousting other nobles happened all the time, but these new lords refused to swear fealty to the Mizuki house.

His enemies were mounting. No wonder he had trouble sleeping lately.

The muscles around his right eye twitched and he rubbed it furiously. This damned tic worsened by the day.

He must get this emitter operational. Then find Fujishin and stick him in a vat of boiling water. Better yet, throw him in a den of blackbeasts and watch his body be torn to shreds.

Deal with these lowly lords and Fujishin's other conspirators next. Lining them up in front of a firing squad should do the trick. Shoot them in the lower extremities, though, and let them bleed out.

After that, emasculate Lord Enomoto, both literally and figuratively. Only then could Mizuki retake the Pentam system and elevate himself to his rightful sovereignty.

A mechanical beep of his office door disrupted his reverie. He straightened his back and hardened his expression. "Enter!"

The entry slid open to reveal a tall warrior with longish black hair on the sides and thinning on top. Bishamon was younger than him, but near baldness made him look like a mangy old blackbeast.

Mizuki curled his lip. Why didn't the man undergo a micrografting procedure? Or, at the very least, wash his greasy head?

Bishamon stepped in with his eyes properly downcast. He stopped a full stride from the front of Mizuki's desk and bowed by the proper degree.

"What do you want?" Mizuki popped his knuckles.

"Your Eminence, you asked me to monitor the young prince."

Mizuki's eye twitched. "What of him? I expected your report at the end of your shift yesterday."

"My apologies, Sire." Bishamon dipped his head. "I came by your office, but you weren't here. I filed it in my report, though."

That was true. Mizuki had trained in his personal dojo for several hours, hoping to work out the tension in his shoulders. He flicked his hand. "I haven't gotten to it yet. Report."

Bishamon cleared his throat. "The prisoners made trouble. The young prince tried to stop it."

Mizuki's eye muscles spasmed. "What do you mean he tried to stop it?" he said through clenched teeth.

"I saw him hurry across the bay. I wondered what he was up to, so noted his direction. It looked like he headed toward a senshi dealing with a pris—"

"Then what?" Mizuki interrupted.

"Colonel Jeruko stopped him before he got there. I could tell they were having an intense dis—"

"Did you hear any of it?"

"No, Sire."

Mizuki rubbed his jaw. "Who was the boy's guard?"

"Tokagei."

Mizuki tapped his deskview screen and opened the reports section. He scrolled to the security division, past the kesatsu to the personal guards, and clicked on Tokagei.

The man's report rolled up into three pages. Mizuki pushed down his annoyance. Thorough was good, but his eyes were too tired to read it all. He skimmed through, catching the highlights of Usagi's obsession with the woman, Jori's approach, Jeruko's interruption, and so on until Terkeshi put a stop to it.

Mizuki exited the report and clicked Jeruko's section. He scrolled down, then up, and back down. *What the hell?* The last time the man had posted anything was the day before.

He pressed the comm. "Jeruko! Come to my office." He closed the channel without waiting for a response. Jeruko would show or be damned.

Mizuki flexed his fingers into fists. *What is going on here?* First his son, and now Jeruko. He expected issues from Jori. The boy's sentiment had always been a problem, and he had a defiant streak that made Mizuki want to throttle him.

But Jeruko? The man had been his closest friend since his youth. He'd fought by Mizuki's side as they cleaned up his father's mess. Jeruko even helped set up the final confrontation that put him on the throne.

Fujishin had served him, too. Then he betrayed him. What was Jeruko hiding? Could he betray him as well? Fujishin and Jeruko had been close friends, after all.

Mizuki's hands shook with the urge to punch something.

"One more thing, Your Eminence."

Mizuki refocused on the mangy man and bared his teeth. "What now?"

Bishamon cleared his throat. "The young prince disappeared shortly after."

"What do you mean disappeared?" A spot of spit flew from his mouth.

"I last saw him talking to Yemon in the control room. After that, he wa—"

"Did you contact Tokagei?"

"Tokagei and Michio. They didn't know where he'd gone either."

Mizuki reopened the reports and confirmed. Surprise—they reported it to Jeruko.

Mizuki slammed his fist on the table. This was unbelievable. How could Jeruko do this to him after all they'd been through together?

He opened and closed his hand, trying to keep from losing his temper in front of this underling. "You are dismissed."

The man left. Mizuki grumbled, then contacted Tokagei rather than Jeruko's son.

"Yes, your Eminence," Tokagei answered in a voice laden with sleep.

"What happened after you reported Jori missing today?"

"Nothing, Sire."

"Why not? Why was no effort made to find him?"

"This happens a lot, Sire. Colonel Jeruko's instructions are to report to him and he will handle it."

"How does he handle it?"

"I'm not sure."

"You've never seen him look for the boy or punish him when he's found?"

"No, Sire."

Mizuki seethed.

"It's not my place, Your Eminence, but…" Tokagei hesitated, undoubtedly knowing how much Mizuki hated it when inferiors reported on their superiors. He let Tokagei continue anyway. "Colonel Jeruko seems too soft on him."

"That will be all," Mizuki tapped the comm, ending the communication.

Jeruko chimed in at the door, then entered at Mizuki's command. "Your Eminence," he said with a fifteen-degree bow.

"Why in the hell didn't you report today's incident?"

If Mizuki's criticism affected Jeruko, he didn't show it. No surprise at being caught, no haste to make excuses. His posture held firm without tension and his expression remained cool. "My apologies, Sire. I followed up with Tokagei and intended to put it in my next scheduled report."

Some of Mizuki's anger sputtered out. The explanation was reasonable. Jeruko's elevated position meant he only needed to make periodic reports, and one wasn't due for a couple days yet.

"Do you still think my son isn't helping the prisoners?"

"I suspect the commotion distracted him," Jeruko said. "I know he struggles with managing the emotions of others, especially when those emotions are strong."

"He needs to learn to handle it," Mizuki replied. This explanation made sense, too. He opened the channel to his son.

"Yes, Sir," Jori answered.

"Where are you?"

"In my room sleeping."

"Get up and report to my office immediately."

"Yes, Sir."

Mizuki tapped his fingers on his desk. "Tokagei says Jori went missing later and reported it to you."

"That is correct, Sire."

"What did you do about it?"

"Not much, my L—"

"Why the hell not? The guards must stay close at all times."

Jeruko dipped his head. "Yes, Sire. It isn't their fault, though. Jori likes to go off on his own."

Mizuki studied the man. Perhaps there was no betrayal here after all. He relaxed his jaw and the twitch in his eye subsided.

"So what do you do about it? What *have* you done about it?"

"I used to reprimand him for it, but it did no good. Your son is stubborn."

Mizuki huffed. Few could get away with saying something disparaging about his children, and Jeruko was one. Plus, it was true.

"This issue has been discussed before," Jeruko tactfully reminded him. "I set up a procedure to document it and we attempted to locate his hiding spots, but he is still small enough to go places we can't."

Mizuki nodded. The boy should be reprimanded, though, even if it didn't solve the problem. However, working on the emitter was more important than being punished. He leaned back in his chair. "I will deal with him soon."

Jeruko bowed. "Will that be all, Sire?"

Mizuki waved him away. His temper cooled, but a nervous energy still reverberated in the back of his mind. Jeruko's even temperament made him hard to read, but the man's loyalty never wavered. Then again, he had believed in Fujishin's loyalty too.

*****

3791:029:07:19. Jori jumped over a shrub, dodged a sapling, and dashed through shin-deep blades of grass. His heart galloped as fast as his stride. What was he running from? A memory tickled his brain, but a coherent image eluded him.

A distinct beep shot him out of the dream and triggered him to alertness. He instinctively tapped his comm. "Yes, Sir," he said to Father.

"Where are you?"

Jori blinked. "In my room sleeping."

"Get up and report to my office immediately."

Jori's heart stopped. "Yes, Sir."

He threw off his covers and jumped out of bed. His quick movement prompted the room's lights to burst to brightness, dazzling his vision.

His mind raced with imaginary reasons his father would call him at this hour. Did he learn about the incident in the bay earlier today? Did he find out he visited Mother? *Did Yemon tell on me?*

He hopped over a cleaning bot and tapped open his narrow closet, snatching a uniform. Muscle memory took over as he undressed and dressed, giving his brain the opportunity to focus on his father.

His senses flew to the distinctive feel of molten steel. Father's lifeforce was constantly hard and hot, and laced with a festering darkness that Jori liked to call impurities.

He hated the invisible thread that always connected him to Father's unpleasant emotions, but it came in handy from time to time. Father was upset about something. Nothing unusual. However, the suspicion that had cropped up recently had grown. Not good.

Jori probed further. Sensei Jeruko was there.

He finished dressing and hustled out the door. Sensei Jeruko's lifeforce made him think of an enduring mountain capped with snow at the top and lush with greenery at the bottom. Now he imagined the mountain with an avalanche charging down. The man's worry flecked with trepidation.

Chusho. Jori's imagination zipped through several scenarios. Each scene played out with Father's possible accusations and Jori's various replies to them. His thoughts moved faster than his pace so that by the time he exited the conveyor to the command level, he had a decent store of responses ready for use.

He reviewed them again as he headed down the hall. A figure approached from the other end but Jori didn't bother to see who it was. When the person didn't step aside to avoid him as most men did, Jori halted and focused on Sensei Jeruko.

"What's going on?" Jori asked.

"He knows you tried to help the prisoners today, my Lord."

"Is that all?" That wasn't so bad.

"He knows you disappeared later."

Jori's heart thumped. "Anything else?"

Sensei Jeruko cocked an eyebrow. "*Should* there be anything else?"

So Yemon didn't tell on him. A wave of relief washed over him.

"Be very careful, Jori-chan."

The chill of Sensei Jeruko's words cut into his anxiety. "Yes, Sir."

Sensei Jeruko moved on. Jori turned the corner to Father's office and paused to settle his thoughts. He filled his lungs and put on a mask of calm, then entered, hoping he projected confidence.

He planted his feet, stood tall, and clasped his hands behind his back. "Reporting, Sir."

Father's eyes bored into him. "You have ten seconds to explain why you helped the prisoners today."

"Usagi is disrupting their work."

"The way I hear it, he was across the bay. What business did you have marching over there just to tell him to stop?"

"Their emotions were keeping me from working, too."

Father's mood turned a shade less black. Jori relaxed the tension in his body without letting go of his attentive stance.

"You need to block those out. I can't have you running amok every time someone's emotions bother you."

"I try, Sir. It's not always easy."

Father scowled and his irritation spiked.

"Especially when I'm trying to concentrate on something important," Jori added, hoping his reference to the emitter project would put Father at ease.

It worked. Father's temper turned down a notch. "Emotion is weakness, boy. Control them, or else."

"Yes, Sir." Shutting off those emotions when he was under so much stress was damned near impossible, but he had no choice but to try. "Is that all, Sir?"

Father's face darkened. "No. Where the hell were you when you were supposed to be working on the emitter?"

Jori froze. He'd played this scenario through his head but didn't expect Father's accompanying emotion. It was like he was leading to something he already knew. Perhaps Yemon told him? No. It couldn't be that. If he had, Father would be raging.

Father bent forward. "Well?"

Jori blurted the truthful answer he'd concocted earlier. "I had a problem to work out and I wasn't able to do it there."

"Why not?"

"The bay is loud. I needed peace." Both statements were true on their own.

Father frowned but otherwise seemed to accept the explanation. "Do not disappear again. You are always to be in sight of your personal guards. Understood?"

Jori hid his relief. "Yes, Sir."

"Dismissed."

Jori left as quickly as he could without making it look like he was escaping.

That was close. Too close.

31

The Attempt

3791:029:10:51. The rat-a-tats and clink-clinks compounded with the din and grated J.D. Hapker to his bones. He raked his fingers through his hair, glancing left where Sergeant Davis worked from his station on the far side of the bay. Hapker hadn't been able to talk to him yet, nor was it likely he'd get a chance today. The last time he tried, the guards asked him what he was doing. He had no answer, nor did he have enough knowledge about this emitter to make something up.

Yemon approached on his right with a cheek-pinching grin that set Hapker's teeth on edge. He turned the dial and re-entered the results on the computer, hoping the man wouldn't notice it was his fifth time doing so.

Yemon's stupid smile broadened. Hapker's spine prickled.

"Still working on the amp gauge?"

Hapker resisted the urge to rub the back of his neck. "I'm double-checking everything."

Yemon winked. "Of course you are."

A chill spread over Hapker's sweaty brow. The man had caught him, so why didn't he call him out on it?

Yemon walked away, whistling a cheerful tune instead.

Hapker wiped his palms down his pant legs. *What in the hell just happened?*

*****

3791:029:15:34. J.D. Hapker stroked his chin as Jori explained the next project. It was a little more convoluted than he was used to, but he managed to keep up. At least he had something new to do.

"Got it?" Jori said in a clipped tone.

"Yes, I think so." He met Jori's hardened eyes. "Is everything alright?"

"Fine."

"Are you sure? Yemon's acting strange today."

"It's not your concern. Now get to work." Jori handed him the MDS and left in a manner more formal than usual.

Hapker wiped the sweat from his brow. He glanced over at Sergeant Davis, whose eyes darted about furtively.

Darn it. He should've alerted Jori. He ran his fingers through his hair again, noting the rawness that spread through his scalp.

How could he get Jori's attention back, or move closer to the sergeant?

He absently tapped the side of his MDS. He might as well be standing at the edge of the cliff hoping the wind wouldn't blow.

He looked over at Davis and froze.

Davis' body tensed like a tiger ready to pounce. The man held a heavy wrench in a tightened his grip. His line of sight appeared tidally locked on the two warriors approaching Canthidius. Davis' knuckles whitened and he stepped after them.

"Watch out!" Hapker charged to the scene as Davis' wrench-wielding hand thrust down at the back of a head.

A blur swept past Davis' legs and the sergeant fell before his strike landed. Jori rolled to his feet. This crisis was averted, but another one rose as Davis stormed against his new opponent.

"Sergeant, stop!" Hapker's heart quickened but events seemed to move in slow motion. He dodged a tool bot and ran on, cursing himself for not talking to Davis or warning Jori.

Davis swung the wrench with a yell. Jori sidestepped, grabbed the man's wrist and flipped, using the weight of his body to twist his arm and make him drop the tool. After that, Jori plunged his knee into Davis' gut. The sergeant buckled but seized Jori's leg, causing him to stumble. At the same time, the man jabbed his elbow into Jori's face.

"Davis! Stand do—" Hapker grunted as someone tackled him and sent him crashing. A heaviness dropped on him, crushing his chest to the cold metal floor. He raised his head and gasped for breath as a knee ground into his spine.

A sea of legs from the other warriors blocked part of his view, but he turned enough to see Davis pounce toward Jori. "Get off! I'm trying to stop my sergeant."

Michio eased and seized his arm. "There's nothing you can do now."

As the man hauled him up, Hapker sprang forward. "Sergea—"

Michio snatched him around the neck, cutting off his air. He struggled but instead of breaking free, Michio clasped his wrist and twisted his arm behind his back. Hapker fought but the chokehold made him as helpless as a hare in a boa constrictor's clutches.

Davis lunged for Jori again. The boy dodged, then punched him in the jaw and pivoted away. Davis tried to grab him, but Jori was too swift.

Davis' face contorted with rage. "I'll get you, ya wanker."

Davis and Jori circled one another. No one stopped the man the way they'd stopped him. They stood like spectators around the two contenders. Their whoops and hollers egged Jori on.

Davis lunged for Jori. Jori ducked under his arm and ended up behind him. Davis turned to him again with a face redder than his hair. Purple veins protruded from his forehead and neck.

Hapker struggled against Michio's grip. "Why aren't you stopping this?"

"The prince has got to learn to hold his own."

"He's just a boy."

"He's a Mizuki prince."

Jori ducked and countered with a jab to Davis' kidney. Davis acted as though it didn't affect him, and likely Jori's lack of strength meant it didn't.

Davis jabbed. Jori darted sideways and hit the sergeant in the ribs, making him wince. Davis swung. Jori evaded and punched again.

The warriors cheered and shouted. "You got this!" "Give that chima what he deserves!" "Kick his ass!"

Jori struck Davis in the nose and drew blood. The sergeant roared like an enraged animal.

The warriors parted. Emperor Mizuki stepped through. Hapker's relief was short-lived as the emperor merely watched. His severe expression could have meant he was angry at Davis for fighting his young son or angry that Jori wasn't winning.

Davis swung and missed again. Jori managed another punch to his jaw and gut. He kicked behind Davis' knee, but Davis moved enough that it was ineffectual. The attempt cost him. Davis threw his fist down onto Jori's face. The pop exploded above the din. Jori fell. Davis bashed the boy and still the emperor remained stationary.

Hapker's gut clenched with each blow. This was his fault. He should have made more of an effort to talk to Davis. He yanked Michio's arm, trying to break the man's hold. "You've got to let me stop this madness."

Michio's muscles bulged and his grip tightened. "The emperor will stop it when he deems it necessary."

Acid rose from Hapker's throat as Davis continued to attack. Jori struggled but had trouble getting out from under the larger man.

Hapker attempted to elbow Michio. The guard pressed against his neck, making his lungs burn. The room spun as he choked for air.

"If you don't stop, you'll pass out," Michio said.

Hapker ceased, but only so he could breathe.

The emperor stepped forward. "Enough!"

Silence followed from everyone except Sergeant Davis. The man cursed and raised his fist to strike again. The emperor grabbed him and threw him into the crowd of warriors. Davis shook himself free and eyed his new opponent.

The emperor stood tall with his broad chest out. His expression seemed to dare the sergeant to try something. Davis charged.

"Davis, stop!" The words ripped from Hapker. "You fool," he mumbled.

"Your friend is dead," Michio said.

Hapker gulped.

Davis threw his fist. The emperor leaned back just enough for the man to miss. Davis tried again. The emperor blocked and grabbed the sergeant by the throat, lifting him a foot off the floor.

Davis kicked and swung. The emperor snarled. His face turned red as the sergeant's purpled. Davis pounded at the crook of the warrior's mighty arms, but the emperor was stone. The veins on Davis' forehead bulged along with his eyes. He futilely clawed at the white-knuckled grip.

Hapker's throat stung with bile. He wrenched himself against Michio's hold. "I can't let you do this."

"You have no choice. You interfere, you die too."

"He's my responsibility," Hapker said through his teeth as Michio twisted his arm upward, making him stand on the tips of his toes.

Hapker's struggle increased as Sergeant Davis' lessened, then ceased. The emperor retained his killing grip. Silence dominated the bay.

Hapker's face burned as Michio's arm around his neck remained strong.

The emperor clutched Davis' head with both hands and twisted it with a sickening crack. Davis' head wobbled like a dead gazelle in a lion's mouth. His body flopped to the ground in an unnatural display.

The warriors erupted into roars and whoops. Hapker's extremities tingled and a wave of dizziness fell over him.

The emperor sneered at the lifeless man. For a moment, Hapker thought he was going to spit on him. He stepped back, though, caught sight of Hapker, and strode over like a tiger in the throes of attack. The emperor stopped short only inches away.

"Was this your idea?" The emperor's tone edged with menace.

"No." Hapker shook off the dizziness and steadied his breathing. "I suspected he was up to something but couldn't stop it."

The emperor's lip curled.

"I believe he's telling the truth," Michio said. "He ordered his man to stop."

Hapker tensed as the emperor's eyes bored into him.

The emperor turned away. "I want all the prisoners taken to the arena. Now."

Hapker caught sight of several of his officers being restrained. Corporal Harley's lip bled. Sergeant Walden's hair stuck out in disarray. Blood dripped from the noses of Corporal Patersen and Tommins.

Had they made plans with Sergeant Davis—without him? He gave the officers a questioning head-tilt. Corporal Harley alone answered with a look. The young man's brow knitted together in a way that could have been guilt or regret.

As the guards led Hapker and the others out, the emperor's glower bored into them. Jori stood at his father's side. Blood splattered his face, but he didn't act hurt. Any emotions he might have felt were masked in a placid expression. Hapker gazed at him as Michio escorted him by, but Jori did not meet his eyes.

Before Michio brought him to the exit, the doors opened and Terkeshi came through. His entire bearing pulled tight enough to snap. Inferno raged in his irises. He caught sight of Hapker and stormed to him.

Terkeshi squared off and leaned in. "I'm done with you," he said in a low tone. The heat radiating from him seemed to sizzle the air.

32
World of Hell

3791:029:16:41. Terkeshi's entire body burned. The agitation in his muscles longed to lash out at the man before him. He clenched and unclenched his fists and forced himself to focus through the red of his rage.

How dare these people act against his brother. Jori had risked his neck to help them and they repaid him with this attack. He should have killed them long ago, especially this man.

Commander Hapker leaned back and shook his head. "I had nothing to do with this, I swear. You know I would never harm him."

The man's words tolled as though through a dense fog but carried no meaning.

"My Lord," Michio said in a calm tone. "He tried to stop this."

"It was Sergeant Davis." Hapker's throat bobbed. "And he's dead now."

Terk was too hot to determine if the man was telling the truth, but his trust in Michio stayed his hand.

"Handle this, boy," Father ordered.

"Gladly," Terk replied through his teeth. "Michio, get this coward to the arena. He will be first."

"Yes, Sir."

Jori and Father followed Michio with Hapker out. Terk's muscles strained to break free of the inferno blazing within. He breathed in and out heavily until the red of his vision diminished.

He made rounds to each of the Cooperative prisoners, staring them down until he felt the quake of their fear. Of all of them, Corporal Harley took the longest to quell. Terk considered beating the shit out of the man right then and there, but he would get what he deserved soon enough.

"Let's go," Terk said to the warriors restraining the captives.

He led the way at a brisk pace. His boots tramped as though keeping the beat to hard and heavy music. Some prisoners grunted in pain. The senshi were undoubtedly rough on purpose. *Good.*

Terk had sensed much anxiety from Jori lately. It was an unusual emotion for him, enough to send him to their mother who he wasn't permitted to visit anymore. If only Terk had noticed the sensation at the time it had started, he'd know the source. Maybe this Davis man had caused it. Since he was dead now, the others had a better understanding of what would happen if they tried the same stupid stunt.

A hard lump formed in Terk's throat. Jori could have been killed, and for what? That wuss of a commander?

He reached the arena where Michio already had Hapker strung up on what the men dubbed the world of hell.

The senshi followed and tossed their prisoners to the floor. Harley growled when he fell while the others grunted or groaned.

"On your knees," Terk said. The strength of his outrage flared through his tone.

He looked to his father for the go-ahead, but the man's attention focused on Jori. His hand pinched into his shoulder hard enough for Terk to sense it. The sensation combined with Jori's beating stirred in Terk's brain. It was sharp, but his little brother also radiated determination.

Father's expression turned stern as he leaned to Jori's ear. His lips moved. Terk couldn't hear, but Father's head-tilt at the world of hell told him all he needed to know. It was the same every time Father made them watch torture. What better place to establish their authority than here.

As before, Jori refused. Terk's rage upped another notch. His brother's refusal usually irritated him, but this time was different. Jori was already under the gun. Now was not the occasion to be obstinate.

Father's eyes burned but Jori's stubbornness didn't waver.

Terk stormed up to him. "Just do it!"

Jori shook his head. His blazing expression matched Father's. The set of his jaw made Terk want to strike it.

Their father growled. "If you don't do this, I will string you up next."

Jori radiated a sizzle of fear, but his determination remained as hard as steel.

"Damn you, Jori! They aren't—" Terk stopped short. He was about to say they weren't worth it. As angry as he was, though, he didn't want Jori's secret exposed. His punishment would be ten-times worse than the world of hell if Father found out what he'd done.

"I won't do it," Jori said, his voice carrying a slight tremble.

Father lashed out, striking the side of Jori's head full-fisted. Jori fell. Terk's heart lurched, but he didn't move to help. His brother deserved this, along with everyone else.

Their father yanked Jori to his feet and shoved him at Terk. "He will go last."

"Yes, Sir." Terk grabbed his little brother by the arm and forced him to walk.

Jori stumbled. His pain sharpened, but it still didn't outmatch his obstinance.

Terk dropped him off by the others, then snatched the lightning rod from the senshi punisher. "I've got this one," he said, tilting his head at Hapker.

Without waiting for the senshi's reaction, he marched up behind the commander and thrust the lightning rod into the man's back, holding it firmly in place. Hapker shrieked. Terk took in his agony and let it fuel the fire burning within him.

33
Fallout

3791:029:22:52. Jori sat up in the healing bed. His body no longer hurt, but the heaviness of his emotions leeched his energy. Something bad had happened. He remained motionless for a while, trying to piece it together.

It had begun with the Cooperative officer's hate. It poured into Jori's senses like alcohol to an open wound. He'd fought well—well enough to sense a bit of pride from Father. His smallness couldn't bring the man down, though. Not even the strike to the man's nose had been adequate. When Davis had returned the same hit, it overwhelmed him. He'd received intense training on dealing with pain, but it was difficult when it came to a heavy-boned hand smashing into a small nose. The searing agony that radiated over his face nearly made him black out.

Father's pride turned sour at that point. The fight ended, but Jori's struggle had just begun.

He lowered his forehead into his palm. His thoughts trudged through the mired mess he'd created. Everything was falling apart. First Yemon and now this. He'd promised to help Hapker's people, only to get one killed.

The intensity of Terk's anger compounded his troubles. Terk hadn't been the one to use the lightning rod on him, but he sensed his scathing judgment.

Jori inched his legs over the side of the bed. His heart throbbed with a slow heaviness.

Terk hated him again. Jori ruined everything. Why didn't he just punish those prisoners like Father wanted him to? His stomach tumbled. Because if he gave in once, he'd have to keep giving in and it would eventually lead to his father expecting him to murder people too.

The thought terrified him. Father didn't understand. Worse, Terk didn't either. Feeling another's suffering was bad enough, but the pain of death engulfed him. It stuck in his brain like a fat tick on a blackbeast and there was no pulling it out.

He struggled to manage the incoming sensations. Sometimes he could push them away. The stronger the emotions, though, the harder it was to do. And the more he cared about the person suffering, the more it troubled him.

Jori swallowed down the hard lump in his throat. Hapker's pain coupled with Terk's rage as he lashed out was like twisting a salted knife into an already festering wound. How did Terk do it? How was he able to ignore the agony of the man who saved his life?

The lightning rod was a welcome respite in comparison. At least he knew how to endure physical sensations. If only overcoming his emotional weakness happened just as easily.

An intense sensation punctured through Jori's turmoil. Terk was headed this way with an anger blazing like a solar flare. With it came a level of violence reaching as high as their father's.

Jori tensed as Terk entered the private room with an expression blacker than he'd ever seen it. His brother's hands clenched at his sides, and his entire demeanor radiated wrath.

Jori's mouth went dry.

Terk stormed forward and pushed Jori against the lid of the healing bed. "I have had enough of you!"

"I'm sor—"

"No you're not! If you were sorry, you would have punished them. They deserved nothing less."

Jori's chin quivered. The intensity of Terk's glare locked him in place.

Terk stepped back and paced, bouncing from wall to wall like an agitated electron. "This has gotten way out of hand."

"It wasn't—"

Terk halted and turned to him with a hateful scowl. "That man tried to kill you!" He stabbed his finger at Jori's face. "No more! I've had to cover your ass too many times now."

Jori held his breath. What did he mean by *no more*? Was he going to expose the secret? Would he kill Hapker and the others? Jori couldn't bring himself to ask. He didn't want to know the answer.

"They're dead anyway," Terk said as he resumed his pacing. "We don't owe them anything. We don't owe them a damned thing."

A memory of Hapker kneeling over Terk's unconscious body after their ship had crashed on the Cooperative planet nudged Jori out of his stupor. "We owe them our lives, yours most of all."

"Damn it, Jori! We can't risk our lives." Terk threw up his hands. "We've kept them alive." He counted one finger. "We stopped Usagi from using the woman. We got Sensei Jeruko, Michio, Washi, *and* our mother involved. And how do they repay us?"

"That was Davis, not Comm—"

"They repay us by trying to kill you!" Spit flew from Terk's mouth.

"That was noth—"

"Nothing? Nothing!" Terk grabbed his shoulders. Heat radiated from his face. "You're being stupid. They are from the Cooperative. They are our enemy, and we should not have to suffer because of them."

Jori's heart thumped as though Terk had punched his chest. A flood of emotions swirled around him. The hurt from his brother's vehemence burned inside him. The dread for Hapker's fate swelled while the sadness from knowing he no longer had his brother on his side poured like a vast ocean twisting down a drainpipe.

"You're growing weak," Terkeshi said with a hard tone. He pinched Jori's shoulders. "Your sentiment is turning you into a coward."

Jori flushed. "If I were a coward, I'd give up… Like you."

Terk slammed him back, making him hit his head against the lid of the bed. "You little shit! I have done nothing but put my neck on the line for you—for you and your foolish sentiment."

The tremble in Jori's chin spread throughout his entire body. It had been a long time since his brother spoke to him like this. That last time, he had also hit him.

Terk looked ready to strike now. He breathed noisily through flared nostrils and the cords of his neck stood out.

Jori's eyes watered.

Terk growled. "You fucking baby." He released Jori and stormed out.

Jori's whirling thoughts and emotions halted. All his senses evaporated into nothingness. Then a switch flipped, and a fallout of tears burst forth.

34

Light in the Abyss

3791:029:23:06. The light of J.D. Hapker's cell dimmed along with his hope. A dark cloud fell over him. Gloom pressed on the pain of his torture, making his entire being roll, rise, and fall like a stormy sea.

Dear god, what was he doing? When he'd first arrived here, Jori had given him a lifeline. He'd clung to the belief that all this would be resolved, and he and his people would either be rescued or freed.

That lifeline was no longer even a thread, though. It had become a spider web that snapped when he passed through and found himself on the edge of an abyss.

The emperor would never let them go. There was no escape and Jori obviously couldn't help any more.

He groaned. What right did he have to put his life and the lives of his crew in the hands of two juveniles anyway? Nothing could save them.

So why continue working on the emitter?

"Sir?" Corporal Harley said with a croak in his voice.

Hapker lost the thought and pushed himself up with a grunt. Every muscle in his body protested, making his movements snail-like. He managed a sitting position with his right shoulder pressed into the hard wall and his legs bent at an awkward angle.

"Harley, you alright?"

"Not bad, all things considered, Sir."

Hapker glanced at Sharkey and Simmonds, who both lay face-down on their cots. Other than the slow rise of their torsos, neither moved.

"What the hell happened?" Hapker asked. "What was Sergeant Davis trying to do?"

Harley lowered his eyes. "He wanted to take out some Tredons before they killed us."

"And you agreed to this?"

Harley snapped his gaze back up. "I asked him what you said. He told me you weren't capable of command anymore."

"So you backed up his plan?"

"No, Sir. I told him I wouldn't do anything without your approval. When he acted and you ran over there, I figured you were in on it." Harley averted his eyes and picked at something on his bed. "What choice did we have?"

Hapker sighed. If only he'd had the chance to speak to Davis earlier. "Did you talk to Lieutenant Sharkey? Did Davis?"

Harley shook his head.

"So he went behind the backs of both his superior officers?" he said to himself.

"Everyone knows you have a soft spot for the boy," Harley replied, "and she has a soft spot for you."

Hapker frowned. "What are you talking about?"

Harley made an emphatic gesture. "Seriously? We can all see how she feels about you."

Hapker's jaw fell. "We're just *good* friends."

Harley's eyebrow rose.

Hapker was too tired to argue and waved away the notion.

"We must do *something*, Sir," Harley said. "Davis' plan was suicidal, but we're about to die anyway. We might as well make it worthwhile."

Sharkey stirred. Hapker's heart lurched. Had she heard Harley's comments about their relationship? He hoped not.

Her hands twitched. One eased her up and the other massaged her forehead. "Sir?" she said in a weak tone.

"Hey, Lieutenant. How are you doing?"

"I feel like I've been struck by an asteroid." She exhaled loudly as she settled into a sitting position.

"We're better off than Sergeant Davis," Corporal Harley muttered.

Sharkey's head fell into her hand. "Oh, shit. Davis. What will we do, Commander?" The dark circles under her eyes revealed how taxing this situation was on her. She carried more stress than any of them. At least Davis had died quickly.

"I'm thinking," he said, even though he was far from a plan.

"It's only a matter of time before Usagi tries something," she said. "When he realizes I'm not contagious..." She shivered.

A mental chill ran down Hapker's spine. "Do you have any ideas?"

"We create a diversion, then run for the hangar bay and steal their fighter jets," Harley replied.

Hapker's brow wrinkled. "*Sounds* simple, but how do we get past our guards?"

"We make a lot of smoke and sneak by."

Hapker closed his eyes and massaged the upper bridge of his nose. Harley had obviously put little thought into this. "Alright. How do we get to another hangar bay? Does anyone know which direction to go?"

"No, but the prince can tell you."

"I doubt Jori can be much help anymore." A hollowness grew in Hapker's chest.

"Why not? You saved his life. He owes you." Harley's tone was almost insubordinate.

"He's only a boy," Hapker replied. "You've seen what his father is like. What do you expect him to do?"

"*Something*." Harley's dark brows furrowed. "More than what he's done, anyway."

Hapker huffed. "Assuming he tells us which way to go, the warriors are armed. They outnumber us and have more combat training. Even if we managed to steal some fighters, how far will we get before the *Dragon* obliterates us?"

"We can take the prince hostage," Harley said.

Hapker's mouth twisted in distaste. "You saw the emperor do nothing when Davis beat him? What makes you think he will care that we have him as a hostage?"

"We can't just sit here without even trying, Sir."

Hapker gave Harley a pointed look. "A plan that isn't likely to achieve anything other than our deaths isn't a plan."

Harley crossed his arms. "I'd rather die than finish the emitter," he said. His bottom lip almost came out as a pout.

"I'd rather die than become Usagi's pet." Sharkey chewed at her fingernails the way she used to before a big test at the PG Institute.

"We'll get out of this, somehow," Hapker replied.

Harley threw his hands up. "*How*, Commander? All I'm hearing from you are excuses."

Hapker tensed and heat flushed through him. "That is enough, Corporal. It is my job to keep you alive and I can't do it if you're making *half-cocked* suicide attempts."

Harley glared but didn't reply. Hapker held his stare. When the man broke eye contact, he spoke in a smoother tone. "I've been running plan after plan through my head. None have even a slim chance of succeeding. So if we can't come up with something to save ourselves, the very least we can do is destroy the emitter."

"Sabotage," Sharkey said.

Hapker's thoughts stirred, slowly at first, then like a blender bringing all the ingredients together into one dish. His death and the death of his crew was certain. The only way to redeem this disaster was to make sure the emperor didn't get what he wanted.

Hapker leaned back. "If we're going to die, we should save the rest of the galaxy."

"What do we do?"

Hapker rubbed his chin. A spark of hope flashed like a light in the abyss. He clung to it and let a plan burn through.

35
Sabotage

3791:030:13:51. J.D. Hapker rubbed the fatigue from his eyes. He had not had a good night's sleep since his capture, and it was taking its toll. His body lagged as much as his brain. None of that mattered, though. The opportunity to implement his plan had come. He forced himself to focus.

What had Simmonds said? Connect this conduit to this one, or was it that one? If he got it wrong, this would all be for nothing.

"Are you sure about this, Sir?" Sharkey said.

His heart thumped at her reminder of the deadly consequences. "We can't let him use this device."

"Okay," she replied with a quiver in her voice. The stress had gotten to her too. Dark half-circles hung under her eyes. Her mouth creased with a perpetual frown, and the usually tidy bun in her hair looked more like a mini haystack.

He put his arm on her shoulder. "I don't want to die either, but we've run out of options."

After turning back to the machine, he connected what he hoped was the correct conduit, then knelt and opened another panel. He poked around toward the rear and found the cable Simmonds had described.

He put out his hand behind him. "Wire stripper."

Sharkey handed him the tool and puffed. "Here we go."

Hapker wiped his sweaty forehead on the crook of his arm. His heart pounded wildly. Movement on his left grabbed his attention. A worker named Pachin claimed the workstation Hapker had manipulated earlier.

Sharkey turned her head in the same direction. "Crap."

Jori appeared behind the worker. Hapker's heart picked up its pace. The time had come, but he couldn't bring himself to do it with Jori here. The boy was a victim too, in his own way.

He wiped his brow again, then brought the wire stripping tool into the opening. His hand trembled, making it difficult to maneuver.

Sharkey clutched his shoulder. "Quick. You've got to do this now."

Her voice sounded muffled through the pounding of his heart. Hapker shook his head. This wasn't right. He couldn't do it. He pulled back.

Sharkey pinched her grip. "You *have* to do this, Commander. I understand why you don't want to, but this is a risk of being Cooperative officers."

"Jori," he said in a shaken whisper.

"It's the Greater Good," she replied. "We must—Oh, no."

Jori approached. "What are you doing?"

Hapker flinched and rose to his feet. "Nothing."

The boy narrowed his eyes. Then the slight shake of his head told Hapker that he knew he was lying. "Step aside."

Hapker stepped back. His stomach did somersaults as Jori examined what he had done.

The boy stiffened. Hapker groaned inwardly.

*****

3791:030:14:08. Jori straightened and willed himself to meet Hapker's eye with a stern expression. Somehow, he was sure his face sagged. He had little energy to muster anything more. "You can't do this," he said in a subdued tone.

Hapker ran his fingers through his short sandy-colored hair. "I don't see how we have much choice. Your father will kill us eventually."

Jori swallowed. The pain in his throat sharpened. Hapker was right but he couldn't have it both ways. Helping Hapker alienated Terk. Fixing this emitter might earn Terk's forgiveness but the commander would certainly die. Hapker was a good man, but Terk was his brother.

Jori deflated. "I still can't let you do this."

Hapker made a pleading gesture. "If this thing becomes operational, people will be murdered. Not just warriors. Innocent people. Women. Children. Slaves. You don't want that to happen any more than I do."

A weight seemed to fall on Jori's shoulders, but a flame burst inside him at the same time and he scowled. "Don't act like you know me."

Hapker opened his mouth as though to speak and froze. Jori followed his gaze to where Pachin and Benjiro worked. He hadn't finished his task, but he'd done enough for it to be dangerous.

"No, no, no!" Benjiro said. "This all wrong."

Hapker lurched toward them. "Stop!"

Blinding sparks erupted, accompanied by a piercing snap that ate into Jori's eardrum. Tendrils of smoke wafted from the workstation. Pachin covered his mouth with his arm and coughed. Benjiro rubbed his eyes.

The coldness of Jori's shock broke into a heat. He clenched his fists and looked back at Hapker. "What did you do?" he said through gritted teeth. "You talk to me about killing innocent people and you pull this?"

He rushed to Benjiro's side. "Are you alright?"

"Eyes hurt," the simple man replied.

Jori scanned him over, not finding any signs of injury on his face or body.

"Can you see?"

Benjiro blinked, then nodded.

Jori glanced at Pachin. The man suppressed another cough but otherwise appeared alright.

"What in the hell just happened?" Terk said, appearing beside Jori.

Jori flinched. His internal emotions were in such turmoil that he didn't realize Terk had come here. "I'm not exactly sure."

He avoided a glance at Hapker, but the man emitted a guilt that Terk certainly felt too. When Terk turned to Hapker with a vehement expression, Jori swallowed.

*****

3791:030:14:20. Adrenaline burned through Terkeshi's veins as he faced his brother. "Don't give me that shit."

Jori scowled. "I'll fix it."

"You better."

Jori returned to Benjiro, who sat on the floor blinking his eyes. "Ben, do you think you can help me?"

Benjiro nodded and moved to stand. Pachin helped him. As they peered inside the emitter component, Terk confronted Hapker. Heat surged through him as he glared with every ounce of fire that burned through his body. "What did you do?"

The commander pressed his lips together.

Terk shoved him against the emitter casing and forced his arm into the man's neck hard enough to hurt, but not enough to choke him. "*What* did you do?"

The commander's emotions fluttered, but he held Terk's stare. "My duty."

Terk let up, but only a bit. "What the hell does that mean?"

"It means I'm doing what I must." As the commander's will hardened, his guilt fled.

Realization struck Terk and he pushed into the man again. Instead of fixing the emitter, Hapker had attempted to sabotage it, hurting Benjiro and Pachin. What if Jori had been injured too? Or killed?

"Keeping you alive was a mistake." He stepped back and evaluated his next move. Hapker must die. The only thing the chima was good for was getting Jori in trouble. Killing him would solve everything.

A storm swelled inside him. He let it build until the crescendo boomed in his skull and snapped him into action. With a flick of his hand, he snatched his knife from its sheath and swiped out with his arm.

Something hard slammed into his side, causing his aim to go wide.

"Don't!" Jori chopped at Terk's arm and the knife clattered to the floor. His face scrunched as he stepped into an offensive stance and clenched his fists. "I won't let you hurt him."

Jori emitted enough fury to puncture through Terk's own emotions. The sensation almost made him waver. Jori had never been this angry before.

Terk's muscles tightened. His fists hardened and he matched Jori's fighting pose. "You want to fight? So be it."

"You're turning into Father." Jori's scowl deepened. "I *hate* you."

The words cut. Terk hesitated, but only for a moment. His muscles tightened and a burning energy coursed through him.

Hapker stepped between them. "Don't do this on my account," he said in a soft tone that didn't match the nervousness emanating from him. "Kill me if you must."

"Fool!" Terk barreled over to him and roared. He struck out, smashing his fist into the commander's jaw.

Hapker's head jerked to the side and he fell with a snap. Lieutenant Sharkey dropped to her knees and slapped the man's cheek to wake him. Terk seethed as he waited for the man to regain consciousness so he could kill him face-to-face.

A tang of dark emotions diverted his gaze as Father marched through the smoke from the device.

"What happened?" he asked the man closest to him. "What the hell is going on?"

"Your Eminence." Pachin bowed low. "It was an accident, I swear."

Terk frowned. Pachin believed this was his fault.

Father's face contorted into a snarl.

"What in the hell did you do?"

"Th-the PFC capacitor is—"

"What the hell is a PFC capacitor?"

Jori stepped forward. "It stores an electric charge."

"Fix it quickly. We don't have time for mistakes."

Pachin's face turned white. He opened his mouth as though to speak but no sound came out. He radiated pure panic.

"It's not that easy," Jori said.

Terk caught a whiff of Jori's own nervousness, but his little brother stood tall and with his chest out like he did when he made a formal report.

Father's face purpled. "What do you mean it's not that easy?"

"We must buy a new part. This type of capacitor isn't something our fabricor can create."

Father snarled. "Take him." He glared at Jori, but Terk knew who he meant. Two senshi stepped in and grabbed Pachin.

"It wasn't him," Terk said.

"Then who the hell was it?"

Terk was about to answer but Jori beat him to it. "It was me."

Terk's jaw dropped. Jori never lied. He always found a clever way to dance around the truth.

Father's fist whipped out and struck Jori.

Terk flinched as Jori fell. Father clutched his hair and pulled him back up.

"No!" Terk said despite their pact.

Father probably didn't hear. He punched Jori twice more, the second sending a splatter of blood from Jori's nose. Jori grunted but didn't cry out.

Terk wanted to intervene but couldn't move. He might as well be standing in the scorching blaze of the arc drive emissions.

Father grabbed Jori by the front of his uniform and pulled him up so they were nose-to-nose. "I have had it with you, boy."

Terk broke out into a sweat. Father's displeasure festered into a gaping wound oozing with the green and yellow of infection.

What the hell was Jori thinking? Why did he take the blame? Didn't he know he put his own life at risk? And for what? That stupid commander? Why? It made no sense.

Terk considered telling Father it was the commander's fault, but a warning bell rang through his head, telling him that Father might realize Jori had taken the blame for the enemy. He tentatively stepped forward. "He made a mistake, Father." His voice quivered as he spoke. He swallowed hard and forced himself to remain steady. "He's smarter than Yemon and everyone else here, but he's less experienced."

Father's nostrils flared and his chest heaved as he glared at Jori.

Jori emanated alarm, but his expression remained void of emotion. He pressed his lips together and met his father's stare.

Terk held his breath and stood as though in the eye of a storm while Father's emotions raged. As a purple vein on Father's forehead throbbed, Terk's heart thumped in his ears. Jori had been getting a lot of punishments lately, and the commander was to blame. As Jori's pain assaulted his senses, Terk's worry turned back into anger. His body shook as his muscles hardened with fury. Each sensation from his brother only made him burn hotter. Jori did this to himself.

Father finally let Jori go and pushed out at the same time. Jori stumbled and fell.

"Get this fixed, boy, or else."
Father's boots clomped on the metal floor as he marched off.
Terk yanked Jori up by his arm. "Get your shit together."
Jori jerked away. "Leave me alone."

36
The Greater Good

3791:031:00:28. J.D. Hapker lay on his hard bed and stared at the dull ceiling. His thoughts spun from one event to the other and back again. Jori's troubles were serious, and his fault. He never should've agreed to let him help. The boy was a hare in a den of lions.

Hapker's stomach cramped as he thought about how he'd regained consciousness only to find the emperor punishing Jori. When it ended and the emperor left, Terkeshi regained his knife. Hapker expected him to attack again, but he leaned in with eyes ablaze. "I hope you're happy," he'd said with rumble in his throat. "Jori just took the blame for you. If killing you now wouldn't make Father suspicious, I'd stab this knife in your eye and end you."

His words had made Hapker's blood freeze, but not from the fear of death. First Jori was tortured, then physically abused. How far would the emperor's temper take him with his own son?

Hapker wanted to prevent hundreds of thousands of people from being murdered by the emperor's new weapon. In this moment, though, the cost of Jori's life didn't seem worth it.

He lay his arm over his forehead and sighed. The Greater Good. It always came back to this. Risk the life of one to save many or protect the one and let many die?

"What do we do now?" Simmonds looked like a lost puppy with his forlorn eyes and his sagging features.

Sharkey hugged her knees. "We're still alive, but to what purpose?"

"If only that little brat hadn't intervened." Corporal Harley's dark brows creased.

"It wasn't his fault," Hapker said.

"He got Davis killed."

"Davis attacked first, and the emperor killed him, not Jori." Hapker sat up and ran his hand down his face. The memory of the way the emperor had snapped Davis' neck made his insides squirm.

Sharkey's expression turned haunted. "Considering how the emperor treated his own son, it makes you wonder what's in store for us."

"It looked like he wanted to kill him," Corporal Harley added.

The emperor had more in common with a deranged bear than a man. Hapker's spine tingled. "If not for Terkeshi, he might have."

Harley sneered. "You mean the one who tortured you?"

An unyielding weight pushed down on him. It broke his heart to see the savagery in Terkeshi's eyes because it meant Jori might end up just like him. "I don't think he wanted to save us to begin with. Jori must have talked him into it and now he's regretting it."

Sharkey picked at her fingernails. "Which means Jori has no allies. If he has none, we have none."

"We knew that already, didn't we?" Harley replied. "It's why we tried to sabotage that thing. We need to take another crack at it."

Harley was right. But how? "We'll never get away with that again."

"We must try," Sharkey said. "I feel like a piece of meat being drooled over. I can't take much more of this."

Hapker swallowed down the rising bitterness. "Simmonds? Any ideas?"

Simmonds shook his head. The slow and dispirited movement reflected in his tone as he spoke. "Not with them watching us like a pack of hungry dogs."

"What if we grab a weapon from a guard and blast the damned thing?" Harley mimed shooting a phaser.

Sharkey barked a laugh. "You'll get your neck snapped before you can press the trigger."

"You're a soldier, Corporal," Hapker replied. "When you look at our enemies, do you see any weaknesses?"

Harley's mouth twisted. "We can't go on like this."

Hapker agreed but couldn't think of a response.

"Maybe we should fall back on the original plan," Sharkey said.

Hapker tilted his head. "Which was?"

"Hope the Cooperative will save us." Her eyes sparked. "Captain Arden won't give up on us."

"The *Odyssey* is no match for a Tredon warship," Harley replied.

"No, but the Cooperative senior staff is no match for the captain's determination," she said.

Hapker smiled. The man could be as dogged as a hound on a scent. He wouldn't disobey orders or do something rash, but he'd argue their case until the end of time. "I can picture him matching wits with Admiral Belmont. If that doesn't work, he'll browbeat the Prontaean Council."

Sharkey's eyes lit up, then dulled again, causing a pang in his chest.

He lay back down with his hands behind his head. "It will have to do for now… Until we come up with something foolproof."

The others settled down to sleep, though he doubted they found any peace in their rest. The end was coming, one way or the other.

37
To Be Brave

3791:031:00:29. Terkeshi stood before his father with his chin held high and righteous anger in his heart. Father tapped his desk with the turbulence of a ship entering atmosphere. The man's eye twitched while the rest of his features stretched tight.

"That boy is a thorn in my side," Father said. "Every time I turn around he's acting like a fool."

"He's made some bad choices of late," Terk replied. "For someone so intelligent, he's being stupid."

"Your brother's actions *have* been questionable." Father's black eyes cut into him. "What do you know of it?"

Terk considered telling him the prisoners' records had been falsified. Father would kill them and this whole mess would finally be over. However, he might suspect Jori's involvement and end him too.

Terk suppressed a shiver. "I think his sentiment makes him weak."

Father jumped to his feet. "What does that have to do with what he did to the emitter? Did he do it on purpose?"

Terk's heart jolted. "No. Not at all. I just meant—" *Chusho*. He almost slipped up. "I thought you were talking about how he helped the prisoners."

His father slammed his fists down on his desk. "He's helping them?"

"No." Terk shook his head emphatically. "That's not what I'm saying."

The muscles around Father's eye quivered. "Then what are you saying, boy?"

Terk took a deep breath and used the lag to gather his thoughts. "Yemon. What Yemon had accused him of before. It made Jori's actions seem altruistic, but they're not. He's making bad choices because—because—I don't know why."

Damn. None of that came out right. He puffed out his chest. "He's not suited to deal with the prisoners. *That's* what I'm saying. Regarding the emitter, he made a mistake. Nothing more."

Terk resisted the urge to fidget as Father glared at him. His heart hammered but he maintained a firm stance, hoping he projected confidence.

Father sat with a melodramatic slowness. Terk steadily released the air from his lungs.

Father folded his hands. His eye spasmed and his nostrils flared, betraying the fury of emotions bellowing inside. "If you were half the warrior Dokuri was or half as smart as Jori, that boy would have been dead a long time ago."

Terk winced as his thoughts warred with being upset at the insult and worried about the threat against Jori. He decided on the former. After all, this was *Jori's* fault.

*****

3791:031:01:32. Terkeshi ducked the holo-man's punch and jabbed his own fist into its ribs. The haptic feedback told him his strike hit true, but not enough to give him the satisfaction of hurting someone real.

The holo-man retaliated with a double-jab. Terk dodged left then right, avoiding both. His rapid movement made the image seem to glitch-out. He righted his position dead-on and it appeared solid again.

What the hell had Jori been thinking, taking the blame like that? It was stupid. Didn't he sense their father's increased agitation?

The holo-man threw another punch. Terk blocked and grabbed its arm, jerking it out of the way. He took advantage of the opening and sent an upper-cut into the holo-man's chin.

Damn you, Jori. Why was he being so stubborn about this? Refusing to torture or kill someone was one thing. Taking the blame for someone else's actions was another—all just to save his enemy.

Terk struck the holo-man in the mouth, forcing it to stumble back. He closed in, punching harder and kicking faster. The haptic image fell and a new one took its place.

Terk's body flushed beyond his exertion. The commander had caused the damage on purpose. He deserved to die for that. Hell, he should have been dead already.

The holo-man jabbed Terk in the gut. He grunted, then roared, and left-hooked the thing in the face in return. His violence increased and the program reacted in kind. It struck Terk's temple hard enough to rattle his brain. Terk's rage surged. He thrust his fist into the holo-man's nose and followed with a swift kick that sent the image to the edge of the field and into oblivion. The next holo-man materialized.

Damn it, Jori!

His body burned as he fought. Opponent after opponent fell, but Terk sacrificed himself to several blows in return. Blood from his nose trickled into the stream flowing from his bottom lip. A sharp pain stabbed into his side every time he moved his left shoulder. His vision blurred from a right cross to the eye. Still, he fought on, pretending the blurry figure before him was the commander.

"You shouldn't fight when angry," a voice said.

Terkeshi sensed Sensei Jeruko but kept his eyes on the holo-man. "I'm doing well enough."

"You're making mistakes," Sensei Jeruko replied.

"I'm kicking ass."

"At what cost? Calm your thoughts, or you'll end up on the floor."

"Leave me alone, old man." Terk spoke through clenched teeth.

"What's your problem, boy?"

"Pause!" The holo-man froze and Terk turned on his heel. "How dare you talk to me that way. I'm old enough now that I don't need you looking over my shoulder berating me."

Sensei Jeruko's scarred brow rose. "No one is berating you."

"Boy?" Terk practically spit the word. "How is *that* not an insult?"

Sensei Jeruko's demeanor didn't change. "You are a boy, whether you like it or not."

Terk balled his fists but held back the urge to strike out. "This boy could kill you, old man." he rumbled.

"Don't be a fool. Besides your brother, I am your only true friend."

Terk huffed and turned to the holo-man. "Begin!" The image came to life and he pounded at it again.

Sensei Jeruko exhaled softly. "Talk to me, Terke-chan. I am always here to help."

"Why should I take advice from a traitor?" Terk continued fighting and spoke between breaths. "This secret you're keeping will get both you and Jori killed."

"I have never betrayed you *or* Jori." Jeruko's tone wasn't at all defensive. Nor did his emotions betray any shame regarding his actions. "My loyalty is to your father, yes. But it's also to you and your brother. When those loyalties conflict, I will choose you two over him any day."

Terk faltered and received a blow into his sternum. "Pause!" he gasped to the computer. He clutched his chest and concentrated on trying to take in air through the arresting pain.

He recovered enough to stand and faced Sensei Jeruko with a frown. "You've fought by my father's side since you were my age. Why would you choose us over him?"

Sensei Jeruko's face gave nothing away but his emotions spiked with sorrow. "I have my reasons. Let's just say our friendship didn't mean the same thing to him as it had meant to me."

Terk's frown deepened, his anger forgotten. Sensei Jeruko had always been the image of perfect loyalty. "*Had meant?* So this isn't something recent?"

Sensei Jeruko shook his head. "It began long before you were born. My loyalty remains, but the more I watch you boys grow up, the more that loyalty turns to you—*both* of you."

Terk's cheeks flushed but he put on a stern expression. "Jori's sentiment is making him weak, and he's turning into a coward. He lied for that man today."

"There's nothing wrong with caring about others."

"It's a weakness."

"Do you really believe your brother is weak? He's one of the bravest people I know." Terkeshi huffed. Sensei Jeruko continued, "Think about it. He let himself get in trouble to save a life."

"It was stupid."

"Was it?" Sensei Jeruko's tone took on a lecturing note. "Sure, you can threaten and hurt people to scare them into following you. However, Jori earned a loyalty far greater. Pachin is not likely to forget what your little brother did. The men who saw it won't either."

"He didn't do it for Pachin. He did it for the commander."

"Ah. So it was the commander who caused it. But he did it for Pachin as well. Your father wanted someone to blame and with his temper the way it's been lately, he was ready to spill blood."

"It could have been Jori's blood!" Terk clenched his jaw and fists. "He's being stupid. I'll be damned if I let those Cooperative bastards get him killed."

"If Jori dies, it won't be because of them. It will be because of your father."

"That won't make him any less dead."

"Then muster up some bravery of your own, Terke-chan, and protect him."

"Getting rid of the Cooperative crew would be a good place to start."

"Killing people isn't bravery. Anyone can do that. Your brother is doing what he feels is right no matter what the consequences." Sensei Jeruko's emotions swelled with an affection that went far deeper than loyalty. "Your father calls it stubbornness. I call it courageous."

Terk frowned. "Maybe taking the blame was courageous, but protecting the prisoners, refusing to torture them, is foolish."

Sensei Jeruko sighed. "Consider this. If Jori gives in and does what your father demands, it means his spirit is broken. I can't bear to see that happen. Can you?"

Terk's ire snuffed out as though struck by a chilling wind. Sensei Jeruko left. Terk remained unmoving. He replayed all the events that led up to this moment with this new perspective. Everything Jori did that got him in trouble with their father, even before meeting the commander, he did to protect people. He never did it for himself.

Jori had covered for others the same way he had done for Pachin. He gave Terena the idea for a pseudo-virus. He discovered Benjiro's talent and made sure he was properly cared for.

Terk rested his head in his hand. How many times had Jori covered for his own shortcomings? This was what his brother did. He protected people, and he did it by standing up to their father. He did it by being brave. *How did I not see this before?*

Realization soothed him like a cool breeze on a hot day. Sensei Jeruko's words etched in his mind. His limbs numbed, then his body chilled. *He* was the coward, not Jori. In his cowardice, he'd let Father guilt him into being a heartless monster. No wonder Jori hated him.

Chusho. How could he fix this?

38
Calamity

3791:031:14:41. Jori sensed his brother headed this way. He halted in the middle of the corridor and considered going another direction. Sorting out his emotions had proved impossible. One moment his eyes flooded at the realization that he and Terk would never be close again. The next, he seethed at Terk's intent to kill the commander.

How could he care about someone who acted like Father? Why should he prefer him over the man who saved his life?

He ground his teeth and pumped his fists while his personal guards waited. Benjiro shuffled his feet, breaking the silence. The simple man didn't have the capacity to ask why Jori stopped. His lifeforce was as straightforward as the man himself.

Terk's essence clashed in comparison. It usually brought forth the image of a majestic black lion but now the animal burned, bringing Jori's blood to a boil.

To hell with him. Jori shook his head and continued on his way. As their lifeforces pulled together, Jori's chest hardened. When he rounded the next corner, his heart turned to stone.

Terk approached with a hesitant stride. Jori sensed his unease and pushed it from his mind. "What do you want?"

"I need to talk to you," Terk replied.

"I'm busy." Jori moved to go around him. Terk grabbed his arm and he twisted from the hold.

Terk raised his hands as though in surrender. "I'm sorry. I'm sorry about all of it."

Jori held his glower. His brother opened his mouth to speak so he turned and left. Terk's emotions tried to follow and poke their way in like wary tendrils, but Jori put up a mental wall to stave them off. If Terk wanted to apologize, he'd have to do better than accost him in the hallway.

Jori entered the cargo bay control room. The cool air stifled his temper but when he dismissed the worker, it came out in a sharp tone. The man squeezed past Jori's guards and cleared out.

As Benjiro and the guards found their places, Jori settled in behind the viewing window and manipulated the controls. Flashing red lights interrupted the shadowed bay. This place was normally quiet, but a cranky alarm blared as the docking bay door slid open. Much of the air had already been pumped out, but a whoosh rolled out with a thump as the remaining pockets escaped into the vacuum.

Jori turned off the alarm and bleak silence followed, allowing him to hear the blood pulsating through his body. Without air for sound to travel, the door seemed to glide effortlessly along its tracks. Only the vibration in the floor indicated how laboriously the mechanism opened.

His mouth hung open as the crack widened to reveal a gaping maw. Though the control room protected him, being on the cusp of utter emptiness sent a tingle down his spine.

He remained frozen as the red lights turned blue and a ragged old cargo ship crawled inside. Once it settled and the docking clamps fastened, Jori closed the door and rotated the dial to allow air to pump back in. The vessel had powered down its engines, but its inner workings seemed to come alive as sound returned.

When the lights changed to green, Jori stepped out onto the dock. He took in the fleeting stale scent of the bay before the metallic tint and oiliness of the cargo ship replaced it.

The aptly named *Calamity* was a miracle of parts. How the captain managed to keep this trash space worthy was beyond him. It was riddled with pockmarks, some the size of Jori; a propulsion unit had bent enough to be noticeable but not enough to prevent the vessel from flying; and a clamp couldn't attach to the mangled starboard-ventral contact point.

The ship's ramp lowered and a lean man with ratty hair stepped down. Captain Jiggerson was just as disheveled as his junker. Of all the cargo captains that delivered supplies to the *Dragon*, this one was the worst. He was more of a pirate than a tradesman. However, Father tolerated him because he had a way of getting him whatever he needed.

Jori stood tall with a scanner in one hand and shipping docket in the other. He kept his face blank and tried not to wrinkle his nose from the man's odor.

Jiggerson's men trailed on his heels and the musky sour smell intensified. Jori suppressed the urge to gag and kept his feet planted despite his desire to distance himself from their oily hair, soiled clothing, and repulsive faces.

The captain smiled. His blackened teeth held a tinge of green. If a maggot crawled out from between, Jori wouldn't be surprised. He had learned some time back to beware of the man's breath.

Jiggerson wore a holster, though it was smartly empty now. What did the man need a weapon for anyway? One puff of air should be enough to make even a blackbeast keel over.

"My, oh my," Jiggerson said with an accent that sounded like he had rocks in his mouth. "What merit have I made to earn me the attention of the young prince?"

Jori bypassed a return greeting. "We need a PFC capacitor, or at least certain parts to repair one."

"Well, I got a mess of different ones inside."

"Benjiro here will look."

Jiggerson waved a crewman forward and directed him to take Benjiro in. Benjiro followed like a puppy. Jori watched him go, though he didn't expect trouble. The captain might be a rogue, but he was no fool. Jori's three personal guards easily outmatched his crew of eight, and the man knew it. It'd be smarter to stick a hand in a blackbeast's mouth.

Thin and straggly men unloaded the ship and Jori investigated each crate. Some were packed with food supplies while others held various sundries needed for day-to-day life. Jiggerson attempted to make conversation with him. Jori gave only noncommittal replies, but that didn't stop the captain from talking. He folded his arms and yammered on as he followed Jori from crate to crate.

Jori let his mind wander as he worked. Nothing was going his way, but it was Terk who dominated his thoughts. His brother always had a temper, but it had never been this frightening. His stomach soured at the memory of Terk almost striking him. When the image twisted into Terk attacking the commander with a knife, his sinuses burned with both hurt and anger.

He closed his eyes and breathed deep. *Accept it. Terk is gone.* He forced his mind to focus and pushed the negative thoughts away.

As he investigated another crate, a slimy sensation entered his brain.

Yemon sauntered in and Washi stopped him. "Where have you been?"

Instead of bubbling out excuses as the clerk generally did when caught doing something wrong, he spoke casually. "Oh, I was running an important errand." He flicked his hand. "The young prince here knows what it's about." Yemon turned a smug grin Jori's way.

The flush from Jori's cheeks fell over his entire body. He clenched his teeth to keep from frowning. He nodded to Washi, confirming what Yemon had said.

Yemon whistled as he went about his work. The sound grated on Jori's nerves. A desire to throw something flashed through him. He imagined it but didn't do it. It would only show the man how well he had him under his thumb. *Chusho! I can't believe he's doing this to me.*

Yemon completed a few pointless tasks, then left again. Washi frowned at his back, then gave Jori a questioning gaze. Jori looked away and fumed.

Jiggerson blathered on. Jori submerged himself in his work until something Jiggerson said snapped him out of it. "What did you say?"

"I said that bugger tried to blackmail me. I got 'im good, though." Jiggerson cackled.

Jori froze. "Who?"

"Fuentes, or Fat Toes as I like to call him," Jiggerson replied. "He's one o' Chepy's henchmen."

Jori knew of Chepy, or Lord Chepy, as he liked to style himself. He was nothing more than slaver—a powerful slaver, but still just a slaver.

"He tried to blackmail me," Jiggerson continued. "Said if I didn't give him a cut, he'd rat me out."

"Rat you out on what?" Jori asked.

Jiggerson barked a laugh. "Wouldn't you like to know." He cackled again. "The point is, he didn't do it."

Jori's heart pattered. "What did you do?"

"Why I turned it around!" He put his hand on his hip and leaned on a crate. "I found his weakness and exploited it. I told him what I knew and said that if he ratted me out, I'd rat him out."

A flash of inspiration erupted in Jori's head. A range of possibilities presented themselves and he analyzed each one as Jiggerson moved on to other topics.

Benjiro exited the ship empty-handed.

"Nothing?" Jori asked anyway.

"No find," Benjiro replied.

Jori nodded and was surprised he had no feelings about it. He should be disappointed. His father certainly would be, but the prospect of not being able to fix the emitter had a certain appeal.

After inspecting all the crates, he tallied the approximate value of the items he'd selected and negotiated a price with the smelly pirate. The captain thought to balk a few times, but Jori didn't budge.

"Why don't I talk to someone else, young one?" Jiggerson said.

Jori resisted the urge to glower and kept his face blank instead. "I will get my father."

Jiggerson's emotions spiked and his body jerked. With awkward movements, he put himself back into his casual position. "Oh, well. I'm sure he don't wanna trouble himself with this. You and I can work something out."

Jori suppressed a smile and renamed the amount he would pay.

Jiggerson scowled but had the sense to keep his comments to himself and accept the payment.

When the pirates left, Jori looked over the list of items he still needed. He checked the shipping docket to see which cargo ship was due to rendezvous next. His heart skipped a beat. The perfect ship will arrive tomorrow. A wide smile pinched into his cheeks as his planning solidified into a single idea.

39
Secrets and Blame

3791:031:22:34. Terkeshi stormed into the workstation room, following his senses to the man who reeked of sneakiness. "Yemon! What the hell are you doing?"

Terk nearly laughed when the skinny little man fell out of the chair. Yemon jumped to his feet and clicked off his deskview screen.

Terk put on his sternest face. "Aren't you supposed to be working on the emitter?"

Yemon licked his lips. "Um, yes. I mean, not right now. I'm doing a task for your brother."

"Really?" Terk drawled, sensing the man's lie. As he leaned in, he hardened his look. "And what might that be?"

"Uh…" Yemon's throat bobbed. "I, uh…"

"Spit it out, damn it! I know you're up to something. I'm told you've been neglecting your work."

"B-by who?"

"Everyone."

"Th-the young prince knows what I'm doing."

Yemon's deception laced with a greasy feeling put Terk's hackles up. He seized the puny man by the neck and slammed him back against the console. Yemon refused to meet his eyes so he grabbed his jaw and forced him. "Tell me the truth or I will kill you."

Yemon trembled. "H-he and I h-have an agreement."

Terk pinched harder. "What agreement?"

"H-he d-doesn't want me to say. That's the truth. I swear."

Terk frowned. The snake spoke truly. What could Jori be hiding from him? He held the man's face and debated whether he should beat it out of him or ask Jori. With his brother refusing to talk with him, it was unlikely he'd learn it directly. Did Terk want to know, though? Jori's secrets had already gotten him in too deep.

Yemon turned white as Terk glared into his eyes. "Whatever you two are up to, it had better not get him in trouble. Do you understand?"

Yemon attempted to nod but couldn't move from Terk's grip. "Yes, m-my Lord."

Terk shoved Yemon back and punched him in the gut. The doubled over with a gasp and cough.

Terk grabbed his hair and straightened him up. "If Father hurts him because of you, you're a dead man."

Terk's comm beeped. He stepped away from Yemon while keeping a hard eye on him. "Yes, Sir," he answered.

"Come here," Father said, then disconnected.

"I'll deal with you again later." Terk left Yemon cowering at his workstation and headed to Father's office. An idea struck him along the way. He trusted Jori to handle the man, but it wouldn't hurt for him to take his own measures against the snake.

*****

3791:031:22:45. A tapping noise echoed as Kenji Mizuki drummed his fingers on his desk and concentrated on the information scrolling down his screen. He leaned in, mentally checking off each option.

His neck and shoulders ached from sitting for so long, but he had to figure this out. He'd been through the list once already. There must be another way to get the part.

He pulled back and suppressed a sigh. "It looks like you will go to Subkojo."

Samuru smiled and Mizuki frowned. How could the man want to visit there again after what Fujishin had done? The place held too many memories of their youths.

The small Subkojo space station had the largest manufacturing facility in Toradon territory. While the slaves and shokukin were poor, the lord and his army of engineers were rich. Their wealth meant they had a harem full of the most beautiful women. Even after all these years, Mizuki daydreamed about the times he and his friends had spent there. Nowhere else did he ever experience week-long orgies.

When Fujishin had betrayed him, he realized he had no friends. Going back didn't just trigger good memories turned sour, it added nineteen days to his timetable. The longer it took him to get to the new ship being built for the emitter, the more likely it'd be discovered by his rivals.

"Have Niashi alter course to the Chundo-port," Mizuki said to Samuru. "Update me on the precise time of arrival."

"Yes, Sire. Should I take Terkeshi with me?"

Mizuki pressed his comm. "Come here." He ended the communication without waiting for the boy's response and massaged his brow where the muscle over his eye twitched. Every time he came closer to having his weapon, something delayed it.

He balled his fist. *What the hell was that damned boy thinking? He knows how important this project is.*

Heat surged through him whenever Jori came to mind. First, the suspicion that he was helping the prisoners. Then his refusal to punish them. Now he'd damaged the emitter. It wasn't a simple fix either. He had to break a difficult component to obtain.

The door comm beeped. Mizuki straightened. "Enter."

Terkeshi stepped inside and took a rigid at-ease stance in front of the desk beside Samuru. Although the boy stood tall, the heavy-limbed Samuru towered over him.

"Reporting, Sir."

Mizuki's eyes bored into him. *If only Dokuri were here instead.* "You and Samuru have a mission to Subkojo soon. I'll get you to the Chundo-port where you'll take a Serpent. And don't crash this one."

Terkeshi scowled. Mizuki glared, daring him to protest and say the last time wasn't his fault. He had no excuse for losing a ship, getting every crew member except Jori killed, and allowing the Cooperative to capture him.

Hell, Mizuki shouldn't even be giving the boy another chance so soon. Samuru would keep him in line, though.

"Make the plans and get Samuru's approval."

"Yes, Sir."

"Don't stay long. There isn't time."

Terkeshi nodded quickly while Samuru frowned and dipped his head with a languid motion.

"Permission to speak, Sir," Terkeshi said.

"It had better not be protesting Samuru's authority. You have a lot to learn yet."

Terkeshi's jaw tightened. "No, Sir. It's Yemon. He's up to something."

Mizuki narrowed his eyes. "What do you mean?"

"He might've been the one who damaged the emitter."

"Why in the hell would he do that?" Mizuki clenched his fists.

"Because he's jealous."

"If Yemon did it, then why did your brother take the blame?"

"Perhaps Yemon set it up in such a way to make Jori believe he was at fault."

"What evidence do you have?"

"None, Sir," Terkeshi replied in a firm tone, "but he wasn't in the emitter room like he was supposed to be when it got damaged—and he's been acting strange."

"Strange how?"

"Nervous. Sneaky."

Mizuki huffed. There was nothing unusual about that. Yemon had always been a sly bastard. "Then it's most likely you're jumping to conclusions for your brother's sake."

Instead of refuting the accusation, Terkeshi's mouth twisted as though he'd eaten something sour. "Yemon is a snake."

"General," Mizuki said to Samuru, "has Bishamon reported anything out of the ordinary to you?"

"Nothing, Sire."

Mizuki pressed the comm button on his deskview. "Bishamon, come to my office now."

Both Samuru and Terkeshi waited in perfect stillness. Mizuki used the time to scroll through his screen. Generally, he avoided the little spats between his crew members. Letting them fight among themselves created the hierarchy that put the best men on top. If Yemon sabotaged the project, though, that was a different story.

Bishamon entered and Terkeshi and Samuru split apart so the man could face him.

"Yes, Sire," Bishamon said with a bow.

"Did you see my clerk the other day when the emitter was damaged?"

Bishamon's Adam's apple bobbed. His mouth opened but it took a moment for him to speak. "No, Sire. I wasn't there."

Mizuki's eye twitched. "Why the hell not?"

"It wasn't my shift." Bishamon glanced over at Samuru.

Samuru dipped his head in confirmation.

"Fine. Tell me what Yemon's been up to."

Bishamon's brow furrowed. "I haven't seen him, Sire."

Mizuki leaned forward. "What do you mean you haven't seen him? He's supposed to be helping with the emitter."

"Um. I assume he's doing other things. He comes in, talks to the young lord a bit, and leaves."

Mizuki clenched his jaw. *Perhaps Terkeshi is right.* "Talk to him," he said to the boy.

"I plan to," Terkeshi replied.

Mizuki glared at them. "Dismissed."

After they left, he leaned back and considered the situation. He held some doubt as to Yemon's involvement. The man was a snake, yes, but also a coward. Terkeshi had his shortcomings, but he'd kill Yemon in a heartbeat if the little man did something against Jori.

Mizuki rested his elbows on his desk and steepled his index fingers on his chin. He put Jori and Yemon from his mind and resumed his search, hoping to find the part he needed much sooner. The emitter was far more important.

The heat of his anger turned to yearning as he imagined blasting Fujishin and Lord Enomoto to dust.

40
Extraction

3791:032:18:29. Jori resisted the urge to fidget while the *Black Adder* drifted into the docking bay. His stomach tumbled and grappled, then pinched like a chokehold.

As the ship landed, his plan took off. *This will work.* He had anticipated every contingency.

His imagination threatened to fling him into doubt. He inhaled deeply, picturing this line of thinking as a target and blasting it into extinction. The remaining positive thoughts zipped around like excited atoms, but none stayed focused.

The *Black Adder*'s feet touched the floor, but the clamping mechanism didn't catch it. Jori huffed and clenched his fists. If this took much longer, he'd scream.

The *Black Adder* finally locked in but adding atmosphere back to the docking bay and waiting for the crew to disembark was like watching someone else take an engine apart piece by tiny little piece. By the time Captain Packwood ambled down his ship's ramp, Jori's muscles twitched with unspent energy.

He masked the jitters and stood tall with his feet planted at shoulder-width and his sweaty hands clasped behind his back. Packwood sauntered over, making his hefty build sway side to side. He greeted Jori with a bow, then took the tablet from Pachin. The list wasn't long, but the man read it with the slowness of a coagulating flow of lava.

Packwood returned the device. "Ain't got nothin' like these. I deal in commodities, not junk parts."

Jori ignored his bitter tone. Packwood's attitude had turned surlier after the devastating injury to his son.

Pachin nodded, then left with Benjiro trailing behind.

"Is there somethin' else I can help you with, young Prince?"

Jori handed him his own tablet. "I need you to do something for me."

Packwood took it. His forehead wrinkled as he reviewed the information on the screen. "What am I looking at?"

"The amount I'm willing to pay you."

Packwood's beady eyes widened. "This must be very important."

"Important *and* secret. Between you and me."

Packwood glanced over Jori's shoulder, undoubtedly seeing Washi and Michio waiting at a respectful distance.

"Not your father?"

"Not my father."

Packwood returned the device. "Sounds risky."

"Hence the amount."

Packwood's mouth turned down and his eyes rolled up as though he was thinking about it, but Jori felt his interest. Packwood and his crew were neater than Captain Jiggerson's and his dealings more honest, but he was still a smuggler. Secrecy was his trade.

"What do ya need me to do?"

"I need you to take someone with you."

Packwood grimaced. "Someone your father wouldn't want me to take, no doubt."

"You will need to disappear after this."

The man's emotions dipped, but his sensations didn't indicate total aversion.

"There's enough there for you to travel to the mine on the Kesanshi asteroid," Jori continued. "Drop him off and use the rest to help your son and alter your identities."

Packwood's frown deepened, but Jori sensed his rising hope.

Jori waited for an answer, but it didn't come so he altered course. "What happened to your son, anyway? How did he lose his legs?"

The captain's jaw worked as he radiated anger. "General Sakon."

Jori tilted his head but didn't push him to say more. He waited as the captain's inner turmoil settled.

Packwood filled his lungs. "It was on Jinsekai, on the outskirts of a smaller city. I had dropped a load off to the city magistrate an' we all headed to a local tavern for some R-and-R. That's when General Sakon's Rattlers attacked."

Jori nodded. Rattler jet fighters were being used on Jinsekai a lot lately where unrest kept flaring up into outright rebellion.

"Their target was the magistrate's estate," Packwood continued. "But it was like they weren't even botherin' to take aim. Bombs dropped everywhere—on the estate, in the worker fields, and in the outer city where we were."

Packwood's expression turned haunted. "We heard them and took cover. A shell detonated less than a quarter-kilometer away. The shock wave hit us, and a chunk of debris struck Jacob below the knees."

Jori tried to stave off the torrent that Packwood's emotions emitted, but the man continued. "It was awful." He hung his head and shook it, as though trying to cast out the memories. "Jacob was knocked unconscious, thank goodness. But the screams… And the bodies…"

Jori swallowed, remembering how Father could have sent senshi to infiltrate the Gonoro space station and deal with the insurgents directly. He said it was important to set an example, though. Jori struggled to understand, but he still couldn't grasp why the collateral damage was necessary. That little girl didn't deserve to die, and Packwood's son didn't deserve to lose his legs.

Jori held back the urge to vomit. How many other undeserving people would suffer if his father used that emitter? "I'm sorry," he said.

Packwood looked him over as though trying to interpret another meaning. Jori let his sympathy show.

The man nodded. "It weren't your doin'." He cleared his throat. "So who is it you want me to take and why the Kesanshi mines?"

Jori had once asked why the Kesanshi asteroid was so special. Any asteroid could be mined but this one had a lot of favorable qualities, making it the most lucrative mining operation in Toradon territory.

"He's an engineer," Jori said. "I figured Lord Vuong would let you through if you brought him someone useful." Yemon could help maintain the machines that extracted the asteroid's rare metals. Since Kesanshi was also inaccessible to outsiders, it meant Yemon would have no means of communication other than to Vuong's space station at the edge of the asteroid belt.

Packwood nodded. "An engineer, you say. Why don't you want him here? I understand engineers are in short supply."

"You will see why when you meet him. He's a conniving little worm of a man and more trouble than he's worth."

Packwood smirked. "Got under your skin, did he?"

Jori raised an eyebrow but didn't respond.

"Worm or not, your father's goin' to notice his absence. Which means he's gonna come after me."

"No one will notice for at least a day. You'll have a head start."

"Even then, I can't outrun a warship."

"You can if the warship doesn't know which way you went."

Packwood scratched his chin. "What's to keep me from killing this man?"

Jori shrugged. "Nothing, but he might be of help to you."

Packwood's mouth stretched out and his brow furrowed into a dubious expression.

"Obviously, you'll no longer work for my father," Jori said. "Lord Vuong will want you back, though."

Packwood scoffed. "Why would he want that?"

"The reason he was so angry when you started delivering here was because he was sure my father would interrogate you about his asteroid mining operation. Give him my engineer and he'll be grateful to have one of my father's assets."

"If I return to Lord Vuong, your father will find me."

It was Jori's turn to make a dismissive noise. "Do you really think Vuong would tell my father about you? He doesn't want that kind of attention. You know how secretive and paranoid he is about his trade routes."

Father inspected the operations once every few years as a show of his sovereignty, and that was enough for Lord Vuong. During the last visit, Jori had nearly given the man a panic attack when he came close to calculating the movements of the asteroids in that belt. Even though the objects averaged about a million kilometers apart, they moved fast. This made the route to the gigantic Kesanshi asteroid constantly in flux. A ship traveling no faster than point-zero-three c's could navigate their way, but it was slow going. Anyone wanting to get to the asteroid in a hurry had to have the route calculated by Lord Vuong's space station.

The security measures implemented by the Vuong family over the generations increased the asteroid's value. Vuong had depots situated all over that section of the asteroid belt. Some housed powerful weapons and others kept track of asteroid movements. The latter's data was then encrypted and sent to Vuong's station, which meant only he knew the ever-changing routes his transport ships should take.

Packwood stroked his chin. "So how am I gonna get this man on my ship?"

"It will be easy enough."

Packwood's brows rose. "Don't get me wrong. I'm sure you can be rather fierce, but I still can't see you pushing around a grown man."

"I won't need force. I'll appeal to his greedy nature."

Packwood seemed to ask a question with his eyes.

"That money I showed you," Jori said. "It's in his account. As soon as you're off, I'll move it to yours."

"You sure you'll be able to hack his account?"

"I've already done it."

"You really thought this through, didn't ya?"

Jori nodded.

Packwood put out his hand. "You got yourself a deal, young Prince."

Jori shook it, then stepped back and pressed his comm. "Yemon. I need you at docking bay seven."

"I'm a little busy, Sir," the man replied with a snippy attitude.

Jori clenched his jaw but spoke in a conspiratorial tone. "It's important. You will want to see this."

Yemon made an exasperated sound. "I'll be there in a minute."

Jori gave Packwood the rest of his instructions. His gut churned as he waited for the clerk. It seemed to take forever for the man's lifeforce to get close, but Packwood's crew barely had half the delivery unloaded when the skinny man finally arrived.

Yemon bowed. "My Lord."

Jori wanted to smack the smug smile of his off his ridiculously round face but restrained himself. "We need to talk."

The man squinted his eyes as though suspicious, but his stupid smile remained. "I think you're forgetting our deal."

"I'm not forgetting." Jori had imagined this meeting several times over and decided being nice to Yemon was the best way to pull this off. He switched to a friendly expression. "We have money to discuss, remember?"

Yemon's eyes lit up. Jori's heart raced as he handed him the tablet with the same information displayed as he'd shown Packwood.

Yemon's eyeballs swelled to the size of loquats. His excitement was palatable, but then his face fell. Jori smiled, both inwardly and outwardly.

"This is too much." The man tossed the device like it had bitten him. "And you removed it directly from your father's account. I meant for you to find a more discreet way to pay me."

"I could have but Father would've found out eventually. Do you really want to be here when he does?"

Yemon frowned and took back the tablet. He practically drooled as he seemed to consider it. "This is a lot more than I expected."

"You are rich." Jori held his smile. Inside, the palpitations of his heart made him giddy.

Yemon's frown deepened. "Yes, but I can't take all this. When the emperor finds out, he'll kill me."

"Then leave now."

"What?"

"Leave." Jori hardened his expression.

Yemon smirked like it was a joke. "You're blackmailing me?"

Jori showed all his teeth when he smiled. "You started it. I'm just finishing it."

Yemon's face dropped into a glower. "What makes you think I won't tell your father about your secret before I go?"

"Because even though it is a lot of money, you'll need more someday."

The man tilted his head. His eyes narrowed but he didn't speak.

"When the time comes, I'll be able to get you more," Jori said with a shrug.

Yemon bit his bottom lip, then leaned in. "Why would you do this for me when you could kill me instead?" he asked.

"You've seen how things have gone in the engine room since you were assigned to the emitter. Of everyone working on it, who is the most competent?" Yemon nodded. Jori suppressed the urge to smile. The man wasn't just greedy, he was arrogant. He truly believed the ship would fall apart without him. "When Terkeshi becomes emperor, I won't have time to work on engines. I will need someone who does." Jori released his smile. *Not a single lie in these statements.*

"Ha! Even if I came back to you for more money, why would I want to work for you too?"

"Status," Jori replied. "Don't you want to be more than just a clerk?"

Yemon's suspicion fled. "Why did you do this for the Cooperative prisoners anyway? Is it true that you're sentimental about them?"

"That's my business," Jori said. Yemon no doubt wanted more information to hold over his head, but he bared his teeth and wordlessly dared the man to press it.

"Am I taking this ship?" Yemon waved his hand toward the *Black Adder.*

Jori nodded. "I've already talked to the captain. He's been paid."

"Do I have time to get my stuff?"

"No."

"What happens when your father finds out I'm gone with his money? He'll come after me."

"The captain here knows how to disappear."

Yemon folded his arms. "How can I trust you?"

"Because you can still tell Father my secret." It was the truth, but only if he didn't get on the *Black Adder.*

Yemon let his arms fall to his sides and looked up as though thinking. "Alright."

The tension that had been riding Jori's shoulders loosened, but not all the way. He still had to make sure his father didn't find out too soon, and Packwood had to keep up his end. The best part was Yemon would never see a single ounce of currency.

"I gave the man in the control room a break," Jori said. "He is on his way back now and knows you will be the one giving the go order. So get situated, then contact him through your comm so he doesn't know you're on the ship."

Yemon beamed and bounced on his toes. "Yes, my Lord."

"I'll leave you to it." Jori turned on his heel and headed out.

His two personal guards met him at the door. "What was that all about?" Washi asked.

Jori's heart double-beat. "What do you mean?"

"Yemon's been acting strange lately," he replied.

"Yeah," Michio said. "I hate the way he's been looking at you, like he's got one over on you or something."

Jori's gut twisted at how close to the mark Michio was. "Yemon is being an ass, but nothing I can't handle."

They both seemed to accept the explanation. Jori's stomach settled down as Yemon's extraction commenced.

41
Courage and Treachery

3791:033:19:52. Terkeshi met his brother in the hall on the way to see their father. "Hey," he said with a slight smile.

Jori stiffened. His resentment lashed out and struck Terk's senses.

A painful lump lodged in Terk's throat. "I'm really sorry."

"Save it for someone who cares." Jori pushed past him and walked ahead.

Terk held back until they reached Father's office. Jori entered first, planting himself on the right. Terk followed and stood to the left. Both faced Father with formal postures and attentive expressions, neither betraying their inner turmoil.

Father sat tall and forbidding. His hard features matched an obstinance lurking beneath. "I've looked over the records of our prisoners…"

Jori's emotions spiked.

"… And I've decided we don't need all of them."

Terk's chest tightened, and he suspected Jori had the same sensation. Jori kept anything from showing, though.

"Terkeshi," Father continued. "Gather them all in the arena. The woman is to be the focus."

Terk twitched as though Father had slapped him. He held no affinity toward Lieutenant Sharkey, but his insides writhed. "Yes, Sir," he said with a strained voice.

"You will kill her. Make it last and make sure they watch."

Terk's mouth fell. "Why her?"

Father's face tightened. "Because she's a distraction."

"Sir!" Jori's eyes rounded. "She's not the least useful of all the prisoners."

"I don't care. I will cure you of your sentiment one way or the other, boy."

Terk's heart pounded like an industrial jackhammer. His hands trembled. The sensation wriggled up his arms, then throughout his entire body.

"You can't!" Jori stepped forward. "I need her help!"

Father bounded to his feet and leaned forward on his fists. "Damn you, boy. I knew you were weak but look at you. You're afraid. And for what? The fate of a mere woman?"

"Father," Terk said, barely keeping his voice steady. "I've heard others talking. She knows more than most of our own workers."

Father bored his hard stare into him. "Not you, too?"

Terk swallowed. Except for the space station he and Jori had destroyed a few years ago, he never killed a woman. Lieutenant Sharkey was a Cooperative soldier, but it wasn't enough in his eyes to consider her a warrior. Besides, he'd gone out of his way to protect her from Usagi. Killing her now felt wrong.

His mind raced, but no explanation his father would accept came to him. Maybe it was his turn to be brave. "Me, too… I guess."

Father's emotions spewed a fury that seemed unreal compared to his unmoving form. "Boy, what in the hell is the matter with you?"

Terk gathered his resolve. "Killing a woman is too eas—"

"Then do it!" Father slammed his fist on his desk.

"It's cowardly."

"It's all you're good for! Everyone knows you can't beat a real man."

Terk's body burned as though pricked by a thousand needles.

"You're useless," Father said. "Both you and your brother."

Terk deflated as his self-worth plummeted. Jori's face reddened with defiant anger rather than shame.

As Terk grasped for his brother's confidence, it flittered away like a flying insect. He didn't have Jori's intellect. Though he could beat Jori in a fight now, it wouldn't be long before Jori's strength matched his skill. What else did he have to offer?

His dead brothers were known for their brutality. Dokuri was a mindless beast—mauling men, women, and children alike. He neither relished in it nor cared which head his heavy boot stomped on. Montaro was weak. He couldn't fight anyone capable of defending themselves. When his victims were powerless was when he unleashed his savagery and fed off their helplessness like a fabled vampire.

Terk mentally shook his head. He didn't want their reputations. He turned back to Father and puffed out his chest. "Dokuri was a dumb beast and Montaro was a coward. Just because we refuse to kill women doesn't mean we're weak."

Father panted as though finishing up a strenuous workout. Jori radiated pride, bolstering Terk's confidence.

Father straightened. "So that's the way it's going—"

The door beeped. Father snarled. "What is it?"

*****

3791:033:20:13. Kenji Mizuki's door beeped. A rumble escaped his throat. His personal guards knew better than to let people bother him when he talked with his sons. "What is it?"

"Sire," Samuru said through the comm. "Yemon is gone."

"What do you mean gone?" Mizuki scowled.

"He's not here on this ship, your Emin—"

"Enter!" Mizuki hated talking through the door.

The brawny man entered. "He's gone, Sire. No one has seen him."

"He can't just disappear."

"I've had my men look everywhere, Sire. The last to hear from him was a dock worker. He said Yemon gave a cargo ship permission to leave."

"Yemon helped me check out the *Black Adder*'s freight yesterday," Jori added.

"Where did he go after that?"

"I left before the *Black Adder* did," Jori replied. "Yemon was still there. I haven't seen him since."

Mizuki frowned. Yemon in the docking bay was not unusual. Both he and Jori often went there to find parts. The clerk should've returned to his work by now, though.

Mizuki sat and opened his deskview. He clicked through to Yemon's section. No recent reports.

"Where the hell is Yemon?" he said to his sons. "Can you sense him?"

The boys closed their eyes. Their faces locked in calm. Terkeshi's eyebrows twitched. Seconds passed. Terkeshi's forehead wrinkled and he tilted his head as though trying to listen to something. Mizuki tapped his foot.

Terkeshi blinked open his eyes. "I can't find him."

"Nor can I," Jori added.

"What do you mean you can't find him? Is he asleep somewhere?"

"I'd sense him if he were sleeping, Sir," Terkeshi replied. "He's either not here on this ship… Or he's dead."

"Dead?" Mizuki's tone laced with accusation. "Who would have killed him, I wonder?"

Terkeshi's eyes bulged, then his brow furrowed in indignation. "I didn't kill him."

"You know me, Father," Jori said bitterly. "I have too much sentiment to kill anyone."

Mizuki glared at him. "You'd better not be lying, boy."

Jori jutted his chin. "I may not be a brutal killer, but I'm not a cowardly liar either."

Terkeshi agreed. "If I killed him, I'd tell you."

"Sire," Samuru said. "I checked with all their personal guards… And another who's keeping an eye out…" He dipped his head toward Jori.

Jori scowled. "You mean Bishamon?"

Mizuki ignored him. The boy likely sensed he was being watched.

"They've been working or sleeping." Samuru indicated the boys. "I'm sure of it."

Mizuki slapped his desk. "Question the crew again. Now. Jori, you check into Yemon's work on the emitter and make certain he didn't do any damage."

Samuru dipped his head. "Yes, Sire."

"Yes, Sir," Jori and Terkeshi said.

They left. Mizuki dropped into his chair and roared until his nerves settled. Then he opened the special comm channel on his deskview and found the *Black Adder*'s contact frequency. "Captain Packwood, this is Emperor Mizuki. Respond now."

Mizuki knocked his knuckles on his desk as seconds turned into minutes. It wasn't long, considering how far the cargo ship had probably traveled since yesterday, but each moment bloated his temper.

"Your Eminence," Packwood broadcasted through static. "To what do I owe this pleasure?"

"Do you have a man named Yemon there?"

Mizuki waited for the transmission to travel to the *Black Adder* and for a response to return.

"Yes, your E—ence."

Mizuki's muscles tightened. "Why?"

"He said he was—ving some—for you—"

Mizuki clenched his jaw. The distance must be too far. "That's impossible. I want to talk to him."

"Cert—ly, y—Emin—" A brief pause followed. "By th—ay, he also—ention—coming—to a l—of money."

"Money?" Mizuki frowned. "Did he say where he got it?"

"No, S—But—ade it s—ike a lo—He s—"

The communication ended. Mizuki stabbed the comm. "Let me speak to him now."

Minutes passed. Mizuki tried again. Nothing. He slammed his fist on the desk. "Chusho!"

The *Black Adder* was beyond range. Mizuki's eye spasmed like a man in the throes of death. Did Packwood say something about Yemon having a lot of money? From where? The clerk didn't have the means.

Mizuki tapped the intercommunication link taped behind his ear. "Biskol," he said.

"Yes, Sire," the man replied.

"See if you can get into Yemon's account and tell me how much money he has."

"Yes, Sire."

*****

3791:033:22:28. Kenji Mizuki stopped rubbing at the ache in his head when Terkeshi and Samuru returned. Both stood formally in front of his desk with no hint of having good news.

Mizuki relayed his conversation with the *Black Adder*. "What did you find out?"

He focused on Samuru but Terkeshi responded. "Washi was with Jori in the cargo bay. He said Yemon looked ridiculously happy about something."

"He didn't know what Yemon was happy about?"

"No, Sir, but he mentioned he's been more arrogant than usual."

Samuru tilted his head. "Do you think he came into some money somehow and left?"

"Doesn't Yemon sometimes handle accounting?" Terkeshi asked. "Have you checked our books?"

"He wouldn't dare." Mizuki opened the records tab on his deskview.

That's strange. His total proceeds from his vassals was a few thousand less than usual. Even Fujishin's stirring up of rebellions couldn't make it go down this much. He clicked through a deposit. The payment was short. He checked another. It was also lower.

Mizuki's shoulders tightened. Either every lord had shorted him or Yemon had taken a little from each.

He jumped to his feet. "That damned snake! He stole my money and ran! I'm going to kill him!"

His body twitched as though an electrical current surged through him. He stepped from behind his desk, took two steps, and turned back. How could this happen again? How many people were out to get him? First Fujishin. Then a half-dozen lords. Now both his sons refused to obey him. Were they plotting against him? That would be foolish, but what if they had help? Jeruko could be helping them. Maybe he was in on it with Fujishin. He and Fujishin had been close. Maybe they were conspiring against him too.

"What was that, Sire?" Samuru said.

Mizuki halted. "What was what?"

Samuru uncharacteristically shifted his feet. "You were saying something, but I couldn't understand you."

Mizuki frowned. He glanced at Terkeshi's wrinkled forehead. The boy shared a look with Samuru, who's brow furrowed.

"What the hell is the matter with you both?" Mizuki said.

Samuru cleared his throat. "I've never seen you this agitated before, Sire."

"Well, of course I'm agitated!" Mizuki clenched his fists. His right eye convulsed. "I've been betrayed… Again!"

"We'll find him, Sire, and make him pay."

"Yes." Mizuki resumed his pacing. He rubbed his chin and let his thoughts run. "We'll catch him and make an example of him. That way, everyone will learn what happens to traitors."

He stopped again. What if Yemon wasn't the only one? What if there were others here who were thinking of doing the same thing? The clerk couldn't have done this alone.

He faced Samuru. "I want all the surveillance cameras operational and men to monitor them at all times—trustworthy men. All cargo bays are to be watched. Show every angle."

"Father," Terkeshi said. "We can't spare any men. They're all working on the em—"

"Then make them work double-shifts! I want everyone so damned busy that they have no time to plot behind my back."

"What of the woman?"

Mizuki scowled. "What of her?"

Terkeshi's eyes darted. "We'll need her to work on the emitter."

Mizuki exploded. He shot forward and slammed the boy against the wall. "You little coward! Did you help Yemon leave so you wouldn't have to kill a woman?"

"N-no, Sir." Terkeshi shook his head emphatically. "I had nothing to do with Yemon. I hate him. Why would I give him money? I didn't even know you wanted me to kill her until after he had already gone."

Mizuki pressed harder into the boy and kept his eyes locked.

"She knows part of Yemon's job." Terkeshi's Adam's apple bobbed. "We need her."

Mizuki ground his teeth. "What if she's the one who helped him?"

"How?" Terkeshi said. "She's never been out of our sight."

Mizuki's chest heaved. He held the boy there a little longer before letting him go. "She lives—for now." He stepped back and made sure he had both his and Samuru's attention. "Both of you get busy with the surveillance. Figure out how to make it work so there's no slacking on the emitter."

"Yes, Sir," they both replied.

"Find out the *Black Adder*'s next destination and find Yemon!"

42
The Hitch

3791:033:23:59. Jori hesitated outside Sensei Jeruko's personal dojo. This place that usually brought him peace, now gave him pause. The two people inside emanated anxiety. Did Terk still have to kill Lieutenant Sharkey? Or worse—Commander Hapker?

He filled his lungs and entered.

Sensei Jeruko and Terk conversed on the far end of the room, just off the edge of the training area. The rightmost shodo loomed above them. *Zanshin*, it said. *Remaining mind*, which meant remain aware even if it seemed the fight was over. Jori discerned a different meaning this time—*the fight is never over*.

His brother and the sensei quieted. They faced him with a radiating concern that struck him like the strike of a staff weapon. *Please don't let it be about Hapker*.

Jori waited at the threshold and bowed. "Permission to enter, Sensei."

Sensei Jeruko beckoned him in. "We need to talk, Jori-chan."

Jori swallowed the hard lump in his throat. He walked tentatively around the edge of the training area until he stood before them. The furrow of their brows deepened but they both seemed reluctant to speak.

"What is it?" Jori looked pointedly at Terk. "He wants you to kill Hapker, doesn't he?"

"No," Terk said in a subdued tone. "The commander's fine. The woman, too. He decided to spare her because of Yemon's absence."

Jori puffed. "Thank you for standing up for her."

Terk nodded. "I was wrong to try to kill the commander—and to call you weak—" He looked away, then down. "—and a coward. You are braver than all of us on this ship put together."

Jori's eyes burned and a warmth spread over his body. He and Terk were on the same side again. He cleared the phlegm from his throat. "So what's wrong?"

"What do you sense from your father?" Sensei Jeruko said.

"He's in a rage."

"Not just any rage." Terk gulped. "This is the worst I've ever felt from him. He's both angry and afraid."

Jori nodded. Father's emotions made sense. Yemon's supposed betrayal wasn't on the same level as Fujishin's had been, but it probably served as an unpleasant reminder.

"Did you have something to do with Yemon's disappearance?" Terk asked.

Jori flinched inwardly, but he kept a straight face. "What makes you think that?"

"The news didn't seem to surprise you."

Jori averted his eyes.

Terk exhaled noisily. "Jori, what did you do?"

Jori frowned. "He blackmailed me."

Sensei Jeruko scowled. "What do you mean he blackmailed you?"

Jori gathered his thoughts. "He found out about the prison—"

"What!" Terk's frame tightened like a compressed spring. "He knew? Chusho!"

"He told me if I didn't pay him, he'd tell Father."

Sensei Jeruko and Terk exchanged glances. "So what did you do with him?"

Jori jutted his chin and filled them in on the details. "Yemon assumed he was rich."

Terk's head tilted. "You mean he's not?"

"No. I moved the money to Captain Packwood's account. He'll take Yemon to the Kensanshi mines and use the funds to help his son walk again."

Terk groaned. "You must stop helping people. It's too risky."

"This is a good thing for everyone," Jori replied. "He'll never get a chance to tell Father anything. I considered every contingency."

Terk rubbed his brow and shook his head. "No, Jori, you didn't."

Sensei Jeruko rested his hand on Jori's shoulder. "Your father's paranoia is taking over his ability to reason. He sees enemies in every shadow."

Terk paced like a caged blackbeast. "It's bad. It's really bad. He's already unhappy with you. Who knows what he'll do next time you try to be brave?"

"And if he finds out about the prisoners…" Sensei Jeruko squeezed his shoulder.

Jori shifted his feet. "What else could I do? I couldn't let Yemon tell Father."

"You should have told me," Sensei Jeruko said.

"I didn't want to involve you. I've already asked too much."

"It's my job to protect you, boy!" Sensei Jeruko's tone was harsh, but his emotions were more distressed than angry. "I'd rather risk the consequences of ending Yemon myself than let you deal with this alone."

Jori glared. "You wouldn't take it that far. You would've told Father about the prisoners."

Sensei Jeruko stroked his chin and seemed to think on it. "I most likely would have given him a half-truth and made him believe it was the Cooperative's doing."

"Hapker would still be dead."

Terk halted and turned to Jori with crossed arms. "You could've let me know. I would have taken care of that conniving snake."

"I need to learn to handle my own problems," Jori replied. "Besides, if I wanted him to die, I would've killed him myself."

Terkeshi scoffed. "No, you wouldn't."

Jori shrugged. "He threatened me, in a way. I considered it, but I decided killing him wasn't necessary."

Terk let out a long exhale. "You and your damned sentiment. Next time let me help. We can figure it out together."

"Then maybe we can figure out how to save the commander."

Sensei Jeruko sighed. "He's already dead, Jori-chan. It's just a matter of time."

"I think there's a way to get them off—"

"Are you mad!" Sensei Jeruko's eyes widened and Jori sensed a surge of his panic. "Your father will blame someone, and that someone will be killed. Which of our men should it be?"

"We can make it look like Yemon sent information to the Cooperative."

Terk wagged his head. "Nobody will fall for that."

Jori looked down. "I don't want the commander to die."

"I get it," Terk replied, "but you are ignoring the danger. If you're caught helping them, Father will surely kill you."

"He wouldn't. He can't afford to."

Terk lifted Jori's chin so they met eye-to-eye. "Do you feel it? Do you sense how out of control his emotions are? He might not set out to kill you, but he could get too carried away one day—like he did with Montaro."

Jori's chest tightened at the memory.

Terk's throat bobbed. "Do you understand now, why I'm so worried?"

"I'm sorry, Jori-chan," Sensei Jeruko said. "You must accept the fact that you can't save these people."

Jori bit his lip. Getting the prisoners away was almost the easiest part, but Sensei Jeruko was right. Father would blame someone and that someone would suffer a terrible death. It was the only hitch in his plan.

"Matters are worse for other reasons." Terk tapped his MM. "Father has assigned me two important tasks. One, I'm organizing a crew to put up surveillance cameras in all the bays and other areas of the ship. It will be impossible to get enough men to monitor it all, but we must be extremely careful of what we do and say from now on."

Jori's head spun. Even if he avoided certain keywords to keep the microphones from focusing on him, the prisoners might talk.

"Two," Terk continued as worry etched his forehead, "Father is sending me on a mission in a few days, which means I can't be here to protect you."

"Chusho," Jori said in a hushed tone.

Terk touched Jori's shoulder. "I'll find a way out of it. I won't let anything happen to you."

Jori's blood flowed again from the warmth of Terk's promise. That he would give up an opportunity to prove himself in a mission meant a lot. At the same time, Jori's mind traced all the possible consequences of their actions to dead ends.

43
Space Station

3791:034:00:24. The cacophony of the Chevert space station assaulted Silas Arden's ears like an out of tune orchestra. The energy of all the shopkeepers, shoppers, and travelers created a never-ending jolt of electricity that ached his bones. One would think he enjoyed group gatherings with his talent for social mediation. He preferred the intimacy of a negotiation delegation, though, to the chaos that reigned here.

The throng threatened to engulf him and his team as they headed to the station headquarters, Director Jeyana Sengupta most of all. Her diminutive figure stuck to his side like a magnet as passers-by pushed and elbowed.

Four PG-Force officers led by Major Esekielu followed in Arden's wake. Not even the major's volcanic bearing kept people from bumping into him. Now and then, the major barked a threat or shoved someone out of the way. Arden rarely condoned such behavior, but the press of so many made it necessary—and the major was here for his protection, after all.

"My baton is gone!" Major Esekielu said, the heat of his dragon breath searing the back of Arden's neck.

Arden didn't bother feigning pity. He'd tried to warn him, but the major assumed he was untouchable.

Once again, he wished he had Major Bracht here. He generally agreed that those involved in close-combat fighting be put on temporary leave, but not this time. Too much was at stake.

The press of people thinned as they reached the security checkpoint. A row of heavily armed guards overwhelmed them instead. They bristled with every sort of hand-held weapon, from sheathed knives holstered on their thigh to pistols in their shoulder holsters to the giant plasma rifles carried in their arms.

These guards in their identical steel-grey armor were the opposite of the mismatched rabble. The individuality of their facial features was evident, but they all shared the same no-nonsense expression that even Major Esekielu couldn't pull off.

Arden beelined to the checkpoint where a tall, lean man wearing a smartly tailored outfit stopped him. The color of the man's suit made him look like a phosphorescent blade of straw and triggered an ache in Arden's eyes.

The phosphorescent man bowed before Sengupta. "Greetings, Jeyana Sengupta. Commander Jax sent me to escort you inside."

She dipped her head and her dark bushy hair flowed forward. "Thank you, Sir."

The man clasped his hands in front of him. "I can only take two of you. Absolutely no weapons."

"We have none," Arden said. Firearms and phasers had already been checked at the main gate, and he wasn't one to carry a weapon anyway.

The major put himself on Arden's other side. "Wait, Sir. I must go with you."

"Only two people," the phosphorescent man replied.

"I will not leave my charges to your—" Major Esekielu's mouth twisted. "—boss."

The phosphorescent man wrinkled his nose as he looked the major up and down. Arden groaned inwardly. "Major, step back in line. I will speak to this gentleman."

Major Esekielu pressed his lips together but moved behind him.

As much as Arden didn't like Major Esekielu, he couldn't take any more chances than he had to with Commander Jax's reputation. He faced the phosphorescent man and put on an agreeable expression. "I understand your caution, sir. I will certainly respect the commander's wishes. However, my superior asked this man to safeguard me. Would you ask your commander, please, if he could make an exception for three?"

"It would be greatly appreciated," Sengupta added.

The phosphorescent man bowed, then touched the comm behind his ear. As he spoke to the recipient on the other side, Arden glanced over his shoulder at Major Esekielu. "Have you ever heard the expression that you can catch more flies with honey than with vinegar, Major?"

The major pressed his lips together until they were white.

Arden turned back to the phosphorescent man, who made a sharp nod. "No more than three people so long as you aren't armed."

"Thank you," Arden replied. Then to the major, "It's a good thing you lost your baton."

Major Esekielu's scowl deepened.

They walked through the hulking scanner. Then the no-nonsense guards searched them. They didn't touch them, but one came uncomfortably close to certain places with his security wand.

The phosphorescent man led Arden with Sengupta and Major Esekielu down a series of bland hallways lined with closed steel doors and drab open offices. The next turn brought them to a colorful area. A couch and several plush chairs indicated it was probably a waiting room. It would have been welcoming if the variegated design was less jarring.

From there, the phosphorescent man took them down a visually dizzying hall. One gaudy piece of hanging art followed another in no particular order of subject or style. It was like walking down a vomit-lined tunnel while drunk on vodka.

The hall led to a great set of doors painted a blaring red. This Commander Jax was either colorblind or had an affinity for vibrant colors.

The phosphorescent man pressed a button on the comm box, and the entrance slid open. An acrid smell tweaked Arden's nostrils. He suppressed a cough as he entered the room. Major Esekielu didn't seem to have his courtesy, though. He hacked and wrinkled his nose with obvious distaste.

Arden faced the source of the odor. A cylindrical-shaped brown thing that reminded him of a turd jutted from the mouth of a massive man. Smoke wafted from the cigar and merged with the haze of the room.

Arden studied the man sitting behind a screen-cluttered desk. He didn't so much sit in the chair as he oozed. His thinning hair was scraped back and laid slick to his round head. Small eyes sank into his skull like two fingerholes of a heavy ten-pin ball.

The man puffed his cigar from an undersized mouth. He seemed to regard Arden with a critical eye, then his gaze darted to the woman at Arden's side. His rotund cheeks bubbled as a thin smile cracked open. "Jeyana!" He put down his cigar and stuck out his meaty hand.

Director Jeyana Sengupta reached out. "Commander Jax," she replied pleasantly, not seeming to mind her hand being swallowed in his grasp. "It's so good seeing you again. I notice you've done more decorating." She gestured at a shelf crammed with figurines.

Commander Jax regurgitated her hand and beamed. "I had to move the viewscreen up there to get that shelf in."

Arden glanced up. The screen above was the largest of many that took up the wall and desk space in this room. Most showed scenes likely streamed from surveillance cameras. No doubt the cameras were enhanced with directional long-range microphones. It would explain why Commander Jax was known as a collector and disseminator of information, as Sengupta put it.

"This one is interesting." She leaned in toward a tall glass statue in the middle of the shelf.

Jax took another puff of his cigar. "That one's from Etena. I confiscated it from a dirty dealer."

Sengupta straightened. "Isn't Etena a myth?"

Jax chuckled. "Not Etena the planet. It's a city on Togala. Of course, I don't tell most people that part. I like them to think my reach goes beyond their imaginations."

"Ah," she said. "You are very clever."

Jax took another puff and tilted his head up in a smug expression. "I'm clever enough to know you're here about the perantium emitter."

"Even Swenson could figure that out." Sengupta smirked.

Jax barked a laugh.

Sengupta gestured to Arden. "This is Captain Arden of the *Odyssey*. We're not just here about the emitter. The emperor has our people as well."

Jax bobbed his head up and down, making his chin wobble. "It's a pleasure, Captain. You have quite the reputation."

Arden dipped his head. "The pleasure is mine, Commander Jax. You have quite the reputation yourself." He let his eyes fall on a small stone box that would have been innocuous to a casual observer. "I see you have a relic of Sanzi."

"You have a good eye." Jax picked it up. "Few know these markings as Sanzi-script."

"I visited their homeworld when two of their world leaders threatened a civil war."

The man leaned back and lazily puffed his cigar. "Ever the accomplished negotiator. Not skilled enough to deal with the Dragon Emperor, I imagine."

Arden clasped his hands behind him and put on what he hoped was an air of confidence. "I might if I had information on where to find him."

"Acht." Jack flicked his hand. "No one knows that. Not even me." He held his cigar in the side of his mouth and talked around it. "Word is someone the emperor trusted betrayed him. He's been holding his cards close ever since."

Arden's shoulder fell. He glanced at Sengupta, a subtle signal that she could take over.

She regarded Jax with mock disbelief. "Surely you know something that can help us. A way to contact him, perhaps? We are prepared to pay for their return."

"Plus a finder's fee," Arden added.

Jax shook his head. "Not this time, Jeyana. Despite how much it galls me to say it, I got nothing."

Major Esekielu stepped forward. "What about information on the emperor's military might?"

"You probably know what I know, as far as the big picture is concerned." Jax took another puff of the turd-like cigar. "The emperor stole the emitter because he wants to turn it into a weapon. His initial plan was to put Lord Enomoto securely under his thumb, then retake the Pentam system. However, the betrayal of his lifelong friend and one of his Five Talons has changed his plans somewhat, considering all the new rebellions."

"Does he have the means to convert the emitter into a weapon?" Arden asked.

Jax shook his head. "I doubt it. He's been calling for scientists and engineers—offering to pay them a fine sum—but I don't see how anyone would be dumb enough to take him up on it. And slave traders almost never come across those academic types."

Arden deflated. His chief engineer, Simmonds, was one of the prisoners. Doctor Canthidius likely was as well. Both could be forced to do the emperor's bidding.

"Sorry I can't help you." Jax's mouth turned down into what seemed to be genuine regret. "You came all this way for nothing, Jeyana."

"Please." Arden put his hands together as though in prayer. "There must be something you can do? Get the whereabouts of the emperor's ship, get us in contact with the princes, tell—"

Jax frowned. "Contact the princes? How would that even make sense?"

Arden glanced at Sengupta. Did he say too much? She knew this man better.

Sengupta's eyebrows lifted and she tilted her head toward Jax as though to say *go ahead*.

Arden cleared his throat. "Surely you've heard they were on our ship for a short time."

Jax choked. "I *had* heard, but I was sure it was a bunch of dogshit. So it's true then? You had those little vipers on your ship."

Arden nodded. "It wasn't as bad as I'm sure the rumors claim. Though we didn't exactly become friends, I believe if I can reach them, they may help."

Commander Jax rolled his head back and forth. "I might have a contact on the ship, but it's unlikely that I'd get a hold of the princes. It will snow on Saurus before they bother replying."

"Sir!" Major Esekielu's dark eyes glared at Arden. "The Admiral's orders were to get information on the emperor's military might and plans. Not to talk to the princes."

"I gave you all I got, son," Jax said harshly. He looked to Sengupta. "Who's this joker?"

"Major," Arden replied in an amiable tone. "Why don't you step outside. It's obvious you're not needed here."

The major's expression tightened, and his face turned nearly the color of Jax's office door. A smile lurked behind Arden's firm air. He didn't want to bring this man along to begin with and Sengupta's relation with Jax seemed even more amicable than she had let on.

Major Esekielu glanced at Jax and back at Arden. His lips pressed into a thin line. He jerked his head down in apparent assent, then turned on his heel and marched out.

Arden reverted to his friendly demeanor and faced Jax.

The big man raised an eyebrow. "That one's got something stuck up his ass, doesn't he?"

Arden almost laughed. "He has his uses."

"Now we can discuss the emperor without interference," Sengupta said. "We desperately need your help. Saving our people is of paramount importance."

Jax nodded. "Anything for you, Jeyana."

Arden's brows rose. Whatever was between Sengupta and the commander, it was obviously something more than just the exchange of information. It couldn't be romance. The two of them were friendly, but Arden saw nothing that indicated intimacy.

"If I can reach my informant, I will ask about your people," he tallied his chubby fingers, "get an update on the emperor's plans to please your stick-implanted guard, and contact the princes. Might be I have better luck with the first two than the last."

Arden bowed. "I would greatly appreciate anything you could do. I'm prepared to compensate you for your trouble."

Jax waved his beefy hand. "I usually have no problem taking money from the Cooperative, but I owe this to you, Jeyana."

Sengupta put her palm over her heart and blushed. "Thank you, Jax. My gratitude is boundless."

"Acht." Jax's rotund cheeks glowed. "Think nothing of it." He cleared his throat and leaned back. "It may be a while, so take advantage of the space station's amenities. I'll be in touch."

Arden bowed. "You have my thanks, Commander."

Jax dipped his head. Sengupta gave her his hand again, and he swallowed it in both of his.

They took their leave. Arden could have floated his way out. The fate of his crew remained uncertain, but at least things moved forward.

Major Esekielu fell in behind them without a word, though Arden was sure the man would complain later.

They cleared the commander's base. "I was aware of your connection to the commander of this station," Arden said to Sengupta. "I didn't know you were on such good terms or that he owed you so much."

She shrugged. "I discovered his sister had gotten herself in deep trouble. I reported it to the PG-Force and informed Jax. Both these things led to her rescue."

Arden put his hand on her shoulder. "You're a generous person, Jeyana."

Sengupta flushed. "Thank you, Sir."

What had he done to deserve such a great crew? She had always been invaluable, but this was above and beyond. Thanks to her, he had a chance to get back his other irreplaceable crew members.

44
Caught in the Act

3791:034:16:43. Kenji Mizuki pinched his lip. The live feed displayed on his deskview screen seemed ordinary enough. The *Mako* just docked and Jori spoke to the captain about a much-needed part. So far, nothing roused his suspicion.

A shokukin ambled in. His odd walk triggered Mizuki's memory. It was that idiot-man engineer.

The captain's eyes fell on the idiot and his face broke into a grin. "Benjiro!" he said, stepping around Jori to embrace him. "So good to see you, boy-o. How've you been?"

Mizuki leaned closer to the video. It was one thing for the captain to recognize a dockworker, but the familiarity with this idiot made his hair stand on end. He studied Jori. The boy didn't seem the least bit surprised with the captain's actions.

Mizuki pressed the contact button on his screen. Jori responded by touching his comm. "Yes, Sir," he said as his eyes fell on the security camera.

"How do those two know one another?"

"Yemon usually brings Benjiro to look over the miscellaneous goods these cargo men collect."

Mizuki relaxed and listened in as Jori and the captain discussed some business. Afterward, Jori inspected the unloaded freight while the captain yelled at the crewmen to be careful as they brought out more. All normal.

The captain put his arm around Benjiro and steered him toward the ship. "Come with me, boy-o. Let's see if I have anything else for you."

Mizuki focused the camera on them and contacted Jori again. "Where is he taking that man?"

Jori frowned. "It's alright, Father. He's showing Benjiro his store of miscellaneous parts so he can pick out what we need."

"Why doesn't the idiot just tell them?"

"He doesn't know how. Benjiro calls everything a thingamabob or thingy."

Mizuki slapped his forehead. "That's the stupidest thing I've ever heard."

"Benjiro isn't very smart in many ways, Sir, but he knows mechanics and engineering."

Mizuki growled. Again, he accepted the answer, but followed the captain and Benjiro with the microphone anyway.

"So what are you up to nowadays?" the captain asked.

Mizuki's hair stood on end.

"Fixing thingamabob."

"Thingamabob, huh? What does it do?"

"Shoots far."

"What does it shoot?"

"Nezumi!" Mizuki called through another channel. "Get to the docking bay and arrest the captain and our idiot worker."

He pointed the camera back at Jori. The boy seemed oblivious. Was it real or a ruse? He reactivated the comm link. "Jori, get your ass to my interrogation room."

He slammed the flat of his hand on his desk. The sting didn't hurt so much as it ignited his anger. He should've known spies would find their way onto his ship. He was sure he'd curtailed unauthorized transmissions, but security protocol couldn't have picked this up. How long had it been going on? How long had that idiot-man been blubbering his secrets?

Was the man truly an idiot or was he acting? *Chusho!* He should know these things. His people should have known. Hell, so should Jori. The boy worked with him more than anyone, and wasn't it Jori who had once convinced Mizuki not to kill him?

He thought back to that day. The idiot-man had bumped into him. He didn't even bother apologizing. He just kept mumbling to himself and moved on.

It had incensed Mizuki that someone so stupid would survive on his ship. He ordered the man killed, but Jori stepped in. He had assumed the boy's weak-mindedness spurred him, but then Yemon confirmed his claim. Were both Yemon and Jori in on it?

Chusho! How did he miss this?

45
The Dog

3791:034:17:02. Hanna Sharkey pressed her hand against Corporal Harley's chest. "No. Don't."

The cords of Harley's neck jutted out and the tension in his body turned harder than steel. He clutched a heavy tool while his eyes smoldered with murder as he challenged Usagi.

Sharkey pinched his upper arm, hoping to divert his attention. "He's not worth it, Corporal. Stand down. That's an order."

Harley refused. Usagi cackled, making her skin crawl. Once again, he had snuck up on her and thrust his bulge at her like a rabbit. She'd let out a yelp and scrambled out of his range. He'd had gotten his cheap thrill. If Harley hadn't rushed to her rescue, he might have moved on.

"Leave her be, you gutless bastard." Harley showed his teeth.

"Come on. Let's go, pretty boy." Usagi grinned, exposing the gap in his mouth, and beckoned with a wave.

Harley took a step and Sharkey pressed harder against him. "Stop!"

"What in the hell is going on here!"

Sharkey's knees almost buckled at the relief of the elder prince's arrival. Harley paused. He shifted the tool in his hand. "Don't," she said, suspecting Harley's temper burned hot enough to strike Terkeshi. "He's helping me, so stand down."

Harley's blazing eyes fell to hers.

She returned it. "You have your orders, Corporal."

"I'm just having a little fun, my Lord," Usagi replied to the prince.

Terkeshi roared. "Damn it, Usagi! I told you to let them work."

"She's only a woman."

"A woman who's a hell of a lot smarter than you. Quit letting your dick interfere with your job or I'll cut the cursed thing off."

Harley stepped back and loosened his grip. The tightness in Sharkey's shoulders lessened. She stayed in front of the corporal but glanced over her shoulder to make sure the prince had the situation handled.

Terkeshi jabbed his finger at the gap-toothed senshi.

Usagi put his hands up. "If you wanted the woman for yourself—"

Terkeshi's fist smashed into Usagi's face with a satisfying crunch. Blood spurted from the man's nose. He cried out, then pinched his nose to stem the flow. He glared with a heat that might have made most men back down, but not Terkeshi. The prince leaned in and growled. "I mean it, Usagi."

The two held like statues until Usagi finally looked away. The knot in Terkeshi's jaw vanished but he maintained a hard stance. Usagi bowed, then left.

Terkeshi faced Harley. His black glare dared the officer to try something. The corporal tensed. His hand still gripped the tool and his dark hooded eyes ignited.

"Put it down," the prince said. "You aren't helping her this way."

Sharkey placed her hand back on Harley's chest. "It's okay now."

Several tense moments passed as Terkeshi and Harley stared one another down. The guards in the room closed in, some with grim expressions and others with interest.

Sharkey held her breath. Harley twitched and her heart jumped. He eased and loosened his grip on the tool but didn't let go.

*****

3791:034:17:17. Terkeshi's glare drilled into the Cooperative corporal. Something about the man made him want to pound his face in. It wasn't anything he'd done. It wasn't even what he threatened to do now.

His essence grated on Terk's senses. The core of it was unremarkable. The man's confidence bordered on cockiness but not arrogance. He didn't carry lust like Usagi or the cruelty of Senshi Kelar—but hatred bloated whenever his gaze fell on Terk.

The man refused to back down. He'd get himself killed if he didn't smarten up and let this go. Terk hadn't been the one to harass the lieutenant. Hell, he just stood up for her. The least the prisoner should do was show a little gratitude.

A beep in his comm broke his concentration and his eye-contact with Harley. "Terkeshi here."

"Boy," Father said. "Get Amarante."

Terk's heart thumped. He stretched out his sensing ability and found Father's emotions in another dark maelstrom. *Where's Jori?* His senses located his brother on the other side of the ship, most likely in the cargo bay. Jori radiated curiosity and nervousness, but they lacked the force to trigger Terk's concern.

"Bring her to the interrogation room," Father added.

Terk tensed. He wanted to ask why but didn't dare with his father's mood. "Yes, Sir. I'll take care of it now."

He finished up with the prisoners and hurried to the harem.

By the time he arrived, he sensed Jori had left the cargo bay and headed in the general direction of the command section. His curiosity had ballooned to an unsettling state of anxiety.

What the hell had happened?

Terk waited outside the doors for Mother. Outwardly, he kept calm and composed. He stood in the at-ease stance and forced his jitters to stay confined to his gut. If Tokagei hadn't been one of his personal guards today, he would have given in to the urge to pace.

His mother emerged. Her forehead wrinkled and he sensed her worry, but she didn't speak. She lay her arm on his and he led her away, toward the unknown. His two guards followed at a respectful distance.

"Is everything alright?" she whispered.

"I don't know," Terk replied.

"Your father has some unfamiliar people with him, but his emotions are too chaotic for me to tell what's wrong."

"He thinks everyone is out to get him. You can't identify those with him either, then?"

She shook her head.

He sensed her uncertainty. "That's not entirely true."

She smiled. "It's nothing, really. One person seems familiar, but only because he is like someone I used to know."

"He's not that person?"

"I don't see how." She spoke truly but radiated doubt.

Terk brushed the feeling aside. "What do you feel from Jori?"

"Worry. Concern." She closed her eyes and a distinctive V formed between her brows. "He's troubled but not deeply—not in a way that makes him afraid."

Terk huffed through his nose. "He could stand at the edge of an erupting volcano and still not be afraid."

She patted his arm. "Maybe it's nothing."

They reached the conveyor. As Terk led her in, an acute pang bombarded his senses. His blood turned hot. *I told that dog to leave her alone!*

"Take her," he said to Tokagei, "and tell my father I'm on my way to stop something going on with the prisoners. Washi, with me."

Terk rushed off. As the heat from the exertion rose, so did the hellfire in his chest.

46
Madness

3791:034:17:35. Jori stood at stiff attention despite his senses flooding with an array of dire emotions. The captain of the *Mako* radiated fright. In contrast to his father's wrath, the captain might as well fly against the buffeting winds of Kazewaki.

Benjiro emitted a nervous energy as he rocked back and forth in the corner. Somewhere on the ship, Terk spewed outrage, though his seemed more targeted than Father's. His mother exuded concern as she headed this way.

Jori felt all these things swirling together with his own confused emotions as Nezumi secured the captain into the interrogation chair. A hunger rose within the man, undoubtedly from the prospect of inflicting torture.

Jori eyed the metal chair with misgiving. How often had he sensed someone being tormented in it? How many times had Father forced him to watch? Too many, and it triggered a rumbling pang in his stomach.

He glanced at Michio. The man gestured with his fist, reminding Jori to be strong. With a deep inhale, he put on a wooden mask and firmed his stance.

"What's wrong?" the *Mako* captain asked. His eyeballs protruded from his narrow head. "What is it you think I've done?"

Nezumi secured the last clamp. "He's ready, Sire."

Father stepped forward and aimed his finger at Benjiro. "Why were you talking to that man?"

The captain struggled against the manacles. "I-I was just having a chat with—"

"You were asking him about my affairs!"

"N-no." The captain wagged his head back and forth.

Jori sensed his lie and his heart stopped.

"Is he telling the truth, boy?"

He opened his mouth to answer when Tokagei entered with Mother.

"Where's Terkeshi?" Father's eyes flared.

"He says the prisoners are making trouble and went to take care of it."

Jori aimed his ability toward the docking bay and got slammed with a jumbled whirl of heightened emotions. Further scrutiny revealed Lieutenant Sharkey's screaming terror coupled with Usagi's lust. The blood in Jori's head drained and a chill dumped over him.

A sensation from his mother yanked him back here. Her jaw slackened as she gaped at Benjiro. "Makoto?"

The simple man bit his fist and whimpered. "Benjiro now. Benjiro now," he said as he rocked.

"You know him?" Incredulity stabbed through Father's rage.

Mother's eyes snapped to his. "I-I thought I did, but no."

Jori flinched at her lie and a knot choked his throat. What the hell was this about? How did she know Benjiro? He glanced back and forth between them and realization struck him like a flash of lightning. Makoto was Mother's brother, but his name was Benjiro now. Could it be?

Father's suspicion swelled into a resurrected monster.

"You lie, woman." Father's eyes turned harried. The muscle over his right eye twitched and his nostrils flared. His posture teetered like a boulder on the edge of a cliff. "I will give you one more chance to tell me the truth."

Mother's panic fluttered. She darted her glance at Benjiro.

"Out with it, woman!" Father's fist flew out and struck her in the jaw.

Jori flinched. His mother yelped. Then she burst into a sob. "That's my younger brother. He's not supposed to be here. He should be at home, safe."

"What!" Father's face purpled. "Lord Enomoto sent someone to spy on me! You knew all along, didn't you?"

"No!" She covered her head as struck her again.

"Chusho! I should have known. You traitor! You fucking traitor!"

Jori adjusted his stance to take a step but decided against it. He should keep to their pact. However, Father's madness lashed out like the claws of blackbeast kept in its cage for too long. He shot Michio a worried look. The man reflected his concern as he depressed his comm, likely contacting Sensei Jeruko. No one handled Father's temper better.

Bile rose in Jori's throat. This was his fault. If he hadn't stirred up his father's suspicion, he never would have put the surveillance cameras up. The captain never would've been caught, Benjiro would be happily working on the emitter rather than whimpering in the corner, and his mother would be safe in her room.

He had to fix this, but how? He tried to think through the surrounding tempest. His heart bounded as the intensity of Father's rage spiraled out of control while Mother's terror doubled.

Mother let out a shriek and with it came a burst of her desperation. "Enough!"

Father froze mid-strike. He straightened and dropped his fist. His body slackened. Confusion emanated from him as he looked from her to his blood-splattered hand, then to Jori and the others in the room.

Jori turned to Mother. Her eyes rounded and her chin fell. She must have used her power on him, though probably unintentionally.

The room stilled. Even Benjiro was quiet. Jori held his breath as the tide rolled into a tsunami. Mother had never done that before.

A shadow crossed his father's face. Jori's heart leapt to his throat.

"How! Dare! You!"

The explosion of his fury sent Jori reeling. What should he do? He had to stop this somehow. Father was lost in a storm. Muscles corded his neck. His fists flew like a tornado as he spewed curses.

A fire of adrenaline fueled Jori's body. "No! Leave her alone!"

He rammed into his father and fell back. Father continued expending his rage, seemingly unfazed by the attempted interruption.

Jori pushed himself up and shoved between them.

"Move, boy!"

"No!"

Father roared and Jori found himself embroiled in the squall.

47
The Pain of Death

3791:034:17:36. Terkeshi entered the docking bay to find it quaking on the verge of a savage explosion. The Cooperative prisoners struggled futilely against the senshi. Two men pinned the commander's arms behind his back and pressed him to the floor. His face ignited as he roared.

Corporal Harley broke free. "Get off me, you sick bast—" His curse cut short by a blow to the gut. A swarm of warriors tackled him.

Terk took in the scene for only a moment before realizing Usagi and the woman weren't here. He followed the thread of the lieutenant's terror until her screams rang out from a supply room.

He barged in to find Usagi with all his weight pressed on her. She struggled but couldn't escape from under him. He held her wrists with one hand and grabbed at her clothes with the other.

She broke one arm free and struck him. "Get off me, you pig!"

Usagi laughed.

Terk snatched a chunk of his hair and jerked. "You think you can go behind my back, you filthy dog!"

Usagi's eyes bulged. He pushed himself off her and twisted from Terk's clutches, losing a clump of hair. "I can explain, my Lord," he said with his arms up in surrender.

Terk's rage fogged his vision. His muscles burned and quivered like an engine roaring to life. He faced the man with bared teeth. "I've had it with you, Usagi." His words ripped through his throat. "You have made your last mistake." He pulled his knife from the sheath at his side and wrapped his fingers around the hilt in a fighting grip.

Usagi let out a nervous laugh. "My shift was over, and they were done for the day."

Terk barely heard him through his ragged breaths. His muscles strained as he stalked over to his prey with deadly purpose.

Usagi stepped back. "My Lord. I'm sorry. I can explain."

When Terkeshi closed in, the man shifted from a defensive stance to an offensive one. Terk lashed out, first low, then high. Usagi blocked with his arms and Terk's knife sliced into them. With a twist and a swift motion, he stabbed at the man's side. Usagi brought his elbow inward, attempting to block. The blade slid across bone and into the hard muscle surrounding his gut.

Terk wielded his knife in rapid cuts and jabs. Each of Usagi's blocks earned him a slice or puncture. Terk's fury moved him like a tempest. Sensei Jeruko had always said he shouldn't fight angry, but his anger made him unpredictable.

He feigned to the left. Usagi parried. Terk cut to the right, stepped around, and jabbed him between his ribs.

The man grunted and flagged. Terk didn't let up. He angled his weapon and stabbed upward. Usagi retreated a step. Terk followed him in and carried the momentum of his thrust under the rib cage and up into the heart.

Usagi gasped and his eyes widened. Terk twisted the blade for good measure, then stepped back. Blood dripped from his fist down to the tip of his knife. Usagi choked and slid to the floor.

Terk reeled as the sensation of Usagi's imminent death flooded his head. The man's lifeforce struggled ferociously as an overwhelming dread pulled it into oblivion. The impact gripped Terk's awareness to a standstill.

Usagi was dead. The pain of his death left a ghosted feeling that kept Terk paralyzed. He knelt with trembling limbs. Sweat dripped from his brow. The vacancy of the man's lifeforce filled with his own surge of nausea.

He retched. Bile burned his throat. His stomach cramped into a twisted knot. He heaved until nothing was left but an unsettling hollow in his gut. He sat on his heels and gulped for air.

His breathing evened out and his head cleared. The shaking in his body subsided. He wiped the vomitus from his mouth, then the bloody knife on Usagi's clothes.

The sight of the lifeless form both lightened and weighed on him. This wasn't his first time killing, but he'd never taken a life without the crutch of his father's orders.

Still, his actions were justified. Usagi didn't deserve to live. All those young girls and women he'd taken over the years finally had their justice.

Terk released a long exhale as the last remnants of his deed fled to the back of his mind. The reality around him came into focus. Lieutenant Sharkey sat in the corner with her knees pulled to her chest. Her eyes gaped and her body shook.

Terk opened his senses and felt both her relief and uncertainty. He stood. The weakness of his legs threatened to buckle, but he willed strength into them.

He held out his bloodless hand. "It's over."

She took it ever so slowly. Her icy fingers trembled. "Thank you."

Terk pulled her up and led her out. Washi met him just outside the room. He dipped his head and emitted a sense of approval.

The situation in the docking bay remained as he'd left it, with the commander pinned down and the other prisoners struggling. He and Lieutenant Sharkey stepped into their midst and it all stilled. "Let them go," he told the guards.

The senshi glanced at one another but otherwise didn't move. Washi put himself at Terk's side. "You heard what Prince Mizuki said!"

Terk mimicked his father's glower to emphasize his authority. The senshi eyed him, some probably noting the blood dripping from his hand, and released the Cooperative prisoners.

Harley jerked away and straightened. His brows hooded over his dark eyes and Terk sensed his harboring resentment. The fight in him seemed to dissipate, though, when his gaze fell on Lieutenant Sharkey.

Terk thumbed behind his shoulder. "Kelar. Pachin. Go glean up that mess and throw the body out into space."

A wave of uneasiness from the senshi rolled into Terk's senses. He pulled his shoulders back. The blood on his hands had earned him his proper place. Maybe now the men would show him respect. Maybe now Father would take him seriously.

His limbs prickled as the adrenaline wore off. He left the bay and headed to the interrogation room. The fog in his head lifted and darker sensations crept in. He wrestled with the tendrils of emotion until they snapped into coherence.

His heart froze. Something far worse than Usagi's death assaulted him.

"No!" Terk stormed down the hall.

"What is it, my Lord?"

Washi's voice warbled through the flood of emotions flogging Terk's brain. He raced on, pushing people aside.

He reached the conveyor just before the doors closed. "Get out," he said to the two men inside. They must have seen the urgency on his face because they exited with haste as Terk and Washi pushed their way in. The conveyor, however, didn't move as fast as he would like.

Terk pumped his fists. Washi spoke again, but the sound was nothing more than a gnat in his ears. He tried to focus, but the terror spewing from Jori and Mother blinded him.

The conveyor jerked to a halt and opened. Terk sprinted down the corridor with Washi at his heels.

Michio met them partway and frantically waved them over to the interrogation room. "Your father's gone mad. He has a knife."

Terk skidded to a halt at the entrance.

Father's face burned like a surge of magma. Sensei Jeruko's bearing held as steadfast as a mountain while he held up his hands in submission. Mother lay lifeless on the floor. Jori hovered over her protectively. Blood oozed from his nose as a torrent of fear enveloped him.

Father clutched his knife like it was a live thing struggling to break free. "She used her power on me!"

Terk's heart skipped a beat. She had never dared that before. What the hell had Father done to make her do it now?

"Yes, Sire." Sensei Jeruko's calmness acted as a wave cancelling device. "It's a good thing you've practiced against it since you broke her hold so easily."

Father's warped expression faltered. "She must die!"

"If you must, your Eminence, but it would be a shame to lose someone with her ability."

"She betrayed me. Did you know that is her brother?"

Terk gaped at the man his father indicated. *What in the hell is going on here?*

A sensation of surprise lit within Sensei Jeruko as well, but it didn't show on his face. "You've located a spy. This is wonderful news."

Father growled "Wonderful? What is the matter with you, man? This is a disaster. He's been spilling my secrets all this time. No wonder Lord Enomoto has been able to block my every move."

"You can use him." Sensei Jeruko's gesture at Benjiro was as sedated as his tone. "You can feed him false information and put Lord Enomoto on the wrong trajectory."

The storm of Father's emotions settled. "She still deserves to die."

"How can she suffer from her mistake if you kill her, Sire?"

Terkeshi gulped as Father considered it.

"Sire," Nezumi interrupted. "I'll make the arrangements for her torture."

Terk shoved the rest of the way into the room. "The hell you will."

Father's ire threatened to reignite.

Sensei Jeruko blocked Terk with his arm. "I have a better idea, Sire. Exile her."

Father glowered at Terk with the fury of a blackbeast, but he seemed to consider it. "Yes, exile. That way her sentiment will no longer be the ruin of my incompetent sons."

Terk embraced the insult for it meant she'd be safe.

Father's wrist snapped with the flick of his hand. "Get rid of her, Jeruko. Send her far away. If I see that bitch's face one more time, I'll kill her. Nezumi, you handle this pirate."

Nezumi's mouth curled in an oily smirk. Father marched out with his knife still in hand. Terk exhaled and his shoulders fell.

Sensei Jeruko knelt beside Jori and eased him away from Mother.

Jori's brow wrinkled. "No."

"It must be done, Jori-chan. She will be alright, I promise."

Terk placed his hand on Jori's shoulder. "She'll be safer away from here… And from him."

Tears streaked down Jori's cheeks. He held her hand and squeezed. "Where will she go?"

"I know a good place," Sensei Jeruko replied. "Trust me."

Jori nodded. He rose, then folded. Terk caught him under the arm and pulled him up. His little brother struggled to regain his feet, but his eyes rolled back. Terk gathered him up while Sensei Jeruko did the same with Mother.

Terk swallowed the lump in his throat. Both lifeforces were strong. Their brush with death had been too close, though.

The journey to the infirmary passed in a blur. Terkeshi's thoughts flitted about. He'd long since accepted his separation from Mother but seeing her like this threatened to choke him. Father had nearly snapped. If Sensei Jeruko hadn't been there, she'd be dead. Jori, too.

A chill dropped over him and stabbed down his spine. "He was going to kill them both, wasn't he?" he asked Sensei Jeruko.

The man betrayed nothing on his face but the distress emanating from him answered the question.

They exited the conveyor and Terena and others met them with two wheeled beds. Terk lay Jori on one. Mother's head hung lifelessly as Sensei Jeruko eased her onto the other. They looked no worse than any other time Father punished them, yet a pain spiked through Terk's heart.

Terena ran a scanner over them as the others pushed the beds through the lobby.

Someone sucked in a breath. "What happened?"

Terk stopped short at the sight of Washi with Lieutenant Sharkey. She had blood on her face from what Usagi had done to her but didn't look to have any major injuries.

"Why is she here?" he said.

Michio bowed. "I noted some senshi resented her for Usagi's death. Since she's injured, I brought her here so she can be refreshed for the next shift."

Terk appreciated his foresight ground his teeth at her special treatment. He threw her a menacing glower. Instead of shrinking back, her brow furrowed deeper. "Is Jori alright? Who's the woman?"

"My mother." His voice came out in a croak.

Sharkey put her hand to her mouth. "Oh my. Oh my goodness, I'm so sorry. I didn't know you had a... You never talked about her."

Terk's anger surged. "Why should I tell you about her? You're the reason she and Jori have been hurt." His fists tightened. "I should have been there to protect them, but I was protecting you instead."

Sharkey looked down at her feet then glanced up with wet eyes. "I'm sorry. Will they be okay?"

"They'd better be." Terk's stomach knotted again. This wasn't the lieutenant's fault. Father did this.

Washi led Sharkey to the small exam rooms in the back. Terk remained and stared at nothing as his inner turmoil churned like the sea.

Sensei Jeruko took him by the elbow. "Have a seat, Terke-chan."

Terk sat. He leaned his elbows to his knees and cradled his head. This was Father's doing—every single bit of it. The man was a menace. He must be stopped.

Terk was no match for Father, though. He'd be a fool to try overthrowing him. Even if he succeeded, he was too young and too inexperienced.

Despite the churning desire to end the man, cool logic won out. If he couldn't stop Father, he should at least keep Mother and Jori safe.

"Where will you take her?"

Sensei Jeruko leaned back. "The best place I know of is with my wife."

Terk frowned. "Wife?" Of course Washi and Michio came from some woman but no one ever spoke of her.

"Well, estranged wife, but I've made arrangements for her comfort. Your mother will be safe there."

"Can Jori go with her?"

Sensei Jeruko hung his head. "No. I'm afraid not."

"He can't stay here."

Sensei Jeruko put his hand on Terk's forearm. "I'd love nothing more than to see your brother safe with her, but your father would never allow it. He wants to quash your brother's sentiment, remember?"

"I just saw you talk him down from murdering them. You have a lot of sway with him."

"Not as much as you think."

Terk deflated. "What if we snuck him on the transport ship?"

"The first thing your Father will do is look for him with her. It would put them both in danger again."

Terk swallowed. There had to be something he could do to help Jori. Father might not have killed him this time, but his temper ticked like a time bomb.

Exile. It could work for Jori too, just maybe not with Mother. Terk stroked his chin and worked out a plan.

48
Dreamfog

3791:034:23:41. The subdued lights of the healing bed roused Jori's subconscious. Memories mingled with nightmares under the veil of dreamfog.

Jori and Hapker played wall ball in the gymnasium on the *Odyssey*. Hapker clapped Jori on the shoulder and grinned. Bodies surrounded them, yet still they enjoyed themselves. Lieutenant Sharkey slumped against the wall with a lifeless gaze. Harley rested in a pool of gore. Other Cooperative prisoners sprawled on the floor with various gouging wounds. Jori turned back to Hapker. He lay dead now too. His neck spewed blood from a gaping wound. Jori ran.

Somehow, he ended up in Mother's room. He fell into her embrace and they both laughed as she tickled him. He was a little boy again, safe and sound in her arms. Her sweet scent warmed him and made him sleepy.

A coldness crept over her. He woke to find her sprawled and unmoving. Blood caked her face. Jori ran.

He found himself in the interrogation room. Like the pistons of an engine, Father slammed his fists on someone in the chair. A sickly red swathed the walls and congealed on the floor. Jori ran.

Hot tears burned his cheeks. He jerked, intending to wipe them away but couldn't move. The dreamfog smothered him like a heavy blanket.

A softness touched his cheek. He twitched. Was this real?

The veil dissipated. His eyes fluttered open. Terk's face appeared. A stew of sensations wafted from him, but the hottest was the sorrow layered with guilt.

Jori eased into a sitting position. The two embraced. The intensity of their emotions commingled and enveloped them in a whirlpool of darkness.

He groped for a hint of Mother's essence and found nothing. He choked, then let out a muffled wail. "She's gone already, isn't she?"

Terk sighed. "Father insisted she not be healed all the way and threatened to kill her if she didn't leave. Sensei Jeruko made the arrangements. She's gone, but she'll be alright."

"I didn't get to say goodbye," Jori blubbered.

"She understands and she sends you all her love."

Jori pulled away. "You talked to her?"

"Yes, but not for long. Father's pissed at me, too, and I didn't want to put her in more danger."

"I wanted to go with her."

Terk rubbed Jori's back. "I know, but Father wouldn't let you. If you try to go anyway, he'll find you. You'd only put her in danger again."

Jori's shoulders fell. Terk was right. Besides, she would be safer away from Father. Somehow, this made him cry harder. The sound of Terk's sniffles indicated he wept too. Their grief engulfed them. Eventually, Jori's tears dried up. The pressure in his sinuses triggered a headache.

Terk let him go. "What happened? Why did Father do this?"

"I'm not sure. I was looking over the cargo when Nezumi came and had Benjiro and the captain arrested. He took them to the interrogation room. Tokagei brought Mother and she recognized Benjiro."

Terk tilted his head. "He's really her brother? I thought Lord Enomoto was her brother."

"He is, but so is Benjiro. She told me about him, except his name wasn't Benjiro then."

"That makes no sense."

"I don't understand it either, but she knew him. Father went crazy. He believed Benjiro was a spy and Mother was in on it. He hurt her. I didn't know what to do."

The tumble of his words halted as he choked up. Terk put his hand on his shoulder. Jori pushed down the urge to cry.

Terk hugged him close. "I have an idea," he said after a time.

Joris stomach did a somersault. He leaned away. "For what?"

Terk sighed. "Since Father will blame someone if the Cooperative crew escapes, the best way to keep that from happening is if the person who helps them also leaves." He squeezed Jori's hands.

Jori tilted his head and frowned. "Who?"

Terk touched Jori's cheek. "I don't care about anyone else. I only care about you."

"Who?" Jori asked again. "Who will take the blame and leave with them?"

"I'll be right back," Terk pecked Jori on the forehead and left without an explanation.

*****

3791:035:00:03. J.D. Hapker's heart thumped dully as the guards escorted him and his team to their cell. He hoped Sharkey was alright. After Usagi forced her into that room and Terkeshi saved her, Michio took her away. He never had a chance to make sure that brute hadn't gotten to her.

As soon as they entered the cell block, he craned his neck to see if she had already brought back. His heart lurched at the sight of her small smile. *Thank goodness*.

A guard opened his cell door and he rushed inside. "Sharkey!"

Corporal Harley beamed Chief Simmonds puffed.

She appeared surprisingly composed with her relaxed bearing and a mouth that neither smiled nor frowned. The blood on her face was gone and her wounds healed. Her ripped clothes carried black stains, but no other evidence indicated what that man had done.

When the guards had gone, Hapker reached out to put his arm on her shoulder but thought better of it and let it fall to the side instead. "You alright?"

"Yeah," she said in a wistful tone. "I'm okay. Usagi didn't get to me."

The muscles in Hapker's body loosened.

"The prince killed him. It was both a relief and…" She rubbed the back of her neck. "I've always known that boy was dangerous but seeing it firsthand was… Scary."

"At least he did it for a good reason," Hapker said, not sure how else to respond.

Her brows rose. "Yeah, I'm grateful. Don't get me wrong. It's just that he's so young."

Harley grunted. "And so much like his father."

"No," Hapker said. "The emperor wouldn't have cared one way or the other about Usagi."

"Thank the stars that man is gone!" Simmonds plunged down on the bed.

The corporal slumped his shoulders and sat as well. Hapker motioned Sharkey to her cot and took a seat beside her. "What else happened? You look troubled."

She wrung her hands. "Jori and a woman were brought into sick bay when I was there. They were both bloody and bruised."

Hapker swallowed. "Is Jori alright?"

"Yeah. I believe so. It's gets worse, though. The woman was Jori and Terkeshi's mother."

Hapker froze as though chilled by arctic waters. "How?"

"He didn't say—"

"Who didn't say?" the corporal asked.

"Terkeshi," Sharkey replied. "He was there."

"Did he do it?" Corporal Harley's dark eyes flared.

She shook her head. "No. He was very distraught. He—"

A swish of the main doors and sounds of movement outside the cell halted their conversation. Terkeshi appeared in front of their door. His tight posture contrasted with his sagging expression as he waved the guards out. One man opened his mouth as though to protest, but he snapped it shut at the prince's glower and left.

Terkeshi entered the code, opening the cage door. He stood alone before them unpretentiously with no hint of his usual domineering attitude.

Hapker rose to his feet. Harley moved to do the same, but he waved him down and met the prince's eyes, noting their surrounding redness. "I just heard about your mother. I'm so sorry."

The young man's throat bobbed. His expression stiffened, as though struggling to hold something back. "You haven't heard all of it. She's been exiled."

"What happened?"

Terkeshi sighed and looked away. "It doesn't matter. What matters is that both she and Jori almost died."

Hapker's skin prickled as a coldness spread over him, then plummeted into numbness. "How?"

Terkeshi's face scrunched up and tears welled in his eyes. "Father," he said in a low tone. His throat bobbed again.

"Oh my god. That's terrible." Hapker opened his arms in a gesture that offered solace. "Is—is it because of us?"

The prince waved his hand. "No—I mean yes, but not directly. Not in a way that puts you at fault." He puffed, then composed himself. "I'm not here to talk about this. I'm here to tell you I have an idea to help you escape."

Hapker blinked. His jaw dropped.

"You do?" Corporal Harley planted his feet and moved to stand but sat again.

"There is one catch, though," Terkeshi said.

"Name it," Hapker replied without hesitation.

"You take Jori with you."

Hapker jerked his head back. "Take him with us?"

Terkeshi's features darkened and his eyes flashed with intensity. "Father almost killed him. A part of me wants to blame *you*." He jabbed his finger into Hapker's shoulder. His glower wavered and his hands fell his sides. "But I realize he had to help you. It's who he is, and he doesn't belong here."

Hapker leaned in. "What about you?"

The ferocity of the prince's gaze died down. "I only want Jori to be safe."

Hapker nodded. The political implications of taking Jori nudged in his thoughts, but he pushed them down. The boy needed to be saved. He *deserved* to be saved. The consequences be damned.

"It's the only way," Terkeshi added. "I fear that if he doesn't go with you when you escape, my father will blame him anyway and kill him."

"What about your mother. Couldn't he go with her?"

"Father would never allow it. He must go with you. It's the only way he'll be truly safe."

Sharkey's expression fell. "But won't that start a war?"

"Father doesn't need an excuse to start a war. If he gets that emitter fixed, it won't be long before he goes after the Cooperative anyway. Besides—"

Hapker stopped him. "Alright. We'll take Jori. What's the plan?"

Terkeshi's demeanor relaxed. "I haven't worked that part out yet. I believe Jori's been working on something, though."

A collective sigh seemed to lighten the air. Sharkey was safe. They were getting out of here and Jori could escape that monster.

49
Psychosis

3791:035:08:37. Kenji Mizuki whirled his staff, snapped it in a downward thrust, stabbed, and swung. He fixated on the imaginary opponent before him and stormed through a series of forms. The weapon bit the air with each move, but not loud enough to satisfy his temper.

Damn her! How long had that idiot brother of hers been on this ship? How long had the dumbass been sharing secrets with his enemies? No wonder Lord Enomoto kept standing in his way.

Mizuki finished the last form. Sweat dripped from his brow and slicked his chest. "I'm ready!" he said to the three men also warming up in the dojo.

As he stepped into the center, Jeruko and Samuru faced him from the left and right. Another senshi that Mizuki didn't bother remembering the name of stood behind him. All four readied their staffs—Mizuki defensively and the others offensively.

Samuru struck first. Mizuki blocked with a crack resounding loud enough to split his eardrums. He swung and halted the nameless warrior's attack with a sideswipe, then ducked under the blur of Jeruko's weapon.

Mizuki parried, followed by a counter cross-strike. Round and round the four fighters went with Mizuki receiving as many blows as he gave. This practice used to be challenging. With Fujishin gone, though, no one else met his expectations.

Mizuki dodged Samuru's swipe and low-blocked Jeruko's. The nameless senshi came at him. Mizuki pivoted and smashed into the man's side. In a combo move, he turned about and clouted him in the temple.

The man stumbled and wagged his head before rejoining the foray. If not for the hard skulls of Toradons, he would've been out of the fight.

The battering continued. Mizuki's moves flowed like a raging river of blood. His sight reddened and he no longer saw the faces of his opponents. Amarante, Enomoto, and Fujishin attacked him instead—and they mocked him. He snarled and roared as a blackbeast's fury coursed through his veins.

"Sire! Sire, stop!"

The words cut through Mizuki's vision. He halted and found himself poised over the nameless senshi curled on the floor. The man coughed. Blood drizzled from his nose and leaked from his mouth.

Mizuki's chest heaved. The muscle over his eye no longer twitched. It was as though it had passed a threshold of endurance and died. The flesh there sagged now, narrowing his range of vision.

He straightened. The warrior rose to his feet. He was a credit to his caste, but not enough to make him a worthy opponent.

"Dismissed!" Mizuki said to him.

The man bowed. He staggered as he put his staff away and left.

"Are you alright, Sire?" Jeruko held his hand out.

Mizuki scowled. "Of course I'm alright. That lout hardly presented a challenge."

"That's not what I mean. You were mumbling earlier." Jeruko's brow wrinkled.

"Pah!" Mizuki pulled a towel from the cubby at the side of the weapon station and wiped the blood from the end of his staff.

"Could this be about the empress?" Jeruko said.

Mizuki turned to him with a glower. "That bitch tried to kill me!" It was her plan all along. Give him sons, wait until they were old enough, then murder him so they could take his place. He should have known.

"Are you sure she wasn't protecting her—"

Mizuki confronted him. "Who the hell's side are you on?"

Jeruko waved his hand and shook his head. "I'm concerned is all. She was an asset. You said yourself many times."

"She's a traitor! And damned lucky I didn't kill her." He slammed the butt of his staff on the floor. Was everyone against him? First Fujishin, then his wife, and now Jeruko!

Jeruko bowed lower than usual. "I understand, Sire. My apologies. I only spoke out of concern for you. Nothing more."

Mizuki eyed the man. His muscles jerked like a cobra ready to strike. If Jeruko, or anyone else, did anything against him again, he wouldn't hesitate to end them. He had enough. No more questioning his motives. No more disobedience.

"Sire?"

Mizuki snapped his glare to Samuru. "What?"

"Do you want to go another round?"

"Get out." Mizuki tightened his fist around his weapon. "Get out!"

Jeruko and Samuru placed their staffs on the rack. Neither looked his way as they left. It was probably best they didn't. Mizuki barely had a grip on himself. One wrong word, or even one wrong look, and he'd jam this staff through their throats.

As soon as the door closed behind them, he let out a mighty roar.

*****

3791:035:09:54. Two cracked staffs and a dozen virtual opponents later, Kenji Mizuki's blood settled to a simmer. His chest heaved and his vision returned to normal hues. Perhaps sending Amarante away wasn't the best choice. He had warned her, though. This was her own fault. Besides, he didn't need her. The emitter would give him the power he needed. Fuck her, and fuck Fujishin, too.

The door comm interrupted his reflections and his heart surged heat throughout his body. *Can I get no peace!* "What is it?"

"May I speak with you, Father?" Terkeshi relayed.

"Enter!" Mizuki tossed aside the broken staff and glowered at the boy as he stepped inside. "What do you want?"

Terkeshi clasped his hands behind him and pulled back his shoulders. "I'm not going to Subkojo."

Mizuki clenched his fists. "The hell you're not."

"Samuru can take care of it by himself. I'm staying here."

"Boy, who do you think you are to disobey me?"

Terkeshi jutted his chin. "You're out of control. You were going to kill her, and Jori too. I won't let you do that."

Mizuki stormed over to his son and towered over him.

To Terkeshi's credit, he didn't flinch.

Mizuki snatched Terkeshi's jaw and pinched. "She betrayed me, used her power on me, and that little brat interfered. They're damned lucky they're still alive."

"Mother had nothing to do with Enomoto putting a spy here, and you—"

Mizuki's fist silenced him. "I've always considered you weak, but this sentiment of yours proves it."

Terkeshi's nostrils flared and his eyes blazed. "Your emotions have become a weakness. You're letting your anger control you."

Mizuki slammed him against the wall. "I have every right to be angry! I told her what would happen if she ever used her power on me!"

"She had no choice! You were being an asshole!"

Mizuki punched him. Terkeshi's head rocked and he stumbled but sucked in a breath and righted himself. "And you say Jori and I are weak because of our emotions."

Mizuki growled and grabbed the boy again. "You dare to call me weak? I will pound you until you are a simpering mess."

Terkeshi's glower reddened as his lips whitened from pressing so hard. "Go ahead! You'll only prove that you can't control yourself."

Mizuki stepped back and shoved him. His chest heaved. "That woman has turned you boys into useless cowards."

Terkeshi's face reddened and he clenched his fists. "I'm no Dokuri, right? Well, I'm proud of that fact. But I'm no fucking coward either. I won't let you hurt Jori."

"If you fight me, boy. I will kill you," Mizuki replied in a deadly soft tone.

Terkeshi's chin quivered but he stood tall. "I'm not foolish enough to fight you, but I'm staying here to watch over my brother."

Mizuki clenched his teeth as a firestorm raged through him. "You will do as you're told, or else."

Terkeshi swallowed. "I will not."

Mizuki bellowed as he swung his fist. He rampaged until his useless son was no longer able to hold his ground. Before the boy lost consciousness, he stopped and stood over him with his heaving.

Let the boy defy him for now. Once this emitter was fixed, he'd no longer be bound by anyone. He could say to hell with the lords and their insistence that he refrain from genetic engineering.

He stepped back and let Terkeshi crawl to his feet. Yes. That's what he'd do. He'd sire better sons than this piece of shit and his stubborn-ass brother.

50
Someone to Blame

3791:035:10:11. Jori curled on his bed and clutched his head. His heart constricted as Father's fury bombarded his senses. It was Terk's turn to face the man's wrath. Jori had to do something but just like with Mother, he wavered with indecision knowing he was no match against the tide of his Father's madness.

He forced himself to rise as Terk's fright bloomed into loathing. The moment his feet reached the floor, the sensations ended. Jori held his breath and focused his ability. His chest ached as the tendrils of Terk's emotions flowed in. He was alive and still conscious. His lifeforce separated from Father's, indicating he walked away. It was a good thing because Jori doubted he could've stopped it anyway.

He expelled the air from his lungs and crawled back into bed.

*****

3791:035:12:49. Jori caressed the small stone and traced the intricate pattern of the surrounding goldwork. He'd given Mother this necklace a couple years ago. The kondentine agate reminded him of the copper flecks in her bronze eyes. The gold chain stood out against her olive skin.

She had loved it. When she opened this gift, her face had lit up and warmed him. At least she was safe now, but it would be a long time before he ever saw her smile again.

His eyes burned with dry tears as he lay in the darkness of his bedroom. He should've been up hours ago helping on the emitter. Instead, he lay unmoving like a stone drowning on the bottom of a lake.

The comm to his chamber beeped. He ignored it, having no desire to talk to Terk and Sensei Jeruko. He blocked their sensations and allowed his mind drift into the emptiness that surrounded him.

The warmth of the necklace intertwined with his fingers was all he had left. He clenched it, not wanting to let go.

His door slid open. Jori glowered at the silhouettes in the doorway.

"Lights." Terk said to the computer.

Jori shielded his eyes from the brightness. Terk sat on the edge of his bed and lay his hand on his shoulder. "You can't stay in here all day."

Sensei Jeruko knelt beside him. "I know it hurts, Jori-chan, but—"

"Emotion is weakness, right?" Jori snapped.

Sensei Jeruko shook his head. "Not for you, it isn't. It's your strength."

"You have things to do," Terk added.

"I'm not fixing that emitter," Jori said. "I won't let him murder more people." Hapker was right. He needed to sabotage that thing. His father was worse than the blackbeast who stalked a fawn because at least the blackbeast only hunted as a matter of survival.

Terk squeezed his shoulder. "We're not here about that. We need to talk about how to free the prisoners."

Jori's slack expression didn't change, but his thoughts flickered. He'd forgotten about them. "Are you sure you're not here to tell me I was wrong to help them?"

"Father's wrong. Not you." Terk's forehead wrinkled, accenting the bruise over his left eye. He had several, but fortunately none that appeared to need immediate attention.

Jori's stomach twisted, sending a pang throughout his body. "This is my fault."

Sensei Jeruko rested his hand over Jori's. "This is your father's doing. I understand you're hurting. We all are. Which is why we can't let him hurt the other people you care about."

Jori eased into a sitting position. Terk put his arm over his back. "You don't want the commander to die…"

Jori nodded.

"And you've been thinking of a way to get him out of this," Terk continued. "So what do you have so far?"

"It won't work." He faced Sensei Jeruko. "Not without Father killing someone else."

"We've got an idea for that," Sensei Jeruko said.

"But let's not worry about that part," Terk added. "What's your plan?"

Jori gathered his thoughts. "The Cooperative is bound to be near our territory, if not already in it. I can get a coded message to the heads of the outposts and space stations along the border, tell them it's for a Captain Arden of the *Odyssey* only."

Terk and Sensei Jeruko's emotions flared with unease. "We can't put secret communications in their hands," Terk said.

"If I code it right, only Captain Arden will know the answers to the questions tied to it."

Sensei Jeruko rubbed his chin. "The heads wouldn't risk passing secrets."

Jori's sluggish heart picked up its pace. "Tell them it's a demand or a threat and hint at a trap. A promise of a reward won't hurt either. They will jump at the chance."

Terk looked up as though considering it. "How do they reach Captain Arden?"

Jori made a derisive noise. "Most heads of those stations are opportunists. They'll find a way."

They exchanged glances.

Terk leaned in. "Then what?"

"You know how the port sensors keep failing?"

"No," Terk said as Sensei Jeruko replied with a yes.

"I'll make sure they go out again. This will allow a ship to get close without being detected. We are on a trajectory to Subkojo, so I can give the information to Captain Arden along with a specific frequency that most ships don't monitor. It's just a ping, but he'll be able to pinpoint us within a few lightyears. Then—"

"Wait." Terk waved his hands. "This sounds too complicated. How much of this can *we* do? Bishamon is still watching you. You can't afford to get caught before—" Terk stopped and looked away.

Jori sensed they were keeping something from him. "Before what?"

Terk sighed. "Someone has to take the blame for all this."

Jori frowned. "You said you have a plan. You *do* have a plan, don't you?"

They hesitated.

"Well. What is it?"

Terk glanced at Sensei Jeruko, then back to Jori. "There's only one person left on this ship who Father would believe can pull this off."

Jori cocked his head.

"You," Terk said.

Jori scrunched his face. "Me? Father will—"

Terk made the halt gesture. "You must go with them."

Jori's chest tightened. "What? I can't."

Terk gently squeezed his shoulder. "I won't let anything happen to you. When I saw what Father did to you…" The words choked in his throat.

Jori blinked the gumminess building in his eyes. "Are you coming too?"

Terk shook his head.

Sensei Jeruko patted Jori's hand. "Just you, Jori-chan."

The heaviness Jori felt earlier rebounded. "You don't want me around anymore?"

Terk's expression fell. "That's not it at all."

"We can't lose you," Sensei Jeruko said with a soft yet gruff tone.

Jori sniffled. He turned away, not meeting their eyes.

"It's the only way," Terk added. "I've already talked to the commander, and he'll take you with him. You'll be safe with the Cooperative. Safe where no one can hurt you."

"I don't want to leave you."

"It won't be forever," Terk said. "Just until I'm emperor. Then I'll call you back."

"We can think of something, find someone else to blame." Jori spoke fast. "Maybe we can make it look like the Cooperative paid Yemon off and this is his doing. Maybe—"

"Jori!" Desperation etched Terk's face. "There is no one else."

"Your father already suspects you," Sensei Jeruko said. "He will assume it was your doing no matter who we frame."

"It's not safe for you here anymore," Terk added.

"You can send me to Mother. I'll hide with her."

Terk's eyes turned down. "If Father finds out you're with her, it will put you both in danger. If you are with the Cooperative, you'll be out of his reach."

"I'll let your mother know where you are," Jeruko replied. "She'll be relieved to know you're safe."

Jori's thoughts whirled. There had to be another way, but he couldn't think of one. This was happening, then. He had no choice. Silence lingered as the realization sank in.

He fell into his brother's arms. "I don't want to go."

Terk held him for a long time. Jori immersed himself in his warmth.

This isn't how it's supposed to end. But it was the only way to keep anyone else he cared about from being killed.

51
Boundless

3791:035:16:39. Silas Arden rested his head on his fist and his elbow on the bar. He sat facing Sengupta and absently stirred the ice in his glass. "I'm beginning to think this is a waste of time."

Sengupta sipped her rainbow layered drink. "Jax is surely trying."

"I believe your friend's sincerity, but the emperor is doubtless being extra careful considering his recent acquisition."

He studied four newcomers entering the establishment. They swiveled their heads as though looking for someone. Their attire was identical—a dark blue jumpsuit probably made of nylon, aluminized polyester, and other space-worthy materials. The black ring at their collar indicated helmets could be attached. These were likely the station's astro-technicians, but Arden monitored them anyway.

They waved to a man sitting at a back table. Arden's shoulder's fell. Two hours had passed since Jax called Sengupta and asked her to visit this bar and wait. His vague message said he had a potential lead.

Arden sighed and took a swallow of his cheap brandy. He rarely drank while on duty, but his nerves vibrated like the strings of a violin. He'd been on this damned station for too long with nothing to show for it. Now hope dangled in front of him like a carrot.

Where the hell were Jax's people?

"We will get our crew back, Sir." Sengupta's brow wrinkled, betraying her lack of certainty.

"I pray you're right. I'd hate to break in a new commander." He winced at his tasteless joke, then took another drink.

Sengupta clutched his arm. He flinched and followed her gaze. The phosphorescent man entered the bar. He wore a green-tinted suit this time. Magenta lapels the size of gigantic hands lay about the collar. Magenta also lined his cuffs and a pocket on his breast. It was a sore sight—*or a sight for sore eyes.*

Major Esekielu, who'd been standing watch at the entrance, planted himself in front of the man. "About time. Do you have any idea how long you've kept us waiting?"

Arden sighed, understanding the man's complaint but wishing he hadn't voiced it. He set down his drink and stood. *The moment has arrived.*

*****

3791:035:17:12. Silas Arden swallowed down his anxiousness and collected himself before entering Jax's domain. The office stank of smoke as Jax puffed another turd-like cigar.

"Welcome," the large man said, though not in the same enthusiastic tone as the last time he'd spoken to Sengupta.

"Thank you for inviting us, Jax," Sengupta said with a warm smile. "I understand you have some news?"

Jax set his cigar down and leaned back with his arms crossed. "I *may* have something. I'm not sure what it is exactly, but it's from the *Dragon* itself and addressed to Captain Arden."

Arden's stomach did a flip. "The princes replied?"

Jax turned his head, making his thick neck wobble. "I never got through to anyone, but surely they knew you'd be looking for them because they sent *you* a message."

"What's the message?"

"No idea." He handed Arden a storage chip. "It's encrypted with a series of questions that supposedly only you can answer."

Arden raised an eyebrow. "You already tried to crack it." This explained why Jax made them wait in the bar for so long.

The man formed a flat smile. "Can't blame me for trying. Everyone in the galaxy wants to know what the Tredon emperor is up to."

"No news on that front?"

"Not a word." Jax pointed at the device. "You should be wary of whatever's in there."

"Why's that?"

"There've been hints that the message is a trap."

Arden agreed. The emperor needed more scientists, and his ship had many to choose from.

"Only one way to find out." Arden pocketed the chip. "What are the three questions?"

"The first asks for a ship's number. I tried yours and every combination thereof, but they didn't work. I also ran a few gathered from our docking records. No luck."

Arden's heart pitter-pattered. If it wasn't a Cooperative's identifier, perhaps it belonged to a certain Tredon ship that had crashed on an uninhabited Cooperative planet.

"Since I couldn't get past that first question," Jax said, "I'm not even sure what the other two are."

Sengupta tilted her head. "How do you know there are three questions?"

"The initial message hinted at it."

"Who sent it?" Arden asked.

Jax's thick neck wobbled again. "Other than someone on the *Dragon*, no clue." He picked up his cigar and took a puff. "The emperor's got specific plans for that emitter. If you learn something there, I'd be in your debt if you told me what it is."

"Ever the entrepreneur," Arden said with a slight curl to his lips. "I must run it by my superiors."

Jax wagged a finger. "That message is for you only. Another reason I suspect a trap."

Arden's heart skipped a beat. "I'll consider your request as well as your warning. I greatly appreciate this. If I can do something for you in return, I will."

Jax waved. "You owe me nothing, Captain. This is my debt repaid to Jeyana."

Sengupta bowed, then grasped the man's meaty hand. "My gratitude is boundless."

52
Countdown

3791:037:15:46. The clock approached the first window. A draft chilled Jori's skin, making him shiver. Each thump of his heart cramped his stomach. He glanced at the time on his MM. Less than an hour left, and Captain Arden still hadn't shown. He might not come yet. Jori partly hoped he wouldn't but the uncertainty hanging in the air wracked his nerves. The sooner the captain came, the better.

Thanks to the nearby communication hub that allowed instantaneous transmission, Jori had sent the message within an hour. There was no way to know whether the captain received it, though—or how far away the *Odyssey* might be.

He tapped open the port sensor application. The sensors were still operational, but he diverted their readings here. This slight change in plan made it so he'd know if a ship approached. It meant he wouldn't have to keep disabling the transport-blockers and increase Father's suspicions.

Jori returned to the auxiliary bay and submerged himself in his work. He must sabotage the emitter before the *Odyssey* arrived. After altering the schematics and changing the distance of the two optical resonators, he reversed the nodes of the CP regulator. It was a subtle change, hopefully subtle enough that nobody would notice. When they used the emitter, the regulator should short out.

This was one of many minor changes he and Simmonds had made. If all went as planned, the prisoners would escape, and Father wouldn't be able to use this weapon. He also wouldn't have enough resources to go to invade the Cooperative and get him back.

His gut spasmed. He didn't want to leave, but neither did he want Hapker to die. This was the only option. He suppressed his rising despair. It wasn't like he'd lose Terk forever. Just for a while. At least he'd be safe with the commander. This was for the best.

"You alright?" Hapker said.

Jori wiped a tear from his cheek. "Yeah," he replied with a croak.

Hapker's brow wrinkled and his eyes turned down. His sympathy shined through his nervous joy. Jori embraced it, hoping to stave off his father's festering hostility as it struck his senses like a barrage of arrows. Father's paranoia had intensified with a string of irrational decisions, including killing three senshi who had made minor mistakes. The constant sensation was almost enough to drive Jori mad.

His MM pinged him and his heart nearly burst. "Something's here."

Hapker's nervous energy spiked. "Is it the *Odyssey?*"

"I don't know yet." He double-checked another application to make sure the interference was still in place for Father's spy microphone, then tapped the comm at his ear. "Terk. The portside sensors have been triggered. If it's who we hope, they should be in range for identification in fifteen minutes."

Anxiousness sprang from his chest and radiated over his entire body. It was too soon for him to go. He wished he'd come up with another idea that didn't involve him leaving, but time was out.

Minutes later, Terk entered the bay and approached. "Do you have an ID yet?"

Jori faced him while Hapker knelt to pretend to work on the conduits on the lower half of the regulator. "Five more minutes, assuming they're headed this direction."

Terk huffed and crossed his arms. A range of emotions flew around him. "Everything's ready?"

"Yes. Everyone has a bio-reader, including me." The computerized disk practically burned Jori's thigh. As soon as Captain Arden or anyone else from the Cooperative pinged for its signature embedded on the small disk, their transport systems could beam the wearer onboard—that was, assuming the transport-blocker went offline as planned.

Terk glanced over at Washi and Michio. "Is everyone ready?"

"As ready as we can be." Jori's chest pounded so hard, his ears hurt.

"Sensei Jeruko has the commander's communication code?"

"I gave it to him," Jori replied. "When things have settled down here, he should be able to call and establish a secret line."

"Alright. Check the port sensor."

Jori hesitated. He moved slower than a stalking blackbeast as he brought up the MM and pressed the application. The information flashed to life. His hands trembled and tingled as he read it.

"Well?" Terk said.

Jori's throat tightened. "It's a large vessel headed this way. I'd say it's an Expedition-class."

Terk puffed his cheeks and blew out. "You're on."

Hapker stood. Tears filled Jori's eyes.

"Knock it off." Terk elbowed him in mock sternness as wetness rimmed his lashes. "I'll see you again someday. I promise."

Jori choked. He wanted to reach out and hug his brother one more time but not in front of the surveillance cameras.

"Go on," Terk said as he emitted a surge of affection.

"We should get going," Hapker added.

Terk's expression turned serious as he faced the commander. "Take care of him."

"I will," he replied with a truth Jori sensed.

Terk dipped his head. "You better hurry."

Hapker took in a deep breath as Terk signaled Washi and Michio over. Their brows creased and Jori felt their unease. They didn't like what was coming, but knew it was necessary.

Terk headed out, back to his bridge duty. Just before he left the bay, he turned and gave Jori one last look.

This was it. Everything was about to change. His old life was at an end. Jori swallowed hard and struggled to compose the rush of emotion welling within him. Then he led Hapker and his guards to the other side of the bay to another exit.

*****

3791:037:16:13. Silas Arden rolled his shoulders. The movement nudged his muscles into a looser state, but not enough to release the underlying tightness constricting his upper body.

He cleared his throat and met the eyes of his intelligence officer and bridge chief. "We have twenty minutes until we are in transport range. So far, it does not appear the *Dragon* has detected us."

"It could still be a trap, Sir," his bridge chief said. She wasn't his usual advisor as her shift took place during his sleep hours, but he was short his commander and Major Bracht remained on leave.

"We have little choice," he replied, ignoring the fact that Major Esekielu had fervently argued an alternative that involved too many days of waiting.

"I am confident of the information in the message," Sengupta said.

They figured out the answers to the three questions easily enough. The first was indeed the Tredon ship's ID. The answer to the second question, date of assignment, turned out to be the day Commander Hapker took charge of the youngest prince. The third asking how many killed referred to the number of people who died when the children seized his ship and escaped. It was an excellent question since no one else in the entire galaxy could have guessed the Dragon Princes didn't kill a single person.

"They might've tortured Commander Hapker into giving us this message." The bridge chief's tone reflected no doubt, however. They had already agreed the video of the commander represented a tired yet hopeful man.

The young prince had been in the video as well. He apologized for everything that had happened and Hapker put his hand on his shoulder. The child's words seemed too sincere and Hapker's actions too natural to have been an act.

"If this is a trap, it's a brilliant one," Arden said. "We get in and get out, and with all eleven of our people, no less."

"That part sounds too good to be true," Sengupta conceded.

"They didn't say the eleven would be *our* people," the bridge chief added. "We could be bringing Tredons onboard."

"If that's the case," Arden replied, "our security officers will take care of them." He put his hands on the table to signal the meeting's end. "We have discussed all this before, so unless there's anything new I suggest we get to the bridge."

Sengupta nodded. "I'm ready, Sir."

"Me too."

They hurried from the conference room. Arden made one step past the threshold when Major Esekielu blocked his path.

"Sir! We must arm our weapons."

"Our weapons are as ready as I intend to make them," Arden said tiredly.

"If this is a trap, we're dragon fodder."

"I'm well aware of that, Major."

"The admiral clearly stated that the next time you engage in battle I have compete discretion, and I say we—"

"I don't give a damn what you say, Major!" Arden stepped into the major's personal space and glared down at his pointed head. "We are not engaging in battle. It's a simple rescue."

Major Esekielu's mouth twisted. "Trusting in that little twerp is a mistake that will get us all killed."

"It's my commander I trust."

"The same one who was nearly dishonorably discharged for—"

"Enough!" Arden glowered. "I've made my decision and if you don't stand down right now, I will have you arrested."

The major's jaw grated. He didn't back down but neither did Arden.

Arden tapped the comm taped behind his ear. "Major Bracht… I hereby release you from leave. Come to the bridge at once."

The major's eyes flickered. Arden hoped it was from unease. Major Esekielu was a major asshole, but even his giant ego wavered at the prospect of facing Bracht.

"If you are not at your station by the time Major Bracht arrives," Arden said in a low tone, "I will charge you with insubordination."

"This is a mistake." The major turned about and stiffly marched to the tactical station.

Arden bit back a scathing reply. He had more important matters to attend to—namely retrieving his own people so he could be rid of this arrogant prick once and for all.

*****

3791:037:16:14. J.D. Hapker slicked his hand down his sweaty face. This was it. It was finally time to leave this nightmare.

Jori led him, Washi, Michio, and Bishamon to the bay exit. "Pachin," he said to the man working on the emitter. "If anyone asks, I'm headed to the aft storage room for another battery."

"That tool bot on the fritz again, Sir?" Pachin asked.

Jori confirmed.

They continued out with no complications. *So far, so good.* Simmonds and Sharkey had acted out an entire scene yesterday where she attempted to use a bot's rotary tools only to not have it work. Simmonds pretended to fiddle with it, when in fact he was reconfiguring the heavy battery so it would run out of juice. Now Hapker and Jori headed in the general direction of the aft storage room, which happened to be near the transport-blocker.

Hapker's blood raced through his veins and every part of his body poured with sweat. He tried relaxing his muscles as they made their way through the ship and into the conveyor. His heart thumped like a rabbit signaling danger as he took a position between Jori in front and the guards in back.

"I heard you had trouble with Kelar yesterday," Michio said to Bishamon to distract him.

Hapker wiped his sweaty palms down his thigh.

"Nothing I couldn't handle," Bishamon replied as Washi discreetly handed Hapker his lightning rod. As part of the plan, Harley had raised a fuss with Jori the other day, which triggered Washi requisitioning rods for all Jori's personal guards.

"That Kelar is quite the bully, but not as skilled as he thinks," Michio said as Hapker turned the device on and checked the setting.

Bishamon grunted. Hapker spun around and jabbed the lightning rod into the man's chest. A blue arc jolted out. The guard's eyes bulged, and his mouth fell open. Then he plunged to the floor like a suicidal lemming.

Hapker puffed. "Alright. You two are next."

Washi and Michio both nodded. They gritted their teeth and braced themselves as Hapker shocked them into unconsciousness.

The story would be that Jori helped take them by surprise. Terkeshi would confirm this as he was the only one left on the ship able to discern whether someone told the truth. The men would get into trouble, but they were too valuable to be severely punished.

Jori and Hapker confiscated their weapons and made sure both were on stun. Hapker's nerves settled as adrenaline flooded his veins. "You ready?" he said.

Jori dipped his head sharply. His steady posture matched his even glare. "Ready."

"Let's do this."

53
All Hell Breaks Loose

3791:037:16:10. Kenji Mizuki massaged his forehead. The ache behind his eyes had grown to an unrelenting throb and lack of sleep shrouded his ability to concentrate.

He should have felt better now that he'd tightened the reins. Punishing the prisoners had made them more resolute in their work. Three traitors found among his own people had been tortured in such a gruesome way that no one could possibly be stupid enough to betray him again. Even his son seemed subdued as he worked on the emitter with a newfound fervor.

Mizuki leaned closer to his viewscreen, watching Jori and Terkeshi as they talked. He tried pointing the microphone in their direction once more, but some nearby activity interfered with the signal. Jori had adequately explained the necessity of this process, but suspicion nagged at him.

Terkeshi parted and Jori left his station with a prisoner. Jeruko's sons followed, as did Bishamon. All seemed well enough, but the nape of Mizuki's neck prickled. He trailed the boy with the camera, the strain in his eyes forgotten.

"Pachin," Jori said as the microphone came back online. "If anyone asks, I'm headed to the aft storage room for another battery."

Mizuki forced himself to relax. The battery of a tool bot had been causing problems. The boy could have sent a shokukin to retrieve it, but perhaps he needed something else from there and the prisoner could carry it all as easily as a worker.

His suspicions waned yet he switched cameras and continued watching. His eyelids hung heavy as Jori made his way toward the aft storage room. The prisoner behaved himself while Bishamon and the guards remained vigilant.

Mizuki's chin sank. His eyes relaxed as the promise of sleep seeped in.

A spark of alertness jolted him. He glanced at the screen. Jori was gone. He sat up and clicked another camera.

There he was, about to get in the conveyor. Mizuki checked through the selection of other cameras. There were none in the vicinity of the exit Jori should take, but the one overlooking the hall leading to the storage room sufficed.

Fatigue hung over him as he waited. He rubbed his brow, hoping it would revitalize him, but the alertness sparked like a blown fuse. He lowered his head in his hand and closed his eyes. *Just for a moment.*

*****

3791:037:16:20. The conveyor came to a halt with a jerk. Jori's heart leapt with it. There was no turning back now.

He overrode the doors to keep them from opening and focused his ability. "Clear. I don't sense anyone around. Along with the transport-blocker, it's mostly storage rooms and passive systems here."

"How far?" Hapker asked.

"When we get out, we go left. Left again down a long corridor, then right down a short hall."

They exited the conveyor. Hapker took point to the corner, then peeked around. "Clear."

They headed steadily yet briskly down the dank corridor where dozens of rusted pipes and ductwork served as the ceiling. Water or some other fluid dripped in places. Jori's heightened alertness meant he heard every plunk and clink.

He halted and put up his hand. "Someone's coming."

"I thought you said no one was down here."

"They're coming from the foundry behind us." He entered a code on a door panel. "We keep replacement parts and ingots in that large room just up ahead."

"I hope they don't need anything from here."

The door opened. Jori motioned him in. "They shouldn't. This is just the filtration system for the fabricor."

This small place smelled of burnt plastic. Jori held in the urge to sneeze as they huddled in the darkness and waited. His senses drifted from the worker outside to the other side of the ship. Terk's sadness impacted his own and threatened to drown him.

His throat constricted as the string of events that led him here flashed through his head. This started with Hapker, yet he couldn't summon a wish that he had let the man die instead. Try as he might, he couldn't think of a single decision that could have saved him in another way.

He sniffled and wiped his nose on his sleeve. Hapker laid his arm over his shoulder, radiating sympathy. "I'm sorry." He pulled Jori into an embrace.

The tears lurking behind Jori's eyes burned. Regret threatened to overwhelm him, but this wasn't the time. He nudged away and closed his eyes, pushing aside any thoughts about what he was leaving behind. His body numbed, and mission-focus took over.

*****

3791:037:16:21. Kenji Mizuki jerked awake. He blinked and composed himself. How long had he been out? He reviewed the surveillance feeds. No sign of Jori. He clicked another camera. Nothing. *Where is he?*

He tapped his comm. "Bishamon." No response. "Bishamon!" Still nothing. He pressed it again. "Washi." His blood pressure increased, making his head throb even more. "Washi. Michio. Will one of you damned people respond!"

Silence.

What in the hell! Mizuki flicked through the cameras. No sign of them. He flipped back to the hallway leading to the aft storage room. Nobody was there.

He was about to click to another camera when a door in the hall opened. He stiffened and kept his eyes glued to the screen. Every moment he waited sent his blood pressure creeping higher.

The prisoner appeared with a phaser in his hand. Mizuki jumped from his seat. "Chusho!" He jabbed his comm, then froze. Jori emerged behind him.

A cold prickling sensation flooded Mizuki's veins. "That little shit. I knew it!"

*****

3791:037:16:22. A searing heat stabbed into Terkeshi's senses and stopped his heart. He jumped to his feet and bolted to the bridge exit.

"Where the hell are you going?" Samuru asked.

"To stop this madness," Terk yelled as he dashed out.

His skin prickled as icy adrenaline surged through his body. His chest ached as the inferno he felt from Father threatened to destroy his world.

Please let me get there in time.

*****

3791:037:16:23 J.D. Hapker took point and they hurried down the empty corridor. Their echoing footsteps set his teeth on edge. Jori claimed he didn't sense anyone here, but he couldn't shake the feeling that this was too easy.

Hapker stopped at the corner with the intent to scope the next hall but a shiny spot on the upper wall caught his attention. "Is that a camera?"

Jori paled. "He knows. We must hurry."

Hapker's heart lurched. He darted a glance down the other hall. "Clear. Which room?"

"The one at the end."

They jogged to its corresponding keypad. Hapker wiped the sweat from his brow as Jori entered the code. The door swished open. Jori gave a military hand signal and he darted in low with his phaser ready.

The transport-blocker dominated the maze of supporting machines. Hapker aimed down each path with the point of his weapon. "Clear."

Jori waved him over to a back corner. "This is where we can disable it." He took the electric screwdriver from the belt at his side. The zing as he unscrewed the bolts seemed to drill into Hapker's eardrums.

"I've got this," Jori said. "Keep an eye on the entrance."

Hapker made his way around the machines. He crouched behind a chest-high machine and watched the door with a ferocity of a tiger on the hunt.

"Chusho!" Jori's voice echoed.

Hapker's heart jumped into what he was sure was cardiac arrest. "What is it?"

"Father's almost here."

Hapker's blood ran cold enough to make him woozy. "Oh, shit," he cursed uncharacteristically. "How much longer?"

"He'll be here in less than five minutes and this will take me at least that long."

Hapker shook off the dizziness and focused on the door. "I've got you covered."

The seconds ticked by. Sweat poured from his face. When it drained away, only a dry heat remained. He forced himself to remain steady as his heart drummed in his ears.

A swish of the opening door sent a surge of adrenaline through his body. He poised his phaser and peeked over the machine. A blast struck the conduits by his head, emitting a flash of blinding light that stabbed into his eyes and seared his senses.

"You traitorous little shit!" the emperor's voice reverberated throughout the room.

Hapker blinked, willing the dazzles in his eyes to clear. He aimed his weapon in what he hoped was the right direction and fired twice. He huddled behind the machine as the emperor's footsteps echoed on the metal flooring. He shot two times more, then listened again.

"You traitor! How dare you!"

The emperor's voice came from Jori's location, which was not in his line of sight—if he had sight. He smacked his palm into his temple, willing his vision to clear.

Something crashed. Thwacking noises, which was undoubtedly the emperor striking the boy, tolled in Hapker's ears. "Hold on, Jori!"

Clouds of color coalesced. Hapker took in ragged breaths as the emperor's tumultuous voice raged.

Then everything silenced. Hapker strained his ears. He caught the whispering sound of breathing. It grew to the heavy wind of bellows. It had to be the emperor.

Hapker groped and scooched down a narrow aisle, then squeezed in between two machines. His heart throbbed as the emperor's footsteps clanked on the flooring. The door swooshed open and steps echoed out. He stayed put until the door closed, then exhaled. The blur of his vision lessened. He inched out from his hiding place and scrambled along the floor until he reached Jori.

His chest hitched as though his heart stopped. Jori convulsed on the flat of his back. A wicked dagger protruded from his breast.

Hapker covered his mouth as tears welled in his eyes. Fadwa, Fresel, and now Jori. How many more friends would he fail?

*****

3791:037:16:36. Terkeshi stumbled as Jori's pain seared his senses. By the time the conveyor jerked to a halt, his chest heaved and his muscles twitched with helpless convulsions.

The conveyor opened. Terk raced down the hallways, hoping to intercept Father. He couldn't move fast enough. Tunnel vision set in as Jori's agony hovered on an imaginary line that he knew all too well. If that line was crossed, his brother would be lost to him forever.

He rounded the corner and crashed into his father. The impact threw him backward and he fell on his ass.

"You're in on this?" Father bellowed.

Terk didn't bother replying. He leapt to his feet and dodged around the man.

"Get back here, boy!"

A tremendous pang shattered Terk's vision. "Nooo!" He roared. With his mind synced to Jori's, the pain of death crippled him. Tears streamed down his face. *This can't happen!*

Somehow, he reached the room and managed to press in the code. Blood surged through his veins as he pushed through the slowly opening doors. He floundered through, bumping into just about every machine along the way.

After taking the last turn, he froze. The commander leaned over Jori's lifeless body.

"You killed him!" Rage swelled in Terk's chest. He pulled his knife from its sheath and lunged.

Midflight, a shimmer blurred his vision. His blade struck air as Jori and the commander disappeared. They'd been beamed away.

Terk collapsed on his hands and knees. Jori was gone. His little brother was dead. He wailed and roared like a dying blackbeast.

*****

3791:037:16:38. J.D. Hapker knelt by Jori's lifeless body. He opened his mouth to apologize to Terkeshi, but a wavering feeling came over him. In a blink of an eye, he found himself and his entire crew on the transport pad of his own ship. He would have sighed in relief if he had not been holding the hand of the dead boy who saved their lives.

54
The End?

3791:037:16:39. Silas Arden held his breath.

"They're on board, Captain."

"Jensin, take us away," Arden said to the helmsman. An invisible weight lifted from his chest as the *Odyssey* maneuvered into position, then took off. The lumbering warship wouldn't be able to keep up. An expedition vessel might not be up for a fight, but it could run.

He fell in the bridge's central chair and glanced at Director Sengupta, who still bit her fingernails.

"It's over," he said.

She nodded and pulled her hand away. Her body remained tense. His too. His gut vibrated like the strings of a violin as they waited for one more thing.

The main bridge-comm beeped. He bolted to his feet. "Captain Arden, here."

"Commander Hapker reporting, Sir."

Sengupta gasped. Arden emptied his lungs. "Thank goodness. Is everyone alright?"

"We lost Sergeant Davis."

Arden frowned. Eleven Cooperative officers had been missing and he just transported eleven people.

"The rest of the officers are alive and well," Hapker continued. "But there's one among us who is not a crew member and who…" He choked. "… Who may be dead."

Arden tilted his head. "Who?"

Hapker's words rushed out. "It's Jori. He saved our lives but I'm not sure if we can save him. Doctor Jerom is on it."

Arden's blood turned cold, and not from the prospect of the child dying. *Why did he bring the emperor's son here?*

*****

3791:038:02:14. The *Odyssey* had crossed back into Cooperative territory hours ago. The rescued officers had rested and been given a good bill of health by Doctor Gregson. Their mental health still needed tending but not before Silas Arden had a chance to speak to them.

He'd met them informally in the medical bay. Now was the time for formality. He sat behind his desk and clasped his hands. Commander Hapker settled before him in a position that usually commanded respect, but Arden noted his sagging features and tired expression. His fatigue became more evident as he told his tale.

Arden laced his fingers. "We owe them both a great deal."

Hapker agreed.

"He will make it," Arden said with a certainty he didn't feel.

Hapker nodded again, though his frown indicated the opposite. "Dr. Jerome is the best."

"And organ regrowth and replacement has a high success rate."

"But not with children."

Arden stared at his hands. Giving solace had never been his strong suit. He fumbled for the words, nonetheless. "If there's one thing I've learned in this entire ordeal, it is this. Never give up hope."

Did you enjoy this novel? Leave a review. Authors love reviews!

The next book is darker. Read it if you dare.
Dragon's Fall: Book Three – The emperor enlists a dubious cybernetic society to help construct the planet killing weapon. Meanwhile, Terkeshi struggles under the weight of his father's lofty expectations and is pressured into becoming a cyborg himself.

Sign up for my newsletter by visiting my website, DawnRossAuthor.com, and get great deals!

By signing up, you'll receive an exclusive short story prequel and get access to the first few chapters of the first four books.

Connect with Dawn Ross online:
DawnRossAuthor.com
Twitter.com/DawnRossAuthor
Facebook.com/DawnRossAuthor
Goodreads.com/author/show/441861.Dawn_Ross
Patreon.com/DawnRossAuthor

Glossary

A-P output – One of the many ship readouts that need to be monitored.

Aki – Sensei Aki is the emperor's old teacher. He currently serves as one of the emperor's Five Talons (aka advisors). Aki also served two previous emperors.

Amarante – One of Emperor Mizuki's concubines and Jori and Terk's mother.

Anaconda – A type of carrier ship on the Tredon warships used to transport troops and atmospheric jets called Rattlers to a planet's surface.

Ankgar – A senshi who enjoys implementing sadistic torture.

Arc drive or arc reactor – This is one of the largest components of a spaceship. It is the engine that allows a ship to travel many light years away without violating the speed of light by bending space-time.

Arc emissions – Emissions from the arc-drive that are measured by the QR gauge.

Arden – Captain Silas Arden is the captain of the *Odyssey*.

Asp – A small Tredon space fighter. While the Asps are directly manned by two fighters, their Cooperative counterparts, the Pterodon jets, are flown virtually.

Astro-technician – A technician who works outside of a ship in space. They work on ships, satellites, or space stations.

Awamori – Major Awamori is a Toradon senshi warrior serving under General Samuru and Colonel Bakuto.

Bakuto – Colonel Bakuto is a Toradon senshi warrior serving under General Samuru. He heads the division of senshi foot soldiers.

Barslow – Corporal Barslow is a PG-Force officer on the *Defender* but serves with Hapker on Thendi and is captured by the Tredons.

Basilisk – A Tredon warship captained by General Brevak.

Belmont – Vice Admiral Belmont presides over both the PG-Force and the PCC. He is in charge of protecting Thendi and is temporarily using the *Defender*, a PG-Force battleship, as his flagship.

Benjiro – A shokukin who is a genius at engineering but doesn't have the capacity to articulate himself well or to do everyday things.

Biometric authenticator – A security measure that uses retina scans, fingerprint identification, voice recognition or other unique biological characteristics to keep anyone but the authorized persons from using certain devices.

Bio-reader – A small device carried or adhered to the body that keeps track of and transmits vitals. It also has a unique embedded signal used to allow the transport to beam the carrier from one place to another.

Bio-scanner – A hand-held device used to scan biometrics.

Bishamon – A Tredon senshi of low rank but one of General Samuru's hopefuls.

Biskol – Biskol is a senshi who usually works on the bridge but is temporarily assigned to work on the emitter. Biskol has skills in programming.

Black Adder – A cargo ship captained by Captain Packwood.

Blackbeast – An animal that Jori often refers to. It is never described but it is hinted that it might be dog or wolf-like.

Bracht – Major Bjornicibus Bracht is a Rabnoshk warrior who is the commanding officer of the PG-Force stationed on the *Odyssey*. He is temporarily assigned as part of the ground force on Thendi.

Brenson – Officer Brenson is a communications officer on the bridge of the *Odyssey*.

Brevak –General Brevak is the captain of the *Basilisk* warship.

Brimstone – A Toradon warship captained by General Sakon. This warship attacked the *Odyssey* in Book One, *StarFire Dragons*.

Burn Barrier – A shield used by soldiers to prevent phaser energy rifle from shooting through.

Canthidius – Doctor Holgarth Canthidius is a lead science officer on the *Odyssey* but is on Thendi and is captured by the Tredons.

Calamity – A junker cargo/pirate ship operated by Captain Jiggerson.

Chandly – Officer Chandly is the head operations officer on the bridge of the *Odyssey*.

Chepy – Captain Jiggerson of the *Calamity* mentions Lord Chepy. Lord Chepy isn't really a lord. He's a slaver.

Chevert outpost – A space station situated between Cooperative and Tredon territory. It has many of the same amenities as a town or city.

Chima – Means vile one or hated enemy in Jori and Terk's language.

Chundo-port – A space-based parking garage for the emperor's cache of smaller spaceships.

Chusho – Means shit in Jori and Terk's language.

Comm – A communication device.

Communication hub – A form of communication that uses quantum entanglement technology for an instantaneous exchange.

Conveyor – An elevator-like car on a spaceship that moves vertically and horizontally.

Cooperative – The agency that governs space. It has numerous treaties with various worlds that provides its charter to keep space safe, ensure peace, regulate fair trade, and colonize new worlds. Its powers are granted by several planets, and the number of planets that are part of the Cooperative continues to grow. The Prontaean Cooperative has two aspects to it. The first is the Prontaean Colonial Cooperative (PCC). This sub-organization handles intergalactic relations, conducts space exploration, performs space-based scientific endeavors, assists travelers, and sometimes provides transportation. The second aspect is the Prontaean Galactic Force (PG-Force). This sub-organization polices space.

CP regulator – An electronic component.

Cycle – A cycle is the universal standard for a year of 360 days. A day-cycle is approximate to one Earth 24-hour period. While each planet might have its own unique standard, anyone who conducts business off-world used the universal standard.

Davis – Sergeant Davis is a PG-Force officer on the *Defender* but serves with Hapker on Thendi and is captured by the Tredons.

Defender – A Tutamen-class battleship of the Prontaean Galactic Force (PG-Force). Captain Richforth is the captain, but Vice Admiral Belmont is aboard and occasionally takes charge as the fleet admiral.

Depnaugh space station – A large space station located outside of Cooperative territory. It has many of the same amenities as a town or city. This station is known for harboring lawless activities and attracting unsavory characters. It's the same station visited by Jori and Terkeshi just before they crash landed on a Cooperative planet in Book One, *StarFire Dragons*.

Deskview – A desktop computer.

Dojo – A place to practice martial arts.

Dokuri – Jori and Terk's older half-brother who was killed by a rebellious Toradon lord about a year ago.

Donal – Mister Donal is Mister Largos' manager.

Dorb – A remote-controlled hovering ball that shoots bursts of low-level energy.

Dragon – The Tredon emperor's primary warship.

Dragon Emperor – Emperor Kenji Mizuki is the ruthless ruler of the Toradon Nohibito/Dragon People, aka Tredons. He is often referred to as the Dragon Emperor.

Dragon People – The Tredons, or Toradon Nohibito, are often called dragon people.

Dragon Warrior – Tredon/Toradon warriors who directly serve Emperor Mizuki.

Edo – Edo is a bridge worker on the *Dragon*.

Emperor's Claw – The emperor's five advisors, also known as the Five Talons. They are Samuru, Jeruko, Nezumi, Aki, and Fujishin.

Energy Cannons – An energy weapon used by spaceships. Some are used to disable or penetrate shields while others have explosive power.

Enomoto – Lord Enomoto is a powerful Tredon lord who serves under the emperor but is dangerously close to being stronger than the emperor. He rules an entire planet in the Tredon territory. His sister is Jori and Terkeshi's mother, Amarante.

Esekielu – Major Esekielu is a PG-Force officer sent by Admiral Belmont to temporarily take Hapker's place on the *Odyssey*.

Etena – A mythical planet said to resemble Eden. It is also the name of a small city on Togala.

Expedition-class – The largest of the Prontaean Colonial Cooperative (PCC) spaceships. It is nearly as large as a Tutamen-class battleship, but only has a few defensive weapons.

Though the officers who run this ship are formal personnel of the Cooperative, they are sometimes considered civilians because they are mostly doctors, engineers, and technicians. This ship has a small presence of Prontaean Galactic Force (PG-Force) officers for security. Expedition-class starships have the broadest scope of responsibilities. They are the ships most often used for exploration and scientific endeavors, but they also provide transport, medical and mechanical assistance, and are used for diplomatic missions.

Fabricor – A replicating machine. There are various types such as a food fabricor, a clothing fabricor, and a parts fabricor. Fabricors work much like our digital printers of today but the types of things that can be made has expanded greatly.

Fadwa – Commander J.D. Hapker's childhood friend who inspired him to work in space. She reminds Hapker of Private Fresel.

Fairyfly drones – Small flying drones that record a scene and send the feed to a military visor. The wearer of the visor eye-clicks the remote functionality of the drones.

Fink – A doctor on the *Dragon*.

Five Talons – The emperor's five advisors, also known as the Emperor's Claw. They are Samuru, Jeruko, Nezumi, Aki, and Fujishin.

Fortis-class destroyer – A military spaceship from the PG-Force. It is smaller than a Tutamen class but still amply armed.

Fresel – Private Fresel is an inexperienced PG-Force officer assigned to the ground force on Thendi.

Fudoshin – Means immoveable mind in Jori and Terk's language. Immoveable mind means don't let doubt creep in and strive to achieve.

Fuentes – A henchman of Chepy's who Captain Jiggerson of the *Calamity* likes to call Fat Toes.

Fujishin – Fujishin used to be one of the emperor's Five Talons until he betrayed him and is now leading a band of rebels.

Gardner – Lieutenant Gardner is a PG-Force officer Hapker calls for only to find he was one of the ones killed in the battle on Thendi.

Ghondorian venascabia – A sexually transmitted disease that leaves an irritating rash over much of the torso and groin.

Gonoro outpost – A small space station attacked by Jori's father about three years ago. Jori had participated in the attack from a distance, only later learning of the death he'd wrought. One of the dead was a girl his own age.

Grapnes – A race of people known for being scavengers. They tend to be greedy and dishonest.

Gravity wheel – This is the part of a spaceship that creates gravity for its passengers. It is one of the largest components that give a spaceship its circular shape.

Gregson – Doctor Gregson is one of the primary doctors on the *Odyssey*.

Greymore – Councilman Greymore is one of the elected council members of the Prontaean Cooperative.

Hanna – First Lieutenant Hanna Sharkey is one of two lieutenants serving under major Bracht on the *Odyssey*. She has temporarily been assigned as part of the Thendi ground force.

Hapker – Vice Executive Commander J.D. Hapker is second-in-command of the *Odyssey*, though he has been temporarily assigned to act as the leader of the Thendi ground force.

Harley – Corporal Harley is a PG-Force officer on the *Defender* but is with Hapker on Thendi and captured by the Tredons.

Harley speedsters – A land vehicle with the reinvented reputation of the Harley motorcycles from ancient Earth.

Hisho – Means secretary or clerk in Jori and Terk's language.

Holo-man – A projected image of a person. This projection uses haptic technology that allows it to be touched and felt. It is used for various functions including as a visual instructor for dancing, exercise, and martial arts. It isn't always a man. It can be programmed to look like just about anything, including animals and objects. There is a more technical term for this, but it is not mentioned in this story.

Huang – Doctor Huang was mentioned as being rescued from Thendi.

Hypospray – Used by medics to inject medicine or nanites.

Imperium-animi – The strongest and most dangerous type of reader. The lowest level reader, called sentio-animi, can sense emotions only. Jori and Terk are a sentio-animi. The second level reader, called extraho-animi, can also pull thoughts. And the imperiums can sense emotions, pull thoughts, and insert thoughts in a suggestive way like brainwashing.

Indivian tarantula – A hissing spider mentioned by Captain Arden.

Inertial dampeners – A device on starships that keeps inertia from throwing and smashing the crew when the starship is being maneuvered or when it is struck.

Jacob – The son of Captain Packwood, captain of the cargo ship named *Black Adder*. Jacob lost his legs in an attack made by General Sakon of the *Brimstone*.

Jax – Commander Jax is the administrator of the Chevert outpost. He is known as a collector and disseminator of information, which means he likes to collect information and sell it to the highest bidder.

J.D. – Vice Executive Commander J.D. Hapker is second-in-command of the *Odyssey*, though he has been temporarily assigned to act as the leader of the Thendi ground force.

Jensin – A helmsman serving on the bridge of the *Odyssey*.

Jerom – Doctor Beck Jerom is one of the primary doctors on the *Odyssey*.

Jeruko – Sensei/Colonel Jeruko is one of the emperor's Five Talons. He is also Jori and Terk's primary military teacher and head of Jori and Terk's personal guard.

Jeyana – Director Jeyana Sengupta is chief director of intelligence on the *Odyssey*.

Jiggerson – The pirate captain of the junker cargo ship *Calamity*.

Jinsekai – The primary planet in Tredon territory.

Jintal – A Jintal master is a master that teaches people how to endure pain.

Jori – Jori is the ten-year-old second and youngest son of Emperor Mizuki.

Jori-chan – The -chan at the end of a name denotes affection.

Kami – Lord Kami of Toradon ruled an estate, which was taken over by one of Fujishin's cousins.

Katharos – Means clear or pure in ancient Greek but has come to mean a type of healing agent that purifies the body.

Kazewaki – A gas planet in Toradon territory with heavy winds.

Kelar – A senshi on the *Dragon* who tends to be cruel.

Kenji – Emperor Mizuki's informal name.

Kesanshi – An asteroid being mined by the Vuong family. It is a lucrative mine that is highly protected. The only communication to the mine is from Vuong's space station, located on the edge of the asteroid belt.

Kesatsu – Means police in Jori and Terk's language. The kesatsu are senshi who keep order on the ship.

Kochuru – The desert-like planet where Sengupta is from.

Kondentine – A type of brown agate rock with flecks of gold. It's used to make jewelry.

Kujira – Colonel Kujira oversees the Rattler division on the *Dragon*.

Lahti – Doctor Lahti is mentioned as being unaccounted for from Thendi.

Largos – Mister Largos is a mechanic that worked on the perantium emitter.

LRS – Long-range sensors.

M-TAK rifle – A phaser rifle with simple functionality.

Madan – Flight Commander Madan is in charge of the Pterodon jets on the *Defender*.

Majimi – A traitor killed by Emperor Mizuki's grandfather.

Mako – A cargo ship visiting the *Dragon*.

Makoto – Benjiro's name before it was changed.

Malkai – A shokukin, man from the Tredon worker caste.

Mamushi – A type of snake.

MDS – This is a read-only device used to access the Main Data Stream, which is a digital public library. Media can only be accessed via a direct-connection port and must be uploaded onto it.

Mendosa – A PG-Force sergeant who is a weapons officer on the *Odyssey* but is on Thendi with Hapker and is captured by the Tredons.

Michio – Michio is Jori and Terk's personal guardsman as well as Washi's brother and Jeruko's son.

Mizuki – The family name of Jori and Terk, and their father the Dragon Emperor. The emperor refers to himself by this formal name.

MM – Stands for Mini Machine. It is a computer that is most often worn around the wrist like a brace but can be flattened and held like a tablet.

Montaro – Jori and Terk's incompetent brother who was killed by their father for being grossly incompetent.

Multimeter – A handheld device that measures electrical voltage, current, and resistance.

Mushin – Means no mind in Jori and Terk's language. No mind means to do your task so well that you don't need to think about it.

Nezumi – Nezumi is a retired general and is one of the emperor's Five Talons. He used to be one of Dokuri's personal trainers and personal guard.

Niashi – Major Niashi works at the operations station on the *Dragon*.

Nohibito – Means people in Jori and Terk's language. It is often used together with Toradon Nohibito, as in Dragon People.

Nordian – Anything that comes from the Norda culture. Nordians are spiritual naturalists. They practice meditations, use alternative healing methods, and are vegetarians.

Odyssey – The name of a PCC Expedition-class vessel captained by Silas Arden. This vessel is the largest type of vessel in the PCC. It has some firepower for protection, but it is a non-military ship. The ship houses hundreds of people and their families. Families are permitted on this vessel because of its non-military nature (except families have been temporarily evacuated in this story). There are military personnel serving on this type of ship, but they act more as security than as a military force.

Orlov – Doctor Orlov is mentioned as being rescued from Thendi.

Pachin – Pachin is a Tredon senshi. He also has some engineering skills that allow him to help with the emitter.

Packwood – Captain Packwood is the captain of a cargo ship named *Black Adder*.

Patersen – Corporal Patersen is a PG-Force officer on the *Defender* but serves with Hapker on Thendi and is captured by the Tredons.

PCC – The Prontaean Colonial Cooperative is the sub-organization that handles intergalactic relations, conducts space exploration, performs space-based scientific endeavors, assists travelers, and sometimes provides transportation.

Pentam system – A star system near Toradon territory. It used to be part of Toradon territory, but the emperor's father had lost it. Now Toradon dissidents were hiding out there.

Perantium emitter – A powerful wave emitter that is powered by a crystal called perantium. It was designed to temper the plate tectonics of the planet Thendi, but Emperor Mizuki wants it so that he can convert it into a planet killing weapon. The perantium device is also called a wave-emitting device, perantium emitter or just emitter.

Period – A period is 30 days. This term is often interchangeably used with the word month.

Perses – A Fortis-class destroyer of the Prontaean Galactic Force (PG-Force).

PFC capacitor – A type of electrical component that stores an electrical charge.

PG-Force – The Prontaean Galactic Force is the sub-organization that polices Cooperative space.

PG Institute – The Prontaean Galactic Institute is a training facility for anyone who wants to work for the Prontaean Cooperative. The institute trains both PCC and PG-Force officers.

Pholatia – Hapker's homeworld.

Pholatian – A proper adjective defining people or things from Pholatia.

Pholatian Protector – A service-oriented military force from Pholatia.

Plat bombs – A defensive short-range bombing weapon used in ground fighting.

Prontaean – It is a word that describes the known galaxy. It is believed the word derived from an ancient Earthen Indo-European language where the prefix pro- means advanced or forward and the suffix -anean means relating to.

Prontaean Colonial Cooperative – The PCC is the sub-organization that handles intergalactic relations, conducts space exploration, performs space-based scientific endeavors, assists travelers, and sometimes provides transportation.

Prontaean Cooperative – The agency that governs space. It has numerous treaties with various worlds that provides its charter to keep space safe, ensure peace, regulate fair trade, and colonize new worlds. Its powers are granted by several planets, and the number of planets that are part of the Cooperative continues to grow. The Prontaean Cooperative has two aspects to it. The first is the Prontaean Colonial Cooperative (PCC). This sub-organization handles intergalactic relations, conducts space exploration, performs space-based scientific endeavors, assists travelers, and sometimes provides transportation. The second aspect is the Prontaean Galactic Force (PG-Force). This sub-organization polices space.

Prontaean Council – The Prontaean Cooperative is ruled by an elected council.

Prontaean Galactic Force – The PG-Force is the sub-organization that polices Cooperative space.

Prontaean Galactic Institute – The PG Institute is a training facility for anyone who wants to work for the Prontaean Cooperative. The institute trains both PCC and PG-Force officers.

Porcupine bomb – A grenade-type bomb that shoots out super-heated metal darts. These darts can sometimes overwhelm energy shields and sear through armor.

Propulsion units – The engines that provide maneuverability for a spaceship. These engines can travel up to a quarter the speed of light but can't sustain that speed for long.

Pterodon jets – Virtually flown spacecraft used for fighting by the Prontaean Galactic Force (PG-Force). They are located on Tutamen-class battleships.

QR Gauge – A gauge that monitors arc-emissions. It is monitored by the bridge crew and to be kept within a certain safety margin.

Rabnoshk – Major Bracht is from the Rabnoshk race. The culture of this race is dominated by warriors. They were once enemies of the Cooperative.

Rattlers – Tredon fighter jets used to fight in a planetary atmosphere.

Reader – The generic term for someone who uses the power of their mind to sense emotions or to read or manipulate thoughts.

Renzo – Captain Renzo is head of the emperor's personal guards.

RF Weapon – A palm-sized device that is thrown against an energy shield in order to keep the shield activated long enough to run it out of power.

Ribisan – Anything from the Ribis culture.

Richforth – Captain Richforth is the captain of the PG-Force battleship, *Defender*. Incidentally, he is the same captain who had recommended Hapker to Rear Admiral Zimmer in Book One, *StarFire Dragons*.

Robo-mule – A hauling machine that uses tracks instead of wheels and has sensors that allow it to follow troops into battle.

RR-5 – A phaser rifle with multiple settings and functionalities.

Ruftbol – A highly competitive and ball sport played on Pholatia.

Rushiro – A senshi working on the perantium emitter.

Safety Depot – When a ship is in danger, non-essential personnel go to one of these many designated areas to strap in. Many safety depots double as escape pods when needed.

Sakon – General Sakon is the captain of a Toradon vessel called the *Brimstone*. He is known for great violence.

Samuru – General Samuru is one of the emperor's Five Talons and is considered the emperor's lifelong friend.

Sanzi – An early civilization of humans who colonized a distant planet but died out hundreds of years ago.

Saurus – A hot planet mentioned by Jax.

Schemster – A complex strategic game.

Sengupta – Director Jeyana Sengupta is chief director of intelligence on the *Odyssey*.

Senshi – Means warrior in Jori and Terk's language.

Serpent – A small transport ship with some firing capabilities. It is often used by the Tredons for raids or pirating.

Sevana – One of the emperor's concubines. She is a little older than Terk.

Sharkey – First Lieutenant Hanna Sharkey is one of two lieutenants serving under major Bracht on the *Odyssey*. She has temporarily been assigned as part of the Thendi ground force.

Shiro – Lord Shiro was killed by the emperor's grandfather for opposing him.

Shodo – Japanese calligraphy art.

Shokukin – The term for members of the Tredon worker caste.

Shovai Canyons – The canyons where the perantium device is located on the planet Thendi.

Silas – Captain Silas Arden is the captain of the *Odyssey*.

Simmonds – Sam Simmonds is the chief engineer on the *Odyssey* but is with Hapker on Thendi and captured by the Tredons.

Subkojo – A small space station with the largest manufacturing facilities in Toradon territory.

Sugi Wood – A type of cedar wood often used in the flooring of dojos.

Swenson – A person mentioned by Director Sengupta.

Tablet – A small hand-held computer device much like the tablets of the 21st century, but with more functionality. Some tablets can be folded around the wrist, and are then called an MM.

Talons – The emperor's five advisors, also known as the Emperor's Claw. They are Samuru, Jeruko, Nezumi, Aki, and Fujishin.

Tamaki – The battle of Tamaki was fought by the emperor's grandfather. It was a historic victory that inspired the emperor.

Telock – A senshi working on the emitter.

Terena – She is the only female on the emperor's ship to have some form of freedom. She used to be one of Jori's grandfather's concubines, which makes her, in a way, the emperor's stepmother. Now she is a medic.

Terk – Short for Terkeshi (see below).

Terke-chan – The -chan at the end of a name denotes affection.

Terkeshi – Terkeshi or Terk is the fourteen-year-old eldest son of Emperor Mizuki.

Terraforming – A process of converting a planet so that it can sustain human life. This process is expensive and takes many decades, so it is only done on planets that meet a very narrow set of criteria.

Thendi – A planet that is having trouble with plate tectonics. The emperor attacks it so he can steal their perantium emitter.

Thendians – People from the planet Thendi.

Togala – One of many inhabited planets in the known universe.

Tokagei – Tokagei is one of Jori and Terk's personal guards. Unlike Washi and Michio, he tells the emperor everything the boys do.

Tommins – Corporal Tommins is a PG-Force officer on the *Defender* but serves with Hapker on Thendi and is captured by the Tredons.

Toradon – Means dragon in Jori and Terk's language. It is often spoken as Toradon Nohibito, which means Dragon People.

Torpedoes – A rocket-like weapon carried by spaceships. Types and destructive power vary. Many have the power of nuclear warheads.

Translator – A device that can translate over a thousand spoken languages across the known universe.

Transport – A device that teleports people or objects from a ship to another ship or to a planet's surface. The person or object transported must have a bio-reader.

Transport-blocker – A device that keeps the transport from working. Since the shields on a ship work the same way, transport-blockers are usually used on planets or other bodies.

Tredon – This is what everyone outside Toradon calls this race of people. It sounds like the words tread on, which is what the Toradons are known to do to people.

TTAC Room – Acronym: Tactical Training Action Center. This room is used for simulated military training and exercises.

Tunrida – A female devil goddess of Scandinavian descent used by Arden as a curse.

Tutamen-class battleship – The largest and most heavily armed of the PG-Force military ships. It houses two squadrons of Pterodon jets.

Tymnar – The uninhabited planet that his father owns and earns a lot of money from mining it.

Usagi – A lusty Tredon senshi with a missing front tooth.

Viewscreen – A large computer screen.

Vuong – Lord Vuong rules the Kesanshi asteroid, which has a highly lucrative mining facility.

Walden – Sergeant Walden is a PG-Force tactical officer on the *Odyssey* but is on Thendi with Hapker and is captured by the Tredons.

Washi – Washi is Jori and Terk's personal guardsman as well as Michio's brother and Jeruko's son.

Wilshire – Lieutenant Wilshire is a tactical officer with the PG-Force and is Major Esekielu's man.

Yemon – Hisho Yemon is the emperor's head clerk. Technically, he's a captain but no one calls him this since he isn't a warrior.

Yushino – Kesatsu Yushino is a low-ranking police officer on the *Dragon*.

Zanshin – Means remaining mind in Jori and Terk's language. Remaining mind means make sure it's over before you walk away.

Zimmer – Rear Admiral Zimmer presides over both the PCC and PG-Force. When Jori and Terk had been on the *Odyssey*, Rear Admiral Zimmer ordered that they be held for questioning rather than be allowed to return home. This order inspired Jori and Terk to fight their way off the *Odyssey* and put many Cooperative people in jeopardy.

Books by Dawn Ross:

<u>The Dragon Spawn Chronicles</u>
StarFire Dragons
Dragon Emperor
Dragon's Fall
Isle of Hogs (a novella)
Warrior Outcast
Dissonance (a novella)
Orphaned Warrior
Fated Warriors
Warriors United
Spire Wilderness (a novella)

About the Author

Dawn Ross currently resides in the wonderful state of Kansas where sunflowers abound. She has also lived in the beautiful Willamette Valley of Oregon and the scenic Hill Country of Texas. Dawn completed her bachelor's degree in 2017. Although the degree is in finance, most of her electives were in fine art and creative writing. Dawn is married and has a wonderful son. Her current occupation is part time at Meals on Wheels. She is also a mom, homemaker, volunteer, wildlife artist, and a sci-fi/fantasy writer. Her first novel was written in 2001 and she's published several others since. She participates in the NaNoWriMo event every year and is a part of her local writer group.